Swoondalini

Thanks for all y'all do down in Ridgeland. There's definitely a little Real Estate turn to this novel, including so much more. Enjoy the Swoondalini ride and pass it along.

— Sutty

Swoondalini

By
Chris Suddeth

©2018 by Chris Suddeth

All rights reserved. No part of this publication may be reproduced, stored in a retrieval system, distributed, or transmitted in any form, or by any means, including photocopying, recording, or other electronic or mechanical methods now available or that may become available in the future without the prior written permission of the publisher.

For permission requests, email the publisher, at:
inquiry@cawingcrowpress.com

Published by:
Cawing Crow Press LLC
Dunlo, PA

ISBN: 978-1-68264-035-7

Library of Congress Control Number: 2018939766

Visit us on the web at:
www.cawingcrowpress.com

This is a work of fiction. Names, characters, businesses, places, events and incidents are either the products of the author's imagination or used in a fictitious manner. Any resemblance to actual persons, living or dead, or actual events is purely coincidental.

Dedication

I would like to dedicate Swoondalini to the angels both seen and unseen. In doing that, I need to start with my mother-in-law, retired English professor at Brevard College, Brevard, NC, Sarah Rhuemma Miller. Without my mother-in-law reading through the unreadable in Swoondalini's infancy, I would not have felt the legitimacy to get past the toddler stage of this novel's undertaking.

   I definitely couldn't have written this novel without the love and support of my wife, Pookie and the home team of my family. My daughter Emma Belle (EB) holds a special place among us Earth-bound angels. Without her placing me under Mr. Mom status shortly after her birth on 9/9/09, I would have never brought to fruition that which was birthed on the rocks of Fripp Island, SC in the mid-80's. Being a full-time stay-at-home father with a six-month-old certainly has its challenges, but Emma Belle afforded me little ten to fifteen-minute pockets of time for Swoondalini's rough draft between feedings, naps, and diaper changes. Thank you to my little bitty E.B, that I swear poots glitter. Thanks to fellow writers Katherine Brown (KTB) and Stephanie Austin Edwards for their encouragement and a point in the right direction to my writing coach, Kathie Giorgio. Kathie was, and is, simply amazing with her memory and writing instincts.

   Much appreciation to the angel that inspired this odyssey of the soul novel and to anyone I may have left out. Thank you from the bottom of my heart. Without the existence of Swoondalini, I would have been left with a death-bed regret.

Chapter 1

I desperately pounded on the door of my favorite Georgetown Law School student until my fist hurt. I yelled, "Eugene, oh, Geney!" Why did I feel compelled to see him?

"Brandy, how nice of you to call first," he said sarcastically while rubbing sleep out of his eyes. He quickly pulled a t-shirt over his head that bore his own likeness with text that read, "If you're gonna play, you may as well score." His image had a lusty, toothy smile, while giving a hardy thumbs up.

"Lovin' the morning wood, and I told you that you may actually use my real name." He was one of the few who knew my given name of Alice. "What you been up to, baby?"

"Studying how to set the guilty free. I know your name preference, but I prefer Brandy as you prefer to call me by my middle name that you only know because you read my driver's license," he shot back. "I also would love it if you'd call first." He scanned me up and down, showing obvious irritation and disappointment at having been awakened and at my being dressed in off-duty attire. A sweatshirt and jeans, a garnet-colored Titleist hat bearing the Gamecock logo on the side that covered my dark brown pixie haircut.

"Hush up," I said as I gave him a peck on the mouth and barged in before he could bar my way. I almost had to rise on my tip toes to kiss him. I was 5'2" and he was 5'7". He always lamented about his problem finding a girl shorter than he was.

"Won't you come in?" Eugene said in mock formality.

Chris Suddeth

"What's wrong?"

"Keep your voice down," he shushed.

A broad grin of realization came across my face. "Do you have a chicky in bed?"

"Yes, damn it. And if you wake her up, you'll be awfully hard to explain," Eugene drawled.

Eugene and I were from the same region of South Carolina known as the Upstate. Just one city to the east of Greenville was Eugene's hometown of Sugartit. It is indeed a real place in Spartanburg County, although I'm not sure this tiny crossroads appears on any map. Spartanburg County is awful anyway, with the county seat being Spartanburg proper. Now that's a real shit-box. People from Greenville just don't go there. I can't tell you a concrete reason why. It's just not done.

"Why would It be so hard to explain?" I asked with genuine interest.

"Because you're a dime, and no one, especially a girl I'm trying to date, will see anything other than tits, ass, and a pretty face when they look at you," Geney fired back evenly.

He was complimenting my looks, but why did it sting? I was beginning to doubt myself about the one thing I never doubted. "Don't worry, Geney, I'll explain our relationship to her," I masked my feelings with a malicious tone.

"Like you did my last girlfriend when you chose my apartment to practice your striptease technique on me?"

"You know I'm a horrible dancer, but at least I practiced my blowjob routine at the same time. I was only trying to help out."

"By sucking me off in front of her?"

Swoondalini

"I thought maybe she would like it and would choose to join in. Tell me that wouldn't make your wildest dreams come true?"

"*Oh my God!* The fantasy world you live in sometimes," he whispered incredulously. "Help?! All I got from your *help* was scathing and blue balls since you neglected to finish the job when she proceeded to break up with me after she slapped the snot out of me."

"Well, I didn't finish you off because we don't have that kind of a relationship and you just seemed so lost and vulnerable. The scathing was an experiment. The snot wasn't so attractive either. I got a little on me," I said, feigning a pout.

"I don't even know where to go with that. An experiment? You're amazing."

"Thanks." I missed the sarcasm. "I can't be expected to try certain things out on clients. I owe you one, okay?" One that I had no intention of delivering, but it had the desired effect.

"Okay."

That seemed to loosen him up.

"Furthermore," Eugene did his best lawyer voice. He'll make a good one. "I was thinking of taking her home to see my loud Italian family for the holidays. I've never dared submit a girl to that type of obnoxious scrutiny before. I think she can handle it and she's worth it."

"Oh," I whispered and looked to the floor. "I'm sorry, babe, I just don't know what comes over me sometimes." I flashed him a seductive look, attempting to recover from the news, and gave him a longer than necessary hug. "I'll go home with you for Christmas if that'll make you feel any better." I surprised myself by offering to go back to Sugartit, South Carolina with him, and meaning it.

"I'm not sure how I feel about that," Eugene said.

"Okay, whatever," I responded more defensively than I would have liked. I had invites to spend the holidays everywhere from Switzerland to Maui, but his family would be one of the few places I wouldn't be paid in some fashion to go. I didn't often think about such things, but the older I got...

"Don't take it the wrong way. Listen, can we talk about this later?" His eyes darted back to his bedroom. "I can't believe she slept through your pounding like a crazy woman."

"Yeah, that's fine." I was still dazed. I pasted my best smile on, lightly stroked his face, and wandered my hand down his chest. "Why don't I go next door and wrap my lips around that Volcano thang of yours until you escort girlie out?" Eugene rented the apartment next door for growing purposes and kept an assortment of smoking devices for our amusement. He also had some farmland close to Camp David, of all places. Eugene had the expertise to be a world class pot grower, which was my initial attraction to him. His skills would unburden him of the two or three hundred thousand dollars' worth of school loans that his peers would spend the first decade or two trudging through their careers. Those are skills he could always fall back on, skills which weren't as finite as I was increasingly feeling mine were.

"Escort her out?"

"Yes, breakfast will not get itself," I explained as I dug in his kitchen drawer for the keys to the Weed Lair, Geney's name for the growing apartment. "And I have to stock up for the Thanksgiving holiday."

Swoondalini

"Oh, yeah, sorry, I forgot."

I tried to lighten the mood. "Duh, it's Christmas shopping time and I can't be doing that sober, now can I? I love for the presents to be just as much a surprise for me as they are to the receiver." My Nana was still not amused by the kite that I sent her a few years back. "I'll have Juicy Fruit for calmness and the Duke University Elvis strain for drooling, please."

"Yes, ma'am." He was relaxing now. "What was it you got the Speaker of the House last year?"

"A big black cock strap-on," I said sheepishly.

That was one of Eugene's favorite stories and he predictably became red-faced as he tried to hold the laugh in. He pointed at his door, expecting me to leave, but I wasn't done casting my spell. It was win-win for me. He would either man-handle me out the door, which I'd like, or I'd put his little girlfriend on notice by alerting her to my presence. At the very least, she'd sniff my scent on or around him.

"That was a bit embarrassing. It was meant as a gag gift for one of my tour pro clients." I had been a golf groupie on the PGA Tour for a long time. Even walked the galleries with the wives sometimes. Not that I cared, but I wasn't popular among the golf wives club. "What was surprising was how much the Speaker of the House actually liked the strap-on." As a strict rule, I gave no details or hints as to who my clients were. Much like a therapist/client or doctor/patient relationship, or what their preferences tended toward, but Eugene was the exception to my rule. I had to have somebody to tell these stories to. He was one of my few friends, but I couldn't--or wouldn't--let him know that. Always at arm's length... "Now chop-chop!"

"Would you autograph your bra and give it to me? I could autograph your breasts with my semen later on, if you want a fair trade," Geney whispered.

I couldn't help laughing at this kid and I didn't laugh at much. Occasionally, I got the autographed underwear request, due to my status within my chosen occupation. "Very fucking funny, I always tell you no, so why do you keep asking?"

"How bout now?"

"No, not now either."

He let a bit of silence pass. "Now?"

"No, damn it!"

"If it's because it's so hard to take that itchy, dirty bra off, then I would help you with it," he offered.

Had I made him forget his sleeping beauty? I felt my face grin at the thought. "I'll bet you would. *No!*"

Long pause. "Now?" he said meekly.

"No. You'd have me spend the rest of the day with my 32 DDD's flopping around?"

"You've done worse with those peanut butter legs of yours. Besides, have you seen what the suckers are going for on eBay?"

"Peanut butter legs?"

"Yeah, smooth and easily spread," Geney explained.

Ouch! I masked the pain that comment caused with a smile I honed to be impenetrable. I had done much worse and I had millions of reasons in the bank for doing so. I allowed the comment to go unchallenged. "Alright!" I said in exasperation. I just wanted Geney to like me. "But lil Miss Molly's going to need to skedaddle and get us some biscuits."

"Her name's Juanita."

"Whatever." The truth was I didn't much like any of his girlfriends he was dumb enough to introduce me to. "Would you please have *Juanita*," I enunciated, "leave for a little bit so we can do some bidness?"

He peered at me sullenly. "Good, I'll see you next door," I said without waiting for a response. "I have some cash for you."

***

An hour later, I was bebopping down the steps of Eugene's apartment with an Obi Wan Kenobi (an ounce in laymen's terms) of the East Coast's finest cheeba and minus one very expensive bra that now bore my Sharpie mark, when I caught sight of a man in a tailored business suit sitting in the passenger seat of my locked M3. Instinctually, my hand went for my Walther PPKS, but just as quickly as my hand found the comfort of my pistol, he was gone.

"What did Geney put in that bong?" I whispered to myself.

If only it were that simple, but I gave it no further thought since I had one of my larger annual functions tonight. My game face gave me very little time for introspection.

Chapter 2

"Good evening, Governor and Mrs. McGowan." The head White House butler bowed slightly with a knowing smile.

"Hello, Harold," I replied graciously. Harold knew full well that I was not Mrs. McGowan but was kind enough not to point it out. We got to know each other casually over the past fifteen years.

"The President and the First Lady should be coming down from the residence shortly. I'll go ahead and announce you. Emil will take your drink orders and see you quickly to your tables. By the way, Miss Brandy, you look lovely this evening."

Lovely indeed. I pulled out all the stops, as usual for events of this magnitude. On this particular evening, I wore a black Chanel vintage: jersey knit evening dress. My size six tootsies sported Christian Louboutin Disco Noeud satin platform sandals in black. An 18k white gold Zebra Safari bangle bracelet graced my right wrist with black and white diamonds for a total carat weight of nearly 66. The matching Zebra safari dome ring added more zing. To balance, I wore a Cartier Baignoire watch encrusted with diamonds on the other wrist and on my left ring finger, my favorite Tiffany Diamond flower of over five carats, valued, I'm told, at nearly nine hundred grand. From my earlobes, hung Tiffany and Co. Legacy. And I carried a Swarovski pure silk DTL evening bag. I was wearing well over a million dollars on my taut bod. BLING!

"Thanks, Harry," the Governor said, patting him on the back harder than necessary. Harold hated being called Harry, but Willy was oblivious.

Chris Suddeth

"Do we really need any more drinks?" I giggled and hung on Willy's arm so that my breast touched him lightly as a reminder. We started drinking much earlier in the afternoon than we should have, not to mention spending an hour riding aimlessly around town in the limo, smoking a J (my drug of choice as I wasn't much for alcohol, besides beer) and fornicating.

"Brandy, honey, as long as we can stand, we'll need just one more round. Tonight is big," he drawled in his silver-tongued Roanoke, Virginia accent.

"Ladies and gentlemen, please welcome Governor Willy McGowan of the Commonwealth of Virginia and his wife," Harold's voice boomed over the loudspeakers. I learned years ago that Harold could just as easily throw you a life preserver if you were drowning or an anvil, depending on how much he liked you.

Polite applause bubbled as the crowd clearly anticipated the arrival of the First Couple. Emil whisked us to our table and seated us next to my old friend, Senator Sam Irving from Montana. Emil scurried away to get our drinks, glad to be clear of the rowdy governor.

I smiled at the senator. "Hello, Sam."

"Hello, Brandy, my dear." His face lit up when he saw me. "Governor." Sam nodded his head and continued speaking to the German Ambassador.

"Senator," Willy responded back perfunctorily.

"Governor Willy," I said, grabbing his package under the table and stroking it at a medium pace, "your next drink order needs to be a club soda if you want to be coherent for your little chat with the President after dinner. Also, you'll want to get your money's worth out of me later."

Unaccustomed to being told what to do, he scrunched up his face and pretended to ignore me.

"You know I'm right," I pressed while tweaking his testicles a little to get his attention.

"I know," he huffed and squirmed. "You've been around here longer than I have. Next drink is virgin."

"Good. We can celebrate later."

At that moment, the President and First Lady made their formal appearance to the Marine Corp band playing *Hail to the Chief*.

"Damn it, Brandy. I can't stand up in decent manner," was drowned out by applause, but I heard it and giggled as I stood to clap.

The remainder of the evening was a blur of foreign dignitaries, lawmakers, and celebrities. All in a night's work.

***

The picturesque mountain church that frequently haunted my dreams simultaneously confused and frightened me. It was discomfiting that a pretty setting could fill me with so much dread. As I sat in the pews, I was completely me; I was Alice, but bearing witness to another personality at the same time. There was never any sound as the preacher breathed fire and brimstone. I marveled at how the sun played on the stained-glass windows depicting various biblical scenes, trembling at what he was saying, although it was only his lips that moved. Whatever other dreamy personality I inhabited merely smiled a lusty smile and was turned on by the control that it, no she, wielded. I felt something stab my leg and looked down to see an eastern diamondback slither under the pew. I was snake bit and no matter what happened, I'd be dead soon. Dead with no hope of salvation.

Beads of sweat and the sound of my shower turning off woke me up. I felt my left leg as always, but always found it without deadly fang marks. I sucked in the air that the dream robbed from my lungs and my eyes blipped open in the momentary confusion that followed my night terrors. This dream came and went throughout my years but was a more frequent specter of the night the last six months or so.

Who was in my shower this morning? I propped myself up on my elbow and rubbed questionable crust out of my eyes. Perhaps Geney? "Guess I'll just have to find out," I moaned to myself as my hangover began to kick in. I was grateful it was only a hangover. A hangover, I could handle.

"Brandy, honey, where are the towels?"

Now I recalled. He could be a bit high-strung and high-maintenance, but he was a lot of fun. "They are where they always are, Governor."

"No, they are *not*," he huffed.

"Well, they should be."

"Goddamn it, Brandy, I should have been in Richmond two hours ago and I'm standing here with no fucking towel. You want me to use all your toilet paper?"

"Hold on," I said as I sprang out of bed. The room spun a little as my hangover shifted into another gear with my sudden movement. "I'm getting you one out of the dryer. Want me to dry you off, baby?" I queried him loudly as I paused to assess myself in the mirror. Despite my short dark hair mirroring a medusa-like image, my frame reflected the perfect recipe for a wet dream. By rote, I checked the small spot on the left side of my head. The roots were showing, but only a little. Only I would notice. I decided to have it tended to while I was out shopping.

"Brandy, please don't. You're getting me worked up." I had him. "I've really got to run." Distress crept into his voice. "Unlike the governor of your home state, I don't have the balls to claim I'm hiking in the wilderness. Where was he again?"

"Appalachian Trail," I supplied. "Feels like you've got a nice set of balls to me, Governor," I said.

"Whatever. I've got to go."

"Not if I have anything to do with it," I said while grabbing his cock and stroking it vigorously.

"Stop it!" He slapped my hand away.

"Stop what?"

"Brandy, you know you're like sexual heroin."

"That just means I'm doing my job."

He pushed me away, which was what I wanted, because I was ready to push him out the door. I hopped in my shower cave before he was able to regain his composure. Move 'em on, but leave them wanting more.

"Bye bye, baby. I'll call you later."

I heard the door slam. "That's what caller ID is for," I whispered to the rain-showerhead. After my shower, I vaguely registered hearing Garth Brooks song, *Thank God for Unanswered Prayers,* playing on my clock radio, but was more interested in smoking a bowl to alleviate the effects of the previous night. This was the week of Thanksgiving, my favorite holiday.

Chapter 3

I possessed everything I could have possibly wanted. I had money I couldn't even conceive of while growing up on a mill hill in Greenville, SC. A little background research about the mill hills and you'll find that the people that lived there were poor and inconsequential for the better part of the 20th century. This fact often spurred its children to great heights as they grew into adulthood. Could I include myself among the successful offspring of the Southeast's blue-collar backbone? I always thought so, but recent events led me to question that.

By the time I came along in 1975, the textile industry was on a downhill slide. Now, it's all but dead. Being a lint-head was never in fashion and I didn't want to end up like my mother. She was and is very passé, very unfashionable. That's my way of saying she was a whack job. The daughter of the 70's version of Jim and Tammy Faye Baker.

For instance, on this Monday before Thanksgiving, my biggest decision was which car I would take shopping. Would it be my ever present M3 convertible, my Porsche Carrera 4S, my 308 GTS Ferrari (that's right, the same model driven by Magnum P.I.), or the Cadillac Escalade EXT that was on permanent loan?

"I'm feeling the M3 again today," I said to myself as I coughed out my Cannabis Cup-winning White Widow. I threw the keys at the front door as a reminder.

Chris Suddeth

My only problem was finding a place to park in this god-awful town. But I couldn't curse Washington D.C. too harshly. It led me to a life I could never have dreamed of in Greenville, SC. I had wealth, power, and privilege. Though I held no office, my constituency was in the hearts, minds, and pants of the men, and the occasional woman in this town.

"Wait," I spoke to myself. I did that a lot recently and in truth, it sort of disturbed me. I put down the bong and walked over to the computer. "While I'm clad in nothing but this little ole towel, better update my website."

My legitimate money came from my website and from my career as the top romance novel cover model in America. I began this business as an elite escort and I still hire out as one on occasion to maintain hands-on contact with the rich and powerful. The real reason I still pulled escort duty was that I was hoping to stumble upon true love. Being grounded in reality escaped my existence. I was also vaguely aware of being in love with Geney but was insecure about being thought of as only a hot piece of ass. Even in my wonderland of cars and money, the irony that I graced the cover of so many romance novels, yet romance eluded me, was not lost on this weed-addled dime. But I'm getting ahead of myself, aren't I?

Being consistently in the top-five most searched women on the web was where it was at. I stayed busy with appearances to maintain that status, but other than that, it was easy. It was genius and I didn't even take my clothes off completely, not that I had any qualms about nudity. In my mind, that's so stupid, but a colleague of mine suggested leaving something to the imagination and I went with it straight to the bank.

Swoondalini

"As long as I'm on the computer," I trailed off and blew out the pot smoke, "may as well check my e-mail." I generally did this about every other week while indiscriminately mashing delete. On this day, when I turned my head to pick up my coffee, my finger must have hit enter. An e-mail from a client from Ohio popped up. Seeing South Carolina in the body of his text kept me from deleting. "Probably wanting a freebie," I speculated. The e-mail read:

Brandy,

I thought of you when I saw this e-mail. It's from a realtor in South Carolina and it should help you through your cold D.C. winter. They're saying it's going to be a doozy. I've never had such good oyster stew. I felt compelled to go visit this place after a friend sent it to me. I can now see why this guy loves the place. I'll probably end up buying some property from him. Have you been there? Anyway, it's got a great story to go along with it. Let me know what you think, and I look forward to seeing you soon.

SEE ATTACHMENT

Anything from South Carolina summoned a bitter-sweet acid taste to the back of my throat. But being on weed auto-pilot...

"Sure, I'll bite. I love oysters," I said aloud as I downloaded the attached recipe.

What I opened was my recipe for redemption. At the time, I barely paid attention to what I thought was a lame attempt to sell real estate in an increasingly tough market. I gratefully include that same recipe here:

Wintertime Stew

By: Jon Sutton

Chris Suddeth

Those who know me know that I am very seasonal in my tastes. Corona in the winter is as much a no-no for me as white after Labor Day is for the ladies. College football just wouldn't be the same in the spring, although I'd vote for it year around, along with a play-off system.

With all that in mind, I sometimes ponder an ideal day from my memory and the recipe it involved. Oyster stew and a cold, foggy Fripp Island winter's day is the answer.

First rule of thumb is not to eat oysters in months without an R. I can't touch them until it has at least gotten cool enough for my favorite gray sweatshirt. Secondly, support your local seafood. Frogmore, South Carolina oysters are the best.

Preparing my oysters is a long, drawn out ritual. I handle each one to ensure it is shell free, wash it, and strain it. You can put some ice on them to make sure they don't get warm. Yes, it is time-consuming, but worth it, because the last thing you want to do is crunch down on a hard shell while enjoying the rich, steamy goodness.

Not everyone can get on board with it, but I will eat oysters raw. Take a Saltine, put a large oyster on top, add a little salt and glop on my homemade cocktail sauce. (I'm still on the fence about releasing that recipe.) My mouth is watering right now, just writing about it.

Once you've done all that prep work, you will probably be tired. Double check to make sure your buddies are iced down, bundle up and prepare for a short golf cart ride to the beach. I find that my inner introvert finds its place during Fripp's winter. I feel the island is at its best when you walk out on the beach and not another soul is in sight. Don't get me wrong, the summertime with sand and sun, girl-watching, and drinking beer on a folding chair is inspirational. But if push comes to shove, I'll take the toboggan, gloves, and a Maker's Mark splashed with Coke on wheels any day.

The winter of 2004 was my first full winter living on Fripp. One day in February, the fog was so thick; you could only hear the ocean from the main Rock Beauty golf cart parking lot. The low cloud cover amplified the ocean's voice. I decided to take a walk down to the water to confirm the Atlantic was still there. After a short time, I made my way up to the top floor of an unfinished oceanfront home nearby to get a better feel for Mother Nature's foggy embrace. It was the sound more than anything that I recall about that day. I nursed my Maker's and knew that it had to be the most peaceful day I'd ever experienced on Fripp. Even now, more than five years later, it's the gold standard day that comes to my mind when someone asks me to tell them about the winters on that South Carolina Lowcountry island.

After an hour, I realized my face and fingers were numb, my drink dry, and most important, the oysters were calling.

You'll need the following ingredients to complete the oyster stew:

--Half to whole stick of butter. I use only half because it gets too oily.

--Ketchup

--1 can of evaporated milk or even some heavy cream, for thickness' sake

--About a quart of milk

--Texas Pete to taste

--Salt and pepper to taste

First, melt the butter and sauté the little jewels. Stay with them so they don't get too done and rubbery. Also, I take this opportunity to sample more oysters. You know, just to make sure.

Chris Suddeth

After about 5 minutes or so, pour in the can of evaporated milk and approximately a quart of milk. From here on out, bring the stew up to heat on low. The slower you bring the temperature up, the better. A couple of years ago, I tried this on a new stove and scorched the whole affair after turning my back for only a few minutes. Pretend you're watching a small child. The thought of that curdled milk still inspires my gag reflex.

While bringing up the stew heat, add seasoning heat with the ketchup, Texas Pete, and pepper. The ketchup combined with the pepper will actually give more bite than you'd think, so add a little at a time and use the Texas Pete sparingly. Maybe even just add some per bowl. I serve mine with six olives (don't know why, but it must be six) and oyster crackers.

By this point in my gold standard Fripp Island winter's day, there was still some light left. I warmed up with two bowls under my belt and wanted to venture out for another golf cart ride before the gray day ended. Though I've been coming to Fripp my entire life and living here since 2003, I never tire of a couple of drinks and a golf cart ride. I turned off the stove and covered up the stew pot. I felt compelled to take a slow ride around Porpoise Road to see the fog and as much as I could of Fripp Inlet. To my delight, neither Hunting Island nor the Fripp bridge was visible on this foggy day. It grew colder as the hidden sun set so I didn't linger long. I needed to write this short story for posterity. This jewel of the Atlantic felt like a world of its own that day. I had a pot of oyster stew calling me home the same way I hope you'll call Fripp Island your home one day too.

I trust you'll appreciate this story about food and Fripp. It came from a special place in my heart and I'd love for you all to build and share any stories *involving our beautiful island. They don't have to involve recipes, but maybe just a little taste of soul.*

--Jon

Had I been there? That was the million-dollar question. I wished that he just sent me the recipe sans the story. Why was this silly story making me feel like crying?

I printed the story out, jammed it in my purse with a bundle of cash for shopping, and promptly forgot about the story. I was good at forgetting. I quickly erased the rest of the e-mails without reading a single one. I held down the delete key and sniffed back a few tears.

Chapter 4

I had a couple of stops to make before shopping till I dropped. The first of these stops was a promise that I made to my uncle Bobby. Uncle Bobby was always concerned about me, but lately his phone calls were incessant. The actual impetus for keeping the promise was the increase in the church nightmares, among other night terrors of various degrees, lately. The most disturbing of the nightmares, besides the church scenario, was the loss of my two biggest assets, my breasts. If I were being honest with myself, I would attribute the dreams to the footsteps of time. Although time wouldn't be visible on my body for years to come, I could hear it, no, feel its footsteps, like a wide receiver bracing for the impact of a defensive back catching me in mid-air. I had been in denial long enough and put this woman off long enough. She was on the kooky, holistic end of the healing world in her chosen field. Seeing her wouldn't be admitting I had a real problem, would it? She was moving to Vermont indefinitely, so it was now or never. I certainly wouldn't follow her to Vermont. D.C. was cold enough for this southern girl. In my hometown, it so rarely snowed, that when it does, people lose their minds. The local weatherman, Charlie Gertz, would broadcast his report right before the storm from the bread and milk aisles at the Bi-Lo around the corner from my house in Dunean. He would say, "Bread's gone, milk's running out, it's going to be a rough one for the Upstate and Western North Carolina."

Besides, the guru's house was on the way to Georgetown and I was out of excuses to postpone her any longer. "Wow, this woman lives in a swanky part of town to be one of these alternative healer types," I whispered to myself as I flicked my clandestine vice out the window. Marlboro Ultra-Light Menthols were my weakness. I was strange about that. Did I care if anyone saw me do bong rip? No. Did I conceal the fact that I was an adult internet superstar and an elite call girl? Nope. Did I hide and sneak my cigarette habit? You bet. I was ashamed of it and it wasn't very sexy to boot.

The closer I got to her home, the more nervous I became. Nervous and jittery was unusual for me, as I considered myself a cool customer. An African-American woman in her mid-60's was sitting on a rocking chair on her front porch, seemingly unaffected by the damp chill in the air. Her white hair was in tight curls. She literally looked like a character plucked out of a movie with that hair, medium brown skin, and a hint of Native American features. She would be easy to envision sitting behind a crystal ball or reading tarot cards to you, but my uncle insisted this medicine woman was the real deal. We would soon find out.

"Sorry to have put you off all this time," I said, walking up her steps. "How do you say your name again?" I asked with a slight snide tone.

"You've only been putting your own journey off," she answered flatly. "You may call me, Ifetayo, and if it wasn't for my respect for your uncle Bobby, I would have put you off indefinitely."

"Is that your real name?"

She only raised her eyebrow in reply to my query then took a deep, calming breath before speaking again. "I see you've shown up to a sacred spiritual event stoned," she said.

Swoondalini

She acted as if she were disappointed in me. Was I that obvious? I quickly checked my face to see if I still had on my sunglasses and I did indeed. "So, can we still do this?" It was off-putting for someone to see right through me as I prided myself on being hard to read and still functional while in altered states.

"Despite my personal misgivings, my spirit guides are giving me the green light on you," she said through tight lips, without attempting to hide her disappointment. Even though this woman was chiding me, she still had a matronly concern about her that was foreign to me.

Who talks to spirit guides? Who does she think she is, talking to me this way? "Really?" I asked. "What else are they telling you?"

"The exact quote that I keep getting is, 'this one's going to get her money's worth,'" she said with a grin of satisfaction. "Speaking of that, I'll take cash or check, but prefer cash."

I didn't like the sound of that but would not give her the pleasure of knowing that I was uncomfortable. I quickly rolled a few hundred-dollar bills off my cash wad and I blithely said, "Shall we get started?"

"Yes, I suppose we should," she responded, turning on a professional tone. "I realize it's chilly out here, but as long as we can stand it, I prefer the outdoors since it encourages grounding. Very important in any energy work and underestimated in everyday life. When life seems to be spiraling out of control, hug a tree."

I didn't know what to make of that statement, but merely shook my head and stared blankly. "Yeah, well, let me get my jacket out of the Bimmer and we'll do *it* out here."

The rest of my visit consisted of a long droning class on hand positions and energy chakras. For the actual attunements, she breathed deeply, waved her hands about, paced around me, slapped the palms of my hands, burned sage, invoked some guy named Dr. Usui as well as spirit guides and angels, and she made mention that I had a very special spirit guide. Her face remained impassive when she spoke of my *special* spirit guide.

Whatever! I paid little attention and claimed to feel nothing after the attunements were done. I kept wondering how this all was supposed to help my dreams, but I didn't bother to ask that key question. As I left, she gave me the amethyst amulet from around her neck. She said I needed it more than she did. I put it on so as not to be rude but took it right off after peeling out of her driveway. I then lit a joint I found in my ashtray and refocused the rest of the day on me.

Chapter 5

Surprisingly, weed made me more cautious behind the wheel. I kept under 100 mph while high. Yes, driving and flying was so much safer than sober driving. I had been fortunate so far to avoid DUI's, but I earned my share of speeding tickets. It was unreal what a beautiful woman could get away with. Not that I was usually in a big hurry, but I had powerful, fast vehicles and it would be a shame not to use them the way they were designed to be used. After all, I had to put them through their paces.

Every radio station I flipped to played *Lyin' Eyes* by the Eagles. What are the odds of that? I was at first relieved to turn the creepy tune off when the cell phone rang, and I fumbled with it while weaving in and out of traffic. "Oh shit!" I cursed and felt my stomach turn over. The 864 area code always made my asshole pucker like I was a scared little girl again. I didn't see that Upstate South Carolina area code very often, but when I did, my heart missed a beat. I chose to ignore the call for now until I got off the highway. At least I had that much sense. Thank goodness for small miracles.

When I reached up to feel my heart pounding out of my chest, I recalled that I gave away my bra and was in dire need of new underwear anyway. Often, I used underwear as my calling card, so I was always in need of more. I suddenly realized that my lingerie store's exit off the highway was coming up in a little over the length of a football field, so I made a radical lane change across four lanes of traffic while gesturing with my middle finger to all the horns.

Chris Suddeth

"*CHRIST!* Americans could take a lesson from the Germans when it comes to driving, and Europe as a whole when it comes to getting flushed over the sight of a boob on the big game's halftime show. "Go fuck yourselves!" I hollered, as if they could hear me. But was cutting across four lanes of traffic in any country a good idea?

I screeched to a halt in front of Bethany's Lingerie after nipping my spoiler on the curb. I nervously checked my cell phone and waited to see if there was a message. No message, but when it started to ring again, I threw the hot potato on the floorboard. Mama often adopted the, "ring-the-phone-until-I-answered-it" routine, whether the call was an emergency or not.

I retrieved the cell from the floorboard in a huff. She wouldn't stop. The woman was relentless. I answered the phone sullenly. "Yes, Mama?"

"Well, it's about time you picked up the phone, Alice," my mother scolded. "Are your fingers broke?"

"No, Mama, my fingers aren't broke. Are you on fire?"

Now that I listened, I could tell she was crying. "Why do I have to be on fire to talk to my daughter?"

"Oh. Now you're claiming me as your daughter?" I challenged in one of our routine gambits of confrontation.

"Listen, Al, your granddaddy's in the hospital."

"My grandddaddy, Pappy, died in Beaufort Memorial a year after Daddy died," I stabbed.

"You know which grandfather I'm talking about. He was a great pastor with a large flock in his day."

Swoondalini

"Jim Jones had a large flock too," I flung back at her like I was throwing a cow patty. I usually liked to press this point but wasn't feeling it today and was glad when she let the comment pass. Strange... "Did him and Granny get in one of their drunken brawls with each other?"

"You know that only happens when they get confused with their meds," Mama said defensively.

"Is that what their excuse is these days?" My *grandparents* had a twisted relationship. I emphasize grandparents as they only claimed you or cozened someone when they had a use for you. Ever since the scandal, they had some real knockdown, drag out fights. Both were devious in their own way. They routinely brought up the sacrifices they made in birthing or adopting their nine kids.

"Don't be disrespectful. They're getting older."

"Mama, please." I could feel myself getting lethargic. "Let's not go there. They've always been this way. They just happen to be getting older."

"Are you coming home for the holidays?" She quickly changed the subject.

"Have I been home for the holidays since I left?" I said with bravado I didn't feel. Despite my feelings toward my mother, I didn't intentionally try to be mean to her. I just didn't know how else to say it.

"A mother can ask, can't she?"

"Ask away."

"How bout I come up there?" She was often oblivious to reality.

"I don't think that's a good idea."

"Why not?" Her voice was plaintive.

"For one thing, you haven't been out of Greenville, much less South Carolina, for the better part of the last two decades."

"Perhaps it's time. Perhaps--"

I cut her off. I needed to have crisp, fall air, and to walk. "Mama, I gotta go. I'll call you later," I said, hitting end before she had a chance to respond. I would not call her later. Whew! Glad I got that call out of the way. I really need to look into getting another cell phone number. I had to do that from time to time to cull out some undesirables who ended up with my number.

"Time for maintenance toking before shopping for undies," I said while cracking the hard top of my BMW. Maintenance toking was what Geney called smoking more while high to make sure you wouldn't come down. Everything and everybody was unnerving me today and the day was young. I would need plenty of maintenance today.

Bethany's became the only place that I shopped for my unmentionables, mainly because Beth and her staff didn't shoot accusing stares up and down my body. By this point in my life, I understood that people looked at me and thought that I must have had tons of plastic surgery. I could be hyper-sensitive about it, depending on what mood I was in. The redneck came out in me at a Victoria's Secret a few years back when a clerk quizzed me about "my work" and I let the girl have it. I gave her my God-given measurements like a resume and threw my money, including coins, at a salesgirl who was all of seventeen. Losing my cool in this manner was unattractive.

As I entered Bethany's, I was comforted to see Beth herself was there. Bethany had a solid business and sold tons of lingerie by the philosophy that there was nothing like quality sexy underwear to make a lady feel like she was in proper command of her day. It's her foundation. Of course, she likely meant surgeons, CEO's, and lawyers. But she always had such a warm smile that put everyone who came in contact with her at ease. The poor woman was getting up in years and the last few had been particularly difficult, health-wise.

"Brandy, darling, how are you?" Beth said, putting her clipboard down and staring at me like a mother peering at a sick child. Did I look as unnerved as I felt?

"The real question is, how are *you*?" I said, attempting to shift focus.

For such a demure, petite lady, Beth could out-swear Joe Pesci's character in Goodfellas. "Chemo is a mudder fucker," she cussed in a thick Jersey accent. As much as I may like a person, and as long as I have lived in the North, the Yankee accent never fails to be nails on a chalkboard to my eardrums. "What'd ya want me to tell ya? But I did get to see my first great-grandchild."

"Awesome! I had no idea." And I really didn't care.

"I don't like the sound of *Great Grandmother*," she said with genuine disgust in her voice. The next second, she melted. "But he is such a beautiful baby," Beth added with proud tears in her eyes.

Before I had time to react, she thrust baby pictures in my face. That kind of wigs me out when I'm high and Beth noticed my reaction. Glad I had on my big, round Gucci sunglasses.

"Sorry, Brandy, I know one of my best clients is ready to get down to business," she said while shuffling away her pictures. I could tell she was hurt a little.

Not wanting to appear uncaring, I said, "No, Miss Bethany," my Southern respectfulness knee-jerking into place, "I'm just feeling a little off my game today." That was the truth, though I always loathed admitting such things. I gave up my bra way too easily to Geney. I only let paying clients have my underwear. I wept over some silly short story/recipe from a realtor, of all people. I thought I was seeing people where there were none. My mother usually got to me, but she didn't often shake me up like this. And then to flinch at baby pictures… "Your grandchild is a very handsome baby, but I am in a bit of a hurry to get to D.C. Vampires."

D.C. Vampires, adjacent to Bethany's, always did my hair. Very convenient. The hurry part was a lie that I don't know why I told. You could now add confusion to my list of symptoms.

Beth seemed to be mollified. "Thanks for leaving out the *great* part. Now what can I do for you?"

"Have an order of my usual calling card panties sent to my condo. Also, will need my special bras."

"Brandy, you've been blessed with tits as taut as an eighteen-year old. You don't even need a bra."

"Thanks." I generally ignored compliments. I heard them often enough, but when I was fifteen, I already had D-cups and Mama was nearly four years into a campaign of covering me to protect me against "sins of the flesh." Even though my body was my best asset, I was still not completely comfortable in my own skin. But I was damn good at pretending. "Beth, here's an odd request. Do you have any golf sports bras?" I asked while ripping the tag off of a sports bra and throwing it at her. Why did I do that? That was rude. And what was a golf sports bra?

Her pencil-drawn eyebrows shot up. "Golf sports bras?"

"Yeah." I felt bit defensive, so I rambled. "I don't see how Cristina Kim or Natalie Gulbis do it sometimes. I'm always looking for an angle." I could see I wasn't getting through. "Yeah, so, just look into it for me. Mmm 'Kay?"

"Sure. I'll let you know if they even exist. Brandy, are you okay?"

I stared at her for a second, briefly forgetting my name. How could I forget the name I went by for the better part of two decades, even if it wasn't my birth name? "Fine. I've got to get to the salon next door."

Abruptly, I made for the door and the crisp, fresh November air. I stood there, eyes closed, breathing deeply and feeling a little better. My shoulders relaxed, and I began to slowly walk to my car, so I could take a hit off of that roach. Maintenance, remember. I was actually smiling. Feeling a little silly at how oddly I acted in Bethany's. *Oh well*, I thought, *why should I give a shit?*

I began to hear the song *Magic Man*, by *Heart*. Was it coming from the salon? As I ducked into the storefront, *Motley Crue's Live Wire* was blaring.

"Hey, Yvonne," I said to one of the partners who owned the place. "I know I don't have an appointment, but I was hoping you could fit me in for a quick color and trim."

"Sure, but Marge is the only one who's free right now."

"Fine," I huffed.

"Go right back then."

There were reasons why Marge was free; she talked too much and smacked her gum incessantly. She confided in me throughout my coloring job how sorry her children were, how she hated working there and how the state of the economy was a commie plot. All I wanted was for her to color me and let me read my *Golf Digest* in peace.

"So, Hun, you never told me why you have this little white spot on the side of your pretty little brunette head?"

I always tried to tune her out and was more than a little miffed at myself for not making an appointment with either Yvonne or Valena, the other owner. "What?" I snapped as she finished trimming the right side of my head.

"I asked, what gave you that white spot on the side of your head? I've always heard that in rare cases, people get these when they've had a shock or a huge trauma in their lives." She popped her gum, clearly waiting for me to answer her.

"Look, Marge, I don't fucking know." I instantly regretted swearing at her. I remembered when the spot started appearing, but didn't care to think of those days, nor could I recall much of that period in my life. "Marge, I'm sorry I cursed. Listen, I don't know how I got the spot. It's been there as long as I can recall. I'm really not in the mood to talk, so could you please just finish me up, so I can get to the mall?"

Marge stared blankly at me in the mirror and popped her gum. *Gawddamnit*, she was clueless.

Magic Man again! The volume was becoming distracting. "Marge, do you think you can get Valena to turn down the volume on that Heart song?"

"What? That's Motley Crue. It's basically all that tatted-up freak plays around here. So anyway, I heard that some of the soldiers coming back from the Middle East have these white spots to go along with a good case of PTSD."

"Marge, I told you I didn't know, and I don't wanna talk about it."

"I understand. It's just that you can't recall anything about it?"

"That's it! That's fucking it!" I said and ripped off the sheet before Marge could ask me any more prying questions.

"But I'm not done," Marge said.

"Oh yes, you are," I said as I wadded up a couple hundred-dollar bills and threw it at the counter on my way out.

I heard Yvonne call after me, but I was done.

As I rushed toward my BMW, I was fumbling through my Louis Vuitton purse for my keys and was stunned to look up and see *him* again. The man I saw outside Eugene's apartment. He was leaning on my hood, arms crossed, looking very amused at my obvious discomfiture. The hair on the back of my neck stood on end.

Magic Man began to play again in earnest. The volume gradually increased to a volume I'd expect to hear in Williams-Brice Stadium while watching my Gamecocks play. I looked around, but no one else seemed to hear it.

As I took more of him in, I noticed that he wore a dark tailored suit and matching dark tie offset by a white dress shirt with platinum cuff links. *I didn't miss money, even when I should have been focused on survival.* I noticed his dark hair and olive-colored skin but couldn't see his eye color behind a pair of Ray-Ban sunglasses. He looked like the Pierce Brosnan version of James Bond sans the sex appeal. Oddly, I could see him, but could not sense him.

Finally, I recovered enough to reach inside my purse for my Walther loaded with personal defense 9mm shorts. Daddy drilled firearms into his little girl. The man didn't even flinch. In fact, he smirked.

"Get the fuck off my car, asshole!" My voice screeched up an octave or two to outmatch the cacophony of the PA system in my head. My nerves were raw, and I could barely concentrate with *Magic Man* blaring. I pressed my hand to my left ear as hard as I could, while my shaky right hand held the Walther.

A family getting out of an SUV parked next to me stopped and stared. "Ma'am? We didn't touch your vehicle," the father said while the mother ushered the children out of my line of fire. I could see her frantically mashing numbers on her cell, presumably dialing 911.

In the instant it took me to look over at the family and look back, the man in the suit was gone, as well as Heart.

"No, of course not, I just thought I saw a former boyfriend who's having trouble letting go." I laughed to try to make light of the situation and save face. But my laugh was forced and high-pitched and it only served to make me sound crazier than I already appeared.

"Okaaaaaay..." The family obviously hadn't seen what I saw.

I looked down and saw my hand was shaking and my pistol was now pointed at an innocent family. I quickly engaged the manual safety and put the pistol away. "Sorry," I called weakly after them.

At this moment, calmness enveloped me. I straightened my unfinished hair and adjusted my purse. I looked around to see if others noticed, the way someone might look after falling on their ass. I just pointed a loaded weapon at children.

I did have enough sense to realize I needed to vamoose before the police arrived to take me off in handcuffs and booked me with more charges than I could come up with at the moment. Brandishing a firearm in the DC area was something even my pretty smile couldn't erase.

Chapter 6

By the time I made it to the mall, I was back in control of myself. I was amazed by the power of weed. Some asserted that I smoked too much of it, namely Geney, but I ignored those assertions. Only Buddha's axiom gave me pause. "Everything in moderation, even moderation." It calmed me so much that I ignored even that sage piece of advice. Besides, pot was a moderate drug. I contended that I didn't typically get drunk and never got into more than dabbling with *real drugs.*

In an effort to put the morning's unpleasantness behind me, I spent the next few hours Christmas shopping and completed about ninety percent of my list. I always allowed the remaining ten percent for odds and ends, though they could cost in the thousands of dollars.

I quickly checked my family in South Carolina off my list, except for Uncle Bobby. What could I get the man who had everything and desired nothing? A carton of menthols was the best I could come up with at that moment. I then shifted all my considerable efforts into my clientele. That was easier. I made all my clients believe they were my best clients and took care of them lavishly. After all, they paid the big bucks for my sweet ass and I learned early on from Mandy Stinger, the woman who started me in the business, that we were the elite in the world, as far as escorts go, and we were to give our clients their money's worth. They were to pay top dollar or barter the equivalent. In recent years, I came to enjoy the art of bartering since I had plenty of cash. Cars, trips, jewelry, and occasionally real estate came from my regulars. The second a client got cheap, a dastardly female malady would come on and he would get put on the shit list. Once a person made it on to this shit list, it was very difficult, in other words, expensive, to make it back into my good graces. This core philosophy made me money and kept them coming back for more.

The most lavish present of a Rolex was reserved for Geney. After all, money equaled love, didn't it?

My Christmas list read as a who's who of politicians, sports stars, movie stars, various other celebrities, millionaires and even billionaires. President Benton was among the notables.

I cut my whore teeth during the Benton years. His White House was party central. The First Lady obviously put up with his shenanigans for the power and prestige; I could respect that about her. The President was some of the most fun this Carolina girl ever deserved to enjoy. I missed those days, perhaps more than I should. As a matter of fact, the Commander in Chief was my first "John." Who would have thunk it? Me at 1600 Pennsylvania Ave. He actually had what he called the "First Bong" and usually, when he said Air Force One in my presence, he wasn't referring to his jet. It was kind of cute, really. We still break out the "First Bong" from time to time together.

I had a soft spot for my tour pros that were dull or cheap. I took part of my payment in golf lessons and golf trips. Sometimes I'd have Congressional to myself and offer private time in exchange. I felt changing a man's perspective on sex was a good trade if my tour pro taught me distance control and how to spin a golf ball to make it look like I was pulling a string to bring the ball back to the hole.

Swoondalini

As a matter of fact, my "to me, for me, from me" present was the new Titleist hybrid and fairway wood, along with the latest and greatest Nike driver. One tight son of a bitch in particular wouldn't even hook me up with the driver after I dropped hints and let him take me on the back side of the course. I made it worth my time, since I was now driving his new Escalade EXT that I claimed as my own. Couldn't really report it stolen, could he? Eventually, he officially signed it over to me while I was massaging his balls at Doral's Blue Monster. After all, I had to draw the line somewhere.

Enough of that. I feel strange even writing vague statements about my work, much less specifics on clients. Doesn't matter whether my writings ever see the light of day or not. It still goes against my professional code of ethics.

Now it was time to deliver a gift to the man that truly was my favorite client. I didn't really think of him in that way anymore as he was more of a father figure to me.

Chapter 7

I gunned my electric blue BMW up I-95 toward Bethesda, Maryland and Congressional Country Club. For the first time in as long as could remember, it occurred to me that in the opposite direction, southbound on I-95, was my home state of South Carolina. I used to think of that all the time when I first moved to D.C. from the south, but now only on rare occasions. I hadn't been back to Greenville since I left in the 90's. I-95 would drop me off directly into the little town of Yemassee, S.C., a former Marine Corp Recruit drop-off point, which one had to go through to get to Beaufort and what was left of my family. Was it time to go back to South Carolina? Why should I?

I had a lot of friends, acquaintances, and clients at Congressional and was even a member myself. I had a little town house with a golf course view and a golf cart's ride away from the clubhouse. My mentor Mandy bought it for business, and I ultimately bought it from her. Something I was proud of. The wives around there didn't care for it, but my "give a damn" was broken when it came to that sort of thing. Mandy required that we all be into some sort of sport and/or activity besides lying on our backs, so naturally I chose golf since my grandfather made me a driving range as a girl. I had a natural ability with the game, and I figured I could just ride around, look pretty in fabulous new outfits, and smoke weed. Golf had the added benefit of placing me around a shitload of older, wealthy, inebriated, self-important men. Love wasn't quite the word for what it became in recent years. Obsession was more like it.

Perhaps a few bags of range balls to clear my mind a little. The weather was warming as the sun shone through the clouds. Yes, this would be perfect, and

I was looking forward to my lunch date with my favorite Honorable Senator from the Big Sky state of Montana.

I felt the braking system shudder and I came in hot in front of the bag stand. "Hello, Miss Hart," Bruce, the valet boy, said. He loved me, as all of the male species did.

"Hey, Bruce," I said, flashing a smile. "Baby, would you take my bag out to the range while I grab some lunch. I believe there's a fifty spot in the front zipper, so take it for your tip."

"Yes ma'am, Miss Hart." Poor little boy was falling all over himself. "Anything else?"

"Not for now. I'll find your sweet little butt after lunch."

There was often a stir when my entitled ass strolled into the grill that was attached to the Men's Locker Room, traditionally male territory. It was an unspoken rule that women belonged in the main dining areas. I called that rule a guideline, which I relished blurring. Besides, it allowed me to be discreet in making appointments with my regulars.

Today was different since Congress was out of session for the holidays and very few clients were around. They were doing the *family* thing.

"Brandy, baby. How are you doing? What are you doing dressed like that?" In his voice, I could hear the joy at seeing me and the disappointment at not seeing enough of me at the same time. So, I shoved the senator's head under my braless sweatshirt for a "brumskee" (the term some loud-mouthed New Jersey boys taught me for the act of rubbing boobs in a guy's face).

"Goddamn it!" He sounded more pissed than excited, but I neglected to care. In fact, I thought it was pretty funny to see his fine silver hair was standing straight up.

"Hey, Senator Sam." Love and excitement bled through my normally controlled veneer. He reminded me of my pappy in that gentlemanly way that only men of an older generation embody. "How are you feeling today?" I truly did love Senator Sam Irving, but he had seen better days and his health was in decline. It didn't help that he was in his 80's, but only recently had he begun to lose the ramrod straight, rough-hewn, cowboy look that was his trademark. "I'm about to change but wanted to eat first. What are you doing? I was going to come by your house later. I have a present for you."

"I like your presents. What happened to your hair?" He pointed with his fork while slicking his hair back in place with his other hand.

I quickly spoke, ignoring his question. "Listen, you know what I want. Order for me, and I'll be right back after I change. I'm going to hit the driving range for a little while."

"Yeah, you better practice up, so I don't whip your ass all over this golf course."

"Are you going to give me some strokes?"

"You're very kind to this old man. The problem is you've come way too close to giving me a stroke on several occasions."

I winked and blew a kiss. "I'll be back in a second, babe." Out of habit, I made sure to sashay on the way out of the grill. Men sometimes forgot my posterior because of my chest size, but I liked to remind people that a size zero waist and an hourglass figure are down below. I was the total package. I failed to notice that I was wasting my efforts on an old man with nerve damage and a strange new bartender who was bent over, stocking a cooler. When did they replace Eddie? He'd been here for years. A total package could be totally obtuse. Eddie passed away nearly a year ago.

While I was changing, I checked out my hair in the lady's locker room mirror, and sure enough, the style bore a slight resemblance to *Flock of Seagulls*. "Holy shit, that busybody bitch Marge. Nothing a hat can't fix until tomorrow."

At any rate, I kept several outfits in my locker appropriate for country club life and was looking the part in my short skorts by the time I got back to our table.

***

"Brandy, not that I don't like your outfit, but isn't it a little chilly for that skirt?" Sam said with a parental tone.

"Sam, it's a skort and I have to look fabulous."

"You'd look fabulous in a potato sack."

"What?" I asked absently while darting my eyes around the Men's grill. My pesky nerves were beginning to assert themselves again.

"Brandy, you okay today? You seem a little off." The parental tone returned.

Was I that off my game? "Yeah, I got a call from Greenville." Sam knew me well enough to know that my relationship with my mother was strained. I decided not to include a ghostly stalker in a tailored suit and drawing my Walther on an innocent family with small children.

"Ah, enough said then. Anything you want to talk about?"

"No, not really. Thanks though. You want to watch my swing a while?" Even though Sam was beginning to get too old to play with me very often, he did provide some good advice on my swing from time to time. Mostly, I just enjoyed his company.

"Yeah, baby, I'll watch as long as I can stand the cold."

Cold? Montana boys never caught a chill.

"Thanks. It would mean a lot," I said in a rare moment of sensitivity.

We spent the rest of lunch talking golf and swapping gossip on common acquaintances we shared in our nation's capital.

***

"Why is he coming so close to us?" I asked. "It's interfering with my practice." The guy in the caged golf ball retriever was coming extremely close to us.

After about fifteen minutes, Sam had enough. "It's too cold, and I'm going in to talk to the executive pro about this guy. Any idea where you are spending the Thanksgiving holiday?"

"None at all," I said slowly. I felt like I had plans but couldn't recall what and where and with whom. "Have a good Thanksgiving, Sam," I said while giving him a quick peck on the cheek. I almost said I love you, but Brandy doesn't waste much effort on such sentiments.

I cringed as the deranged guy picking up golf balls buzzed me again. I shot him a bird and took dead aim at his cart with my driver off the deck. *Clank.*

I watched Sam amble off. In retrospect, he seemed glad to be walking away from me. I knew Sam cared for me, but there was a distance that emerged between the two of us lately. Even with this important male figure in my life, I chose to remain wrapped in myself. What could be more fabulous than that?

I glared back at the ball retriever cart as it sped away from me and fired two more drivers off the deck that found their target as well. The ball retriever guy yelled back something that I'm sure was very nasty in a proper British accent. Exactly what he said was drowned out by the ball retriever driving faster and more erratic than I ever saw one go. He was everywhere and nowhere, like a determined horse fly. This guy was too much and was giving me a dull headache. Perhaps a nap at my town home and then I'd call in to complain about this loser.

Chapter 8

DEATH

In the fifteen minutes it took for me to pay my tab for lunch, get Bruce to load my clubs up, and drive around the corner to the town house, I was feeling really *funky*. I didn't care for using the word *funky,* but I'm not sure how else to describe a headache followed by confusion over whether I needed to puke, crap my pretty little skort, cry, or run. Run? Where in the fuck would I run to? And run from what? So, I suppose *funky* would cover that if no other word would.

I managed to keep myself together until I could get in the house. I made chit chat with the neighbors who lived and died by my comings and goings. I waved at the teenage boy and his father across the street that loved when I was there and was in the door. That's when things ratcheted up a notch.

I locked the door and leaned against it for an interminable amount of time, breathing heavily. That stopped the downward spiral briefly. I thought a beer would further calm my nerves, but it had the opposite effect. I saw that my old answering machine was flashing. Not many people actually had this number. I hit the play button and heard the sonorous sound of my uncle Bobby's voice. I heard that he left the message earlier today about Thanksgiving or something but heard no more as an intense wave of nausea hit as he was getting to the point. My mouth started sweating and I knew I had to run for the toilet.

I lay there on the floor, spent after puking for a solid four minutes and twenty seconds. I know because I made note of it when I cleaned part of my

Congressional Club sandwich off of my platinum Rolex. There had to be something ironic about the amount of time I puked, but I didn't care to dig deeper. I rarely did. I began to feel a little better as the nausea subsided and the cool floor soothed my bare legs.

What the hell was wrong with me? I didn't think I could be pregnant. Was it food poisoning? A virus? Could be. I hoped it was. Should I go to the doctor? What a pain in the ass that would be on a holiday week.

As I gathered my wits, I realized I vomited all over myself. A shower wouldn't be so bad and might just make me feel like a new woman. The master shower at my town house was the most unique shower I ever scrubbed my svelte body in. I had my D.C. condo's master shower fashioned after it. It was more like a shower cave and was the deciding factor in buying the place.

I slowly got to my feet and steadied myself. I was definitely coming around. Maybe I purged my system and got "it" all out.

I stripped off all my clothes and admired myself in the mirror, as I always did. I felt it akin to checking to see if your wallet was still there or that your door was locked at night before bed. I always checked out my naked body to satisfy myself that I was holding up, that I was still a sculpture of perfection at 32DDD 19 34. I remained unchanged since my teen years. If anything, the years added more tone and refinement to my body. Never thought that could be possible.

I began to feel the calmest I felt since getting up this morning. Gazing at my reflection usually had that effect. But then I felt a desire to grab my old 1911 Colt .45 out of the nightstand and end my pretty total package right then and there. What was that? Was suicide really painless? I never pondered the question until now. Merciful was the first word that came to mind.

Swoondalini

I willed my lungs to inhale deeply, and then marched into my shower cave. My shower never failed to ease any tension. I turned on all seven shower heads as steamy as I could get it, then slowly released my breath. I placed my head and body under the harsh caress of water that was just this side of scalding.

Then "it" started. The nausea came back full force. I assumed the arrest position and wretched out what little was left until I was dry heaving. Then extreme fatigue and confusion set in. Time ceased to have meaning. Thirty seconds or thirty minutes passed, for all I knew. Unwisely, I came out of the arrest position to wash the puke off my front side. When I stood erect, I had a brief flash of normalcy before I felt his presence.

The last thing I saw with my physical eyes was him walking through the wall of my shower cave. At that point, the shock set in, and I went down like an elephant being darted on Mutual of Omaha's Wild Kingdom.

In what was probably the amount of time it took for my body to hit the river rock shower floor, I experienced a memory of my pappy that I hadn't thought of since his passing. This was my daddy's father. A man that spoke only when something pertinent had to be said. Pappy took me on one of his nature walks, in particular, the nature walk when he taught me about the resurrection ferns that grow on live oaks. He removed his ever-present cigar and spoke. "Resurrection fern is one of the wonders of Lowcountry's nature. It grows on live oaks, a tree that can live for hundreds of years, and will appear dead after a dry spell. Then, when the rain falls, the miracle happens."

"What's that, Pappy?"

"It returns to life, like the phoenix from the fire. Like Jesus himself."

Pappy jammed his cigar back between his teeth and faded into the shroud of Spanish moss.

Then darkness steamed my vision.

Several loud heartbeats passed, and I opened my *new* eyes to see him emerge from the steam of the shower. He bent down over my crumpled form, examined me head to toe, and unceremoniously jerked my arm.

It seemed like an instant of forever. I had out of body experiences before. (Not that I confided that to anybody.) There was the typical "sound" of metal upon metal grinding and squealing without lubrication. I heard hushed, whispering tones that I took to be voices. This was way more intense than any of my previous experiences. And then a loud pop, and I was on my feet, light as air. I felt great. No pain. No nausea. The confusion subsided, but the clarity brought a new realization.

My back was to the intruder. I forgot all about him during the time I was apparently being forced out of my body. He was between me and my body on the shower floor.

"Oh, shit!"

"You can say that again, sister," replied a British voice.

I stood there, mouth agape.

"What, no quip? Thought you had an answer for everything?"

"Your suit's not getting wet," I pointed out weakly.

"That's the best you have?"

"Yep, okay, you got me. I'm standing here, and my body is apparently over there. I guess I'm dead, so excuse the fuck out of me if I'm off my game."

"No, you're not dead." He paused and added, "Yet," with relish.

"That's good, I suppose. Who the hell are you? The grim reaper?"

"No, he's extremely busy, and he is a lot gentler than me."

Swoondalini

"What's that supposed to mean?"

He leered at me, but not in the way I was used to having men leer at me. "You'll find out. Oh, get that pout off your pretty little face. We'll be fast friends before too long. You'll see."

I stood there, staring at my body again. Mercifully, the steam all but obscured it. Was it the shower or was he doing it? "Fine. Whatever. Who are you then?"

"You needn't be concerned about who I am. You'd be better served pondering what I am."

"Maybe so, but I feel like we need to get to know each other a little better. After all, you just popped my death cherry."

"As I said, you're not dead yet, and you've already died hundreds of times, so don't get dramatic with me." He paused for effect. "I have gone by many names throughout time, but just for today, you may call me Nigel," he pontificated.

"Nigel, like a butler, or a limo driver?" I couldn't help myself.

He smiled a patient little smile one might put on their face when witnessing a three-year old hold its breath in a tantrum. "Pretty cheeky for the situation you find yourself in. We'll soon find out how long that will hold true."

"What do you intend to do with me? Rape me?"

"You've done quite well at raping yourself for a long time now. I'm here to give you your money's worth. Of that, you can be sure."

"What's that supposed to mean?" I demanded.

I just pushed him too far. He was nose to nose with me quicker than I could blink. He definitely grew a little larger to loom over me. Before speaking, he looked up and around as if to say I told you so to someone in the background I couldn't perceive. "I make the rules here, *Brandy*—you pathetic piece of shit. You can't even use your real name and you make light of mine. You're the one whose body lies impotent on the river rocks over there. If you don't hop to, you will not return to it."

It wasn't just him looming over me that was intimidating, it was the massive amounts of energy being thrown my way from every direction. Even from within. It was as if he was holding back the power of an atom bomb, and one false move from me would unleash its fury.

"Okay. Okay." I held up my hands in submission. "What do you have in mind for me? What happens now?"

He backed off and began studying my various shower heads, body washes and shampoos. Cool and calm now as if we were ordering cocktails. The energy dissipated. "I'm glad you asked. Finally, we're getting somewhere." He turned to look pointedly at me. "Time is money, is it not?" I bobbed my head. No need to stir him up again. "The journey you are about to embark on is an experience that can be likened to going through Marine Corp Boot Camp in that little backwater home state of yours. I am your drill sergeant, and you are my recruit, or "boot" if you like. The major difference between me and the Marine Corp is the Marines tend to coddle their boots. You know, build them back up to be proper Marines after they've torn their humanity completely apart. *I DON'T CODDLE!*" he seethed.

"No, I wouldn't take you for a coddler." I always had a little jab even when I would have been better served keeping my mouth shut.

"Shut your hole, whore."

Swoondalini

I had been called a whore countless times, but it never bothered me or cut to the bone the way it did now. I was a whore, but I reasoned that I had so much to show for it. What if I was really dead, then my actions up to now would be all I was remembered for. This was a sobering realization.

Instinctively, I responded, "Sir, yes sir." Where did that come from?

"May I continue?"

"Do you need my permission?"

He simply raised an eyebrow. "As I was saying, the Marine Corp builds you back up after tearing you down. I do *NOT*. That will be completely up to you."

His last words to me blurred in my mind as the shower dissolved around us.

Chapter 9

KUNDALINI RISING

I could not have been more surprised at what appeared before my eyes next. More accurately, I smelled and felt the vibrations of artillery, all in an instant before I heard and saw it. *War.*

I even knew the size of the shells by the sound. I knew the difference between ingoing and outgoing artillery, naval versus land-based.

What I felt was blood, bones, brains, guts, and Pacific Ocean spray as I waded through waist deep water surrounding the volcanic island of Iwo Jima. How did I know it was Iwo? I looked to my right, where Frady just took a direct hit from a mortar and there was a red greasy film on the surface of the water where he was only moments before. McPherson and I looked at each other in shock, but that lasted only a second.

"They've got us zeroed. Move!"

How did I know the Japs had us zeroed and what zeroed meant? How did I know their names? I felt like I was on a nightmare episode of Quantum Leap, sans the lusty, kind, and helpful hologram, Al. Instead, I had some British psychopath who ambushed me while I was taking a shower. Where was Nigel, anyway?

"What the fuck?" I yelled above the din of battle. Barely audible.

"I know, Sutton, I got him all over me too."

"How did you know my name?"

McPherson looked at me as if I just grew a second head. "Stop fucking around. We need to get to the beach, Marine."

Chris Suddeth

We finally made it to the beach, but it felt like I was back on Parris Island running through the salt marsh. I looked down and the reality struck me all at once when I saw the black volcanic sand. The sands of Iwo Jima. I was holding a M1 Garand and it was February 19, 1945. Bullets and shrapnel were zinging all around, but I was in shock. I felt my chest with my hand. Why was my hand so large and heavy? My heart was pounding out of my chest. I looked down again and realized my beautiful breasts were gone. In their place were powerful pectoral muscles. Man hands? I felt thick hair on my usually baby soft legs. I felt my crotch as I squeamishly squenched my eyes. I had a package, and a rather large one at that. So, this was how the other half lived?

What did he do to me? I felt like I was me on the inside; kind of. Was I still me? Speaking of being zeroed, mortars and artillery began to burst all around me with an intensity that isolated me from the rest of the Pacific Theater in 1945. "No man is an island?" Whoever wrote that obviously did not live through what I was living through right then. A wall of volcanic ash and metal that could cut a man in half surrounded me. There was nowhere to run, nowhere to hide. I heard the last shouts and whimpers of Marines all around me, but I remained mostly untouched.

When I thought, "This is it? I can't even die the way I was born, a girl. I have to die on some rock thousands of miles and thirty years away from where and when I was born." Nigel emerged from the chaos, unscathed.

"Of course, you are still you, my dear lady. Or should I say my fine fellow." He was having a chuckle at my expense. "Ha, get it?"

I stared at him, dumbstruck, and flinched at every little sound.

"Oh, don't be melancholy. You are still you," Nigel said in a teacher to student sort of way. "But you're him, too."

"Him, who?"

"You should probably duck or something," he said, feigning a yawn. "Those are indeed real bullets."

I tripped over a body and fell face first into the warm, putrid guts of another Marine who was unfortunate enough to still be living.

"And do you know who this man you appear to be is?" Nigel inquired.

Wait a minute. I did know who HE is, or was, rather. I knew it without knowing how or why. I just simply knew that I was Corporal Elmer Sutton, United States Marine Corps, 4th Marines, 2nd wave ashore, from Pelzer, SC. We already distinguished ourselves in battle at Roi-Namur, Saipan, and Tinian (famous for being the take-off island for the Enola Gay).

Anticipating my next question, Nigel said, "Yes, souls often choose to incarnate in the same locale over the course of several lifetimes." As if reincarnation was a foregone conclusion.

After that statement, he began to walk toward Mount Suribachi, and away from me lying in the lifeblood and guts of a fellow Marine.

To quote a favorite movie of mine, 'cause what can you do but laugh in certain situations, "I couldn't have been more surprised if I woke up with my head stapled to the carpet." But this was no holiday comedy, and I wasn't talking to Cousin Eddie. This was real. At least it felt real.

"Oh, it's real, alright." He was still getting his jollies off my predicament. "Check your right cheek to see how real it is, old boy."

Come to think of it, the right side of my face was stinging. I reached up and removed what appeared to be a bit of skull from Frady, presumably. I felt I received this particular wound before.

Nigel turned and began slowly walking away again.

"Wait a goddamn minute! Just where the fuck do you think you're going?"

"Search that thick noodle of yours. How long were you on this glorious rock, fighting for America's freedom?"

Instantly, the answer came to me. "Thirty-six days, but I can't recall if I made it off alive."

He grinned from ear to ear. "I know. It's fantastic, isn't it?" he said rhetorically. "I blocked that little tidbit of information to make it more exciting and *educational*." Nigel enunciated educational proudly in his prim parlance.

"Tidbit! Educational!" I said incredulously as I squinted through the sand blasting at me by another near miss mortar.

Nigel ignored me and walked on through the battle smoke. Before disappearing into the smoke, he yelled back, "As you can see, I'm a very busy man and have much work to attend to." With that he was gone. Vapor.

"Come back here, you limey son of a bitch!"

But it was no good. He was gone. What work did he have to *attend* to?

***

Really, it's hard to say, but I believe it took us a few days of fighting before we established the beachhead and got inland enough to dig a foxhole. We were all running on pure adrenalin. Kill or be killed.

Swoondalini

When I finally crawled in my foxhole and began to settle down as much as one can in such a ludicrous situation, I began to worry if I had my monthly out here with all these men. How was I going to shave my legs? Brush my hair? I was usually at my best when surrounded by men, but never dreamed it could be a disadvantage, and a deadly one, at that.

"Sutton?"

I would generally own a type A, man's man such as this Sutton fellow. I would envelope him inside of me and he would give me his children's college fund if I so desired. I was now inside of him on a whole other level. I couldn't believe two such different people could dwell in the same body.

And boy, did this body smell. Blood, guts, sweat, dirt, and various other things… A bubble bath would be luxurious right now.

"Psst! Sutton! I need a lighter. My Zippo took some shrapnel…"

Where am I going to find some weed around here?

"Sutton, you big-assed ape, I know you can hear me!" McPherson whispered, although it sounded more like a scream since we'd all lost our voices to some degree, or another, from having to shout above the din of battle.

McPherson snapped me out of my reverie. I was not a woman, despite walking like one when I wasn't paying attention. No one noticed since it was life and death here. I needn't worry about my monthly, and if I could find weed… Well, let's just say I definitely needed to keep my wits about me with all these little fuckers trying to kill me. "McPherson? Is that you?"

"Yes, it's me, goddamn it. We've been together the whole time. Why are you acting so weird? I mean, other than the Nips trying to kill us again."

"Sorry." I shifted suddenly in my foxhole to get to my Zippo. When I shifted, my legs went one way, and my balls went the other, tweaking them.

Jesus, that hurt! So that's what it felt like. I would endeavor to be gentler down below with my men, if I ever got back to Brandy.

The anger at having to leave visions of bongs and bubble bath and the discomfort in the crotch pushed Corporal Sutton back to the forefront, making Brandy little more than an observer. I grabbed the lighter and flung it at McPherson, catching him in the forehead, right below his helmet and drawing blood.

"Was that necessary, asshole?"

That was definitely not a throw Brandy could have executed.

Chapter 10

It would, in fact, feel like thirty-six days of living hell that would be known as the battle for Iwo Jima, because it was. Because of what we Marines did (yes, I just said we), many American Airmen would live to eat Mom's apple pie again.

My incarnation did survive Iwo. It was touch and go several times, but after I learned what a Jap (I understand Jap is not PC, but I never was PC to begin with) smelled like, it got easier at night. Night was when they came out of their holes and really tried to do you in. I was wounded in other battles in the Pacific Theater, but not Iwo. I was fortunate to have only gotten my front teeth knocked out by the butt of a Japanese rifle. I would have them replaced with gold teeth.

It was on the last day that I saw Nigel emerge from napalm smoke burning off of enemy bodies that I knew he was coming back for me. Brandy was nearly forgotten. Nearly. I was so consumed with surviving Iwo that all else took a backseat. Now that the battle was winding down, I was taking pride in being a Marine. Surprising, given the hell I just went through, but sharing in the camaraderie of my fellow Marines, mourning my fellow Marines, protecting and being protected by my fellow Marines was what I was all about. I loved being a Marine. What was it I loved? Hell, I even knew Ira Hayes, the fourth Marine in the famous photograph and statue. I desired to visit that statue so many times in my years in Washington, but never did. I always had the odd sensation that I wasn't brave enough. I even recall being entranced by it as a little girl when Pappy used to take me over to the Parris Island version. If I ever returned alive, I'd never take it all for granted. Probably end up visiting it all the time.

At any rate, the second I saw Nigel, Brandy began to reassert herself. I took care not to walk like a woman. It was odd being two distinct people at once. One thing the two of us would take pleasure in, was that we'd both like to throttle Nigel. Nigel was inciting rage in our minds. We wanted to kick his teeth in.

I considered myself strong for a petite female. I was mostly muscle, despite the only exercise I got was on my back and my obsession with golf, but this guy, this bear of a man, had more muscle in his little finger than I had in both my arms.

I was having an orgasmic vision of wrapping my talons around his throat when he said the last thing I expected he would say. "You're most welcome, my dear. No need to thank me," he said earnestly. He might as well have sucker-punched me with brass knuckles.

With those words, 1945 and Iwo Jima were left to history.

Chapter 11

I was back in the vortex, for lack of a better word, that transported me to the Pacific Theater of World War II. I could sense Nigel with me but could not see him. I heard him speaking in muffled tones to others that were much further away. Although, I didn't get the impression that distance had much meaning here.

Suddenly, the voices became more animated. I heard snippets here and there. It sounded as if they were making this up as they went along.

"You think she can handle that?" a gruff-sounding voice said.

"Positively," Nigel asserted.

"Very well, proceed," a birdsong-like voice said.

"Cheers," Nigel said as a sendoff. Then he turned his attention to me and I could see him. "You ready for your next stop?"

"Do I have any choice?"

"Sure, you do." His expression did not match his words.

"Where to next then? The Crusades, Spanish Inquisition, Salem Witchcraft Trials?"

"Interesting you would bring up religion. Would you like to visit any mountain churches? Hmm?" He then lost himself in thought, ignoring my discomfiture at the mention of my frequent night terror.

"You're not sending me to any of that, are you?"

"What? —Hmph… Oh no," he stammered, as if it was far worse than being on an island for over a month with thousands of suicidal Japs. "Those are all excellent ideas that we will take under advisement though."

"I was being a smartass."

"Doesn't make your ideas any less valid."

I always needed a lesson in how to hold my tongue which now seemed very poignant. "So seriously, where are you taking me now?" I asked timidly. I didn't want the same atomic energy that ended the war I just left to be directed my way again. I could tell the vortex was slowing, and it was adding to the anticipation along with Nigel's sudden quiet, pensive mood. What was Nigel up to? What had I done to deserve all this? Maybe Geney put something in my weed as retribution for the scathing blue balls incident. He could be a sneaky little fucker. "Taking me back to the shower?" I asked hopefully. Not only would the shower mean that this, whatever *this* was, would be over, but I hadn't properly showered in over a month. I crapped in my foxhole, or wherever I was hunkered down for fear of exposure to the enemy emerging from nowhere as they were known to do on Iwo. I didn't even feel human. I never desired a shower so badly in all of my life.

"No, I'd be doing you a disservice to send you back there this early in the game," Nigel replied with a knowing, arched eyebrow.

"I've been gone thirty-six days," I offered weakly.

"Time, schmime. When are you going to learn? No, you can take comfort in the fact that you're going someplace very familiar to your current incarnation."

"Can I really?"

***

Swoondalini

Twin Peaks Gentlemen's Club in Columbia, SC materialized around me. Funny that my younger self thought it was a sign from God that I was in the right place when I spotted the letter board out front that read, "Now Hiring the Class of 1993." My body was back, a younger, long-haired version of it, at any rate. I was so glad to have at least some version of my body back. I got lost in myself, looking in the mirror. I would miss the strength and coordination of my Marine incarnation, but this body was home.

I remembered leaving home at seventeen in a vague typhoon of emotion before graduation that was still ambiguous nearly two decades later. My diploma was mailed to my employer's address, and I enrolled in the University of South Carolina. I kept my grades up but piled up demerits in my junior and senior years of high school, mostly out of an intense desire to be undesirable to Bob Jones University and to piss off my mother.

I lied about my age to get the job. I knew that I was attractive, but never dreamed of it as a meal ticket until right before I left Greenville, SC. I figured it was my only shot at a new life and the best strip club in the state would lead me there. The manager took one look at me with my clothes off, and another at my pathetic attempt at a fake I.D., then hired me on the spot, never even asked me if I could dance. I did have what people in show business called stage presence, so I suppose that's either something you have, or you don't.

"Can't help getting caught up in yourself, can you?" My reflection spoke back to me in Nigel's haughty voice and snapped me out of my self-ogling. He was here with me, in what I believed was June of 1993.

"What?"

He then appeared beside me, momentarily throwing me off as I kept looking back and forth between my reflection and his, and the Nigel by my side. "You have a job to do."

"You haven't explained exactly what that job is yet, now have you."

"Are you really so dense? Can you not get past your tits for a minute and see you're fighting for your life?"

"I just got done fighting for my life for thirty-six days, remember."

"Wrong, you feckless excuse for a quaintrelle! You just got done surviving for thirty-six days."

"I don't see the difference."

"Somehow, that doesn't surprise me. You'll either sink or swim. We're throwing you a life buoy, but we cannot make you grasp it. I would tell you not to waste my time, but time is irrelevant, other than in the physical sense. You're going to have to figure it out on your own, sweet-cheeks. Ta ta." He slapped me hard on the ass, walked through the full-length mirror in the dressing room, and faded out.

I was stunned by the sting his hand left, and the fact that it was a flesh and blood hand that spanked me. Perhaps I really could choke him. Sweet-cheeks? Quaintrelle? What's a quaintrelle? What did he mean by that time comment? Did he think he was doing me a favor by putting me through the wringer? Evidently so, but with favors like this, what if he really chose to do me harm?

I was brought out of my thoughts and back to reality as I heard the house D.J. announce, "Braaaaaaaaaaandy HAAAAARRRRTTT on deck." I just came up with that name on this particular evening as I arrived for my first shift. I felt it fitting for my new life. Brandy was definitely a stripper's name and Hart was the name of one of the most powerful families in Greenville, so it made sense.

"Holy shit!" I cursed since I was still naked. Being naked in a strip club comes with the territory, but first, you have to have clothes on to strip off. I needed to hustle.

I ran to the back of the dressing room closet where we kept the standard strip club outfits and ran right into the woman that would become the Heidi Fleis of Washington D.C., and the United States, by extension, Mandy Stinger. She was fifteen years older, and no doubt threatened by my looks. Still, to this day, I had yet to decide if Mandy did more to help or hurt me. She was an enigma. The closest I came to an answer was the fact that I would not have made my millions had I not started with her. I never allowed myself to stop and think what the true cost was.

"Baby cunt, you'd better get the fuck out of my way. I own this place. I hope you can dance; otherwise, it's going to be a real quick trip here for ya. I don't care if those things are real or not." She thumped my nipple so hard, it made me wince. She took satisfaction from my pain before walking off.

I was now remembering back to Mandy's dance skills. They were top notch where mine were sorely lacking. Just a few years from now, Mandy would be forced "behind the desk," so to speak, as she became more and more cartoonish with plastic surgery. She said it herself, "An elite escort should be slurring her words from the effects of top-shelf alcohol and not botched collagen injections." That coupled with the fact that her 38J's made it look as if she had two bowling balls strapped to her chest brought other, more devious talents to the surface. I suppose all this served us well enough as she built an empire and took me and a select few along for the ride. She even brought along a couple guys.

I blasted at her the way I did that first night, "Mandy, honey, when you look like this, you don't have to know how to dance." I said all of this with a confidence I didn't feel.

"Keep thinking that, smartass."

"Oh shit," I muttered under my breath as my stomach lurched. It hit me all at once. This was indeed my first-time stripping. I remembered a boyfriend in high school that I gave my cherry to in what I felt was a sweet, touching, and poignant moment in a young girl's life, but this was not high school, and this was not the Upstate I fled for unremembered reasons. Even though I was thirty-four, in my head, I felt the reality of seventeen. It's all about how you feel, isn't it? And I was feeling positively uneasy and nauseous. Did this mean I was going to pull out of this body the same way I did in my shower cave?

The old saying, "if only I knew then, what I know now…" was total bullshit. At least in this case, it was. Unless…

I barely made it to the trash can before I lost my lunch. Got some in my hair too. Nice…

Trudy heard me and poked her head in to check on me. "Baby?" Damn, she had a thicker accent than me, being from Cleveland, GA, "You okay? My name's Trudy. What's yours?" she said in a voice so calming. "Baby, you've got a little vomit in your hair." Oh, sweet Trudy. Poor thing had a heart so big, it sucked all her brain power away, aside from basic functions like eating and breathing. She had this wild finale where she'd slap her whole body against the stage to draw even more attention to her athletic figure. It elicited jaw-dropping shock among those who had never seen the routine and demanded respect from the rest of us.

"Yeah, I'll be fine. Name's Brandy Hart," I stated naturally. It wouldn't take long to get used to the new persona.

"Good to meet you, Brandy. Sweetie, you've got to pull yourself together. You're on right after this song," and she shook my hand despite a little vomit. She didn't appear to mind. "Honey, how old are you?"

"Eighteen," I said a little too quickly.

"I'm not the PO-lice."

"I turned seventeen last August."

"Well, you look twenty-five, but your eyes say innocent as a newborn fawn. I suppose Hector took one look at the skin you're in and decided being old enough to vote didn't matter."

She began dressing me in a nurse's outfit and cleaning me up. I allowed her to, as if I was a little girl being helped into her Halloween costume. Why was I feeling seventeen again? Shouldn't this night be a breeze? Certainly, I should feel fear in battle, but this was my territory. Peddling flesh was my bread and butter.

The music halted for a second before the DJ did his build-up routine to introduce me. I thought I was going to pass out.

"There it is, babe, the stripper's anthem," Trudy said. It was true. I could never hear *Def Leppard's "Pour some Sugar on Me"* without thinking of a strip club, and in particular, Twin Peaks Gentleman's Club. "Brandy, let's go. Give them a shoe show they'll never forget," she said as she finished dressing me and gave me a gentle shove on stage. "Shake that ass."

My stripping career was off and running. Visions of what my father would think blasted through my head with an intensity stronger than the first time I careened through Twin Peaks. But they were the same sequence of thoughts.

One thing was a little different though. Given my relative objectivity, I noticed the men, and some women, gawking in a way they didn't do with the other girls. It certainly wasn't my dancing and all of the other girls here were very attractive. I had something. It wasn't until a few years later that a high-profile client told me I had the "it" factor. I ignored it as I ignored most compliments after I left South Carolina, but I never forgot it. I never realized until this moment and took it for granted all my life. For better or worse, people were drawn to me.

Finally, one guy, about my age, came up and gave me a hundred-dollar bill. It was obvious that the older gentleman he was with gave it to him, put him up to it, and snuck him in. Who was this kid? I couldn't discern his face in the lights and cigarette smoke. He felt familiar, but he had a sad, disappointed look on his features that confused me until I was forced back into the moment by the sensation of money being shoved in my g-string.

The lights and the smoke produced a bleary, astral impression on my senses. No matter, I just had to survive this song. Who would have thought that four minutes and twenty-four seconds could seem so long?

The boy sparked something in me, a remembrance of sorts. I caught a flash of red hair and then he blurred quickly into the crowd. He ran and the gentleman he was with trailed directly behind him through the door. I didn't even recall the hair until this moment. I did recall that I didn't remember much at all after this dance. Why was that? It was as if someone used White-Out on large portions of my memory of this night.

Typically, a girl would dance two songs: warm-up for the first song while dancing seductively, then lose her clothes except for the g-string by the end of the first song or the first part of the second song. But since I removed my entire outfit, g-string included, which was frowned upon, within the first thirty seconds, the DJ mercifully said, "Let's hear it for Brandy, ladies and gentlemen. Brandy Hart. She's worth every dollar you put in her g-string, folks. Wait, she's not wearing a stitch, ladies and gentlemen. She let it all hang out. Awesooooome! Show some love to our freshest meat direct from Heaven's market. She's here all night." Patrons wadded up money and threw it at me. Trudy came on stage, roused me from being a fawn in headlights, and helped me gather up my booty.

"I don't know why they didn't pull you off stage," Trudy said.

I can only attribute it to the aforementioned "it" factor. Hector just gawked at me and I'm sure he'd seen it all.

"Why? What's wrong?"

"Full nudity and a liquor license don't go hand-in-hand in the state of South Carolina. I wouldn't do that again," Trudy chastised.

Despite my awkwardness, I made almost five-hundred dollars while at Twin Peaks that first night, which was totally unheard of.

***

After my dance, the time came where one trawls the club like a shrimp boat. A dancer must try to entice, or up-sell, the customers into lap dances or the VIP rooms where the real money was made. Due to my obvious rookie status, Mandy was assigned to show me the ropes in that department. Why couldn't it have been Trudy? She seemed much nicer.

Mandy warmed to me after she saw my earning potential on stage. We worked the room for a few minutes without any takers, and then reeled in a group of gentlemen from Knoxville, TN. I lined them up for the VIP room for the next hour or more.

Mandy inserted herself in my life for the first time. "Would you gentlemen like a two for one deal to go back to your place?"

"Huh?" was all I could get out as I played with one fellow's hair and sat in his lap. I encouraged his growing hard-on by slowly writhing up and down on his lap and giggling. I was growing tipsy with this newfound command over those who desired me.

"Don't stop, baby, we were just getting warmed up," the oldest gentleman complained, and grabbed my breasts firmer than I liked.

The shock of Mandy busting up our little party didn't last long as they realized that they could really have me. Rusty, the flashiest and drunkest of the four proclaimed, "Why not? How much we talking?"

"Ten grand for three hours."

"How much for the whole night?" Rusty tossed back.

"Twenty." Mandy hit him back with the number so quickly, my head spun.

"Fifteen. I like it when we meet in the middle," he said, obviously proud of his sly little comment.

"Sold," Mandy said with an avaricious grin on her face.

Swoondalini

"We'll meet you out by the limo as soon as we settle our bar bill," the man I would come to know as the Preacher, decreed.

"Ah, ah, doll. Have you got some cash in that limo?" My, Mandy sure was pushy. Must have been the Jersey girl in her. To her credit, she said it in a sugar sweet way as she sat in Preacher's lap and started grinding as if in heat.

"I've got five grand on me right now, and the rest is back in my room," the one they called Beefcake slurred.

She jumped up quickly. (Always leaving them wanting more.) "Let's go then. Get yourself together…" she trailed off, making a rolling motion with her hand, hinting for my name.

"Brandy Hart," shot out of my mouth so quickly, it surprised me how quickly the ebbing current of my memories was washing Alice out into the foggy Atlantic.

"Alright, Brandy, follow my lead when we get there and be professional and courteous, very courteous."

"Hector said we weren't supposed to leave the premises with customers," I stuttered with uncertainty. Christ, I sounded like I memorized the rules or something. I was about to get my first demonstration from the force of nature that was Mandy Stinger.

"Listen, little girl," she said as she grabbed my nipple in what felt like a vice grip. A sharp electric pain shot up my neck and into my jaw. She maintained a perfect smile on her features for the gentlemen still departing. She sucked snot in quickly before responding. "Don't fuck this up. You're lucky I'm letting you have five grand out of this deal."

I forgot about Mandy's blow habit… Scarface had nothing on her. It was as if all this was happening for the first time. "Five grand?" When I questioned the number, her grip clenched a little tighter. Good God! It felt like a stone crab attached to my chest. Beads of sweat popped out on my forehead. Her smile permeated pleasure as she asserted herself further.

"Damn, girl, you've got a lot to learn. It's called a finder's fee. You were just going to sit around here with your thumb up your ass, make a few hundred in the VIP lounge, and dance, if you want to call what you did on stage back there dancing. This is where the real money is made. Be lucky I don't take more than that. Now get your shit together. Our gentlemen await us."

"But how do we get out of here without Hector noticing?"

"Follow me in the back, put your clothes on, walk around the corner of the dressing room, and out the back door. The fire alarm hasn't worked for years and Hector always stays up front by the bar."

I looked to find Trudy, only to see her busy on stage. No help there… Mandy arched her eyebrow, waiting for me to acknowledge her marching orders. A simple nod of my head changed my destiny.

Business attended to, she released her grip on my nipple. It throbbed as the blood rushed back to it. That would leave a mark tomorrow.

As soon as we got in the limo to go back to their hotel, we started getting the party warmed up. Rusty was apparently in charge of the drugs, owing to the fact that as soon as the limo door closed, and Beefcake nodded, Rusty threw a bag of ecstasy pills, a bag of coke, and a bag of weed on the floor. I smoked weed and dropped acid for rebelliousness' sake, but never saw the likes of cocaine and ecstasy in my life. Everybody made a grab for the trick or treat of their choice. I noticed the oldest gentlemen, the same one I was perched on when we started this deal, was really hitting the white powder hard.

Swoondalini

"Gentlemen," I said with confidence I didn't feel. "I think introductions are in order. My name is Brandy Hart." I wanted to slow things down. Everything was happening far quicker than I liked.

The oldest leered back at me for one uncomfortable moment too long, then decided to humor me with his name. "Name's Buddy. People call me Bud, ma'am, like the beer" he drawled, in a forced old-world Southern accent to cover his wrong side of the tracks upbringing.

I smiled and offered my hand, then asked the crowd, "Somebody throw me that weed please," so I'd at least sound into it.

"Better listen to him, Brandy. He is a menace to society."

They all thought that was very clever for some reason.

"Weed is for pussies," Rusty slurred, without taking his eyes off of Mandy. "Preacher over there asked me to get it."

"The Israelites grew hemp on their farms in Biblical times."

"Preacher?"

Before I could let the fact that a preacher was among this crowd sink in, a portly man of around forty jammed a glass of Beam into my hand. "None of these fuckers call me by my real name due to a lifelong battle with pudginess. Call me Beefcake. Take it, baby, it's mostly Co-Cola." I sipped and started coughing which elicited raucous laughter. It was evidently not mostly *Co-Cola*. It was mostly Jimmy Beam spiked with ecstasy for good measure. I would not find out until later about the E. Beefcake came across as an individual one just wanted to trust. "That's Rusty over there, who has eyes for your partner. And this handsome, silver-tongued devil right here is Preacher."

"Very nice to meet you, my dear." Whoa! He definitely was the looker of the crowd, with plenty of charisma to spare.

Chris Suddeth

The party calmed when we got to their hotel as we all concentrated on getting buzzed. I began pounding Beam and Coke in hopes that I would pass out, therefore foregoing any further commitments. I chatted it up with Preacher and Beefcake while Dennis the Menace disappeared into the bathroom. I fell under the spell cast by Preacher's baby blue eyes and decided then and there that I would follow him to the very gates of hell.

Mandy and Rusty suddenly disappeared to get down to business. This briefly left me with Preacher and Beefcake. Not so bad. Then, all but forgotten, I saw Dennis emerge from the bathroom. I swear I saw flames in his eyes. I tried to shake off that visual and resume my conversation with Preacher and Beefcake, when I noticed Dennis circling me as if doing a parade ground inspection. Wonder if Nigel could return me to my Elmer Sutton incarnation for just a couple of minutes? The conversation stopped, and the mood shifted palatably. Even young, naïve, and intoxicated me knew I was in trouble. This might be another situation where being surrounded by men might not work to my advantage.

"Come on, girlie, shake it. It's time to get down." If I heard this once, I heard it slurred and belched a hundred times. By this point in my life, I was used to men gawking at me. But I was not used to the leering and zero attempt at eye contact.

Dennis suddenly grabbed my arm and said with a devilish smile, "It's time to get down. It's time for the train."

Inexplicably, I started doing what passed for dancing in my world. That's a skill of mine that did not improve with age. I did this in spite of the lack of music. I suppose I figured on being able to dance my way past three large men and out the door to safety. I couldn't help myself, it did feel good to dance, although I looked like a decapitated chicken, even on my best days. This prompted the preacher to fumble with his boom-box's tape player, and out of it came the greatest rendition of "Amazing Grace" I ever heard. "That's me singing, fellas…" I didn't notice the strange looks his partners cast his direction. So enthralled was I with every word of the song, that I breathed in the "Grace" through the pores of my body rather than heard it. Once they noticed my reaction, they quickly forgot about the deviant musical choice.

The fear and anxiety slipped away from me, and feelings of empathy and compassion were placed front and center, as my only yearning was to quench their obvious need. I began to feel a distinct split of selves similar to what I felt on Iwo. My seventeen-year old self and thirty-four-year-old self-coexisted. Foreboding and euphoria coexisted. "The train? What's that?" Damn, why was I so slow on the uptake? The E was obviously kicking in. I was grinding on the Menace.

"Don't worry. It'll be fine. You'll be able to figure it out as we go along." He abruptly jerked me up off my feet, slung me over his shoulder, and threw me on the bed in the opposite side of the suite from Rusty and Mandy. Beefcake ripped the shirt and bra right off my back in one swipe while my jeans were removed in another deft motion. This stunned me as Beefcake appeared too much the mama's boy for me to see this coming. I'm not even sure my thirty-four-year-old self would have caught it. Had they practiced this?

"You get that on tape, man? That was awesome! Nekkid in less than five fucking seconds," he said to a round of high fives.

"No, it was not *fucking* awesome. It hurt. Those were not break away clothes like basketball pants."

"The E will smooth out the pain, baby. Just enjoy the ride," Beefcake said as he pulled his little banana-curved pecker out of his pants and began to stroke himself. "Those titties are screamin' for a creamin', gentlemen."

They thought this was hilarious. I was being filmed? Wow, that's cool. I was determined to play it that way. Act really foxy for the lens. Make love to the camera, like you might hear them say in the fashion world. I whipped my hair about, attempting to mimic what I thought sexy was.

I was largely ignored at this point as the conversation turned to the business at hand. "Has anybody got any rubbers? Here, baby, lemme warm you up a little bit. One in the pink, and three in the stink. Boys, my fingers smell like prom night."

The peanut gallery burst into another round of guffawing, but I wasn't laughing. I was too busy trying to look sultry as a defense mechanism and Dennis was sticking his fingers up my ass. Again, the pull of my two selves, coupled with heaven knew how many intoxicants, rendered me flustered, to say the least.

"Nope, no rubbers."

"Fuck it."

"I'm not leaving my DNA up in there, and I don't want your jizz on my tallywacker. I've got a family and a flock at home to think about."

He was a pastor of the largest Southern Baptist church in Knoxville, I found out after the fact. His sermons were indeed televised throughout the Southeast and other parts of the country.

DNA? I was still trying to act like I was having fun, but the E and the Jim Beam only numbed me so much. I was getting worried.

Swoondalini

At the same time, I decided to make a run for it, clothes or not, Dennis lost all restraint. He pushed me hard to the bed and nimbly tied me up to the bed post with his belt, but not before giving me a few brutal lashes. "Gotta get our money's worth."

I sobered a bit when he took his penis out. He was already almost fully erect, with probably the biggest package I've ever seen on a man and I've seen so many that Geney could legally call me to the stand to be an expert witness on penis. He slowly circled the bed, as if stalking prey. He finally put one knee up on the bed and shimmied up to me at an agonizing pace. I still had my legs free and saw my chance and took it. I kicked him in the nuts as hard as I could. This was a mistake. It was also my first lesson in life that there's no accounting for taste.

"Yeah, baby, daddy like," he said, as his face turned beet red from the pain. He then backhanded me so hard, I saw stars. The stars ended quickly as he roughly inserted himself and started pounding.

Since I had not been properly turned on, I was nowhere near being moist. "Oh God!" I winced in pain. "That hurts. You're so big."

I chose my words poorly, causing him to plow into me harder and harder. I heard the other two giving each other high fives. "You got that on tape, right? Awesome! Menace, hurry up, old man. I don't care if we don't have any rubbers, I'm about to nut my pants," Preacher sniffed after taking a bump of blow off the nightstand.

"You're hurting me."

He ignored me. "You're so beautiful. I've never seen such a beautiful girl," he proclaimed as drunken spittle landed in my eye and on my cheek.

The other two agreed as if they were saying "aye" at a county council meeting. It also turned out the old man was a real estate developer, and the other fellow was a county councilman, and was considered a pillar of the Knoxville community at large. They all were.

"Oh my, GAAAAWWWD!" he drawled. "Your tits are so big, taut, and seem natural. Are they store bought?" He gave the same breast bruised earlier by Mandy a hard squeeze and jerk to confirm that I was, indeed natural. I yelped in pain and could feel him getting even more engorged and pounding away. I felt myself tear. The E and booze faded quickly, as the exquisite pain asserted itself, demanding my full attention. I never dreamed such pain existed. Then I realized I didn't remember this nightmare happening to me in Columbia, SC.

I mercifully grew delirious from the pain. I heard screaming but wasn't really sure that it was me.

Next came the preacher. I heard something about, "making me scream for Jesus," but that was a blur, and before I knew it, the third man was about to enter me when I saw Nigel standing in the corner. He watched the entire scene unfold with a decidedly neutral and dispassionate expression. He opened his mouth as if to say something, then turned his attention to the door as if waiting for someone to enter.

How did I suppress this dire situation, much less how I got out of it? What else was hidden between my ears? I felt myself swoon, but I sensed that Nigel prevented it so that I could bear witness to this painful event.

I could feel every stab of cock down to my core. I looked over to my right and saw the other two working themselves up for another go at me. I wanted to drop into a coma. I would have begged for someone to end my lamentable life, if I was able to find my voice. I couldn't feel my forearms and hands, as the belt dug into me and I bled. It was then that I heard the commotion outside the door that Nigel was listening to.

The voices were muffled, but I did catch Mandy's gravelly voice saying, "What the fuck is going on in there?"

Was Mandy Stinger, the tit wringer, going to be my savior?

"Nothing, baby. Just the boys having a little fun," Rusty said too quickly.

"Doesn't sound like fun being had by all in there. Better check it out…"

"No, it's fine. Everything's good in there," his voice became more panicked.

"No--- it's NOT!" Mandy said forcefully. "Now move."

My hearing became acute and focused, like you'd see in a Superman movie. I was able to hear them pushing each other outside of a closed door with three men riding the train on me. I heard Mandy rustling for her purse and the click of a Walther PPKS safety going red, apparently the same pistol I now carry and point at families in parking lots.

"What are you going to do with that?"

She answered with a shot. My ears rang from the *hyper hearing*.

"You shot me in the leg, you fucking whore!" Rusty shrieked in pain that I could feel over and above my heartfelt injuries. Was this what it was like to be an empath? What in the hell was I doing even contemplating another's pain in my hour of need?

Preacher stopped pumping me while all heads turned to the closed door that led to the suite's living area and kitchen.

"That's right. I'll shoot your other leg if you don't give me all the money you four ass-clowns have."

"Dennis, you'd better go see what's going on. Was that a gunshot?"

How could they not know what was happening when even I knew and felt it?

Mandy never let pain, especially other people's pain, get in the way of making a buck. I was getting jack-hammered by three of Knoxville, Tennessee's finest, and she wanted to make sure she got paid. She had an ability to focus on money when the world was coming down around her. She taught me everything I know in that regard.

I heard Mandy say, "I'll be right back, Rust-man, and when I'm back, I've got seven more reasons why at least ten grand better be on that bar."

To carry out his marching orders, the Menace opened the door to bowling ball boobies and a .380 up his nose. In her other hand, she produced a stun gun that caught him square on his big dick. Needless to say, "daddy" became a crumpled mess on the floor. His bowels released a smell that was nauseating.

"What you boys doing in here?" Mandy said casually as she watched The Menace squirm in his filth. She dug her heel into his cheek for good measure. "Looks like everybody but one person is having a grand ole time... Boy, you better get up out of her, and don't make me ask twice."

I welcomed the wilting of Preacher's erection as their romp came to an abrupt end. I could feel shock setting in as the blood began to flow from me when he pulled out and then suddenly the blinding pain began. With the preacher getting up in a hurry, he mashed my sore breast again to add insult to injury.

Swoondalini

"Brandy, can you walk? Don't look down at yourself, we can do that later. You boys get in the corner and slowly pull out and empty your wallets. Throw all the money here at my feet. Brandy!"

"You're going to fucking rob us at gun point?" Preacher denounced.

"Is that a video camera?" Mandy lit up, ignoring the preacher's question. "Yeah, we'll be needing that too. Insurance, you understand. Rust, honey you still with us?" she said as she peeked around the door to check on him. "Looks like the poor guy's going into shock just like Brandy. Brandy!"

"What? Who's Brandy?" I said in a haze of pain and blood loss.

"I know you're hurting, but this is no time, trust me. Suck it up and walk it off," Mandy recited the gym teacher's mantra. "We'll get you to a doctor as soon as we get out of here."

"We're going to call the cops as soon as you leave." The Menace pointed at her with his left hand as he grabbed his crotch with his right hand. He was coming around.

"That looks like a nice watch. What is that? A President's gold model Rolex? Very nice," Mandy said as she popped his outstretched arm with her stun gun and removed his watch. "That's right, Brandy. Get up very slowly. Boys, any valuables and keys on the floor, too."

Somehow, the Menace was still alert through the pain. "My wife gave me that watch."

"How nice. I'm sure she did, just as sure as I know that the quickest way for all of Knoxville to find out about this is to call the cops after we leave. Rusty's already struggling with the pain of the gunshot. You know gunshots are pretty hard to explain to hospitals. They tend to ask a lot of questions. It's only a matter of time before hotel security gets here, so we need to think quick, gentlemen."

"Fuck you, we're going to sue and press charges."

"How do you people rise to such high positions in society by being such dumbasses? You tore her hoo-hah while riding the train on her. Oh, and don't forget, I believe we have the whole act on this tape right here. Let's see, how would a letter to the parishioners or stockholders go?" Mandy mocked.

"We got it," Beefcake growled as he flung his car keys at her. I was wrong to judge that book by his cover.

"Wow, BMW. Very nice." Mandy nodded admiringly. "Looks like a good get-away vehicle. I don't think you do get it, smartass. This will be fun:

Dear Stockholders:

I raped and ripped the hoo-hah of Susie Q's. Even though she was only seventeen, the coke, booze, and ultimately the devil made me do it...

"See how this will go?" Mandy said patiently.

"You'll never get away with this," the man of God (Gawd if you're from the South) postured. I managed to get to my feet and put my jeans on. They quickly soaked with blood.

"Looks like you ripped her shirt, so she'll need another. Wow, this is literally costing you the shirt off your back," Mandy said with glee.

Beefcake, having just lost his new M3, had to give me the shirt off his back. He threw it at me with scorn in his eyes. I caught it with my face but was alert enough to enjoy the shoe being on the other foot.

"Mandy, I'm okay for now, but I need to get to a doctor soon." My voice cracked with pain and fear.

Swoondalini

"Alright then, boys, we must take our leave of you. It's been real. Brandy, can you hold this gun while I gather up our belongings? You know how to work a gun?"

Do I know how to work a gun? It's not a gun. It's a pistol. "Yes, I can handle it. My father taught me," I said, breathing through the pain.

Mandy quickly gathered up our booty, stunned Dennis the Menace one more time for good measure, and patted down everybody to make sure they weren't holding out.

Two bloodied, barely dressed strippers got away with robbing four large men, firing one round and taking cash and jewelry in the amount of fifty-five grand, not to mention a brand new M3 convertible.

Mandy always said that I earned that car, and my "worry-free humping," but I never knew what she meant until now. To the best of my questionable memory, Mandy stopped at a doctor client's house on the way out of Columbia, SC, to have me patched up.

I can now recall an argument about me travelling in such a condition, but when he said I probably wouldn't die, the decision was made.

"Give her all the pain pills you have in the house, Jim. Brandy. Brandy, baby, (she never used terms of affection) I don't think those fuckers will come after us, but better safe than sorry. We're done with this shithole. I've got things working in D.C."

I always wondered how I came to live in D.C. Now I know it was more than just randomly bouncing from city to city. I always heard people could suppress traumatic events, but figured that only happened to other, lesser people. People who weren't as pretty and rich as I. How could I have become so deluded?

Chris Suddeth

"I promise we'll get you to the hospital as soon as we get to town," I heard her say as we got on I-77 and drove past Williams-Brice Stadium in the distance.

"The power of denial is an amazing thing," I heard Nigel whisper as the vortex closed around me. The banjo music of the song made famous by "Deliverance", *The Dueling Banjos*, began to swirl around me.

Chapter 12

You wouldn't think it by looking at this pretty face, but I am a closeted Trekkie. I suppose, at its core, and at my core, I hoped for a world like Star Trek portrays. Anyway, I've forgotten more Star Trek trivia than most people know. Sad, but true.

That's why I appreciated the flair with which Nigel executed my next jump through time and space. When I awoke, I saw two sliding doors before me, fashioned in the way that the holodeck doors were on ST:TNG (that's "Star Trek: The Next Generation" for those not baptized in the ways of Kirk, Spock, and Picard). I looked down to find myself totally nude again. I did a quick once-over of my girly parts to make sure that everything was the way it should be and that I didn't have anything that I shouldn't.

I breathed a sigh of relief, but quickly returned to reality, or what passed for my reality these days. Why was I always ending up naked? I checked my right hand and left knee and found the scars from a fall I took last New Year's after overindulging. I felt my head and felt the pixie haircut I adopted upon my arrival in Washington, D.C. I was back in what seemed to be my thirty-four-year-old self.

"Okay, Nigel, what's next?" I looked around, and he was nowhere in sight. Everything was white, aside from the "holodeck" doors in front of me. There was no answer to my question, and I felt frozen in place. Realizing there was no place else to go, aside from forward through the doors, made the decision for me. I could hear muffled banjo music as I stepped closer to the doors. The next dubious step activated the doors to reveal a mountain wilderness.

I stepped through and took a few more steps and spun around quickly to take in the majesty of nature. It was breathtaking. The doors vanished as they did in the old television show. The music was louder now that I was inside the "holodeck."

I looked down and felt all over once again to confirm that I was still in the buff. I took in a luxurious breath of crisp, mountain air and closed my eyes. The music abruptly stopped, and it made me jump as I turned to find that Nigel was within arm's reach. Whomever he was "dueling" with was nowhere to be seen.

"Mighty revealing, ain't it?" Nigel drawled.

Nigel was Nigel, but he was much different-looking. Gone was the expensive tailored suit, replaced by worn overalls with a wife-beater shirt, no shoes, and missing teeth.

"Ain't what?" I queried, truly perplexed.

He spat tobacco juice uncomfortably close to my bare feet and went back to playing the banjo again as if I didn't speak and was no longer there. I still couldn't see who he was dueling with. My emotions began to get the better of me as I could feel the last several "weeks" events begin to congeal in my throat. I thought of all that time spent on Iwo Jima, and not a single other man in my company escaping without a wound of some kind. Obviously, many Marines remain on Iwo. I could even recall being sent back to Maui after Iwo for R and R. After R and R, the 4th Marines were to prepare for an assault on mainland Japan that thankfully, would never come. Memories of the Pacific segued into memories of getting gangbanged against my will at the young age of seventeen.

Swoondalini

I couldn't take it anymore. My body began to shake from head to toe as the music fiddled on. I lost it and yelled until my throat hurt.

"Ahhhhhhhhhhhh…….!!!!!!!"

I snatched the banjo from Nigel's hands, taking pleasure at his face contorting in shock and anger. I admired the instrument as one might look at a fine painting. Then I swung for Nigel's head as if going for a short risk-reward par four. He made no move to duck as the banjo passed cleanly, and regretfully, through him.

That brought me zero satisfaction. I was bored with his parlor tricks. Then I noticed a boulder and a pine tree close together and bashed the banjo back and forth against each until nothing but strings and splinters remained. Oh, it felt so goooood. I let out a heaving breath and calmly handed him the remains of his banjo back, as if presenting a fine bottle of wine in a swanky restaurant.

He took it, stared dumbstruck at the broken instrument, and glowered at me. I took note that the other banjo ceased playing, and I thought I perceived faint giggles off in the distance.

Still maintaining his version of a Southern bumpkin accent, he said, "My pa gave me that, and it was his pa's, papa's, pa's…"

I fluttered my hand at my heart and exaggerated my natural accent, "Oh, I'm so terribly sorry, suh." I only spoke Southernese when I was drunk, upset, or calling home. "It seems to have slipped from my little butterfingers. Oops. I do apologize," I batted my eyelashes. "I so hope you can forgive me."

"Mm hmm," and an eat shit and die stare was all I got in return.

So, I felt it wise to change the subject. "Now, if you're done stroking your little instrument," I glanced down meaningfully at the remains of his banjo, "I'd appreciate it if we could get on with it."

"Get on with what?" Still with the accent.

"You know, stake me out, pour honey all up and down my body, and leave me for the ants, bears, and buzzards."

Nigel's accent reemerged gleefully. It was oddly offset against his backwoods appearance. "Don't forget the nearby pack of wolves." He let that hang in the air to take effect. "No, no, my dear, this session will be a little different, but no less entertaining."

"Session? Entertaining? How will it be different?"

"You do come up with some good plans, but as much as I'd like to tie you up and do any number of things to you, that's beside the point."

"What is the point?" I asked petulantly, with my face inches from his.

He took a deep breath while contemplating that question. "My hope is that you will uncover that very nugget of gold for your soul at some point along this journey you're on."

"Journey?" My temper was still running hot. "How much longer is this journey going to be? It's been one bad trip so far, and I'd like to exit this ride while I still can."

"Take my hand," Nigel ordered.

"I just got my womanhood ripped, in what was such a horrible memory that I forgot it the first time around, until you dredged it up in living color, no less, and you won't even have the decency to tell me how much more I have to endure?"

"What have you got better to do? Got a date with a bong? Believe me, we'll get to that! NOW TAKE MY HAND," he said balefully, leaving little room for choice.

Knowing I was pushing my luck far enough, I did as I was told. The instant I took his hand in mine, I was whisked off my feet and over the cliff by my guardian poltergeist, Nigel.

"Tell me, do you know where we are?" he asked.

"Yeah, we're thousands of feet up in the air, and I don't much care for heights."

I received a stern look for that comment. "I would think by now that you'd know better than to be tart with me. Now, where are we? What state are we currently flying thousands of feet above?"

I felt the answer to that question the moment I stepped into my third scenario. "We are in the mountains of Northern Greenville County, better known as the *Dark Corner* because of the clannishness of the moonshiners up here. Even the law has a very limited reach up here. "Deliverance" didn't take place here, but it could have."

"Very good. How did you know where we were?"

"I just knew."

"Now, we're getting somewhere."

"What?"

"Never mind, what does this neck of the woods mean to you?"

"Well, all of my mama's side of the family came from here. For generations, they were part of the only industry around to speak of---White Lightning. They eventually made their way down the mountains to the booming metropolis and county seat of Greenville itself."

"And how did your mother's forbearers fit in up in the Dark Corner?"

"I suppose they got along well enough to have my mama and eventually me," I offered weakly.

"You don't know very much, do you?" Nigel said with a hint of sympathy.

"Come to think of it, my grandmother has always been very vague about the family's past. I always found that odd, since most Southerners take pride in tracing back their family tree. But I've never put much thought into it." Table Rock passed leisurely under us as I pondered the question. "She would always steer things back to politics of who screwed who. My grandmother was a master of misdirection."

"Yes, your granny could also be very single-minded."

"That's one way of putting it."

"Don't judge so harshly, my dear."

"Why?"

"As they say, the apple doesn't fall far from the tree."

I didn't have a moment's notice to reply to that barb. I noticed the hand he was holding beginning to turn opaque and watched it quickly spread over my body. "Hard to hold you this way with my butterfingers," Nigel did a poor job of mimicking sympathy before I plummeted toward the earth and a run-down mountain cabin. I left mocking laughter in my wake as I flailed helplessly.

What shocked me the most wasn't the fall, but what awaited me inside the dilapidated cabin. The fall was akin to the most intense falling dream I ever dreamed, ratcheted up by the fact that I wouldn't wake up the split-second before impact.

I fell straight through the metal roof like I was an apparition; hell, I was an apparition and was able to note the inside of the metal and wood particles as I passed through. This was somewhat like out-of-body experiences in my past. I only told my uncle Bobby about those. His reaction was one of extreme interest, but very little surprise which strangely discouraged me from speaking more of them. I never wanted to reveal too much, said the nude girl.

As I thought that last thought, Nigel projected inside my head in a reproving tsk-tsk, "You realize that some people... How can I put this kindly? Dense is good. Yes, some people less dense than you have used astral projection and near-death experiences as a springboard along their path of bringing body, mind, and soul into sync."

Before I could give some weak excuse for not taking advantage of the clues offered me along the way, my descent came to a halt mere inches from the dirt floor I could vaguely feel with my opaque breasts. I opened my eyes and stared down my nose. I exhaled in relief and then was summarily dropped the remainder of the way.

"Stop toying around and pay attention," Nigel said, clearly amused.

I righted myself off the floor in an instant, without knowing how I achieved it. I just merely willed it to be so. "Is that what this is, a very long out-of-body experience in which I'm haunted by a torturous spirit?"

Ignoring my barb, he replied, "How do you know what you call your pathetic everyday existence isn't an out-of-body experience and this is actual reality?" He made a broad sweep of the cabin with his arms as a piece of straw appeared in his teeth.

Not to be deterred, since I placed astral projection on the dusty shelf along with the rest of issues pertaining to my heart and soul, I impatiently asked, "Well, is it?"

Nigel shushed me and gave me a librarian's look. "Pay ATTENTION!" he said through clenched teeth while stabbing his index finger in my third eye before pointing at the door.

Third eye? Why in the hell would I call my forehead that?

I began to take in the stark interior of the cabin. It was only one small room with a loft. The cooking was done in the fireplace, and there was a pump for a kitchen sink. The winters must be rough up here as I could see through cracks in the walls. The table and mismatched chairs were centered on the fireplace. There was a bed made out of birch in one corner, a double barrel shotgun, a .22 Remington, and Colt .45 wheel pistol in the opposite corner. Also, there was a lone window by the door with a broken pane of glass.

"What am I paying attention to?" I demanded.

"You might try showing a little gratitude," Nigel said with a hurt tone.

I raised an incredulous eyebrow at that comment but held my tongue.

Nigel merely smirked and nodded at the door a moment before a teenage girl burst in, half-carrying a man. The girl was all of fifteen and looked much like I did at that age. I felt this must be my grandmother.

"They didn't have hormones in chickens back then, did they?" I whispered, referring to her small chest.

I got an eyeroll in response.

"Jenny—git me my jug, girl," the man I took to be Paw Paw slurred.

"Diddy, you've had enough. Now go to bed and sleep it off," Granny said plaintively.

She didn't get the backhand that I expected after being told of his drunken cruelties. Instead, she received a hug, followed by sobbing from the big man.

"I'm so sorry, Jenny. I know I've been drunk nearly every day since your mama's funeral…" the sobs were coming harder now, and Granny rolled her eyes as if she'd heard all this before. "Aye never would've laid a finger on you."

"Then how did I get this baby in my belly?" Granny said.

I instantly looked down at her midsection. She wasn't showing, but I could sense a heartbeat, a definite presence there.

"You've been lusting after me in your heart ever since I became a woman. And you know how you take drunk all the time. How do you know what you've done?" she accused. I felt she was just as confused about the identity of the father of her child as the confusion she intended to illicit within my great-grandfather.

Paw Paw struggled to remain standing upright as he mulled over what his daughter was implying. He then responded in a surprisingly succinct and caring manner for one so drunk. "You look so much like her, and I miss her so bad that I can't help but stare. It's not a damn thang more than that. You're all I got in this world, and I just want to protect you."

I felt Granny believe all of what he was saying but she just didn't care. She knew he legitimately thought he was having relations with her mama and she decided it'd be fun to play along with her pathetic broken father. "Protect me from who?"

"Your cousin down the mountain for one. I've seen the way Billy looks at you."

"He's just lookin'."

"That may be so, but it seems like more than looking. I know it's done all the time round here, but I tell ya, it just ain't natural. Not to mention that side of the family is bat shit crazy."

Nigel broke the fourth wall of the scene with a barb. "He's ahead of his time with those ideals... Ain't he?" He was very proud of his little joke.

I moved around the small room, found that I could walk through things, but chose not to. I was impressed by seeing my grandmother and great-grandfather on my mother's side, and I took it all in, mouth agape. Then I walked through Paw Paw as he continued to plead incoherently. I felt his confusion and his liquor. It felt like my own when I imbibed too much of one substance or the next; many times to get through one client's body odor or odd request. The apple didn't fall too far from the tree.

I couldn't take my eyes off of my great-grandfather. "He is not at all like my grandmother portrayed him. Yeah, he's a drunk, but he has a kind spirit."

"History is written by the victors."

"Victors?" I questioned as I spun on my heel.

I looked down and realized that I was doing a rough approximation of holding Paw-Paw's hand, except that my hand was literally in his. I pulled back in shock, held my hand up to my face, and placed it over my heart. I noticed upon my hand's removal that Paw-Paw looked in my direction, then our eyes met briefly; two familiar souls greeting one another, but it seemed to further befuddle Paw Paw, so he quickly put his attention back to my ranting grandmother.

"Are you sure they can't see us?"

"Not entirely sure. It happens with small children, animals, and other more perceptive people on occasion or it happens as a person approaches death. The soul will begin to see as they once saw," Nigel explained.

"Death?" As the word left my mouth, bits of brain, blood, and skull passed through my body. She stood over him and shot him squarely between his navel and sternum for good measure. "Holy fucking shit!"

Swoondalini

Several heartbeats later, Nigel replied solemnly, "More like unholy."

I quickly felt myself for bits and pieces of my great-grandfather as I watched him fall. Dead before he even touched the ground. At least she made it quick.

My grandmother didn't miss a beat, as she immediately began gathering up belongings without as much as a moment of silence for her slain father. This was obviously premeditated. Wow, I always knew there wasn't a matronly bone in my grandmother's body, but I never realized she was a cold-blooded assassin.

The door burst open during her packing to reveal an out of breath boy no older than sixteen. It was my grandfather.

"Goddamn, Jen! I thought you were going to wait until he passed out?"

She whirled around, grabbing the Colt and leveling it at his chest. "No more taking the Lord's name in vain. Justice is mine, sayeth the Lord."

"Alright, Cuz, easy. Put the pistol down," Granddaddy said.

"And no more calling each other Cuz," she said, clearly establishing who wore the pants before she slowly lowered, decocked, and tossed the Colt onto the bed.

Granny busied herself packing what little there was of value from the sparse cabin and missed seeing my grandfather retrieve the pistol and methodically level it at Granny.

His hands began to shake almost violently as he recocked the hand cannon. She raised an eyebrow to the sound, but didn't turn to face him, instead concentrating on counting the white lightning money.

"What you planning on doing with that Colt, Billy?" she asked casually.

Chris Suddeth

When Billy didn't answer, she turned her small frame to face him. Her green eyes burned with intense irritation at having been interrupted.

Timidly, my grandfather closed the distance between them until the pistol was inches away from blasting my granny's heart from her petite chest.

"Answer me," she demanded.

"We're not killers, Jenny," he said deferentially.

"I had no choice. He was crazy-talking about building a hot-rod to run all his shine in," she quickly said. One could tell that she didn't even believe that there wasn't another choice. Would Granddaddy believe that lie?

I made a scoffing sound at her lame answer.

"As ludicrous as it sounds, she felt she really didn't have a choice in the matter," Nigel spoke morosely. "You can sense it in the situation if you learn to listen closely with more than just those two things on the side of your head you hang expensive trinkets on. Their family obviously wasn't the same since her mama died in the Great Flood and her daddy was a constant living memorial. Even when her father was inside of her, he was calling her mama's name. It was a partly vengeful act to murder Paw Paw, but a large part of this scene was a rare act of mercy on your grandmother's part, akin to shooting a horse with a broken leg, except your great-grandfather had a broken soul."

Apparently, my grandfather did buy it as evidenced by his lowering the pistol.

Confident in her victory of willpower in hand, my grandmother turned back to her inventory of ill-gotten gain, but before she made a complete turn, her face was met by the full force of my grandfather's backhand. He was a large boy and she, as all the women are in my family, was slight of frame. I could hear her teeth chatter as she was knocked off her feet and left dazed on the floor.

"I like it when you're tough, baby," Granny said, obviously punch-drunk off the taste of her own blood.

"Listen to me, Jenny. I'm happy to let you wear the pants. No doubt you're smarter than me, but we are not killers. You got me?" he commanded. His backbone emerging, he loomed over her and raised the pistol once again. "Are we together on this, Jenny?"

In answer, Granny slowly moved her bare foot up his leg and began massaging his growing manhood. A sinister smile played across her features that beckoned, "I want you right here, right now."

"OH, MY, GAAAAAWD," I exclaimed in hushed disgust. "With him here?" I pointed to the lifeless form of my great-grandfather.

"I'm so wet right now." Granny moaned.

"They are quite the pair, aren't they?" Nigel offered as he observed me getting green around the gills.

"I think I need to throw up."

Nigel simply grinned his understanding.

There was so much wrong with this scene, I didn't even know where to begin. My head was spinning. "Can I throw up here? In this form, I mean?"

Nigel attempted to answer but was interrupted by the throes of passion playing out across the room.

"La, la, la, la, la…." I hollered with my fingers in my ears and my eyes squeezed as tight as they'd go. "Can't you show me anything nice for a change, like kittens, butterflies, or better yet, how about some unicorns?"

"Unicorns do exist, you know."

"I don't give a flying rat's ass. Get me out of here."

"I can see that I now have your attention," he said in a maddeningly understated tone.

"You captured my attention when I saw you sitting in my BMW." A part of me still couldn't believe that this was all real.

A smirk that made my insides churn appeared. "I think you're right. Maybe we have gotten off track with this little detour. The time for graphic remembrances and demonstrations is coming to a conclusion. Before we dash from this idyllic setting, let's do some follow-up work."

"Okay," I said, not liking the sound of that at all.

"Shall we?"

Without waiting for my permission, as if that mattered, the cabin melted away.

***

The cabin faded to reveal woods and mountains again. Only we were in a different locale.

A few notes of the banjo began to play, and I noticed Nigel was back in his tailored suit. He acted as if he couldn't hear the music. In answer to my unasked question, he said, "Now we'll see your paw paw's white lightning recipe."

"Really? I've always kind of wondered how it was made."

"Really," Nigel mocked. "Can you not come up with a question more intelligent than that? You really just figured like almost every other attractive woman ever to walk God's green Earth that since your tits are big, you've got a tight ass, and have a winning Mentos Freshmaker smile that you don't have to attempt to be intelligent?" He was jabbing his finger roughly into my breastbone, deliberately trying to goad me. It wasn't working.

"I read."

"Harlequin Romance novels that you grace the cover of don't count, babe."

I wanted to tell him that I read more than that and didn't even like those ridiculous novels, but they paid me top dollar, so I let it go.

"You don't even want to know why they wanted all Paw Paw's white lightning money?" he asked.

"Because they're mean and greedy?" I answered gamely.

"Well, yes," he granted, "but that's not it."

"Okay, why?" I huffed.

He made a broad sweeping motion with his arms. "That, you'll have to find out for yourself," he said, his voice heavy with implications.

We turned around, and the mountains warped in my field of vision. Suddenly, there it was, the church that haunted my dreams, although, to my knowledge, I never physically visited there.

I heard the click of a lighter and the smell of cigarette smoke as Nigel fired up a Marlboro Menthol Ultra-Light. He made smoking look sophisticated, like in the movies of an era gone by. He studied it intently and said, "These things are so bloody good. Christ, I miss them so." He then blew smoke in my face as if he'd just nutted his pants.

"You smoke?"

"Yeah, it's done me in a couple of lifetimes," he replied nonchalantly. "I don't normally smoke, but it's the 50's, and it didn't hurt you back then." He chuckled at his sarcastic joke.

I held my shaking hand out for the pack and noticed my hand was solid again. A cigarette would ease my frayed nerves. In truth, I loved cigarettes, and these were my brand, but they scared the shit out of me; thus, I only smoke weed. At least that's what I tell everybody, myself included.

"We'll get to your habit soon enough," he said, tossing me the pack and offering to light my cigarette like the gentleman he appeared to be.

What did he mean by my "habit"? Did he know what I was thinking?

"Let's just take on one thing at a time, shall we? For now, you've got to go in there," he said, pointing at the church building, and I noted a bit of sympathy in his tone.

"I would, but I've got no pockets," was the only lame response I could summon to excuse me from what I felt was coming.

"So, I see," Nigel said. "It's been nice, but now I'll let you in on a little secret. The nudity up until now has obviously been a metaphor. You didn't get it, did you?"

"Not really," I said, feeling embarrassed. "I thought it was just another one of your ways to torture me and get some cheap thrills for yourself all in the bargain."

"Oh, it was, but I don't torture at random. Really, you're going to have to be quicker on the draw from now on. We're entering the lightning round."

"The lightning round?"

Ignoring my question in his usual maddening way, he pressed on. "You may assume clothing anytime you wish or maintain your present non-attire as I know you feel very much at home and in command this way. But, be warned, people perceive you as they want to perceive you or, more accurately, how you project yourself. It's not any different in your everyday physical life either, you know."

I was not as in command as I would have people believe. Don't get me wrong, I was well aware of what I looked like, but there were the inner demon insecurities that every girl faced regardless of looks. I just wore a prettier disguise to conceal my demons. Was this whole trip showing me that there was more going on with me than just your run-of-the-mill insecurities?

Before I could take time to think too deeply, I ran through a few snazzy outfits that appeared on me with a mere thought. This was the coolest thing I ever experienced. Versace popped on me as if I was Barbara Eden on *I Dream of Genie*. In the end, I chose the buff. I didn't want to reveal my weakness and figured I began the journey in this manner and would finish it.

Observing the wheels turning in my head, Nigel said, "Don't put too much thought into it. There's no right or wrong answer. Besides, command over others is an illusion. You can only control your own free will."

"There's a reason I began this odyssey this way."

"Maybe so," he conceded with a knowing smile. "Shall we move on?"

"Yes, let's," I said, trying to sound chipper. "What's inside that church?"

He merely bowed in deferment to my choice and motioned for me to proceed.

"Not going to tell me, are you?"

"Nope. But to quote a fictional Zen master, 'Only what you take with you.' Yoda was based on a real person, you know."

Not wanting to be the butt of another joke, I ignored the Yoda revelation and steeled myself for what was to come in the house of worship. I took a long pull on my menthol and flicked it. It disappeared before it hit the ground.

My still shaking hands turned opaque again as I reached through the doorknob. I quickly pulled my hand back and looked over my shoulder to Nigel. He was studiously lighting another cigarette when he saw me looking at him. He made a shooing motion and went back to his smoking.

I turned back to the door and was startled when it opened up to reveal a small forty-something year old man with a collar, peering outside suspiciously to see if the coast was clear. He quickly slammed the door in my face, and I heard the sound of the deadbolt slamming home. It was obvious he didn't see me. I looked back once more, didn't see Nigel and proceeded to walk through the locked door. As in other out-of-body experiences, I experienced every grain of wood as I passed through the door. That's something I don't believe one ever gets used to.

The small chapel was lit with only the waning light of day. The sunlight shone through the stained-glass windows, featuring various saints and biblical scenes. I walked down toward the vestibule and noticed that there were three lit candles beneath an ornate statue of baby Jesus being held by the Virgin Mary. I looked to my left and saw light streaming from under a closed door. I was drawn there as if I was on tracks and found myself standing before the door and listening to muffled staccato voices.

Swoondalini

Before proceeding through the door, I again looked over my shoulder and scanned the church. It appeared serene as night assumed its reign over day.

I was startled to see Billy, my grandfather, spirit in the back door without making a sound. He must have had a key. What was he up to?

Then I noticed his right hand held a cage. I felt the desire to know its contents and instantly my being was transported into the cage. In it were probably a dozen or more cottonmouths and mountain rattlers. Yuck! Just as quickly, I was back across the room and away from the serpents.

Billy padded across the heart of pine floors without so much as a pop or a crack from the wood. Very impressive, it was now apparent to me how my grandfather got into black ops in Vietnam, before there was a "Vietnam". He opened a closet to the rear of the church and switched cages that appeared to be identical.

They were not, indeed, identical. Both contained dangerous serpents, but upon closer inspection, Billy's cage did not contain snakes that were defanged. Wasn't he the one taking the moral high ground by saying they weren't killers? Before I could ponder the question any longer, the voices behind the door became even more animated.

" Why don't we have a drink?" I heard my grandmother say, ice calm.

I needed to find out what was transpiring behind that door. I tentatively stepped through, knowing full well I was likely to see something I didn't want to see. When I emerged from the forest of splinters in the door, I was not disappointed with the shock factor.

My grandmother sauntered nude around the reverend's office, clearly in command. I recognized that same walk in myself and it made me cold, even though temperature seemed not to be a factor in this environment. She flipped open his large pulpit Bible to reveal that most of its contents were sliced out to make room for a bottle.

"A drink?" asked the reverend, clad only in his collar. He was surprised, but pleased she found his stash.

"Yes, a drink. I have here some strychnine that we can mix with a little R.C. Cola," Jenny said with a wink.

"Yes, let's drink to us." The reverend obviously thought it was our family's white lightning.

"Yes, let's," Jenny said while lowering herself to sit primly behind the reverend's desk.

"Bottoms up, my child," the reverend said, tossing back straight strychnine.

My grandmother merely poured hers out on the desk and smiled approvingly.

Mortal understanding passed over the reverend's face.

"Yes, we thought it only right that we replace all that, less than potent, strychnine from the faith closet with something that has more of a bite. It seems your faith has been strained of late," my granny explained.

"Why? I love you, Jenny."

"Why?" she derided. "You told my cousin, Billy, the same thing. Did you really think Billy does anything without checking with me first? Billy likes girls, reverend. Sodomy is a sin, you know. Remember that powerful sermon you delivered about Sodom and Gomorra? We had to keep a check on your pillow-talk to see if you were double-crossing me. We couldn't have all that money we helped you get for the poor uneducated children, of backwoods America to go to anybody other than poor uneducated children of backwoods America, now could we?"

He fell to his bare knees in supplication.

Jenny merely ignored his dying sputter and began to dress. She looked at her clothes in disgust and said, "With all that money, I'll be buying the latest fashions from Main Street, Greenville. We may even buy a house on Crescent Avenue."

"Sad, really, she thinks of Greenville, South Cackalacky as her fashion Mecca," Nigel mocked.

"So that's how they came to live there?" Realization dawned. "I suppose to a couple of kids who have rarely stepped foot off of the Dark Corner mountains, Greenville, South Carolina could seem like Paris," I said to no one in particular.

"But you don't..." the reverend choked out.

"But I don't know where you put all that money?" Granny supplied. "You taught me every trick I needed to know."

Quickly, and thankfully only briefly, I was in two places at once. I remained witness to the dawning of my granny's con artist career and was back in the main part of the chapel, witnessing my grandfather Billy kick over the statue of the Virgin Mary to reveal what must have been several hundred thousand dollars. It gave me a migraine to have multiple viewpoints.

"Quite the family you have there," Nigel remarked. I was beginning to get used to his sudden appearances. "Not two hours ago, she killed her father and now she just tricked a man of the cloth into consuming poison."

"This is not funny," I said in protest.

"I never suggested it was."

"Why are you showing me this?"

"Take a closer look at the priest."

"I'd rather not."

"Suck it up," he ordered.

"Yeah, I see him dying an agonizing death."

"Look beyond the obvious."

I walked around him, turning my back to Nigel. I stooped down and tried to look the priest in the eyes, but they were shut in anguish. I was about to stand straight up when I felt a firm shove in my backside from Nigel's Italian leather shoe.

I was instantly trapped inside the priest. I felt the pain he was feeling from literally having a hole burned from the inside out. Aside from that, I was astonished to feel a familiarity with this priest. Was he another incarnation of mine?

Nigel jerked me out of him moments before death, so I could witness his soul, and apparently my soul, as well, leave his gravely damaged body. Too close for comfort.

"Yes, he was one of your incarnations," Nigel answered my unasked question.

"No, it can't be."

"But yes, it can be. Moreover, you know it's true. We can't all be saints all the time. Sometimes we must be the sinner. Then there are the grey areas," Nigel waxed wistfully. "Come with me," Nigel said softly, extending his hand like a lifeline. "I've got something else to show you."

I was done. I needed a break. "Nigel, please! I can't take it anymore. You've broken me. I'm out of witty remarks now. PLEASE no more."

"You will be done when I say you're done, but I am a merciful spirit, and I can see you need a respite. That's why this next little aside will be very informative and truly painless. No little surprises, I promise," he said, holding his hand up as if he were swearing on the Bible.

I tightly crossed my arms over my chest and sucked in a resigned breath. There's no getting around one's demons. "Okay. Let's get this over with."

***

We were gently transported to a Japanese Buddhist monastery. The time period was difficult to ascertain at first glance. Monks generally wore similar clothing century after century and shunned technology, but I would hazard to guess late-1800's.

"That is precisely when and where this is. See, you're much better than you give yourself credit for."

"Thanks," I said warily. Was he actually paying me a compliment?

The gong sounded from atop the hill, and the monks quietly filed out of afternoon meditation for their evening meal. This was the most serene place I ever visited. The scenery was like stepping inside a Thomas Kincade painting, except the mountains and forest in the distance were authentic. The gardens were meticulously kept, with not a weed in sight or leaf out of place. Ponds fed by little waterfalls were populated with hundreds of koi. But moreover, the men were, well, they were monks. They spent their entire lives in dedication to meditation.

Chris Suddeth

The leader of the monastery wasn't made obvious by his outfit, nor was he the object of adulation or special treatment. He was simply the calmest, most centered part of the sea of tranquility. He was the oldest, but that wasn't it. Why was I so drawn to this elderly gentleman?

"I see the master has caught your eye."

"Yes, who is he?"

"Master Usui, but it doesn't matter what his name is. Who or what do you think he is to you?"

Instantly, I knew. "He's me! That is, he is one of my incarnations."

"Bingo! Tell her what she's won, Johnny."

"But how did I get from all this to where I am now? And why didn't you allow me to spend time as the monk and force me to spend more time as the reverend?"

"The first question you need to answer for yourself, but I am pleased you are asking. As to your second question, sometimes I do things just to make you ask questions. You've seen enough here. Now---"

There was more to Nigel's choices than just making me ask questions, but that was probably the best response I was going to get. "I want to stay here for a while. How about thirty-six days here?" I attempted to bargain. I literally could spend my entire life here and be at peace.

"You did spend an entire life here in seclusion and look where it got you. You need more stimulation than what this monk could provide," Nigel responded with a smile that could be interpreted a variety of ways.

"What do you mean by that?" I intuited what he was talking about, but I sensed he was holding something back.

"Indeed," he huffed. "Back to what I was saying... Now it's time to even you out a little. Take the edge off. Round off the corners. You get the picture?"

Not really, but Japan's serenity disappeared in a blaze of light.

Chapter 13

When the blinding light dissipated, I found myself back in the cloying fog of my shower cave. Was it all a dream? So, it seemed. That would be preferable, wouldn't it? Just one more fucked-up dream I could brush off with a bong rip. I could see the steam, but I couldn't feel the warmth. At first, it was too thick to make out anything at all, and then the veil of steam dissipated surrounding my supine body. I was still there, where I fell, my body contorted in an unnatural shape, and the shower was still spraying on me. I was breathing, and I could hear my heart; odd that visiting the shower was comforting. I tried to nudge my body's shoulder with my foot, but that proved ineffective. Perhaps I could stay here with my body, try to shake and wake myself out of whatever was wrong with me.

Then I felt my shoulder being nudged. I looked down at my shoulder and saw it moving without my having willed it to move. I only had a moment to wonder what was happening before I woke up in Eugene's apartment, with him shaking my shoulder. To my left was Nigel, holding my SpongeBob SquarePants bedroom shoes. He threw them at me harder than necessary, but I caught them despite his intent of zinging them off my head.

"What was that?" I asked.

"Get comfy," he said in a forced monotone voice. It was obvious I wouldn't get an answer to my query.

"Why?" I replied tentatively. "What could you possibly do to me that you haven't already done?" Why did I ask these questions and deliberately bait him?

"Nothing you haven't done to yourself," he parried back.

I stared blankly at him and sat up on the sectional. I noticed Eugene was busy packing his volcano. It also looked like we had plenty of DVD's.

"See, you're still not getting it." Condescension dripped from Nigel's lips. "You're acting like all of this is my doing. Let me remind you of one universal constant, baby cakes. It's called free will."

I opened my mouth to protest my unfair treatment, and he quickly did an about-face and charged through the wall. I got up to follow and viciously banged my shin on the coffee table. There would be no walking through walls in this leg of my journey. He left me again with my impotent rage. On the bright side, at least I wasn't stranded on Iwo Jima this time.

I looked over at Eugene, noticing that he was done packing his volcano with what was no doubt the best weed the little Italian boy could grow. He didn't even acknowledge me yet. This was doubly bewildering, as I was still naked, and Eugene practically groveled around me, even with my clothes on. I waved my hand in front of his perturbed face. "Can you see me, Geney?"

He stared daggers at me. "Yes," he said flatly and proceeded to heat up the weed. We both raptly watched the plastic bag expand with pure THC. I thought, damn, I need this worse than I've ever needed it before. He unlatched the mouthpiece and offered it to me. "Greenies?" It was the courtesy of the first toke that he usually gave me, but he didn't even take his eyes off the TV.

"Sure," I said as I tossed my slippers on the floor. Eugene, of all men, should be reacting to my nudity. "Geney?"

"Yeah," he replied distractedly. "Could you please move and stop calling me Geney?"

I was taken aback. Was I losing "it"? When I didn't move fast enough, he started shaking the volcano mouthpiece and bag violently at me, making the plastic crinkle loudly. "Christ almighty! Hold the fuck on." I jammed my feet into my slippers and noticed my favorite sleeping sweatshirt and comfy shorts appeared on me. My sweatshirt was "cut all to pieces" as my nana used to say. I cut the bottom off to my navel, the sleeves off, and the hood off. It was so careworn one could barely see, Carolina Girls: The Best in the World stenciled on the front.

"How about NOW?! You want greenies or not?"

Coming out of my shock, I said absently, "Yeah—yeah," plopping down on the couch next to him.

I took the bag o' pure, heavenly, Juicy Fruit pot smoke, and he started our first DVD.

As soon as I inhaled my first toke of purified cheeba, the tension began to melt and release from my shoulders, and I slumped into Eugene's cavernous couch. It was reassuring to be in the familiar environment of what seemed like Eugene's apartment. I took a deep breath, closed my eyes and took mental notes of my body as I relaxed. That's right, my body, or at least what felt like my home for the last thirty-four years. Who could be sure after all I had been through?

After centering myself, I opened my eyes and noticed a large clock on the wall, the kind of clock one might buy at one of those snazzy, home accessory stores. I was intrigued by, and began to study this clock, but was interrupted as an impatient hand shot in front of my face.

Startled a little and beginning to be put off by his attitude, I grumbled, "Goddamn it, Eugene, what is wrong with you? I've been through a lot lately, so can you take it easy?"

"You're fucking up the rotation. Puff, puff, give." He retorted back the popular line from Chris Tucker to Ice Cube in the movie *Friday,* but there was zero humor behind it, only an expectant stare.

"Alright, sorry." He was never like this with me. He usually kissed my ass. "You're not gonna tell me what's bothering you?"

"I told you," he said through clenched teeth. "Puff, puff, give!"

"Okay, here. Christ!"

He yanked it out of my hand.

"You need to get your head out of your ass."

He chuckled derisively at that comment and asked, "Do you realize how long I've been here waiting for you?" He sucked down the rest of the bag and hooked it up to the volcano for a refill. The buzzing, burning of the weed filled the room's silence for a moment. Then he looked me in the eyes, rare for him, or any other man, for that matter, waiting for a response. He sucked down the bag again, quite a lot of THC mainlining into his body. I don't believe I ever saw him hit it that hard. I'm not even sure if it would be possible to inhale that much pot in what passes for our everyday lives.

"Impressive set of lungs you have there," I ventured, trying to break the ice. It didn't work. "I don't know, but I'm gonna need another hit, and may schedule a date with Mark, Maker's Mark." I rarely drank liquor, but when I did, it was Maker's Mark.

He relaxed slightly at that comment and exhaled. "Yeah, no shit," he conceded. "I think there's a bottle in there, and I don't know either."

"You don't know what?"

"I don't know how long I've been here. That's how long I've been here."

"What do you mean you don't know how long you've been here?"

"I mean I've been here so long, I've forgotten. That big clock on the wall doesn't tell time in the usual sense. I haven't figured it out completely yet."

I opened my mouth to inquire further about the clock but was interrupted by the doorbell.

"Chinker dinker food is here." And with that politically incorrect ethnic slur, he darted for the door and tossed me the mouthpiece. "Mind repacking that."

"Nah, I got it."

Funny, I was just thinking of Chinese food. The restaurant on this side of town was the best I ever tasted.

"Ten dollar, dis food make you holler," I heard the delivery man say. His voice sounded familiar.

"Wait, was that Nigel?"

"What?" Eugene said absently. His mind was on food only.

By the time Eugene came back, I already had the bag inflating again. "So, tell me what's up with the clock, and why are you acting so testy?" I concentrated on pulling another toke out of the bag to allow him time to speak. I noticed that he was tearing into the eggrolls as fast as he could. He was starving.

"You don't understand," he said with a full mouth, as he shoved the bag of food in my direction. "That Limey motherfucker told me I could have anything I wanted as soon as you got here. So, I asked when that was going to be, and his response was 'only time will tell.' He motioned at the clock, like he was some lord or count, and then the fucker walked through the damn thing. Weird... Wonder if somebody put something in our weed, Brandy? Cause all this is really strange. Did you buy that clock and put it in here? Cause it's about to get taken out into the woods so I can try out my new tactical Mossberg 12-gauge."

"Yeah, that's fine," I rasped with a little pot burn. I didn't know what to make of the fact that Eugene was apparently communicating with Nigel, so I chose to let it be, for now. I didn't believe Eugene was completely grasping the situation. For that matter, I didn't believe that I was completely grasping the situation, but I was tired of trying to figure it out. I grabbed a blanket to cover myself and said, "Look, can we just eat, smoke, and watch a movie?"

"Sounds good to me," he said between bites of his third eggroll.

"Good. What movie we got in there?"

"*English Patient.*"

"That movie makes two hours feel like two days. It's crap."

"But it won all those Oscars," he said, with unconcealed sarcasm.

"I don't give a rat's ass," I said as I laid down the volcano's mouthpiece. I was relieved that we were starting to get along again. I noted that I actually cared that we got along...

"Yeah, I realize that the movie sucks. Matter of fact, I walked out when it was out in theaters originally."

"Then why are we watching it?"

"It seems that we have plenty of time…"

"Don't tell me all we have are lame movies to watch. Nigel fits his little humor in any which way he can."

"No, nothing like that. We actually have an extensive collection."

"Then why?"

He held up his hand to keep me from going further. "Oh, see, I've got this aunt that took offense to me walking out of the movie only twenty minutes in, all those years ago."

"You gave it ten minutes more than I did."

"Yeah, well, I just wanted to give it another chance. We can watch something else?"

"No, actually, that's fine."

"Kay, there's another blanket and a pillow over there."

He was encouraging me to cover up?

"You want?" He offered me the bong with a mouthwash and ice mixture in the chamber.

"The menthol effect? No thanks. Remember the last time you had to pick my ass up off the floor."

He shrugged and exhaled a little. It was true. The first and last time I tried mouthwash in the bottom of the bong, it did not agree with me. I think it was a combination of being shut up in a room, with zero ventilation, and it just being too intense. The movie, such as it was, blazed on.

***

"*English Patient* still sucks," I said, sitting up as the movie credits rolled.

"Pot didn't make it bearable like I thought it would." His voice squeaked agreement in an effort to hold smoke in and speak at the same time.

I snorted laughter, then did some yoga stretches, mostly for Eugene's benefit, and took stock of the situation. My eyes went wide at the clock. I think it actually moved backwards.

"Apparently, the biscuits got themselves." Eugene was sounding like himself again. "Found them in the kitchen, with a note that read: 'You're welcome'."

"Wonder how long we'll be here and how long we've already spent here?" I pondered aloud.

"I don't know, and it doesn't really matter," he said as he pitched a biscuit and jelly packet my way.

"Thanks," I said as I tore into a jelly packet with my teeth. How odd it was that we were doing things in much the same way we did in our waking life. If I didn't know any better... "But why do you say it doesn't matter?"

"It's best that you don't ask," he said with liquid pleading eyes that took me aback.

"Alright, I'll leave it alone for now, but what can you tell me?"

"Let's see: I'm here for as long as you need me—"

"I need you?" I snorted sardonically. I mustn't allow him the upper hand. Why did I push away one of the few that cared?

"Look, I'm just telling you what I was told. Gonna let me finish?"

"Yep, sorry, please continue."

"We have all the food, weed, and movies we want..."

"And Maker's," I supplied. "Sounds heavenly. What's the problem? You and I have always fantasized about this sort of thing. Any outside contact? Cell phones? Internet?"

"No, no, and fucking no. We fantasized about a day or two. I guess we should be careful what we wish for, because I'm stuck in here with you. Even though I don't believe in this sort of shit, it's become evident to me that I'm in one of your out-of-body experiences or lucid dreams."

I forgot that I confided my nocturnal activities to him once. "Maybe I'm in yours." I intimated I was the woman of his dreams. I got a raised eyebrow in response, not doing much again for my self-esteem. He was "stuck" in here with me? Was I that annoying and repulsive?

"I am open to suggestions on what to do. In the meantime, I suggest we enjoy the ride while we can," I pointed out. A very valid point, but the situation was beginning to dawn on me, and I didn't like the direction this was headed. I should have known I was still doing whatever it was I was doing when I couldn't wake up back in my shower. "I suppose you're right. Nigel has done worse to me."

"Do you think Nigel's really your problem, *Alice*?"

"What do you mean, and why are you being so irritable?" He really was starting to hurt my feelings. At least he called me by my given name. I guess that's a good sign, isn't it? "Who are you? Y'all butt buddies, now? He let you in on his plans?" He made to answer those questions, but I waved him off. "What about your foul mood?" I didn't even want to think about the mind-bending effects of me reliving all the gory details of my journey so far. I involuntarily shut my legs as events threatened to flood back. I really wanted to focus elsewhere.

Eugene raised another knowing eyebrow at my legs closing and responded, "Look, I'm sorry about my mood, but as you're always telling me, it is what it is."

"I'll accept that for now, but I'll need that menthol bong," I said with an outstretched arm and mouth full of sausage biscuit. "I just want to be out of my mind…"

"You sure about that?"

Yes, I was sure about that. Numb became my default mindset when life got too touchy feely. "What's in the bowl?" I asked, ignoring the question, but secretly relieved he cared to ask.

"Only our fav, the 1995 Cannabis Cup winner, White Widow. Very strong and soothing, sure to make you drool," he said as if he were the industry pitch man. Hell, he did get invited to Amsterdam every year as a judge.

"Cool. Here goes… Catch me before my head goes through the glass coffee table there, please."

"Will do, but that's what has been bothering me and making me irritable. Sorry," he added quickly, but not really explaining himself.

"It's okay," I said as I eyed the bong one last time to check that the bowl was packed properly. I took a deep breath, steeling myself. "I've been on one bizarre little journey myself. I don't know how long I've been on it, nor when the ride will be over." I inhaled as much as I dared. "All in," as Clemson's latest bullshit head coach, Dabo Sweeney says. Go Darth Visor!

"Well, here's the thing." He was now talking over my pot coughs. "So what if your head goes through the coffee table."

"Excuse me?" I managed to squeak out.

Swoondalini

"No, now I didn't mean it like that. Are we asleep or not? Dead or alive? If we get hurt in this room, does it hurt our real bodies? Is what we see and do real? Will we remember it? Does this happen all the time? Am I me, and are you you?"

"Stop! Let's just answer one question at a time. Now, you've made my head hurt with all the questions. I think I'll just be content to pick out the next movie since it's my turn. My vote is *North and South*."

"Deal, but that's really long. Shouldn't that count for several votes?"

I responded with a, "does it really matter at this point" look.

"Guess you're right. Orry Main it is. Still can't believe Patrick Swayze is gone. Maybe we'll run into him."

"Just put the movie in, please."

There we sat and smoked, drank, ate, laughed, and cried, through all three books of *North and South,* even the crappy one that Patrick Swayze wasn't in. That's about twenty-one hours in real life time.

"What's next on the movie agenda?" I asked Eugene as we both seemed a little startled that *North and South* was actually over. I observed both of our emotions were more on the surface here. Eugene was the typical male and, therefore, not a crier, but he was now, and he was so angry earlier. I suppose it could be attributed to all the weed and alcohol, but it was more than that. I was surprised at feeling a pang of insecurity that he didn't notice me being naked earlier. Ever since I hit puberty, I never failed to turn a straight man's head; even made plenty of gays take a second look.

"Not sure." He yawned and stretched. "How about a rousing game of dick or scroat?"

I ignored his attempt to get me to play his game of identifying which part of his manhood he was showing me. "Why don't you tell me what the deal is?"

"What do you mean? How about the gobbler then?"

I wished that more of the many men I knew possessed his sense of humor. Senator Sam was a riot sometimes, but other than that... I actually thought the gobbler was hilarious. It brought me to tears the first time I saw him put his balls through his zipper and make turkey sounds. Was he the first guy I saw performing this gag? "The gobbler is fine."

He ignored me and on went his gasmask. The thing with Eugene was that he didn't like using a pipe or rolling a joint. It needed to be a fancy apparatus. I usually drew the line at the gas mask, as it made me feel utterly ridiculous.

"Perhaps I like to savor my cheeba, and these 'fancy apparati' provide a bit of a ceremony for me."

"Fair enough." No surprise, we were starting to read each other's thoughts. "Give me the mask."

"Cool. Bout damn time..."

Pressing the point that I couldn't let go, "I mean, I was naked earlier, and you didn't even make a comment, look my way, or make a move. I know you think that I'm just *pretty*, and no one sees me otherwise, but you're causing me to doubt my hotness. Am I losing it?" I couldn't believe how much I actually cared what he thought.

Not commenting, he took his thumb and index finger and gingerly pulled up my cut off sweatshirt to reveal my breasts. He held my shirt up an inordinate amount of time, studying them. "Nope, you've definitely still got it. I just didn't even think about it much due to my predicament, nor was I able to see you very well because of your purplish glow. That's not to mention the fact that I swore to myself, from now on, I would only look at those sea green eyes of yours."

"You rarely look me in the eyes..."

"Yes, I know. I'm sorry; I just decided that the rest of you hurt too much to look at. Of course, when I would look into your eyes, well..." he trailed off as we suddenly found ourselves nude.

I chose to take it as a compliment, but I was becoming more attentive to things. I realized that he was talking about more than my looks. What was the purple glow he mentioned?

He must have noticed the hurt confusion that registered on my face. He pulled the gas mask off to gently dry a tear with his thumb that I didn't realize I shed. He slowly lowered his hand to the blanket that covered me from the waist down and caressed my breast with the back of his hand, sending shock waves of ecstasy to my core. When he removed the blanket, I could no longer be contained. I was so wet, but it was more than that. I closed my eyes and took a sharp, shuddering breath in to steady myself. I had to have him. Upon opening my eyes, I could see his confusion at his own sudden nudity.

"Go with it," I said in a heavy bedroom whisper.

We both stood up in unison and touched each other's hands in a mirroring motion. I began to feel white hot electric energy passing between us. I looked down to see his erection awaiting me with anticipation.

The excitement was more than I could stand between my own legs. It wasn't often I felt this way, if ever. For an eternity, we both stood staring at each other, neither wanting to make the first move for fear of ruining the moment, but unable to stop what was set into motion. I could feel my breasts heaving up and down with deep, expectant breaths.

Finally, our starvation for one another demanded feeding. He slammed me against the wall and penetrated me. The "electricity" arcing between us intensified with each thrust until we inexplicably merged body and **soul**. It was like we were pioneering a different way to have sex. This was more than sex; it was new and foreign and completely blissful.

I now know that if we viewed ourselves from the outside, we would have been unrecognizable to our everyday selves. I heard of astral sex in my studies of new age material, but never thought much of it. After all, I already cornered the market on sex. Didn't I?

We went on and on in this astral embrace for who knows how long? Time was meaningless. Minutes, hours, days, who gives a fuck, literally? I never knew pleasure like this.

Finally, there was one large, heavenly surge that I could only take to be astral orgasm. I couldn't conceive that it could get more intense than it already was, but it did.

When it was over, Eugene pulled out of me, and we both fell to the floor, spread eagle and panting from the release. I was still tingling all over, but as the feelings began to wane, I lifted up on my elbow to face Eugene. "Can I call you Geney again?" I asked playfully.

"You can call me whatever you want to call me after that. What was that? Never knew the Thundercock had it in him..." he said with his eyes still closed and breathing hard. He called his penis the Thundercock in reference to the *Thundercats* cartoon. He asked me all the time if I needed some "thunder down under" or if I wanted a little "thunder and lightning." Those comments were usually followed by him bellowing, "Thundercock HOOOOOOOOOO!" like in the cartoon. I thought it was funny but would never give him the satisfaction of giggling. Now I found myself wanting nothing more than a lot of "thunder and lightning," especially the lightning part.

"I don't know what that was, but I know I want more. Want to go again?"

"Damn right I do! Lemme catch my second wind."

"Yeah, me too."

I lay back flat on the floor and took it all in. I was brought back to the moment by a hand groping my breast. That was all it took to turn me on again. I leaned up and firmly grabbed a hand full of nut sack before looking Geney in the eyes.

He responded with words I never saw coming. "You know, people only see that you're pretty, because that's all of you that you put out to the rest of us," he said kindly, running his fingers through my hair and touching the area where my hair was shocked white.

Realization began to dawn on me, and my entire way of life, but for right now, I would be right here.

I began to massage his manhood vigorously until his eyes registered pleasure, and then quickly went to slightly worried and surprised, before giving way to a distant gaze. He then disappeared before my eyes, leaving me more than wanting, my hand grasping air.

I was left in a bad way. I couldn't go on any further until I got more of what I just tasted. I wasn't a fan of the c-word, but the only way to describe it was that I got cunt-bunted, given a dose of the same medicine I dealt out to Geney and numerous other men to "leave them wanting more."

I fell back to the floor with a huff. "I'd like some more of that please," I muttered in a far-away voice, as if asking for a second helping of mashed potatoes.

"That can be arranged," Nigel said, interrupting my frustration. He was eating popcorn as if watching a movie and there were a couple of dirty socks tossed to the side of his chair.

I cracked one eye open to glare at him, hoping he simply came and went, but no such luck there. "You would have to come and ruin this."

"This den of sin will always be here, and you may return in time. Tell me, have you learned anything yet?"

"Blue balls really suck."

"Yes, that's true, but we still have work to do before you can see the forest for the trees. But don't worry, we're going to get you there. I'm hopeful now."

"So, tell me again, what I was supposed to get from thirty-six days on the volcanic sands of Iwo Jima?"

He responded with a snap of his fingers and we were gone again.

Chapter 14

Wherever we were going, we weren't in a hurry to get there.

"That's because we're headed to the "Slow Country" of South Carolina, and I thought I'd get you into the pace of things down there," Nigel responded to my passing observation.

The term "Slow Country" was used by some when they referred to the Lowcountry region of South Carolina, and it was true, things did move at a much slower pace there. Maybe it was the heat and humidity, but it was a fact of life in this neck of the woods.

"Thanks, my father's side of the family is from here. I am aware of its pace of life." I was feeling defensive suddenly.

"Ah yes, but you seem to have forgotten."

I wasn't ready to face why we were circling like a buzzard over I-95's Exit 38 to Yemassee, so I asked, "What happened to Eugene? Why'd he just disappear on me?" I demanded, letting my frustration seep out.

"Geney woke up from his wet dream to end all wet dreams, when all that pent-up baby batter exploded into his skivvies. Quite a gooey mess."

"That's what that was, a wet dream?"

"Is that what you think it was?"

"No, probably not..." I said.

"No, probably not..." he parroted.

When my face bled hurt, confusion, and admittedly much sexual frustration, he backed off a little. "Look, you'll have time to sort all that out. For now, and always, be in the *now*. Savvy?"

"Savvy," I echoed back. Funny thing was that, by this point, I was beginning to realize that Nigel was trying to help me out in his own sadistic way. I just hoped that it wouldn't kill me before he was finished.

"It won't, or rather it shouldn't... do you in."

Damn it, I hated him horning in on my thoughts.

We quickly drifted to the east, and it seemed for a brief second that time blurred a little. I looked over at Nigel and saw him point toward Highway 21 and a red car as it was going over the Whale Branch River. I hadn't seen that road in years, but I knew it instantly; even from the air. I took a moment to breathe in the salt marsh and marvel at the majesty of the ACE Basin before spotting a '65 Mustang convertible like the one that meant so much to my father. He loved it so, because it was from a much happier and simpler time in his life. He always told me the car meant so much to him because he used to drive Pappy around town in it.

Pappy rarely spoke if it wasn't pertinent, or he wanted to share a humorous little aphorism. When he took me fishing or to the driving range he made me, he would speak of odd things like holding my mouth right in my follow-through and where certain squirrels would be at a particular time of day. Pappy just saw the world from a different perspective than the rest of us. Truth be told, I, one day, would like to see life as he did, provided I lived through this ordeal. He also took his naps in his aqua blue '66 Rambler station wagon and prescribed himself three cigars a day as his only vice. The cigars produced the added benefit of keeping the ubiquitous insects at bay in this part of the Palmetto State.

We descended rapidly on Northern Beaufort County. I heard Nigel giggling over my shoulder, but his little games were bothering me less and less. I wondered if that was a bad thing or good thing. As we rapidly closed in on the Mustang, déjà-vu began smacking me in the face.

I was headed straight for a dark-haired teen girl sitting in the passenger seat. "Oh my God, that's me and Daddy," I exclaimed gleefully. The glee gave way to tears as I realized that this was the first time that I can recall him bringing me to his hometown of Beaufort, SC since my mother had her final falling out with what she termed the "Lowcountry White-Trash Devil Clan." She ended holidays and summers along with the only real stability I knew as a child. Sure, there was my daddy, but he was outnumbered and outclassed by the sheer volume of bat-shit crazy that was my mother and her kin. I was fourteen the first time I was allowed to go alone, with my father, for four hours down the road to see his family.

I felt a flush of excitement as I looked over at my father. I never truly recovered from his death and never fully understood how or why it happened.

Right now, I wasn't concerned with that. Right now, I would be in the here and now. Maybe I was learning something.

I looked down at my body to confirm that I was indeed me, albeit a much younger me. My essence then merged with my younger self. I gave myself a quick once-over. I was a little smaller all the way around, sported three Swatches on the left arm, and several jelly bracelets on the other.

I was wearing shorts, which was a rarity back then since Bob Jones High School didn't allow them and only allowed a casual denim skirt to the ankles.

Even though I was olive-skinned, it was obvious my legs didn't often see the light of day. Daddy even allowed me to wear a bikini for the first time ever on this trip. I was to be a normal girl on my trips to Beaufort from now on, Daddy proclaimed. Mama equated normal with worldly and therefore sinful.

"My skin is itching with excitement. Thank you so much, Nigel."

"What's that, baby?" Daddy slurred a little.

"Nothing, Daddy," I said as I reached down to turn up Cyndi Lauper's *Girls Just Wanna Have Fun*. "Did you know that 'The Noise You Hear is the Sound of Freedom'?" I read the quote from the front gate of the Marine Corp Air Station.

"Can't hear ya. Wind's in my ears and somebody just jacked up the radio," he said with a smile on his face. I forgot how truly handsome my father was. One tends to obfuscate what those that have passed over looked like as the years pass by.

I quickly noticed that I was burning all over. Looked like I stepped on a big ant hill. My muscles ached, I was bruised, sprained and it felt like my shoulder was about to pop out of its socket.

"Yeah, you're a hot mess," Nigel yelled over the wind and the radio from the back seat, then chuckled at his little play on words. "Do you remember how it happened, or why, for that matter?" he asked after regaining his serious tone.

I was scratching a lot by now. I needed Benadryl and apple cider vinegar to salve my wounds in a bad way. "I remember that it happened, now that I'm here again, but not really where, or why, or how. I guess you're about to show me?"

"My, you're getting good at this, aren't you?" he praised without any of his usual sarcasm. "Let's go back in time about thirty minutes or so to where you played bumper boobies with the fire ants."

***

In a blur, we pulled up and stopped in a large clearing surrounded by woods. In the middle of this clearing was a large mud pit. "This is where they hold the Yemassee Mud Run every year," Daddy announced. "Your uncle Bobby and I had some good times here."

Why did I not remember this?

"You are a master of denial, rivaled by few. It's a family trait that you took to new levels. Don't get me wrong, it has allowed you to survive into your mid-thirties without putting a pistol between your dentist office poster smile, but it's only a matter of time," Nigel quickly whispered all this in my ear, with real concern behind his words.

Memories were starting to trickle back in. Daddy pulled over on I-385 to roll a joint and tugged on it for the last few hours. He told me that he was rolling his own cigarette, but even though I was cloistered in Bob Jones most of my life, I knew it was more than tobacco. Then around Columbia, he started in on the pills. By I-95, he cracked his first "homecoming celebration" beer and was on his fourth celebration beer thirty-five minutes later when we pulled up to the property in Yemassee.

"What we doing here, Daddy?" I was becoming a little nervous.

"It occurred to me that you've never learned to shoot," he said while relieving himself on the back tire.

"But I don't like guns," I heard my fourteen-year-old self say. I owned plenty of them in my adult life, but I was beginning to recall that I didn't care for my first experience with firearms. I loved my father, but this was not a memory of him I cherished, so I simply forgot it until Nigel dredged it back up, in living color, no less.

"Doesn't matter, everybody needs to know how to handle them. Not enough girls do, and some men take advantage of that. You're old enough now." His last word was muffled by the sound of him slamming his door and unlocking the trunk. I smelled weed as my father was finishing off his roach.

"Alice, you gonna get out of the car, babe?"

"Nah, I'm good here."

"Alice, get out of the car and come back here. I need to show you something."

My father's tone left no room for argument. He never yelled at me like my mother, nor did he ever spank me like her. He simply possessed a tone and a look that made me hop to.

"Come on, it's okay," he said in a calming manner.

I slowly climbed out of the Mustang and stretched before making my way to the trunk. What I saw would have turned a much older me on, but I was looking through innocent eyes at a small arsenal. Before me was the Colt 1911 .45, that I now keep in my nightstand at my town home by Congressional, a Remington Mini-14, a sawed-off Mossberg 12-gauge, and a Smith and Wesson

.44 Magnum. I always liked that Colt because it reminded me of a much simpler time of sneaking to watch Magnum P.I. when my mother wasn't around.

"Good, those shoes should work," Daddy said as he looked down at my jelly shoes, then cracked another beer. How he figured plastic shoes were appropriate where snake boots would have been recommended, I don't know.

"But I'd really rather not do this right now."

"Now's as good a time as any. First lesson, always wear eye and ear protection," he said, jamming plastic sunglasses on my face and Kleenex in my ears.

"Okay." I had no choice but to go along with this.

"Let's start with something that won't have as much kick. You know, to kind of give you a feel for things."

In my adult life, I was comfortable with firearms and developed an appreciation for quality weapons, took comfort in having them in my homes, on my person, and even wielded them in the line of duty. But I didn't always wield them for protection. (No accounting for taste, remember.) There was this one time that some fellas paid me a pretty penny to come topless to a bachelor party and shoot machine guns. Now, those boys knew how to have a good time. Some real *Soldier of Fortune* shit.

"BRANDY!" Nigel yelled in my ear, to bring my attention to the matter at hand. He intentionally used my alias. "Focus, girl," he admonished.

But now, as in Twin Peaks before, I felt the unease of my younger self rising up. Apparently, fear and unease could be implanted in the very physical structure of the body.

"It's also how issues can be transferred from one soul's incarnation to the next if karma isn't done with its lesson," Nigel tossed in.

"This is the Mini-14. Fires a .223 round," he said, cursing under his breath as the roach burnt his fingers. "Now, one quick word about firearms before we get started: You can only fuck up once. Understood?"

"Yes, I think so," I stammered as I realized that this was the first time I heard my father drop the F-bomb.

"Good. Safety first," Daddy said with a serious face as he opened yet another Milwaukee's Best. "Alright, babe, take these milk jugs and watermelons over there to the tree line."

"Daddy, what are all those watermelons for?" I knew but was compelled to ask.

"Oh, you'll find out, pumpkin. I'm saving the fun part for last. Kay, run along."

We got about fifty yards away from the jugs and Daddy presented me with the Mini-14. "Didn't that fruitcake down in Texas, back in '72, use one of these to kill more than twenty people?" Daddy asked, like I'm supposed to know that.

First off, the rifle was heavy. I mean, I picked up some A-Team toy guns the boys in Dunean used to play capture the flag and Tour of Duty with, and there was just no comparison. It was hard too. Daddy jammed the stock in my shoulder. "Hold it firmly," Daddy instructed. "Now, you don't pull the trigger, you squeeze the trigger. Aim down the sights there and squeeze off a round."

I hesitated.

"Go ahead, it won't bite. Just keep the business end pointed away from anything you don't want fucked up," Daddy said languidly, like he was medicated. Hell, he was medicated! And there was the F-word again.

Swoondalini

"Okay, here goes." I squeezed just like Daddy told me, but it didn't return my embrace. Instead, it cracked my eardrums. Kleenex is no substitute for a real set of shooting headphones. My ears rang from the first shot. Is this what tinnitus feels like? Would I be like this for life? My shoulder definitely felt it. I'm glad I held it firmly.

"You missed, but that's alright. It's only the first time. Go ahead; you've got twenty-nine more in there. Keep shooting until you hit a melon."

I fired five more rounds until I hit my first melon. It exploded. I was starting to have a good time and was wondering when the other jelly shoe was going to drop.

"You know, that's what would happen to somebody's head," Daddy mentioned nonchalantly. "Walk down there and look at it while I reload."

When I arrived downrange, pink watermelon brains produced flashbacks from my life as a Marine. I could recall Corporal Sutton's memories of enemy dead and him conveying matter-of-factly that the Japs kept coming and he didn't mind killing them. What was worrisome was when you'd have to push stacked up bodies away from a machine gun nest to be able to dispatch more of the enemy. At that point, there was a real fear of the machine gun seizing up due to the barrel overheating. The sheer numbers of slant-eyed muthafuckers that hurled themselves at a machine gun with only their glorified over-sized letter-openers for protection in honor of some unseen emperor was unsettling and gooseflesh inspiring. What teen girl even thinks this way, much less gets flashbacks of a war fought three decades before her birth? The girl that was excited over wearing her first bikini and how she was going to look in it was horrified and sickened, but Elmer Sutton had a hard-on that only a Marine could appreciate.

Chris Suddeth

"Alright, now it's time for something with a little more kick," Daddy hollered from up-range just in time to divert bile from rising up in my throat. We walked to each other. "This is a Colt .45 1911 model. It's been a key instrument of freedom for American armed forces in the 20th Century. It's not very accurate, but the bullet is big and slow, which means you're probably going to knock down a molester no matter where you shoot him."

I followed orders and banged through some clips with the 1911, so I didn't notice that Daddy was setting up an obstacle course of sorts for me, complete with silhouette targets.

"Let's get you started by firing another clip or two before we turn it up a notch."

The pistol rocked violently as I went through the last rounds. When that clip was done, my father shoved the .44 magnum in my hand. "Now, listen up, baby, this is the most powerful handgun made by man," he said proudly with an unmistakably glazed-over look in his eye. "You'll see it if you ever watch those shitty *Dirty Harry* movies. Go ahead, she's loaded."

I fired, and on the first shot, I could feel a little bruising going on in my palm. The second shot jammed my wrist, and I stopped there to shake it off.

I didn't hit anything, but Daddy didn't notice. "Okay, that's fine. Here, put this on," he said, throwing the shoulder holster for the .44 at me, while he replaced the two rounds I fired. I was getting a renewed education in the Lowcountry humidity and as a result, was sweating profusely. Not to mention being devoured by mosquitoes that swarmed me as if they never saw virgin skin like this in their entire lives.

He jammed the .44 in its holster and snapped it shut. "Oh, I almost forgot the Mossberg. Yeah, better let you fire it a couple of times before you run the gauntlet."

"Gauntlet?"

"Don't worry about it. Here, I've loaded it with alternating double ought and slugs. It holds six 2 ¾" shells. This weapon makes big holes, and you don't have to be very accurate with it. Point in the general direction of the *asshole* and blow his fucking guts and spine out his back." The way he said asshole led me to believe he was speaking of someone specifically.

I had some experience with shotguns but had not shot one since this time in Yemassee. I remembered that now. But, I did own one and kept it loaded with alternating double ought buck shot and slugs. No matter what, I needed that power, didn't I? I fired and it about knocked me over. Ouch, I forgot the kick they give your shoulder, especially when you neglect to embrace it.

"Alice, aim for the jugs over there. You've got five more shots. Fire away. Unload on the bastard," Daddy slurred and guzzled another Beast.

I fired, and the first jug exploded. The glee was gone.

"Fire, goddamn it! Fire! Fire! Fire!" Spittle flew out from his mouth. Daddy was yelling now and beginning to scare me. I unloaded the rest of the Mossberg despite the shoulder threatening to leave its socket.

"Daddy, I don't like this. I'm too small for this shotgun. Why are we doing this? Is everything okay?"

"No, it's not okay, and I don't care whether or not you like it. You're going to do this, because a girl has to know how to protect herself when her father can't." He looked so pained and haunted that it scared me. Where was this coming from? I never remembered us being like this. So serious, so... so life and death.

"Fine, let's get this over with."

"Watch your tone, young lady."

"Sorry." I glared at him while briefly considering "accidentally" shooting his precious Mustang.

"Here's what we're going to do: Load that shotgun back up the way it was."

"Kay. How?" the fourteen-year-old child in me asked.

Daddy threw shells at me and pressed on. "Now, I've set up all these targets, and you're going to have to pretend you're training for the FBI or something. You're good at pretending since you're an only child... You will use the shotgun first and then lay it on the ground."

Daddy shoved the .45 in my little cloth Esprit belt, after showing me how to cock and lock it. He then forced two spare magazines in my small pockets.

"After that, you'll grab the Colt..."

Blah, blah, blah. It was all becoming a blur with what he wanted me to do. Then a moment of cold fear struck when I considered that I might have shot and killed my father—but forgotten. Was that how he died? It would make sense that I would suppress something like accidentally shooting my inebriated father. No matter, since I went on autopilot on the rare occasion that Daddy actually raised his voice to me. He was like Pappy in that manner. "Go, go, fucking go, I want all those goddamn targets taken out like your life depends on it, cause it just may."

Swoondalini

What followed was a train wreck in the annals of father/daughter bonding. I almost popped my shoulder out of the socket, again, screwed up both wrists diving and/or shooting the magnum, and jammed a couple of fingers, simultaneously ripping off a few Lee Press-On Nails, while landing solidly on the Colt 1911 to make a big blue version of the pistol on my hip that would last a week or more. I wouldn't be looking my best for my first outing in a bikini. This was not to mention the skinned knees from dropping abruptly to the ground several times and the piece de resistance: suddenly, my body erupted with a fiery sensation in dozens of different places all at the same time. I rolled on top of one of the ubiquitous ant hills without noticing.

"Holy hell, Daddy! I'm on fucking fire."

He stared at me in confusion before realizing that my chicken dance was indeed for real. I actually thought I was going to get a reprimand for cussing, but he just looked through me before finally helping me brush off the little fireballs. "Walk it off," he said in his typical gym teacher's response for every injury. Break an arm, walk it off. Get kicked in the nuts, walk it off. Take a tumble down the bleachers, at field day, in front of the most popular kids in school, and you get a dust off and yes, you guessed it, walk it off. I did two out of three of these in this lifetime, and I suppose I experienced the other one too. Now I could add target practice while rolling around in fire ants to my list. I'm sure that's something that Navy Seals or Army Rangers did before they got tucked in at night. What was next? Sleep deprivation? Forced marches with fifty pounds on my back?

"You ready to go, Alice, or would you like another run-through? You missed a couple of targets."

"I thought we were going to see Nana, Pappy, and Uncle Bobby?" I winced. I just received an ass-whipping without anyone laying a hand on me and those fire ant bites would itch for weeks after this. How could I have forgotten?

Suddenly, Daddy grabbed the Mini-14 leaning against the car and swung it toward the woods. The muzzle raced by my gut, and I noticed his finger on the trigger with the safety off. If somebody filmed all of this, it would be a great video on how not to teach your daughter gun safety.

"Daddy, what are you doing?" I yelled at him in surprise and admonishment.

"Did you not hear that?"

"Hear what? I didn't know you could hear fire ants chewing on skin." Again, my attempt at levity in the face of pain fell on Daddy's deaf ears.

"Somebody's watching us."

"Okay." I was unsure of what to do next. Would he leave here willingly, or did he have more in store? "Daddy, you're scaring me."

"I'm scaring myself."

"Let's go." I crossed my fingers behind my back that he would agree.

"Maybe we better head on to Uncle Bobby's."

"Yes please. I think that's a great idea. Daddy, why did we do all this?"

"I told you, a girl has to learn to protect herself. Maybe we'll get you some karate lessons too."

"I'd prefer golf lessons. There's more to this than protection. Something happened, didn't it?"

Swoondalini

I could see tears forming in his eyes as he packed up the car and lowered the top. "Yeah, baby, something happened," he said quietly and tenderly before turning over the engine. "Do you not remember?"

"Remember what?"

His face froze in anguish before he could explain any further.

"You're not ready to hear this just yet," Nigel said softly.

***

Nigel hit the fast-forward button on the VCR that is my life again. We were back out on Highway 21, some twenty minutes removed from the shooting incident. How did I forget so quickly? I wanted to press my father for the information that Nigel said I wasn't ready to hear, but my lips were compelled to refrain. In fact, I was inexplicably losing the urgency to press that particular matter, no doubt due to Nigel's pesky influence. I would let it go for the moment and live in the moment. I was again feeling the excitement of just being with my father. "Thank you, Nigel," I whispered.

"What's that, baby?"

"Nothing, Daddy."

Nothing could ruin this day. I didn't even care that my father was hammered while driving me around. That was merely frowned upon during the 80's, right?

"Can't hear ya with the wind in my ears and the radio turned up as far as it'll go." Daddy grinned. His ears must have been ringing too. "Look, there's the sign, *The Noise You Hear is the Sound of Freedom*. That quote says it all."

"Read it in Pat Conroy's book about his father," I said.

"When did you become a reader? You never liked to read."

"Er... there's lots of things you don't know about me, Daddy," I said with my best smile. Reading anything outside of the Bible and schoolbooks was frowned upon as worldly by Bob Jones and my father just assumed I stuck by that rule. Besides, Daddy was old school. Why would a pretty girl need to read anything she didn't have to read anyway, right?

"Really now?" he questioned, giving my shoulder a playful shove. I winced a little, but quickly focused on the joy that I'd feel when I saw my father's family again. I always loved seeing my nana and Uncle Bobby and longed for the unassuming kindness and simplicity that was Pappy.

Truth was that I became quite the little reader after I left the Upstate. First, because Mandy Stinger required all her girls to be well read. She didn't just want pretty faces. That could be found anywhere. I read grudgingly at first, and then developed a great affinity for it. I got to where I kept two or three books going at the same time, ranging from military history, to new age, to the smut novels that featured my image on the cover.

"Okay, maybe I didn't read *The Great Santini*," hedging now. "We watched the movie with Robert Duvall at school." Knowing we did no such thing. Bob Jones students were encouraged to sell out other students to the administration, if they spotted their classmates going into a theater. "Can we ride around town before heading to Uncle Bobby's and out to Fripp Island?"

"Absolutely." Daddy sounded thrilled. "I'd love to show you around my old stomping grounds. Be careful, doe, the Lowcountry'll get in de blood." Daddy chuckled at himself feebly attempting a Gullah accent.

Swoondalini

Daddy should have seen through my lie, but he was obviously drunk, high, and upset. His parents actually sent him to Greenville to attend Bob Jones as well. Their hopes were to calm down the rebellious streak that lived in my father and make a man out of him. The Marine Corps with a tour in Vietnam would have been a better choice, my nana admitted, but hindsight is 20/20.

She stopped short of saying that her largest regret about Bob Jones was that's where her son met my mother. Some things don't have to be said. It went without saying that Bob Jones was one of the most conservative and backwards colleges in the country. (It had an entire school system built under it.) Despite that, kids from as far away as Hawaii and even further would attend. Mama all but stole their son and eventually their only grandchild from them.

There are two classes of people who attend Bob Jones: (Even up into the 80's, they didn't allow blacks there either.) There were those who were serious about being the most square, pious, Christian assholes possible and those who just knew how to work the system. My mother was from, at least on the surface, the former, my father the latter.

My mother was the type that tattled on couples holding hands on campus, a strict no-no. What was wild was that even married couples were discouraged from the simple practice of hand-holding.

My father, on the other hand, was a master at manipulating the system. He knew how to say all the right things, charm the right teachers and fellow students. According to Uncle Bobby, his charm allowed him access to the panties of the loveliest preacher's daughters on campus. Given a lifetime of Divine oppression, it wasn't so difficult to give into his devilish smile.

When my parents got together, my mother was the only girl that presented a challenge to his charms. The thing about Mama was that she possessed my grandmother's looks, featuring a smoother edge in personality than my granny. People just didn't see her coming. She didn't have my exotic flair, but pound for pound, she was probably the prettiest girl in the Upstate and probably still is. Mama always did a good job concealing her looks beneath the standard issue school marm look that the BJU ladies sported. But just like you can't put lipstick on a pig, you can't hide beauty like that. Believe me; Mama tried it on me too. Daddy finally put his foot down when I hit puberty and she took me out in public wearing a muumuu.

I'm convinced that hormones and the thrill of the chase are what sealed the deal with my parents. By the time he realized just how whacked Mama was, I was well on my way to this world.

I digress. I could feel my father's excitement over visiting his birthplace for the first time in years. I could sense his pride at being able to show me off to old friends and family. My pappy would pass about a year after Daddy died. Nana said his heart blew apart after losing a child. I got to know Uncle Bobby fairly well, as he would often endure my mother's family to be with us on the holidays, especially Thanksgiving. Although Daddy's loss aged my nana, she never lost her sweetness and offered her unconditional love. Admittedly, I failed as a granddaughter—

"Are we having a gut-check moment?" Nigel asked from the backseat.

I chose to ignore his peanut gallery comments being lobbed at me. "We going to Uncle Bobby's first? Thought we were going to ride around a bit?"

"Can't wait to see the old boy. Probably best we get on to his house."

"He's only four minutes and forty-five seconds older than you, Daddy."

"I know, but I don't ever let him forget it. We're going to pick up the key to Bob's Fripp Retreat, then head out ahead of him and do a little fishing. Sound good to you, sweet cheeks?"

"Fishing!?" I made a crinkled-up face at the thought of it. "Gross, you're not going to make me touch them, are you?"

"Take it easy, Alice. We'll be surf fishing, and that's just an excuse to drink beer. All you have to do is lie in the sun and ride that raft."

"Sure, you want to let me drink beer?"

"Not you, silly. Me and your uncle Bob. And don't tell your mother or Nana that I had a celebratory beer as soon as I hit the Lowcountry."

More like a six-pack, some unknown pills, and a joint, but who's counting? "Okay, Daddy. I don't understand how you got Mama to agree to this little trip for just the two of us, anyway."

"That's none of your concern, little girl," he said with a deflecting smile. "We needed some father/daughter time and that's all there was to it. You just sit over there and look pretty. But not too pretty, okay?"

"Daddy," I squealed.

At fourteen, I was just beginning to realize what I looked like. Granny said I was an early bloomer, and she and Mama proceeded to make me feel shame for my body, most likely as a means of manipulating me in one way or the next.

Daddy just laughed the nervous laugh of fathers with their daughters. "Here we are," he said with obvious, beaming pride.

My breath caught at the sight of Uncle Bobby's home. So much time passed since I visited there. "Wow, this must be the prettiest---"

"Home in the entire downtown Beaufort historic district," he finished for me. "Yes, indeed it is."

Daddy bounced out of the car and stretched all at once. I rarely saw my father this loose and happy, especially lately. Buoyant would be the best way to put it. I supposed he was able to file away and compartmentalize what just occurred in Yemassee. Like father, like daughter.

Evidently, Uncle Bobby was looking for us, as he bounded off the front porch in excitement as soon as our car pulled in the driveway. He stopped short once he got a look at the two of us. "What in the hell happened to the two of y'all?"

I didn't realize how bad we must have looked. Daddy was hammered, and I must have looked like I had been jumped in gym class.

"Target practice," my father said a little too quickly.

"Target practice? Ah haaaa. Was she the target?"

"A girl needs to know how to use a firearm. Doesn't she?" I asked, attempting to defuse Uncle Bobby's well-placed concern.

"I'll agree with that, but it looks like the only things you forgot was the pig guts and barb wire. You take a detour to Parris Island, Alice? And you… You straight enough to drive out to Fripp?"

"Yeah, Bob, I'm fine. What's with all the questions?"

"Never mind, we can discuss all of this later." My uncle looked eager to change the subject in front of young ears. "For now, I'm going to need a big hug from the future Miss South Carolina."

"Uncle Bobby!" I blushed.

"Yeah, you're right. You are sure to go on to compete for, and ultimately win, the crown of Miss America." At that, he did a dramatic little twirl, curtsied, and grabbed me for a huge hug that promised to reinforce my recall of target practice.

Other than the ponytail, my father and uncle looked exactly alike. Their resemblance is the main reason for my self-imposed exile from South Carolina during my adult life. I couldn't take seeing a mirror image reminder of my father, even if it would help my grief, so I just didn't submit myself to it. Uncle Bobby's voice was gay enough that I was able to maintain a sporadic phone relationship with him and keep a check on Nana from time to time. Other than Thanksgiving, Uncle Bobby stopped pressing to see me years ago.

"You know Mama would never let me in those sinful pageants. Besides, I just hate those things. You know, 'I want to be an American, not an American't.' Puhleese."

"When did this little one become so serious, Jim? I was only kidding. You're too good for those stuffy contests any ole way. You've got a point, but I just meant that you're destined for great things." He let go of his embrace and looked down at my legs. "Girl, you wanna come inside and wash off? I'm sure Nana will have some salve."

"Thanks, Uncle Bobby," I said, trying not to sound stung. Destined for "great" things? If he only knew I spent my entire adult life selling my body, and apparently my soul, in various forms, he might not be so complimentary, even if I was worth millions.

Uncle Bobby looked through my physical façade and saw my essence.

"Can I, Daddy? I've got to pee." I was also eager to get away from this potentially volatile reunion.

"Yeah, baby, go ahead. I'll be right out here."

I sprinted. My legs and heart knew where to run, even if my memory was questionable.

"Go on in the back door to the kitchen, and Nana will fix you up," Bobby yelled after me.

As I was running toward the back door, I heard my uncle question Daddy more firmly.

"What the fuck happened?"

"I told you. Target practice."

"You know that's not what I'm talking about..."

***

Sometime later, I came back outside from getting administered to by Nana. She fixed me a Duke's mayonnaise and tomato, on Captain John Derst bread sandwich and we caught up. Poor thing cried when she saw all of my bites and bruises but administered to my wounds as only a grandmother can. I could tell the two brothers were having a heated discussion. I chose to ignore the angry red faces.

"OMG, Uncle Bobby, is this really your house? What do you do for a living?" I knew where Uncle Bobby lived, of course, but this house, in 2009 dollars, was probably over two-million-dollars, not to mention the historical aspects of it. What did my uncle do for a living? These things were only just occurring to my younger self, while my older self was curious as well.

"OMG?" Bobby said in confusion at slang that wouldn't be adapted for another fifteen or more years.

"Oh, my goodness," I explained. A good Christian girl would never use God's name in vain, after all.

"Yes, it is my house, and I am a highly sought-after witch doctor and healer, although you wouldn't know it by my behavior right now. Nothing like family..." my uncle trailed off, giving a meaningful look at his brother.

"Right," Daddy said quietly.

Uncle Bobby took a deep breath to collect himself. "Okay, love you two, so I'll see you both later?"

"Absolutely," I said for the two of us.

"Good, and we'll all continue our conversation with cooler heads prevailing."

"Are you really a witch doctor?"

The brothers laughed, and it seemed to ease the tension. "Some people say that..." He looked at my father who simply shrugged and stuck out his bottom lip. "Well, to tell you the truth, it's a long story that I'm not sure you'd completely understand at your age."

"Try me," I shot back respectfully.

"Alright. I tell ya what. I've cleared my schedule for most of next week to spend with you and your daddy. So, if you'll allow me to get a few beers under my belt and some of those angels on horseback your daddy does so well, we'll chat. Deal?"

"Deal," I affirmed. "But what are, 'angels on horseback?'" I was attempting to ask some of the same queries I did all those years ago, except that twenty years ago, I didn't have a smartass imp, in the way of Nigel, riding around Uncle Bobby's property on a neighing steed, with a large golden halo on his head. Did my father and uncle really not see Nigel? I observed Uncle Bobby cock his head as if heard something, but the brothers were so focused on each other and I wasn't sure just how far Nigel's powers of agitation extended.

What was it Geney told me a couple years back that went in one ear and out the other? "Fear the angelic-looking ones?" I just got it. He was referring to me, but I'm generally so self-absorbed… Was this Nigel's way of reminding me? I saw him nod.

"Jim!" Uncle Bobby shrieked at my father. "What have you been teaching this girl?" Sincere worry was in his voice.

"You know how her mama's side of the family is."

My uncle raised an eyebrow and turned back to me. "Angels on horseback are scallops wrapped in bacon and thrown on the grill. Don't worry, you'll find out and fall in L-U-S-T."

My father retreated in to his worries. "I hope we've been teaching her the right way to live." Self-doubt crept into Daddy's voice. Nearly broke my heart to hear him torn up inside this way. I remembered the words but was too young the first time around to sense their meaning.

"I'm sure you've done the best you could, Jim."

My father seemed not to hear him.

"Listen, I've got a quick meeting, then I'll be on out to Fripp in a couple of hours. I've called you in a pass, here are the keys, so go on out and open up. Jim, you sure you're okay?"

"Yeah, man," Daddy said and made to get in his Mustang.

"Jim, what are you doing?"

"Heading out to Fripp, what do you mean?" Daddy said, obviously confused.

"Um, I understand you're a little hammered and may not want to see our mother right now, but you really should try. She's getting up in years..." Uncle Bobby patiently explained.

"Of course,... Don't know what I was thinking. Where's Pappy?" Daddy leaned down to check his hair in the rearview mirror.

"Out on the water, catching us some shrimp, so you'll have to see him later..."

After Daddy left, Uncle Bobby asked, "So, how long has your father been this way? What happened?"

Wow! Weren't those the sixty-four-thousand-dollar questions? "Ummm... I'm not sure how to answer that, Uncle Bob-O," I stalled and told more of the truth than Uncle Bobby would ever know at the same time.

He put a comforting hand on my shoulder and said, "It's okay, baby, we'll sort it out this week."

We spent the rest of Daddy's uncomfortably short visit with Nana in mostly uncomfortable silence, punctuated by probing questions that I had no clue how to properly answer.

"Uncle Bobby, do you realize that Pappy can float on his back for as long as he wants to? I can a little bit, but my legs keep sinking. He does it without struggling."

This was a safe subject and something about Pappy that I always remembered fondly. I still can't make my legs float, hard as I try.

"What can I say? He's a magic man, baby. But the answer appears in your question," Uncle Bobby said enigmatically.

"What? He is definitely magic, but I'm not sure how I feel about that song."

"What?" Uncle Bobby asked, but we were interrupted by Daddy coming back outside.

Uncle Bobby asked with a knowing smile, "She give you the old one-two?" Nana was a matronly, sweet lady, but also blunt and direct in making sure you knew exactly where you stood.

"You know it," Daddy said softly. "Kay," my father said, coming out of his blank stare. "It's good to see you, Bob-O. Been too long—Obviously..."

"Damn right! It's been too long, but all that matters is that you're here now."

"Alright, let's break this up before we start blubbering," my father said, inhaling sharply.

Daddy and I proceeded on to Fripp after stopping at the Lady's Island Winn-Dixie to pick up provisions for three. On that twenty-five-minute car ride, I wanted to ask my father so much, but I asked him nothing. I knew all I needed to know, didn't I?

Instead, we talked about how good the pimento cheese was at Winn-Dixie. Daddy explained to me the reason the tomatoes are so much better from the St. Helena soil. (St. Helena was the largest island in the four-island chain that ultimately deposited the fortunate few on to Fripp's shores.) We even touched on what we were going to do with ourselves for a whole week without Mama.

***

Swoondalini

Fripp Island is very different from what one would expect from a typical beach resort. I went to the Redneck Riviera, otherwise known as Myrtle Beach, with a church missionary group a couple of years back from my current teenage perspective, and this was night and day.

For starters, Fripp was as far out as one could drive from the mainland on the coast of South Carolina. Highway 21 deposited serendipitous souls in need of respite on to a wildlife sanctuary that was literally the end of the earth. It was almost twenty miles out in the Atlantic, nestled in between Hunting Island State Park and Pritchard's Island that's now owned by the University of South Carolina. Deer, alligators, loggerhead turtles, raccoons, osprey, bald eagles, among other fascinating feathered friends, were your neighbors. Even during the 4th of July, there's breathing room on the beach. Fripp's property owner association puts on a fireworks show that turns the evening of the 4th into daylight over Fripp Inlet.

We pulled up to the house, and both chuckled at Uncle Bobby's name for his Fripp house. There was a large brown-gray sign with white routed letters reading, *SEREN-FRIPPITY*. I spotted a red E-Z-GO gleaming in the driveway when we pulled up. "Is that for us?" I asked excitedly. That golf cart would be awesome at any age, especially a teenager without her driver's license. The main modes of transportation on the island were golf carts and bicycles.

"All for us, sweetheart." My father's strange mood began to pass as soon as we hit the "thump-thump" heartbeat sound that Fripp's concrete bridge made as one crossed over. The half-mile bridge across the Fripp Inlet was the only thing connecting Fripp to the outside world. "Explore to your heart's desire," Daddy said, and gestured grandly.

Not quite understanding, I asked, "So are we going to play golf?" If I allowed it, my mouth and my body would go on autopilot, much like breathing, and I would act fourteen rather than thirty-four. Not unlike my normal life, I thought, beating Nigel to the punch.

"I guess we can. I haven't played in years, but that'd be nice. There's a beautiful course on the ocean. We'll talk to your uncle Bobby about it when he gets here."

"Cool."

***

I spent much of the following week exploring the island on that red '83 E-Z-GO. I had to blast my jam box at top decibel range to be able to hear my *Bon Jovi* tape above the wind and gas engine. Even though Fripp is only three miles by one mile at its widest, one could spend hours before mapping out all of Fripp. I did grow tired of boys, and sometimes men, following me and enjoyed employing loudness to ignore them.

When not exploring, I spent afternoons on the beach, watching my father and Uncle Bobby fish and catch up with each other. "Bob-O" had a calming effect on my father. That and he had better pot but didn't allow his brother to overindulge.

I had my fill of overindulgence during my countless days with Eugene. Altogether gluttons we were to the extent that boredom kicked in. However, that boredom finally culminated in the most pleasurable experience I ever had. My nipples became hard just at the mere thought. I had to bite down hard on my fist, and in uncharacteristic modesty, I covered myself with a towel and asked, "When are we going to play some golf?"

"I dunno, baby," my father slurred. It was taking some time becoming accustomed to seeing my father drink more than a glass of wine here, or a quick beer there.

"Jim, the girl wants to play the greatest game there is and you 'dunno'. You ought to be excited. She could grace the cover of *Golf Digest*." That would be much cooler than a bodice and the covers of romance novels. Uncle Bobby sensed my father's reluctance to leave the freedom the beach offered. "Why don't you let Uncle Bobby take you tomorrow? I need to dust off my game anyhow. That okay? I think your daddy needs some alone time."

My father's shoulders sagged. What was the deal? "Do y'all mind going without me just this once?"

I did, but Uncle Bobby was right. If ever a man needed some alone time, it was my father.

"As long as Uncle Bob-O doesn't mind me taking him downtown with a little beginner's luck." I poked him in his bare ribs with a cold beer offering for emphasis.

"Sounds like we've got a little smack talker on our hands here," he said, as he grabbed me and messed up my already windblown locks with a noogie.

***

The next day brought my first official round of golf and was the day that the seed of obsession with golf was planted. How often does a person get to go back to the birth of one of their true loves of life? Pappy, the keen observer that he was, recognized before anyone, especially me, and fostered this obsession of little white balls with the driving range where I now find my game "in the dirt". This day also brought my first unofficial beer, the official first beer coming on my twenty-first birthday in the White House, of all places, and poured by President Benton himself after we romped down in Nixon's bowling alley.

"Now, this course isn't the best one to start out on. Ocean Point has water on seventeen out of eighteen holes, but we're just going to have fun and sweat, okay, Hun?" Uncle Bobby was trying to prepare me for the heat and frustration. Normally, this would be good advice, but I knew how to handle both. In fact, I always felt my best when on the golf course. I was a scratch golfer at any age.

Instead of commenting, I just asked, "Think Daddy'll be alright? What has he told you?"

"Absolutely, your father's a survivor," Uncle Bobby said quickly. His voice didn't match his confident words. At fourteen, I bought that, but now…

I raised a questioning eyebrow, and my uncle pressed on. "Yeah, sweetie, your daddy's a strong man and a good brother. I've missed him since he moved to the Upstate. We were so close growing up, and he was the only person who ever really got me."

"You know I wish we could visit more often. Maybe we could live here. I—"

"I know, babe. Time just gets away from us, and your mother can be a difficult woman. I don't mean to run down your mama, but it's a fact. I'm just thankful for this time that we now have."

"To say that my mother is difficult is being kind. Yeah, it's not a problemo. I know how she can be."

"She's never approved of my professional or personal life so..." I could see tears welling up in his eyes. "Sorry, I just want to hang with my niece, and miss my brother. I probably won't have any children of my own because I'm a faggot. It's also difficult because Nana and Pappy are getting up in years, and they miss their son and granddaughter."

I listened and lost myself in the emotion of it all. I so missed Uncle Bobby. What did he know? If I ever get done with this journey I'm on, I'm going back to South Carolina.

"I'm sorry again. My use of that word was wrong. It's just... I'm a little emotional is all. I'll stop now."

"It's okay, Uncle Bob-O. Let's play some golf."

"Right, I'm just glad we'll get an opportunity today to spend time with one another. That's the silver lining in all this."

"Silver lining in all what?"

"I think you better go ahead and grab me one of those beers."

"Don't worry about me. I'm okay. I'm not sure what to think about the maternal side of things in my life either. I—"

"Lemme stop you right there. Gimme that koozie, baby. Thanks. Yeah, just keep in mind that you are a smart young lady, who will be able to think for herself very soon, if not already."

Uncle Bobby teed off after this statement and had too much club in his hand. He caught all of the ball and rolled it into the water about forty yards in front of the green. "Damn it! Anyway, what was I saying?"

He turned around to find me already running up to the lady's red tee markers. I usually played from the men's, or at least the senior men's tees, but I figured since I was a little smaller and these were borrowed clubs...

I gotta say that the feel of real spikes and hitting a balata ball with a persimmon head club is all it was cracked up to be. I started playing golf full-time after the widespread adoption of soft spikes, and I loved the feel of all this. Now I knew why many of the professionals still clung to metal spikes.

"Holy shit! Where'd you learn to strike the ball like that, Hun?"

"I'm full of surprises and even surprise myself sometimes. You must watch your language around such young ears, Uncle Bobby," I said in a very cheeky manner.

"Evidently." His mouth was agape as he watched my opening tee shot. This was going to be fun. "You might need to give me some strokes."

Playing golf to my full potential could be liberating. I felt I could be myself with Uncle Bobby. "You were saying," I prompted.

"What? Oh, sit back, listen, observe and make your own decisions about life. Don't ever let anybody tell you how to think. Understand?"

"Yeah." But I really didn't at that age and wasn't sure if I did now.

"Good. I'm going to throw down with you and take a stroke."

"Kay," I said, sticking my tongue out, Michael Jordan style, as I pulled the string on the ball to spin it back down to the hole. Uncle Bobby completely missed it. Another thing he missed was his fourteen-year-old niece cracking a cold beer.

After this exchange, we stayed pretty quiet for a couple of holes. I was enjoying my beer and my first taste of golf; in other words, freedom, in quite some time. By my estimation, it was several weeks since I passed out in the shower, but if there was one thing I learned was that time was much more fluid than I dared to dream.

Swoondalini

By the fourth hole, which was a par five that I drove in two, my uncle was growing suspicious. "What the fuck?" He cupped his hand over his mouth, signaling his apology for the use of such language around a child.

"Whatever do you mean?" I said coyly.

"You know exactly what I mean. I know I'm out of touch with my Upstate family, but I'm not so out of touch that I wouldn't know if my niece was ready to join the Furman Lady Paladin Golf Team, followed by a quick graduation to the LPGA."

"The LPGA?" This sent me deep in thought. I never even considered professional golf.

"Yes, the Ladies Professional Golf Association."

"I know what it stands for, but I never considered those four little letters."

"What do you mean, you never considered it?" Uncle Bobby said, as I tapped in for my gimme birdie while he skulled one out of a sand trap, which skidded across the narrow green and wound up in another sand trap.

"Damn it, girl! There I go cussing again. Sorry for my potty mouth. Run get Uncle Bobby another beer for his wounded pride, would ya. Looks like I may be here for a while."

"LPGA," I breathed as I fetched Uncle Bobby his beer and popped another for myself.

"Put me down for a double."

"Did you get a double?"

"Please have mercy on me."

"Okay. How bout a triple?"

"Fine, but you still haven't answered my question," he said with a piercing look.

"Would you believe that I'm actually thirty-four, but stuck in a fourteen-year-old's body for an unspecified period of time?" I asked with the smile of someone admitting they just ran over the neighbor's dog. Maybe I could be myself for the first time since I met Nigel. Hell, this could be the first time I was honestly myself since my childhood abruptly went down the shitter and I ended up working in a titty bar then promptly for Mandy Stinger, before I could legally vote. My childhood simply ceased. I looked the part of an adult, but I never really became an adult. Limbo was a fun game, but no way to go through life. My adult ego just caught up to that.

"Hmm, I have a very open mind. More than you could imagine, but I'm not sure that I can hop on board that one."

"Better hit, Uncle Bob. You're about to get some pressure from those two blue hairs back there," I said with a hint of glee in my voice. I wasn't a huge smack talker on the golf course, preferring to let my clubs do the talking, but I knew how to choose my moments.

He sliced into the woods on the dogleg left par four and drove me up to the women's tees in brooding silence. I shaped my drive around the ancient live oak on the left that I figured protected the green from direct attack.

A puzzling smile spread across Uncle Bobby's face. "Alice, that was beautiful, but I'm afraid you'll be in the little pond in front of the green," he said, taking obvious pleasure in my first screw-up.

"You didn't tell me there was a pond."

"You didn't ask. But I did ask you a question…" Damn, he was being persistent. "There's something odd about you. You do have the presence of someone much more seasoned."

Really, what's that supposed to mean? "Well, I feel like I've *seasoned* a lot lately," I tossed back weakly. That was the truth; I was getting thoroughly seasoned of late. Pour some sugar on me, sprinkle a dash of volcanic ash, and voila, I was blackened with dark grill marks on my fine ass. "You'll need another one of these..." I cracked another cold beer, took a big swig and handed it to him.

"You trying to get me hammered so you can beat my butt on this golf course?"

"Uncle Bob-O, I don't need to get you hammered to beat your butt," I said as pleasantly and as matter-of-factly as I could. "May I ask you a question?"

"Sure, why not," Uncle Bobby said, sounding resigned.

I felt that Uncle Bobby was just the person I needed for a heart to heart. He seemed so open and easy to talk to. Quite the opposite of my father... After me chipping tight and one putting to save par, Uncle Bobby needed a breather, and I needed the potty on six's tee box. We also needed to get the blue hairs off our tails, so we waved them through. That was a little embarrassing.

As an aside, one thing was for certain, I could get used to my slightly more compact frame. I love my boobs and they've made me a lot of money, but I never realized how much I adjusted my swing to accommodate my chestiness.

"Alright," Uncle Bobby bellowed in the old lady's backswing, as he burst out of the restroom onto number six's tee box. He seemed not to notice, so I waved an apology in their direction and got nothing but dirty looks in return. "I will answer your question honestly and completely, provided you answer my question honestly and completely."

"Er—honestly and completely?" My voice trailed off.

"Tit for tat, girlie. Quid pro quo..."

"Alright…" I hesitated.

"Aht," he tsk tsked. "Fair is fair. And we have a little time now as those old Yankee bitches play through."

"Okay then, but don't be surprised if you find my story ludicrous," I warned.

"We can all sound ludicrous, depending on who you're talking to, can't we?"

"I suppose so."

"That's why we must learn to discern. Given your Bible Belt background, you would seem, on the surface at least, to find my occupation odd. But I have a feeling about you. What's your question?"

"All we can do is trust one another and be supportive. I was going to ask you what you knew about my father and obviously still want to know what you know in that regard, but now that you mention it, I've been wondering what you do for a living. You seem to be doing well, whatever it is." As an adult, I still really didn't have a grasp of what he did. The teenager in me didn't care, and, up until recently, the adult wouldn't have either.

"Preach on, girl. In the meantime, let's start pushing those ladies for shits and giggles."

After teeing off on six, my Uncle Bobby began telling his life's story. He left Beaufort for college right after high school. Turns out he didn't have a wild streak in his teens quite like Daddy.

"Now it looks like they're putting on the brakes," he commented half-heartedly, as the ladies studied a harrowing eighteen inch, straight uphill putt. "Yeah, I think they let us tee off in the middle of lady's day. We should find a lot of golf balls. Wanna play it as it lies?" Uncle Bobby asked. I allowed him to improve his lie without saying a word up until now, but if that's how he wanted to play, then so be it. I didn't care that he was moving his ball around, but I guess he thought that it would help him out in some way to put that restriction on me.

"Anyway?" I prompted him to continue. "Sure, we can play like that." I was so fascinated to hear his story. Mama never allowed Daddy to speak much of his family, especially Uncle Bobby.

"So, I got a scholarship at USC and attended. Not the real USC in Columbia, mind you, but the one out in LA-LA land on the left coast. I always had to remind them that Carolina was a college before Cali was a state. A whole other planet, as far as the South is concerned. I eventually became a practicing psychiatrist and stayed out in California for a dozen or so years. The book learning came easily to me which, consequently, left plenty of time for experimentation. I discovered I loved boys, rather than girls."

"I liked all manner of drugs and alcohol, but never enough to become addicted. It did, however, afford me the opportunity to study addiction up close and personal. This, in a strange twist of fate, led to my investigation into alternative methods of healing. Not healing of behaviors, mind you, but healing of the actual beliefs and feelings that led to the behavior in the first place. Something that traditional therapy often skirts around, if it's acknowledged at all. While in L.A., I was given the opportunity to meet, and eventually treat a couple of major Hollywood players and their families. Word of mouth works there just like anywhere else, and when word got around that I was successfully treating everything from blow to cancer, to tennis elbow, with bunches of stuff in between, I became very much in demand. So much in demand, that I started charging a premium for my time and expertise. This was an effort to give myself a much-needed break. It produced the opposite effect by making me more exclusive and branding me as 'Hollywood's healer.'"

"That's absolutely wild. What exactly do you do?" I was mesmerized.

"That's the million-dollar question, isn't it? I'll get to that in a minute," he said. "Now, where was I?"

"Demand…" I prompted.

"Yes, demand was very high. In fact, it got so I could hardly keep up and had little time to myself. That is dangerous for a healer, especially an introvert such as myself, so I began training others to do what I do to allow me to be even more selective in my clientele. I was known as the miracle worker of Hollywood, their best kept, open secret. No surprise, I burned out. Doing what I do, if one does too much of it, can make you into a crazy person. I felt like---"

"Uncle Bobby, what do you do?" I squealed impatiently.

He inhaled sharply. "As long as I've been at it, I've never really been able to describe it exactly in words. It's only understood after experiencing it. It's something every human can do if only we'd put our energy in to 'it'."

"What is 'it'? Can you force Daddy to come to 'it'? I think he needs a bit of the 'it'."

"It's up to you what 'IT' is," he answered with a wry smile, ignoring my silly question.

"Right," I said in a frustrated huff. I took my frustration out on the Royal Maxfli, with a crisp long iron shot.

"I'm not trying to be cagey but let me get to that in my own time. Besides, 'IT' is up for you to decide what it is anyhow. Oh shit!" Uncle Bobby shrieked as he realized that his ball was less that a yard from an eleven-foot-long hissing alligator. "You gonna make me play that ball?"

I didn't answer immediately, as my head tried to wrap around what he was saying. I was not used to thinking in the abstract. I snickered and waved for him to drop elsewhere.

He pressed on. "So, even before burnout, I could feel something coming, a need for a change. Change is the only constant in life. I made a lot of money, so I began to send it back home to the parents. I could sense in phone calls that Pappy was starting to miss a few steps, but his mind was still sharp, so to give him something to do, I asked him to help me out with the purchase of some property around the county, as I knew that one day, I would return here for good. You can leave the Lowcountry, but once you've been here, it gets in your blood and always beckons you back to its timeless ebb and flow.

This must be how Pappy came to get that property out on St. Helena that he's made into my driving range, complete with my own commercial lawnmower and a four-wheeler to retrieve the golf balls. That begs the chicken and the egg question as it relates to the already questionable nature of what we think we know about time. Did the spark of my burning passion for golf originate by my future self-coming back to this time and showing off? After this trip until my father's passing we made frequent trips to see my father's family in Beaufort.

Uncle Bobby raised a questioning eyebrow as if he knew where my thought patterns were unfolding. "Finally, in my year of catalysts," Uncle Bobby blazed on, "more aptly described as the dark night of my soul, however one chooses to look at it, I caught my long-time boyfriend cheating on me with a hot young starlet, of all things, and I reached burnout. I thought I was losing my ever-loving mind and falling off the face of the earth. The South Carolina Lowcountry beckoned me back, and I answered its marshy call. It was time to come home before I lost myself."

"I can identify with falling off the face of the earth," I said. My head was spinning with all the revelations he was spilling.

Uncle Bobby merely nodded and pressed on. "Still, it was a big decision to leave that booming business to come back here, of all places. Don't get me wrong, I love it, but the hustle and bustle of L.A., it ain't. I was assured by many highly placed clients that they would actually come to me. Look, they installed a phone so that we can place our lunch order to the 19th hole."

"Cool, looks like we'll need more beer," I suggested with a hopeful smile.

"Right, well, anyway. They were as good as their word. They did indeed come to me, and some actually have stayed, at least on a semi-permanent basis. Although they maintain a low profile while here, they were not immune to the charms of beautiful Beaufort by the sea. So, I suppose I can take indirect credit for many of the motion pictures made in this area."

"Are you shitting me?" I was truly impressed, and I wasn't easy to impress. I knew that gobs of movies were shot here, but never gave it much thought. I was beginning to realize that Nigel was right. I didn't think much past my own tits, and it was apparent that it was a fault of mine, a fault that I would endeavor to repair.

"Watch your language. It's bad enough you're drinking, but we can't have you developing a potty mouth. It's not ladylike."

"Sorry. So, what exactly is it that you do that is so special for these people?"

"Well, there's the trick, isn't it? I don't do it via a bunch of pills, I can tell you that. In fact, most of the time I tell people I let my license lapse. I do help people with addictions," he said, thumping my can. "So, in some extreme cases, I have to prescribe to help ease the transition, but that's where it ends."

"Alright, you've got me on the edge of my seat. I can't concentrate on my round of golf anymore. Out with it, Uncle Bobby," I demanded in exasperation.

"Shaking up your golf game, am I?"

"Don't worry, I can still take you."

He laughed loudly. "The art of non-doing is an accurate description, besides knowing the right questions to ask at the right time, along with an inner knowing of where to place my hands. Simply put, I think organized religion has made us forget how to pray properly. It seems often times that religion was created to separate us from God, and not the other way around. Please don't take offense to that."

The fourteen-year-old in me might have taken offense, but I certainly didn't. "Don't worry, you have a point."

"Well," he continued, "I've always been a touch psychic. You know, hearing and seeing visions, not to mention out-of-body experiences. I know that sounds crazy…"

"Not really, I think I might be having the ultimate out-of-body experience right now," I deadpanned. I wasn't quite ready to go there.

"Really?" He studied me up and down, and then pressed on with his story.

"What do you mean by praying properly?" My interest was genuinely piqued.

"For starters, most people are taught and/or believe that you need a church, mosque or synagogue to pray in, or some sort of idol to pray to. Really, though, God, or whatever you care to call him, or it, or her, is all around us and in us," Uncle Bobby said sagely, pointing out a large live oak with a heaping helping of old man's beard, and then pointed past the tree to a large flock of about three dozen pelicans in V-formation. "He or she or it, is also us," poking my arm. "He made us all, so all we need do is look within and know how to listen to find the answers or proper questions to our prayers."

"I think there would be members of my family who would probably like to take you up to the Dark Corner, tie you to a tree, and let you find Jesus the old-fashioned way for saying something like that. That's not me, per se, but I'm just saying..."

"Yes, I know. That's why I'm very discerning about who I tell. You know the difference between being labeled a crazy man and being labeled the Yoda type, don't you? Hmm?"

"No," I said, giggling at his Yoda reference, along with his Yoda impression.

"Who you tell," Uncle Bobby answered.

"But you trusted me, given my background?"

"A feeling I had. You even sound different than when I speak to you on the phone. Your language and diction, for example."

"I know. But I still don't understand how you use it to help others." I wasn't ready to plow into my story yet either.

"Because people live their whole lives being burdened by beliefs and feelings that have no place in their current day to day life or this particular incarnation. People in traditional therapy only focus on their behaviors, while giving lip service or passing thoughts to what caused them to behave in a certain way to begin with."

I gave him a light bulb look. In a fit of weakness, I tried therapy in the past with limited results, and gave up quickly for that very reason. That and I found it good sport to lie to my therapist, then seduced him into a loyal client.

"Yeah, I know it never occurs to most people, and if it does, they probably receive a blank look from their therapist." Wow, did he hit the nail on the head with that statement. That summed up my experience with therapy. "Do you realize people will stay in therapy for years to work on issues that I can handle in five or six sessions?"

"No, I didn't," I replied with a faraway look out over Fripp's north end, otherwise known as Ocean Point. I gazed at the Atlantic but saw none of it as my head swam.

"Yep, and I'm very expensive in the short term, but in the grand scheme of saving time and money on years of therapy, I'm a bargain. So, if you make that short gimme putt, you'll be even on the front, right?"

Broken out of my reverie, I said, "You gonna give me that?"

"I need all the help I can get, so **NO**!"

"Didn't think so."

I stepped up to putt and missed like Angel Van Der Bon choking at the British Open. That was one of my fonder memories as a golf fan. As a client and a lover, Angel was very generous, but he was an even bigger douchebag when the cameras were off. Hope he ends his career majorless...

Uncle Bobby ran in to get our food and beer but was gone a long time. Long enough to make me nervous about telling my tale.

"Damn it, I placed that big lunch and beer order, and when I got in there, the girl showed me the piece of paper she wrote the order down on but didn't lift a finger to start. Anyhow, so we spent the front nine talking about me. Now it's only fair we spend the back nine talking about you," Uncle Bobby prodded.

I spent the back nine struggling to make up for the dropped stroke on number nine but ended up adding four more bogies to my card. I decided to take it easy on myself for dropping all those strokes since I don't typically spend my rounds of golf spilling my guts. That's right, past lives, Nigel, my attunement that may have precipitated my fall in the shower, and all the gory details of my current life. It felt good, it was much needed, and he seemed to take it all in stride. He seemed to believe me, or was he being polite?

By the time we were cutting the dogleg right corner on number seventeen, a hole that would become my favorite, although I often struggled to par it, I couldn't stand it anymore. "You do believe me, don't you?"

"I believe, as your father does, that you've always been a special little girl since the day you were born. I believe your soul is an old soul born into a difficult family for one last challenge. I've been around the world, seen many interesting and wondrous things in my work, and am convinced that the last great frontier is within us, not some trillion-dollar trip to Mars and beyond."

Unsure as to what to make of these statements, I let them lie as we finished out the round. Number eighteen finishes along Fripp Inlet, with the Atlantic in the distance beyond. As we walked up to putt out, I spotted *him* looking out over Fripp Inlet toward the Hunting Island Lighthouse. Nigel turned back to look at me and gestured with his head. "Beautiful, is it not?" I heard him in my head.

"Yes sir, it is," Uncle Bobby intoned, paying little attention to Nigel. Uncle Bobby then reached out to shake my hand to congratulate me for a good round.

"Can you see him?"

"Yeah. Why?" He regarded me with a strange look.

"Well, that's the fella who's been showing me around." I gestured with my thumb.

"Really?" Uncle Bobby made to go over to talk to him.

"No, wait." I grabbed his elbow. "Let me."

I walked across the green to Nigel who did not turn in response to my approach. "Beautiful place this is…"

"Yes, I forgot." I suddenly felt nervous about what was to come next. "Thanks for reminding me."

He ignored my last comment, "Magical, some would say," he said, still gazing at Hunting Island and Edisto Island in the distance.

"May I stay one more day?"

"Sure, why not," he mumbled absentmindedly before finally looking at me.

"What does all this mean for me?"

"It means that I've nearly gotten your full attention and the rest is up to you."

"Kay. Well, I'm going now."

He dismissed me with the wave of a hand like he was shooing away a fly that kept buzzing his ear.

"What was that all about?" Uncle Bobby asked as he fumbled to get his keys out of his golf bag.

"Apparently, I can stay another day."

"Bully!" he said, intoning a little Teddy Roosevelt.

Although 'I' would still be here since 'I' was here the first time. I rubbed my temple as it was throbbing slightly from all the heat, beer, but mainly the heavy issues discussed during the round. "May I have some of your weed, Uncle Bobby? This is really making my head hurt," I said in a leaden tone, momentarily forgetting my appearance.

His face flared briefly with a sudden shot of irritation as he stabbed his index finger to my forehead. "Now you listen to me. It's bad enough I let my fourteen-year-old niece drink beer, but I allowed you to kick my butt all over my home course."

I opened my mouth to point out the fact that I was no more fourteen than he was and that he allowed nothing on the golf course.

"Don't interrupt your uncle."

"Yes, sir."

"I believe you, especially after the way you played golf and how you said things, but you've gotta admit this is pretty out there."

I nodded.

"You look fourteen, and your daddy won't understand. So as soon as we get back, you march straight to the shower and get the beer smell off. Then brush your teeth and drink water. Savvy?"

"Yes, sir." I couldn't help smiling. I missed having a father figure in my life to guide me. "I'm sorry, I'll try not to blast you off your home course next time."

"Thanks, smartass." He smiled and put his arm around me.

Swoondalini

***

We got back to the house and Daddy was nowhere to be seen, at first. He was supposed to be preparing his famous angels on horseback for the entire family and whatever he caught surf fishing. My mouth always watered at the thought of succulent scallops wrapped in bacon with lemon pepper seasoning. They truly were angelic when they galloped off the grill.

Nana and Pappy were coming out to Fripp Island from town. I headed straight to the shower, as instructed, when I heard my uncle's sharp swearing. "Damn it, Alice, you'd better come out here." I remembered instantly what he was hollering about. I buried bunches of stuff between my two ears, but not this daddy issue inspiring event. Despite the gravity of the situation, I liked being called Alice again.

I ran out to the back deck overlooking the ocean and pulled focus on the prone form of my father. Like father, like daughter. Families strolled by and gawked at my father, folded up in his beach chair. Mothers shooed their children the other way. The closer I looked, I realized that I could see my father was bright red all the way from here. He passed out and was evidently so drunk that he didn't feel the tide pounding on him. At that moment, a wave nearly knocked him out of the chair he was enmeshed in, and he still wasn't coming to.

"Don't think we need to worry about Jim smelling beer on you now. Come help me get his ass up to the house before he embarrasses the family," Uncle Bobby deadpanned.

When we got down to the water's edge to fetch Daddy, there was a half-eaten sandwich on his knee and a death-grip on a Corona that was way too hot to taste decent anymore.

"Jim!"

"Daddy!" His foam cooler began to float away with a myriad of other cans and liquor bottles. "Did he clean the house out?"

"Appears so," Uncle Bobby responded slowly while surveying the situation. He seemed to be considering what, exactly, to do with his brother.

I caught the cooler from the surf and peered inside to see a satisfying bit of ice water still in the bottom. I handed the top to Uncle Bobby and dumped the ice water on top of my father. Seeing my father like this was disgusting.

"Holy shit! That's cold!" he slurred, flung his Corona past my head, came up swinging at some imagined person, and then did a face plant before either of us could catch him. It was one of those situations that would be hilarious unless you were living it up close and personal. We let him writhe around in the waves for a little while, not knowing what to do.

Uncle Bobby then became decisive. "Alice, clean all this shit up off the beach, and I'll carry him up to the house." As he hefted his brother up on his shoulder, my father retched all down his twin's backside.

"Nice," we both said in unison.

Apparently, someone called security, as there was a white Nissan truck, with a blue and red light bar, flashing and heading our way on the beach. It kept getting better. "Goddamn it," Uncle Bobby cursed under his breath as security pulled up to us.

"Hey, Bob," the chief of Fripp's security called out over his radio. "What's going on?"

"Oh, not too much, Joe. My brother's not used to this Lowcountry heat anymore and got too much sun is all." My uncle tried to underplay the obvious.

"Alright then. Make sure he gets out of the sun. Wouldn't want to have to get Beaufort County out here to apply sunscreen."

"No problem."

"Alright. See you next Thursday?" Joe asked.

"Next Thursday."

"C'mon, Alice."

"Okay, what's up with next Thursday?" I asked Joe pulled away.

"Joe's one of my long-time clients and chief of security here on Fripp," he trailed off, clearly irritated and straining with the added weight of his twin. Apparently, my uncle didn't want to expand on the topic. I became curious if the chief was a celebrity in hiding.

When we got up to the house, my uncle threw his twin in the bathtub and turned the cold water on full blast. It was like the old Star Trek Original Series episode where Captain Kirk and three members of his crew get sent to the mirror universe where their doppelgangers are deranged. This was all just too surreal and upsetting.

"Damn it, Jim!" Uncle Bobby grabbed him with one hand by the hair and picked his head up. My father wasn't doing much other than grunting, so Bobby allowed his head to drop with a thud that startled me. Finally, after an agonizingly long time, my father started to come around.

"What's going on?"

"What's going on is that you're losing your shit, Jim."

"Tell me something I don't know, *doctor*," my father replied petulantly.

"You're going to lose it all, if you don't pull yourself together," Uncle Bobby said while giving me a meaningful look.

"I know," he said and made to pass out again before he was brought back by a crisp slap from me. I surprised even myself and stared at my right hand in disbelief. Unless my job demanded it of me, I wasn't the type that hauled off and hit a person, much less my father.

Bobby placed a calming hand on my shoulder that felt as if it remained there long after he removed it. "Baby, why don't you let me finish up here," he whispered firmly. "Go get that shower, and I'll use the outside shower…" Bobby grabbed him roughly by the cheeks. "Jim, clean your sorry ass up, drink some water, and go to bed. We'll sort all this out tomorrow. You hear me in there, boy?"

"Yes," he replied weakly, and Uncle Bobby allowed his head to drop with another thud and slammed the door, leaving Daddy to puke on himself.

I only walked around the corner, within earshot, so we were both startled when Uncle Bobby nearly barreled over me as he came out of the bathroom. "Sorry, kid. Alright, show's over. Call Nana. It'll sound better coming from you, and she's not likely to grill you about why they can't come out. Tell her and Pappy to come out tomorrow. Then go shower up and we'll cook."

When I came back down after my shower, I found my uncle staring off toward Pritchard's Island, Lil Capers, and Hilton Head in the distance and smoking a cigarette. He didn't turn around at my approach. "Guess you caught me?"

"Caught you doing what?"

Swoondalini

"My chink in the armor. Menthol cigarettes. Every other drug, I can lay down without a single thought, but menthol cigarettes always rear their ugly head when I'm worried. How was Nana?"

"Suspicious, as she should be, but placated, for now."

Uncle Bobby only nodded.

"Well, I must admit to having a similar love-hate relationship with lung darts myself," I said, grabbing a smoke. "Funny that I don't hide how much weed I smoke, but I will sit on a can of paint, in a corner of a dark garage, behind a parked car, in an evening gown, before I'll let somebody see me smoking one of these," I mumbled as I clenched the menthol with my lips. "I even have this perfume and mouthwash routine before I feel decent for the public again."

My uncle only raised an eyebrow, flicked the lighter for me and said, "Interesting."

"Why? Seriously, I can't remember the last time I smoked a cigarette in front of somebody."

"Me too, but that's a discussion for another time. Glad you feel comfortable enough with me, I think."

"What's on the menu?"

"Angels on horseback, my dear," he reminded me.

"I love those." I paused. "How's Daddy?"

"Your daddy is done. D-U-N. Dun! He's as cooked as those scallops are gonna be."

"What's wrong with him? I've never seen him this way." Although, apparently, I had.

"No, neither have I," he replied absently. "I mean, when we got a little older than you are now, we did as kids do, but this is different."

There was a long quiet moment as we sat and smoked.

"You still haven't answered my question."

"I know, honey. Listen, if you're really as experienced as you say you are, then you'll have no problem making cocktail sauce from scratch," he challenged. He still wasn't completely convinced, and I couldn't blame him. I was living it and I still struggled to wrap my head around it. A little skepticism is healthy as long as it doesn't blur into cynicism.

"No problem at all, since you will show me in this very kitchen," I said with confidence. "My hobbies are golf, reading, and cooking in that order," I offered. "I would cook more, but rarely have anyone to cook for."

"You call what you did to me on the golf course today a hobby? I'd like to see what you do when you put your mind to something."

"No, you wouldn't," I said and flushed for a second when my chosen profession came to mind. "What's wrong with my father?" I persisted as I lit another cigarette. "I remember him being this way, but can't recall why and, therefore, chose to remember him with rose-colored glasses. Something awful happened," I said, but wasn't sure it was a statement.

My uncle only stared at me for a while, and then abruptly rose. "It's time to go in and make the cocktail sauce. C'mon, this isn't usually a smoking house, but it is today," he said, leaving me a trail of cigarette smoke to follow.

We walked in through the large family room/kitchen combo that overlooked the deck and the Atlantic beyond. It was a really simple house, but very inviting and functional. I busied myself with the cocktail sauce and prepping our meal. The air was thick with the unsaid. I mean, really, how do you talk about these issues?

"So, what you were saying out there..."

Here it comes. "What?"

"First off, let me apologize for doubting you earlier, but you have to realize that you do have a wild story. Probably the wildest I've heard, but I learned a long time ago not to question whatever feels right, no matter how incredulous something sounds," Uncle Bobby said.

I nodded and waited for the rest of it.

"The tone you took implied that Jim didn't make it to whatever age you claim to be."

I let out a huff of air and grabbed one of the few remaining beers my father was probably too hammered to find. "Yeah, I'm not entirely sure what happened, but he does die in a few years from this point."

"You serious?"

"Yeah," I said gravely.

"James... It'll kill our mother..." he trailed off.

He was mistaken about who it would kill, but not far off the mark.

"I know. I have not returned to Greenville since."

"I don't know if I should be hearing this."

"But you feel it's true, don't you?" I asked. I was heartened to have someone to talk this out with.

"Yes," he said after a long pause.

"Here's the cocktail sauce. *Real* lemon and Worcestershire sauce with a, and I quote, 'a shitload of horseradish. You control your heat with the amount of ketchup you put in,' end quote."

"Bingo. Very good. You wanna tell me what happened?"

"Not ready to go there," I said and could feel the pain emanating from my face.

"You know how to roll a J?" My uncle quickly shifted gears when he sensed me venturing too close to the flame.

"Of course."

"I want to make sure you're not like my child-star client that's about your age, or rather appears to be your age. She turned fifteen in February and has done every drug known to man. Hope I can get her straight one day."

"Might help if he didn't smoke up with her," Nigel tossed in from an unknown direction. Bobby cocked his head as if straining to hear something, then appeared to make a note of it and returned his gaze to me.

I did my best to ignore Nigel. "Yeah, we would seem to be the same age, wouldn't we?"

"You're exactly six months younger," Bobby said, doing the math in his head. "We'll need a joint for the ride to T.T. Bones to get more beer. I'll tell you in the golf cart," Uncle Bobby said. He threw papers and a bag of high grade cheebah at me.

"Good, good, can't be sobering up now, can we? Why don't one of you at least check on pukey papa in the bathtub before you go get more intoxicated?" Nigel reminded us.

Nigel was like a gnawing no-see-um you couldn't just mash, but he was right. "I'll roll this if you go check on Daddy, then we'll go."

"Good idea," Uncle Bobby said. He flushed red like he should have known better.

Swoondalini

The red '83 E-Z-Go was loud and smelly. I smelled like fumes, like I hadn't showered at all, but I loved it. This was one of my favorite parts of Fripp, the fact that one could park their car and not drive it for days. I heard *The Eagles: Life in the Fast Lane* blare from a passing car.

Uncle Bobby bought a six-pack to see us through the evening. "Good God, you have to take out a loan to buy anything in T.T Bones." After that preamble, Uncle Bobby plowed right into it. "Ever wonder how your family paid for the house in Dunean, paid for the property in Thornblade, paid for the cars, paid for your school at Bob Jones?"

Again, with my thoughtlessness. "I—I never really put much consideration into it."

"Certainly, wasn't from your daddy being a gym teacher."

I suddenly felt very far away. "What did she do?"

"What did she do?" my uncle repeated, stalling for time. "Alice, you know how convoluted your mama can be sometimes," he explained.

"Right," I said slowly, still not quite catching on.

"Fire up that hogleg and be smooth about it. Keep it down between your legs when you're not toking."

"I know how to be discreet," I said briskly, growing perturbed at being sidetracked.

"Sure, you do. So, does your mama. I'm convinced she's the queen of obfuscation." Uncle Bobby said knowingly. It made me shift nervously on the seat. "And do you know how much of a devoted mother she is?"

"Evidently, I don't. I know I'd remember Thornblade... Snazzy." Thornblade was a swanky country club on the east side of Greenville, where a celebrity Nationwide Tour event is now played.

"We need to work on your memory gaps. It may be because that's where your father chose to draw the line in the sand. You never built the Thornblade house."

"My memory gaps are alarming, Uncle Bob. At least I am becoming aware."

"Yep, that's the first step to healing. Anyway, you know how attractive your mama is. Based on looks alone, she's one of the few women who could make me rethink being queer."

My mother was the only woman that made me feel ugly. "Right. So, what's that got to do with Thornblade?" I passed the joint to my uncle as an old couple coming the other way gave us a warm wave.

"They must be some of the handful of people on Fripp from the South. They also must not be able to see very well."

"What'd she do, Bobby? Out with it."

"Just so you know, what she did, she did years ago."

I crossed my arms huffily and glared expectantly.

"Okay, long story short, she paid for it with her body. Likened it to the prostitute in the Bible, no less. She is very adept at her justifications with the good book."

"Really?" Guess the apple didn't fall as far from the tree as she would have me believe. "Where and when did this all begin?"

"Not exactly sure. It's really hard to wrap one's mind around. Besides, some of this isn't my story to tell. You're gonna have to ask your daddy. But it seems that it started with your grandparents pimping her out."

"Wow!" I was so stunned, I didn't have anything to say but 'wow', and I'm not a person that uses the words *wow* or *great* at all.

"Are you surprised?"

"Yes and no."

"And, of course, your daddy finally wised up to it all when you all 'won' the Thornblade property, and he's devastated. He suspects your mother and grandparents have designs for you, too. Hence the drinking."

"Can you help him? What was that last part?"

Uncle Bobby was spoke in a hurried barrage, likely to ward off one question too many from me. "You seem more ready for help than he does. Yeah, I think that's why your daddy's been acting so weird. It's only a theory, but my intuition tells me it's got some basis in fact. You remember anything like that?"

"Maybe. Perhaps. I don't know," I huffed. "My memory is apparently at Alzheimer level. I wouldn't be surprised if I remembered The Great Depression as if it were yesterday."

"You have no idea," I heard Nigel whisper gently.

I pressed on because I really wasn't ready to go there. "I'm getting my share of help right now, remember?"

"Yes, I can help him, but he needs to wallow some more, then he'll need to come to me, and then, only then, can I show him how to help himself. We all have free will. And I don't offer a magic pill, and it's *not* a tent revival."

"Always wondered why we ended up staying here until time for me to go back to school."

"Yes, that's an excellent idea, an idea that I was going to suggest when he was sober tomorrow. So why was part of you not surprised?"

"Well—by the time I leave home in a few years, I'll look to be more like twenty-five and have natural 32DDD's."

He looked at me appraisingly. "Looking at you now, that part is not hard to believe at all," he said, nodding for me to continue.

"Right," I inhaled sharply, "so, I felt that I needed to use everything at my disposal to get out after Daddy died. So, I went to a strip club in Columbia for a minute, then got my real start as a high-priced escort in D.C. and ultimately became a cover model for romance novels. I'm worth millions," I added quickly.

"It doesn't sound as if money bought happiness or peace of mind," Uncle Bobby threw back just as fast.

"That's a fair assessment." Introspection made my stomach turn. I put my hand out for the joint again. "Yeah, so you can imagine that Mama wasn't in full support of how I led my life, probably since she never got her cut. But I always felt there was more to it. Anyhow, I've only spoken to her on the phone since leaving the Upstate and never went back."

"Now you know."

"Yes, now I know what a hypocritical cunt she really and truly is. Why…" I trailed off as I saw Nigel pass us on a golf cart going the other way. His cart was full of inebriated women on a long weekend escape from their husbands. He simply waved, and I put the joint to my lips in response.

"Wasn't that that Nigel fellow we saw on the 18th green?"

"Yes," I answered. Interesting that Bobby could see Nigel. As far as I knew, nobody else had been able to see him during my odyssey.

"What about after the anger with your mother fades away?"

Swoondalini

"Hasn't faded in twenty years, so what about it?" Now I was sounding the age that I appeared to be. I felt the effects of the marijuana numbing my system as I spoke the words. Perhaps I should consider if numb was all it was cracked up to be.

"You should give it some thought."

"I've thought about it, and I hope she rots in hell." I was mad, but I didn't mean that and we both knew it. "It sure is pretty here," I said, taking in live oak and the marsh in the distance.

"Yes, it sure is. Don't change the subject," he commanded gently. "Your feelings are certainly natural, but you're going to have to get past it."

"Why?"

"I dare say that if you don't, you'll be thirty-four with nothing but millions of dollars and big tits."

"Funny you should say that."

"Honey, there's nothing wrong with the money or the beauty, but there is obviously something amiss on the inside."

"I guess that's why I'm here."

"You must have a pretty special guardian angel for all this."

I caught a glimpse of Nigel straightening his halo in our parabolic rearview mirror, but when I turned, he wasn't there. "Special is one way of putting it," I said.

"If all this is true, you're getting an opportunity that most of us don't, so suck it up buttercup."

"Would you hand me another beer," I said sulkily.

"Thought so."

"Yes, sir. It's getting late and I'm starving."

"I second that emotion," he said.

We got back to the house and grilled up those heavenly angels on horseback, something I still cook to this day and wax nostalgic. My father woke up to the smell, ate a scallop, puked, and then retired to his bedroom again. Uncle Bobby and I chatted around the heavier issues that took up the better part of our day. We ate, and then I was introduced to music that my uncle and father grew up on, music I still listened to in adult life, but not without thinking of Uncle Bobby. Beach Music, Motown. I never stopped to think just how important this trip to the Lowcountry was to a high school sophomore.

He introduced me to the Temptations, General Johnson and the Chairman of the Board, the Spinners, The Tams, The Swinging Medallions, Earth, Wind, and Fire and everything in between. I was never allowed, much less interested, in the melodic way of life that spoke to my very soul. I learned to Shag, or at least my version of it. Learning South Carolina's state dance was when I first discovered that while God was overly generous with my beauty, he made up for it by holding out in the rhythm department.

Finally, by one in the morning, the beds called to us both. I slept hard until nine the next morning, when a ray of sunlight shone directly into my eyes to awaken me. I was startled when a figure stepped into the beam of light and sat down gingerly on the bed.

"Oh... It's you." I yawned. "Come to dig a hole in the sand and bury me up to my neck for the tide and the crabs to take care of?"

"None of that," Nigel said with a chuckle. He seemed a little stung by my jab, and that made me feel a little guilty. "We're leaving soon, and I figured you'd want to say goodbye to your father."

Swoondalini

"Sure, that'd be nice," I said, taken aback.

Sensing apprehension, Nigel volunteered, "Don't worry, since you're starting to get 'it', it won't be nearly as vexing as it was previously."

***

Surprised that Nigel was being courteous, I took advantage of my time and placed myself fully in the "past" while I was in the past. If I could keep my father sober today, then perhaps we could have some quality time.

I found some blueberries given to my uncle by a neighbor from Mill Springs, N.C. and began to cook up some blueberry pancakes and sausage links. Sop the flapjacks in Mrs. Butterworth's and we were well on our way to one of my favorite breakfasts. Sadly, a breakfast that I usually only cooked for myself, or for others that were anything but friends or family.

"Whew!" Uncle Bobby startled me when he exclaimed, "Just by the smell, I thought I woke up in heaven."

"Thanks," I said, blushing. "Coffee?"

"Yes, ma'am."

"Since you have a medical background, wouldn't you say that the best way to wake someone up after a sloppy drunk would be chest compressions?"

Uncle Bobby missed my joke. "No, I don't think you want to do that to someone."

"Soooo—you wanna go wake up Daddy before this heavenly breakfast gets cold?"

"Right," he said, finally getting my joke and hoisting a dramatic finger in the air.

I heard my uncle's dead-on impersonation that about made me wet my pants with laughter. "It's the Nature Boy, Rick Flair. This ain't no garden party, brotha, this is wrestling, where only the strongest survive. WOOOOOOOO!!!!"

I heard Daddy writhing in agony as my uncle applied the Nature Boy's signature finishing move. "That's the figure four, brotha. Ya mess with the bull, you get the horns, son. WOOOOOO!!! Nature Boy! Woo!!!"

"Get off me, you old fucker!" Daddy squealed.

"Only by four minutes and forty-five seconds," Uncle Bobby reminded his brother. "I may be the oldest ride in the park, but I got the longest line. WOOOOOO!"

I heard my father's sternum pop as Uncle Bobby gave his brother vigorous chest compressions.

Uncle Bobby came back and calmly announced, "Your father should be joining us momentarily, as the prince has emerged up from his slumber," he said in a mock formal tone.

"Thanks, Nature Boy," I said, giggling.

"WOOOOOO!!! You know he's actually a very sweet and sensitive man..."

"Really?" Again, this made me wonder about my uncle's client list. I was interrupted from further questioning about my uncle's business by my father's arrival at the breakfast table.

"Well, hello, sunshine!" Uncle Bobby said jovially and far too loud. "Need an elbow drop, bitch?"

"No thanks, and would you please turn down the volume, Bobby?" my father said in a weak, gravelly voice as he poured himself some coffee.

"Fine," Uncle Bobby stage-whispered. "What the fuck were you doing yesterday?"

Daddy looked genuinely confused. "What do you mean?"

"What do I mean?" Uncle Bobby seethed. "I mean, when we went to play golf, you were fine and dandy. 'Fixin to go put a couple of lines in the water,' you said."

"Yeah, after y'all left, Janie called."

"Right," my uncle said in a drawn-out manner to prompt my father that more explanation was required. "So, your wife calls, and you decide to drink nearly the entire alcohol stash out of this house, which was considerable, and pass out on the beach in the middle of the day?"

"Just had a few too many."

"Few too many?" Uncle Bobby's voice grew incredulous. "The tide was coming in on top of you, and it didn't wake you, big crashing waves, mind you. Women and children were pointing and staring, so much so, that someone called security."

"Security?"

Uncle Bobby was starting to get through the haze. "Security. Here, have some pancakes. Your daughter worked hard to cook them," Uncle Bobby said, flinging a plate down the table with Mrs. Butterworth's sliding behind.

What might Mrs. Butterworth say about this little family gathering? When I was really small, I always thought that she could talk just like in the commercials. Mama always told me that it was sinful to wish for magic like that.

"What did Janie say to set you off?" Uncle Bobby inquired gently.

"What?"

"What did she say, Jim?" Uncle Bobby's soft professional voice took over.

Daddy looked at me in a way that made it clear that he didn't want to get into it in front of me.

"It's okay, Jim. Your daughter is a lot more grown up than she appears." We exchanged knowing glances. "Due to your odd behavior, I clued her in. More coffee?"

"Yeah, so you know, baby?" Daddy asked with a gruff hung-over voice.

"Yes, I know most of it, Daddy, but don't be mad at Uncle Bobby for telling me. It wasn't that I knew specifics, but it's not too hard to put two plus two together."

"I'm not mad." The relief was evident in his voice, and his shoulders relaxed as his burden of protecting his little girl eased. "I wanted to tell you in my own way, but just didn't know how to go about it…"

"That's why she'll be kicking *your* ass all over the golf course today, bud."

"In a nutshell, she said she did it all for the family and that I needed to turn the other cheek. Forgiveness is a virtue, you know," Daddy said as he dug into his pancakes.

"Wow!" Uncle Bobby exclaimed incredulously.

"Yeah," Daddy said. One word said it all. He looked up from his plate, his face chalky white with hangover and slack-jawed from confusion and defeat and said, "She pretty much confirmed my suspicions." Daddy nodded meaningfully at me.

Uncle Bobby breathed in sharply as the gravity of what my father said sank in. "Well, you know I'm here if you want to talk, bud, but no more antics like yesterday, okay?"

"Thanks, Bob. No more antics."

"That's what brothers are for."

"Wait a minute! Either of you assholes want to fill me in about these *suspicions*?" I asked hotly.

"I guess I deserve that after the scene I caused yesterday," my father admitted. "Let's do it on the golf course, Alice. Fair enough? I want to get a shower to get my head on straight, then some hot, wet, fresh air. Kay?"

"Fair enough, I suppose."

***

The rest of the morning passed by in loving, family banter. I didn't realize how much my soul needed that. Uncle Bobby proudly recounted my prowess on the golf course, and I downplayed the previous day's prowess as much as I could. I didn't think my father would believe the truth, much less be able to handle it. I wanted to remain Daddy's little girl while I still could.

That did not mean that I could dial down my natural instincts once I got to the golf course. "Holy shit," was the refrain I heard most of the day. By number eight, I was on fire. Lack of beer and being more familiar with the course from the previous day contributed greatly. "Baby, when, where, and how did you learn to play golf like this? Perhaps Pappy can make you a driving range on Bobby's St. Helena property."

Was this where the driving range idea came from? He wouldn't buy beginner's luck. "Mallory's dad takes us out all the time." I threw out the first school friend name that came to my Swiss cheese mind. And that was a stretch since I didn't have many friends in school. "I suppose I'm just a natural."

"Really?"

"Daddy, I'd like you to tell me what's going on in our family."

He opened his mouth, but no words came out.

"And I mean the whole story. Please don't leave out anything. Lives may depend on it."

"You're finally beginning to see past those buoyant boobies of yours," Nigel's voice sibilated to me from nowhere and everywhere.

Shock and awe lit across Daddy's features, but he remained silent, unsure of where to begin.

"I only have the rest of the day, so everything you can think of would be helpful," I prodded. I cut the ball out over the corner of the pond from the men's tee box on number nine for an exclamation point. I stood, staring at him in askance.

"Alright, alright. I hear you. Let me hit first."

I stepped out of his way, and he proceeded to plunk two balls in the pond about fifty yards in front of us. "Wanna throw down with me and take a stroke?" I asked sheepishly.

"Yeah, okay," he said, a little quicker than I might have expected. "What do you want to know?"

"For starters, why have you been acting so strangely? What happened between you and Mama?"

"Thought Uncle Bobby told you all about it," he replied with a hint of irritation. He clearly didn't want to talk about it.

"Uncle Bobby was trying to do what he thought was right. He was trying to help," I said defensively.

"I know," he admitted.

Swoondalini

"You know, Mama relies on your desire to keep her secrets," I said so incisively, it cut me too.

He was silent for a moment. "I think that realization is what led to my beach outing yesterday."

"I want to hear what happened from you. Moreover, I want to hear all the family history that led up to now. What you don't know, I'd appreciate you sharing your best guesses with me... MUTHAFUCKER!" I swore, as I thinned my approach shot off the back of the green into the bunker.

"You may be more adult than I ever gave you credit for, but I am not ready to hear adult language coming from my little Alice," he chided. I was quiet but pleased by the rebuke. I missed the discipline my father instilled in me. After he was gone, discipline was forgotten, along with a great many other things. "You hear me?"

"Yes, sir... Can we get some beer at the turn?"

"No, smartass, you're fourteen," he replied, with authority that his grin did not convey.

"How about if I hole it out of the trap for a birdie?"

"Are you serious?"

"Only slightly less serious than wanting to know why my crazy family is getting a one-way ticket to Marshall-Pickens. Yes, I mean it."

"I can't believe I'm gambling with my daughter."

"It's not gambling if you know you're going to win," I fired back with a confident smile.

"Fine. You make this, and I'll get us a six-pack. I could do with some beer for this hangover."

"Make it a twelve-pack. Are you telling me that a hangover is why you're playing golf so badly?" I taunted.

"Hit the ball," he said, not amused.

The harder the shot, the less time I tend to take to pull the trigger. I simply walked up, dug in, looked once and fired. My ball looked like Tiger's on number sixteen in the 2005 Masters except the Swoosh was replaced by a Royal Maxfli balata.

"Muthafucker," Daddy cursed. "Excuse the same language I just got on to you about, please."

"You are excused. That's a sandy and a birdie, Daddy. I love sandy birdies," I trilled. "Please write down a three, and I'll take Michelob Light or Coors Light, since ultra-light beers haven't been invented yet. Oh, and be a doll and grab me a hotdog with onions, mustard, and ketchup."

"Listen at you. You little hustler," he said, clapping me on the back so hard, it left red marks of pride. "Can't believe my little girl can play golf like this."

"Well, believe it, and when you get back from Hugo's, it'll be time to fill in the blanks," I reminded him.

"Bob was right. You are more grown up than I gave you credit for."

As we pulled up to number ten, I gave the word, "Talk to me, old man." And talk to me, he did. He proceeded to pour his heart out over the remaining nine holes. Some was shocking, some not so much. It merely confirmed issues that I already suspected. Most interesting was the fact that Mama intentionally got pregnant by another man and allowed Daddy to think I was his until just recently. The official reason was to get out from under her parents' thumbs.

The feeling remained that there was more to the story that he didn't know or wouldn't tell.

Who was my real father? What did he look like? What were his strengths and weaknesses? They could explain some of my unique personality traits.

"Would that be your unmatched narcissism or setting the record for being potentially the youngest, most beautiful Alzheimer patient ever?" Nigel projected into my mind.

"Fuck off," I muttered.

"What?" Daddy asked.

"Nothing, Daddy."

Wonder what my real grandparents were like? Could they make up for the freak show that was my mother's parents?

"Baby, I don't ever want you to think that I didn't want you," he said with sincere, misty eyes.

"I know, Daddy," I replied mechanically.

My head was swimming. Talk about some daddy issues… I always sensed something beneath the surface with my parents, something perfunctory in their day to day relationship, quiet resentment from my father. I always found it interesting that even though my father was a handsome man, he didn't look like the male equivalent of me or my mother. Then again, I spent a lifetime battling between beauty and substance, with substance taking the ass-whipping nine times out of ten.

"You believe me, don't you?"

"Yeah, but you're not happy about it."

He inhaled sharply. "You're right. I'm not, but it has to do with your mother and not you. I always wanted kids, but never so early in life. Know that I wouldn't trade you for anything. Well, maybe for another kid who wouldn't beat me so badly on the golf course."

I laughed just as I started crying. I never knew how much I needed to hear that. I reached out and gave him a hug and refused to let go.

"Baby, are you okay?"

"I'm going to be." That's when I saw Nigel in the distance, waiting for me on the eighteenth green again. Only this time, he would be taking me with him.

Just for shits and giggles, I yanked my approach shot over to the left side of the green where Nigel was standing on the seawall. I couldn't resist giving him some airmail. My ball landed and bounced through him, hit a rock and ricocheted into the edge of Fripp Inlet. He shot me a bird, but there was no anger behind it. The animosity was fading between us.

"Ha! That's the worst shot you hit all day. A chink in the armor," Daddy said with glee.

Didn't have the heart to tell him I meant to hit that ball there. "You don't have to be so happy about it."

He flipped me another ball. "Sorry, Alice, but this grown man just got his butt kicked by a fourteen-year-old girl," he said, laughing. "But I couldn't be prouder. Wait till I tell Bob-O." I waved him off with an embarrassed flush. "I'd like to be your caddy on tour," he added with enthusiasm.

"May I finish high school first?"

"Absolutely, but there appears to be no need to finish high school," he said as my ball landed for a tap-in bogie.

"I need to attend college," I said. I tried to conceal the sting that always rose up when I thought of a higher education. I kept a smile on my face, but I've always been ashamed of the fact I never even walked in my high school graduation, much less matriculated to the big campus in Columbia, SC. I was probably one of the wealthiest high school dropouts in the country, but it really bothered me.

"Absolutely, but not BOB JONES!" he said with surprising ferocity.

"Think Mama will approve of anything but Bob Jones?"

I only received a steely glare in return.

"Alright, Daddy," I said with my hand held up to stave off yet another taboo subject. "Their golf team doesn't compare to Furman's, as they don't have one," I said, trying to lighten his sudden darkness. He didn't answer and appeared to lose himself in the view of the Atlantic and his thoughts. "Daddy?"

"Yeah, babe?"

"I love you and that was the best round of golf ever," I said through restorative tears that started flowing so heavy that I could barely see, and the words came out choked. I always knew I needed to mourn something, but never knew what it was until this moment. The sadness I hid so adeptly from even myself was erupting to the crust of my being in this moment.

"Aw, I love you too, sweetheart," he replied, taken aback by the amount of emotion. "You okay?"

"I could ask you the same question."

"What?"

"Yeah, I'm peachy. It's time for me to go."

Confusion flashed across his face.

"Bye, Daddy." I sniffled, gave him a big hug, and handed him my anser-style putter.

With a befuddled look on his face that clearly indicated he did not grasp the finality of what I said, he responded simply by saying, "Bye."

And I ran as fast as I could toward Nigel. Nigel waved his hand and motioned for me to turn around. I witnessed the scene unfolding as it had originally. We replaced the head covers on real woods, cleaned out the club's cart, and I heard Daddy console me on how tough the game of golf is. So apparently, he was now remembering things differently despite the fact that we just completed an altogether different round than the one he was discussing with the "real" fourteen-year-old me. How often were our memories shaped in this manner? Remembering one thing when clearly something else just occurred. I heard mention again of the land on St. Helena Island and how it would be good for Pappy if I spent some time with him. Nigel mercifully snapped his fingers in dramatic fashion before the stew pot of my emotions boiled over. We quickly soared out over the Atlantic. We didn't slow down until we got over the shipwreck *Savannah* that went down during the great hurricane of 1893. The Lowcountry of my South Carolina past was left behind.

"I know what you're wondering. Did your father realize or remember you leaving in this manner? The answer is yes and no."

"Not sure what you mean."

"We all assume a certain veil of ignorance when we come to this Earth plane."

Nigel sensed that I wasn't quite ready to leave and backtracked to fly us down Fripp's north side toward the bridge and then out over Hunting Island. We travelled silently for a while before he spoke. "Well?"

"Well what?"

"Are you quite alright?"

Do you really care? I asked with my expression. I needed reassurance.

"Wouldn't be here if I didn't," he responded.

"Where to now?" I asked, because I didn't know how else to respond to kindness. I was only versed in the art of taking. The art of receiving gracefully with gratitude was beyond me at this time of my life.

"I don't want to spoil the fun," he said coyly.

"Fun? I'm beginning to appreciate the fact that this has been very eye opening and for my own good, but 'fun' wouldn't be the word I would choose."

He chuckled and replied, "Fun was obviously not the objective of this little exercise. Do you even know the meaning of fun?"

Ignoring his question, since I didn't even know where to go with it, I asked, "Really? What was the objective?" The earlier acidity that I displayed toward him in my voice was gone and replaced by raw emotion and genuine curiosity.

"You may not believe this, but I wish I could tell you. Most of it's for your own good, but a tiny portion has been solely for my entertainment. I can only tell you that this is not done for many souls in this day and age. In fact, it's rarely done any longer at all; probably can count them on two hands in the past couple of decades. At any rate, the point is for you to determine. Recall that free will is a license that can never be revoked... Ah, here we are. Your last stop, in one sense of the word."

In my emotional state, I failed to realize that we entered another vortex.

"What happens after this 'last stop'?"

"Worry about right now, NOW and worry about then, THEN," he said enigmatically.

Chapter 15

"Re-examine all you've been told. Dismiss what insults your soul."

--Walt Whitman

When I gathered my wits and looked around, I found myself in my media room with a couple of glaring differences. The walls and many of the accents around the room were an indigo color that emitted a purplish haze. My peripheral vision was even an indigo hue, very trippy. The most notable difference was a large snowy owl perched on top of my ninety-inch flat screen. The owl stared placidly at me like any other owl might, but this could not be an everyday hoot owl when Nigel involved himself. She peered, unmoving, straight through to my very soul. For a few seconds, I wondered if she were real until she whirled her head around to track my movement around the couch.

I looked down at myself and noted that I was once again thirty-four and back in Brandy's body. Alice was out over the Atlantic somewhere. I was naked as when my journey began. Being back in Brandy's body made me think of Geney and the unparalleled sex we experienced together. "I'm starting to think you like me this way. Where's Geney?" I asked nonchalantly, trying to distract from my breasts reflexively heaving with excitement over the memory of time spent with Geney, but I knew this metaphor all too well by now. Who was I kidding?

Physically, I long ago took the European view on nudity, but the metaphor of baring one's soul left me wanting a flannel nightgown that would swallow me. Nigel ignored my bestial breathing and motioned regally to the coffee table, and there beside an unfamiliar remote control was my care-worn sweatshirt and jeans along with a fresh pair of period panties. The same outfit saw me through many lonely off-nights. The sweatshirt bore the Greek letters Gamma Phi Beta and was worn and tattered from years of comforting. I always dreamed Gamma Phi was the sorority I would have suicide-bidded. I planned to wear it until it literally fell off me. Even though I became richer, better read, and travelled more that most my age, I had the female version of "little-man syndrome." Dropping out was a secret that few knew, and to my knowledge, no one in D.C., besides Geney, had an inkling. I've always harbored a deep-seeded jealousy of college kids and people with college educations. I had a dream of one day finishing my education at the University of South Carolina. Of course, that meant I would actually have to go back to South Carolina and face whatever demons that entailed.

"You mean you're going to allow me to wear clothes?" I asked.

"I didn't put those there. You needed them and therefore they became."

I marveled at this but didn't let on. I quickly pulled on my granny panties, then the old *Lucky* jeans and flopped down on the couch. "What's the deal with this room?"

"Have you noticed a theme yet with your travels?" Nigel tossed a question back to counter my question.

"A theme?" I repeated to stall.

He stared back at me for a while, then mercifully answered, "Yes, a theme. Think hard. In putting you through your paces, I can promise you that those paces have not been random."

"Kay," I said tentatively.

He sucked in an exasperated breath. "Right. Then, I'll be off. Cheerio! You'll be here as long as you deem necessary. When you're done, simply turn off the monitor and that will summon me."

Nigel whiffed out of my existence before I could ask another silly question. I leaned up, grabbed my sweatshirt, and quickly pulled it over my head while studying the odd remote. Where the channel up and down would be, it said Years + or -. Where the volume would be, it said Intensity + or -.

I leaned back on the couch with the remote in hand and said, "What the fuck?" in wonderment to nobody specifically. The owl moved a little on her perch at my question and caught my eye. In her stillness, I forgot she was there. She was unnerving, as she studied my soul, yet comforting at the same time, like she would make me search out and stand up to my demons but was there to take me under her loving wing all at the same time.

"Care to explain this remote to me?" I asked as if an owl could talk.

"We can talk. It just depends on whether or not you choose to listen," she said with indignation.

I suppose I should have been shocked by a talking owl, but time travel and a man in a tailored suit walking through my shower cave wall, among other oddities that were now my life, left me a little jaded. "Okay, sorry. Would you please explain this remote to me..."? I let my sentence trail off to prompt for her name.

"Pallas is my name, but you may call me Pal. How bout I just tune this thing in to some regularly scheduled shows, and we'll go from there."

"You mean like the Greek Goddess of Wisdom?"

She ignored my query, and the TV flashed to life and tuned in to VH1's Sex Rehab with Dr. Drew. My friend Amy Smith came on the screen. I say friend in loose terms since we really just partied together on occasion. She liked pills a little too much for my taste, but she was a nice enough girl. The show followed her on a sober night out to a club and revealed how socially awkward she was without alcohol or drugs. The show could have easily followed me on a similar outing. I never thought how much I relied on substances to get me through social settings. Here was a woman, nearly as attractive as me, not knowing what to do at a club when she was sober. I thought about it before, but dismissed it as quickly, as I knew others would. Who would ever buy that a pretty woman would have social anxieties at a nightclub? Was this why I smoked so much pot?

"Got your attention?" Pal asked.

I noticed that Pal was projecting her thoughts to me. Communicating in this manner was becoming more comfortable for me. Verbal communication can bog us down so. Pal did the telepathic equivalent of clearing her throat. "Have I got your attention?" she repeated.

"Yes, ma'am."

After I gave her my answer, Pal seemed to be lost in grounding herself. She was daydreaming about sequoias and live oaks. I decided to do the same. It's not often we try to listen to every sound, smell every smell, sense every ounce of our weight on our feet as we walk, feel the cotton against every pore of our skin. It can be invigorating to the physical body. How much do we miss in our everyday lives?

"Now you're getting it," Pal said. This ended my moment of meditation.

"Thanks, I'm glad you approve," I said aloud with a trace of sarcasm. In truth, I was flattered.

Swoondalini

With astonishing alacrity that made me recoil suddenly and draw my feet up on the couch, Pal darted from her perch across the room, and had the remote in her talons, then dropped it by my side. She then flew silently back to her perch on top of the TV.

She commanded my attention now. "I get it. Stick with the matter at hand."

I focused on figuring out the remote. It had a little screen where one could type in a desired location. Numbers were on a dial that read months, days, and years. It even had a smaller dial that read OPTIONAL: seconds, minutes, and hours.

Not knowing where to begin, I began at my beginning. I dialed in August 22, 1975, and set the location to Greenville General Hospital, Greenville, SC. "SYSTEM Searching…" the viewer read. The monitor blazed through the decades, starting with the roaring 20's. The stock market crash, then the Great Depression, the New Deal, the Dust Bowl, Pearl Harbor, FDR's funeral train, and a fly on the wall view of Adolph Hitler's suicide. Quickly after that came Chuck Yeager, Korea, the Cuban Missile Crisis, both Kennedy assassinations bookended Martin Luther King's demise, the Space Race, President Johnson escalating the War in Vietnam, and Neil Armstrong.

By the time we got to President Nixon's resignation, it was slowing up and becoming more detailed. Then we got to President Ford's State of the Union. Saturday Night Live's premiere. Jack Nicklaus winning his fifth Green Jacket (Now we're talking). "Can this thing give me all the highlights and behind the scenes action of the 1975 Masters?"

Pal looked at me as if I just grew another head. Funny, I never thought an owl could make an expression so human.

Chris Suddeth

"Sorry I asked." I turned my attention back to the monitor, and it became like when one types an address into Google Earth and hits enter. The Earth was shown as we saw the moonrise from Apollo 8 on Christmas 1968. Then the monitor quickly accelerated to show the United States, and then the east coast, then South Carolina, and then the Upstate of South Carolina came into focus. I got a bird's eye view of Clemson's Death Valley and rocketed through the little town of Pendleton and wound up on the I-85 corridor heading north to Greenville, G-Vegas as the locals call it.

The monitor then zoomed in on a large brown building off of Pendleton Street in the heart of Greenville proper. Greenville General would be eventually replaced by St. Francis and Greenville Memorial, but for generations of people in Greenville, this is where they entered the world.

The TV took me through walls where one could observe all the brick, mortar, and wood as the "camera" passed through. When the "camera" passed through a person, one would see all the flesh, blood, bones, and organs.

There would be only two births at Greenville General that day. This was a slow day by any standard, but really slow, considering nine months ago, most people were celebrating the holidays. Tis the season to make babies. People tend to have more time, and more of everything in their systems, to lay the groundwork for the spark of life.

The new baby boy was represented by both sets of grandparents, the father, and various other family members and friends from both sides. The monitor scanned and rested on my sole family member present. The camera then pulled a slow focus as the doctor walked up to my father with the gait of a tired man. "Jim, Janie had a rough go of things, one of the roughest I've seen in my twenty-five years of delivering babies. Miraculously, they both survived, and you have a healthy baby girl," the doctor said in a hushed tone.

"You struggled from the very start," Pal pointed out.

My father contemplated for a few beats and asked, as if he hadn't heard, or cared, for that matter, that we were both lucky to be alive, "Doctor, is there any way of knowing if the child is mine?" I could feel my father's resentment as he recounted their wedding day. A shotgun was indeed present, and my grandfather Billy conducted the nuptials.

"Well, she's not black."

Daddy stared daggers at the man.

"That's a joke, son."

"I know."

The doctor cleared his throat and pressed on past the awkwardness of the moment. "No, sir, I'm sorry to say that we've got a little ways to go in the science of determining paternity," he said in a business-like manner. He probably got this question from time to time.

I had no inklings over the years that my father ever doubted whether or not I was his. One of the few times that my thoughtlessness was legitimate. There was never a doubt that I always was Daddy's girl.

"I understand," he drawled out and went spacey for a second until the doctor cleared his throat. "May I see them?"

Where were my grandparents? I figured at least Nana would be here. I've never thought much about the day of my birth, but always pictured more of a gathering like the baby boy.

"I'm afraid you can't see them. Not today, at least. They're both exhausted, and we've got your daughter in a little oxygen tent," he added as he lit a cigarette. Yep, this was definitely the 70's. "Best to go home and rest up. You'll need it with a new baby, and your wife's going to need lots of help in the beginning due to the tearing. Any other questions?"

"None. Thanks, doctor," Daddy said, running his fingers through his frazzled hair.

The doctor spun on his heel and proceeded to the other family in the waiting room. My father looked so lost in comparison to the eager faces of the other family. He slowly walked down the long hall and exited the hospital. The camera followed him until I absentmindedly muttered into the remote resting under my chin, "What made Daddy suspicious from the beginning about paternity?"

The remote's dials whirled into action so abruptly, that I flung the remote across the coffee table. The TV went blank, leaving me with the image of my lonely father walking out of the hospital on the day of my birth.

About fifteen or twenty silent seconds passed before the screen returned to life as the camera pulled away from the hospital and shot up in the air as if attached to a grade school kid's rocket project. The distance was not far, nearly walking distance. The locale was McDaniel Avenue. "That's right around the corner from my grandparents' current house on Crescent Avenue."

People from the Mill Hill didn't typically go over to McDaniel Avenue on social calls. I always felt out of place there in so many ways, and my grandparents never belonged, despite all their posturing.

"But your mother belonged," Pal projected with a raised eyebrow.

Swoondalini

What I was beginning to notice about these thought projections was that barely a split second after I thought something, Pal was able to think a response back to me. It was a disconcerting convenience.

Ignoring this as best I could, I picked up the remote again to take a look at the date. It read December 1974. This would obviously be around the time of my conception. The camera pulled up in front of the most ornate house on McDaniel. An orchestra was playing all the holiday favorites to perfection. My perspective was led through the large oak front door with hardware that I'm sure was gold. The house was packed to the gills with the wealth and power of the Palmetto State.

The mayor of Greenville, both U.S. senators from South Carolina, the governor of South Carolina, owners of the local mills, were all being served by African-Americans with white gloves in formal wear.

Apparently, by the mid-seventies, my grandparents and mother learned how to look the part of the elite belonging to the deep South but lacked the subtle art of belonging. It was akin to a Yankee that spent decades in the South but would never have the manners or mannerisms of a Southerner. The northerners became friends and neighbors but would knowingly and unknowingly remind the natives that they were not native. What was also apparent was that my mother would always be the most beautiful woman in the room. For better or worse, she demanded full attention be paid to her, no matter the situation. However, Mama was barely a woman at this point in her life. In fact, she was around the same age as I was when I left Greenville.

How on Earth did my family snag an invite to this soiree?

"How do you think?" Pal shot back.

I felt the answer via a deep knowing in my gut. I noticed that my mother was dressed rather unconservatively for this conservative gathering.

"Now it's time to show you what this latest and greatest in flat-screen technology can do," Pal said in her mock salesman's voice.

I was afraid to even ponder what that meant, but it didn't take long to find out as the camera quickly rushed to my mother standing nervously in the corner and assumed her perspective. I could feel what she'd felt, hear and see what she'd seen and heard. I even smelled the cigarette smoke and expensive single malt scotch from the power broker get-together beside us.

"There he is," Granny said, and I felt a sharp nudge in the small of my back. Odd…

"I know what he looks like, Mother. We go to the same high school, remember?" my mother said in a petulant whisper as she dashed away after him.

The gentlemen next to us lost concentration on what they were talking about to watch my mother promenade across the room. This was something that I was so accustomed to happening to me that I rarely noticed it anymore, unless intentionally doing it to my advantage. Would there be a day that I would miss it or become uncomfortable with it?

"Yes and no. Now pay attention," Pal demanded.

There he was indeed. Adam was tall, with olive skin, and an awfully expensive leisure suit on that was just awful. Adam was a Herb Tarlek wanna-be with a white belt and white leather shoes to finish the look. But unlike Herb, he owned the top of the line Rolex model that was about ten grand even in 70's money. Mama was very taken with Adam's suit and Adam as a whole.

He was handsome, I'll give him that, but he was also the son of Greenville's wealthiest family, the Harts. Ironically, I assumed that name because it adorned the side of a building in downtown Greenville and it was the first name that popped in my head when I arrived at Twin Peaks. No wonder Mama reacted so strongly when she heard it.

The more I looked at Adam, the more striking I found his movie star looks. He was the seventies version of a Paul Walker with a smattering of Eric Dane thrown in for good measure. Adam was, in short, the male physical version of me.

"Paaal," I said plaintively. "I see where this is going, so we can skip this part."

"Hush and pay attention. Things are about to get interesting," Pal said.

"I don't need interesting. I have had my fill of interesting."

Pal answered me with her silence.

Apparently, my granny was trying to pimp my mother out to add legitimacy to the family. My racist grandparents used the term "nigger rich" so much, it became obvious to me that they were what they feared. Thou dost protest too much.

I might have felt bad for Mama, if I just took in the surface of all this, but I was feeling it too. Mama didn't completely agree, but she didn't completely disagree either. She was eager to take one for the team. Had they tried to run this same game with me?

Even though I could feel the conflict and uncertainty from my mother, I could also feel the confidence that she exuded. She didn't care for the way she was dressed, but she knew it was a tool, maybe her only tool. But did it have to be that way?

As she crossed the room and caught Adam's eye, it was interesting to note that Adam maintained eye contact with Mama, something neither of us is used to.

"What a beautiful home your family has here," Mama said in her politely perfect drawl. "I realize I've been here a few times to study, but I've never been to one of Mama Hart's power parties…"

"Thanks. It's something, all right," Adam said. "May I get you a drink?"

My mother was a teetotaler, but I could feel her decide she would hold a drink, sip it, and pour out the majority at the next opportunity. That's where the two of us differed. "Yes, please, that would be nice."

Adam kindly asked an old black gentleman to bring them two spice punches. "So, are you going to college next fall?"

"No, not right away," Mama said quickly. I felt the shame and embarrassment she felt at that statement. The same shame and embarrassment I felt for not going on to higher education. She sounded proud and resolved though. "Are you?"

"Oh yes, headed to the University of South Carolina, much to my father's chagrin," he said.

"Your father doesn't like the Gamecocks?"

"No, it's not that. Sports and education are two different things. Most people don't get that. Anyway, he went there. It's the fact that I got into Harvard and Notre Dame, among others."

"Why wouldn't you go to either of those schools? They're better, aren't they?"

"Sure, they are, but that would make him happy." The old man arrived with our drinks. "Thanks, Moses." He raised his glass in salute to Mama. "You look very pretty in that new dress of yours. You wanna go somewhere a little less stuffy to talk?"

We were all waiting for that move for various reasons. I knew what was coming. Mama had her prey within her grasp. Adam, for his part, genuinely wanted to chat with a friend.

"Absolutely."

"We'll go to my upstairs study."

"So, you have a downstairs study, too?"

Adam merely raised an eyebrow at that question.

When Adam closed the door to the study, he immediately asked, "Why are you here?"

"Adam, we've known one another since we were little, and your parents invited us." Mama masked her bitter venom for the way Adam's parents always treated them as "white trash with money" with a honey sweet smile.

"You're being coy," Adam observed.

"Fair enough," Mama said, crossing the room toward him, closing the distance between them. No breathing room. "Why did you ask me up to your study?"

"Not for the reason you may think. I'd like to talk. One can never have enough friends."

Mama wasn't interested in talking, much less cultivating a friendship unless there was a gain to be made. "Really? You never wanted to be friends at school." Mama's small, tight frame was now inches away from him.

"Not true, my parents didn't want that, but now I'm my own man."

"That's funny, because guys ask me to their study all the time and it's not to study. Except for you, that is."

"Well, I'm funny."

"How do you mean?" Mama was certainly confused within, but still exuded confidence on the outside.

"I'm gay," Adam blurted out.

"We've known each other for a long time, so I've had my suspicions. I can help you with those sinful urges," Mama said, maintaining laser beam eye contact while her hand cupped his face.

This was way before the time when such things were just blurted out, and there is still a degree of stigma in 2009. I could feel a rush of confusion and anger coming from my mother. Mama spoke to Adam as if she were speaking to a naughty child. "Well, I don't suppose you'd mind if I did this?" She reached out for Adam's manhood and began to stroke it. He was rendered speechless but didn't move. "Doesn't feel like you're gay to me. In fact, you feel very straight. You know what happened to the faggots of Sodom and Gomorrah."

So typical of Mama to say something like that while she's sexually assaulting someone.

"Where the hell do you get off judging me?" Adam pleaded his case as he retreated behind his desk and flopped down in his chair. He wasn't able to walk very straight, and the embarrassment showed on his face.

Mama ignored him. "You don't find me attractive, Adam?"

"Of course I do," he stammered. "But—"

"But what? Wouldn't I provide legitimacy for you? Make life a little easier?" We could both see this hit home with Adam. Mama never missed an opportunity and taught me as much. "I'd be the perfect cover. No one would ever think you were 'funny' with me on your arm. In fact, you'd be lucky if they noticed you at all," Mama explained.

Adam wasn't answering, and his gaze drifted out the window. I knew my mother, and knowing her, she would now turn things up a notch. One ignored Mama at his peril. She went behind the desk and wheeled him around to face her. "Why don't you give me a ride? You might find that you like girls," she whispered as she dropped her panties out from under her short cocktail dress. "Even if you don't, we can still work something out."

"Pal, I think I'm going to be sick, and it's not just because I'm watching my mother put the moves on some gay kid that is obviously my father, but will NEVER be my daddy," I complained. All at the same time, I felt like I wanted to cry, puke, and run, an uneasy combo, to say the least.

"Yes, that's natural," Pal projected, as she paused the unfolding debacle.

"Natural that I feel like a caged animal? What do you mean?"

"All of what I'm showing you is an exercise in developing your third eye, not to mention educational. Two birds, one stone." Pal guffawed at her own joke and placed her wing on her stomach.

"What if I don't want my third eye developed?"

"Then you wouldn't be here. The nausea you're feeling is just a touch of Kundalini syndrome. Same thing that put you on that shower floor."

I read a little about this sort of thing and used it as one of my battery of excuses not to spread my wings in a spiritual sense, so to speak. After all this time, this was the first explanation as to what happened to me.

"How about we jump out of the frying pan and into the fire," Pal said, in what was cruel delight from my perspective.

"How bout we don't, and say we did," I said, fearing what surprise lay around the corner. "I like the frying pan." Alas, it was too late. I looked down at the remote and noticed the intensity button mashed down in the up direction. I could now feel not just my mother, but Adam's emotions as well. "How is this possible?"

"Don't worry; it's only natural that you feel a little off-balance. Brilliant, isn't it?"

"I thought we were going to be friends, Pal," I said, making one last plea for mercy. Did I get demoted? I mean, Nigel was one thing, but now I was being tortured by an owl.

"Oh, we have been friends for longer than you can imagine, but friendship has nothing to do with this."

If only, I thought, as Pal hit the play button again.

"I've been with girls before," I heard Adam claim.

No, he had not.

"No, you haven't. I can spot a virgin. Takes one to know one."

"I'm not a virgin. At least, I'm not in the strictest sense of the word. I sincerely doubt you're purity as well."

He was telling the truth there.

Mama's face morphed into chaste innocence. "I've been a babe in the woods and lost my virginity several times over now. Do you find me so unappealing?"

"It's not that, it's just…"

"Just that what?" Mama interrupted impatiently.

Swoondalini

He stammered, and Mama took the initiative by jamming her knee between his legs and into the chair. I felt him startle at almost having his nuts mashed down into his fine leather chair. She had no intention of hurting him, especially there. "EASY!" he shrieked, but I could feel his growing excitement.

Mama started rubbing with her knee and then reached down and took a firm grasp. "Stand up," she commanded. Adam swallowed hard and did as he was told. I could sense his unease and confusion at having lost control of the situation to a "little girl." The desire and throbbing of his penis against the confines of his tighty whiteys and tight polyester slacks was an interesting sensation for the opposite sex to experience. I felt his heart rate go through the roof as he gazed upon my mother's exposed breasts.

Mama looked meaningfully at the growing bulge in his pants. "That's more what I had in mind." Adam looked genuinely confused. Mama possessed a tsunami-like way she could turn someone's world upside-down. It sometimes took months or years to completely dissect a two-minute conversation with her.

I began to see with his eyes and hers all at the same moment. I could feel his yearning for her, as more blood rushed from his brain to his crotch. No wonder men could be so easily led by their penises. Once turned on, they would pursue pleasure at almost any cost. From a strictly biological stance, it made sense. Would his tight leisure suit pants stand the pressure on their seams? I could feel Mama enjoy her control, as she jerked his pants down and gently stroked him until he had a full-on erection. When he began to groan with pleasure, Mama tried to guide his penis into her and hit a road block.

"No, I don't want to go all the way," he said, trying to sound reasonable.

"I won't get pregnant the first time, baby," she purred.

"I know better than that," Adam said, breathlessly.

Her sweetness dissolved as she grabbed his nut sack with just enough force to make an impression. Again, she really didn't want to damage the fun bag. I inhaled sharply, as I felt his shock and discomfort and yes, exhilaration.

I simultaneously felt that familiar rush of power as Mama began to drive her point home. I sensed Mama's pleasure at having her large prey so easily off balance and on the ropes. It was the same kick of pleasure I enjoyed so many times as I massaged egos, among other things, with one hand and emptied wallets, jewelry boxes, and "borrowed" flashy car keys with the other hand, all in plain sight. Mostly, I wouldn't, or couldn't, get off with my clients, but this was another type of orgasm all together. Like shooting fish in a fucking barrel. It was no fair and no wonder I yearned for that time with Geney again. A girl has her needs, regardless of her looks. Why was I so slow on the learning curve? Until I viewed manipulation from the outside, I never realized how repulsive it was.

I even added what I called a "love" fee. I charged more to clients who fell for me because I saw it as a weakness that needed to be punished. *Caveat emptor!*

"Now, listen up, *Adam*. We're having sex, and you're going to love it."

"Or what?" Bold words for a man with his testicles in harm's way. Adam was playing with fire, and he knew it, but was excited by it all at the same time. It was intoxicating, and I could feel his erection become harder. An erection was a breathtaking and new experience for me. I mean, I was a male for thirty-six days, but Iwo Jima was hardly inspiration for boners.

"The possibilities are endless for me right now to get what I want." He didn't suspect it, but Mama was willing to cause a scene downstairs that would be the talk of South Carolina for years to come if she didn't obtain his full cooperation. Adam thought he was dealing with the same little girl he saw in the halls of high school. That little girl died right before his lust-filled eyes. He was now witnessing the birth of a siren, a man-eater.

Adam had no clue what she wanted but was relieved that he wasn't completely gay. Granted, Mama didn't give him much choice, but he allowed that relief to cloud his judgment. "Okay, alright, over on the couch." His voice sounded resigned, but in truth, he was eager for that sullied beaver.

Almost as soon as he entered her, he came, and felt no remorse about it. Mama's momentary victory came to an end with frustration. I could feel urges within her screaming to be slammed against the wall and worked over by Adam's carved frame. Everybody needs to hurt so good from time to time. I could also feel something else in the deepest part of her, something she wasn't yet aware of. "Adam, you better keep that cock out and ready if you know what's good for you," Mama commanded.

She said cock...

"But we probably need to get back downstairs."

"I'll tell ya what we need. That's for you to throw me up against that wall and have your way with me." It was so strange hearing this from my seemingly straight-laced mother. Adam hesitated a moment too long. "I'll walk right out that door with tears in my eyes, jizz running down my leg, and my dress ripped if I'm not walking with a limp tomorrow," she said as she leveled her eyes at him. It was not a threat, but a promise.

"Yes, ma'am."

"Good boy." The threat left her voice and turned all sugar.

Adam did as he was told, but for all intents and purposes, all it took was once. My mother felt it on the subconscious level; in the deepest part of a woman's soul, she knows the instant she is with child. I could feel it too. Sadness bubbled up from the canyon where I kept my soul buried. This scenario may be the only time I feel that miracle of life within that I've heard other ladies drone on about. I could feel the life already expanding inside my mother as Adam "overpowered" Mama and penetrated her once again.

Adam was oblivious, as most men are, even gay ones, to the ways of women, especially predatory women like my mother. And yes, like myself.

"Admitting it is the first step to recovery," Pal tossed in.

Between the emotions of all three of us, it was becoming too much. "Look deeper," Pal prodded.

"I'm done. I don't feel very well."

"Just one more minute. What do you feel?"

"Eggs splitting?"

The camera focused quickly to my mother's womb to show on a microscopic level Adam's sperm fertilizing Mama's egg and it splitting in two. Just as quickly, the focus backed off.

"Life! Me?" I said in hushed wonderment as I keeled over and blacked out from overstimulation.

***

I awoke to a pleasurable sensation between my legs and groaning in stereo. I was confused for a second until I opened my eyes to see my mother and this boy in the midst of coitus. I shuddered in revulsion and ecstasy in the same moment as they both, as we three, achieved orgasm. It was too much; I thought I was going to pass out again.

"What a ride this has to be for you," Pal said, with too much glee for my taste.

"Yes, quite a ride. I must look green."

Intentionally dense, Pal said, "You look the way you want to look."

"I know, I know. It's all up to me. Well, I've got one for you. If it's all up to me then, why do I have to sit through this?"

"Why do you think?"

I didn't have a ready answer but followed my intuition for once and felt it out. The throes of passion and persuasion were waning, leaving cold hard facts in their wake. Mama was pregnant with me...

"Bingo!" Pal lauded. "For lack of a better way to put it, do you feel your essence now?"

"No, I don't. Why?"

"The long and the short of it is that you signed up for an ass-kicker of a life, so you chose to stay among the azaleas for as long as you could," Pal explained.

"Azaleas?"

"You'll see," Pal said, enigmatically. "Anyway, some souls incarnate, or at least visit, at the moment of conception, while others wait until the very last minute like you did. Most start integrating into their bodies around the fourth month."

I didn't know what to make of that tidbit that would put Roe vs. Wade in a whole new light, so I chose to focus on Daddy. I now knew Daddy wasn't my real father. But I should have been told the details.

"Yes, you should have been told, but you also shouldn't have to have been told. Would you have been ready for these details at fourteen?"

"What the fuck is that supposed to mean?" My emotions were getting the better of me now, and I was lashing out in the wrong direction. From the outside, it would appear as if I were a crazy woman berating an owl. Who did that? Funny how I wouldn't have cared about my path of destruction in the past.

"What do you think it means?"

"How am I supposed to know?" The venom was leaving my voice.

"But you are supposed to know, or more accurately, to *feel*," Pal said patiently.

"I know. A little warning next time please. I'm sorry I yelled at you."

"I know, and you won't need my warnings. Things unfold as they're supposed to."

My attention was drawn back to the TV, as I felt my mother think, now we don't have to worry about losing the house on Crescent Avenue, and the next thing that flowed from her mind was, that was easier than I thought it was going to be, and I must be prettier than I thought I was. There was a fleeting thought about if she actually were to stumble upon some poor straight fellow to fall in love with and then a shoulder shrug. There wasn't so much as a tinge of regret as the thrill of Mama coming into her full power served to get her off. I was much like my mother for the best part of two decades without realizing it, and it sickened me that I became what I most detested.

"I've seen enough," I said weakly.

Mercifully, the screen went blank, and Pal and I bathed in silence for Lord only knows how long. Pal broke the silence. "Now it's time to learn to filter."

***

The remote whirled back to life, slowly and meticulously like a combination lock, as if it felt my anxiety at where it would take me next and wanted to draw it out to an agonizing pace.

Finally, the dial landed ten years before my birth, 1965. "We're taking this route because of your appreciation of history," Pal volunteered. A black and white image of President Johnson popped up on the screen. Being an amateur historian, I correctly surmised that this had to do with his justifications over escalating the war in Vietnam.

"Now, America wins the wars that she undertakes," he drawled. "Make no mistake about it. And we have declared war on ignorance and illiteracy. We have declared war on poverty. We have declared war on disease. And we have declared war on tyranny and aggression. And we not only stand for ending these things, but we are willing to stand up and die for these things." The President was now becoming more heated as he ramped up to the bottom line.

I felt that the President believed in what he was saying as much as a disdained part of him feared it would fail. He wasn't ready, much less willing, to face it even as it destroyed his legacy and ripped the country to shreds that could still be felt at times in 2009. This wasn't hindsight; it was foresight, but he never admitted it to anyone, especially himself. It jammed bamboo shoots under his figurative fingernails and haunted his dreams.

"Feel the difference?" Pal asked.

"Difference?"

"The difference between his feelings and yours, his beliefs and yours, his life and yours," Pal droned on in my head.

"Sort of," I said uncertainly.

Ignoring my uncertainty, Pal pressed on, "Good, let's turn the speed of the pitches up a bit. The screen is merely a safety net to keep you objective. After you feel confidence in your ability to filter, you may step through."

The screen went blank briefly, and the remote advanced a little over three years. It was shocking, but the President looked as if he aged more like fifteen years…

"…Accordingly, I shall not seek, and will not accept the nomination of my party for another term as your President."

I could feel the failure, the defeat, the utter disappointment and confusion of this beaten man. He would go from being the most powerful man in the world to obsessing over counting chicken eggs on his farm before his death. Micromanagement of the mundane and a premature death were his future.

Now that I thought about it, I could literally feel with my whole being where he stopped, and I began. The sickness in the pit of my stomach was not mine. The sense of betrayal by his closest advisors was not mine. The feeling of the country tearing itself apart was no fault of mine. I was surprised to find a sense of relief in handing this pile of shit to the next guy. That's something one wouldn't see in the old films and history books on the pivotal Johnson administration. I remembered that this speech came in March, which meant that things were actually about to get worse. Still to come were the assassinations of King and Kennedy.

"Good that you've learned the line not to be crossed to maintain your highest and best health. Even advanced students can have trouble separating themselves from the whims, wishes, and woes of others," Pal explained.

"Thanks."

"Now you're prepared to step through the screen into 1968."

"But that's one of the most turbulent years in American history."

"Don't worry, you'll be invisible."

"I wasn't worried about that."

"I know, so perhaps you'd prefer 1865? 1919? 1929? 1941? 2001?"

"I get it," I said.

My mouth went dry, as I steeled myself for what was to come. I regretted my choice of clothes. I was sweating profusely. I reluctantly walked toward the TV as if it were an executioner. It must have sensed my apprehension and decided to rip off the figurative band-aid. Suddenly, the TV lurched in my direction and swallowed me whole. I found myself in the Oval Office, facing President Lyndon Baines Johnson as he signed off to America. I quickly noted the difference between this Oval Office and the one I came to know during the Benton Administration.

As soon as the television cameras went off and the lights went down, Lady Bird and their two daughters rushed to the President's side. The First Lady actually walked right through me, and I felt her pain at seeing her husband's downfall.

I could sense the turmoil in the room. More than a few of his top advisors were angered over their reign of power coming to a close. L.B.J., for his part, was resigned and was left as a tired, beaten, withered shell of the man who took the reins on that fateful November day in 1963. Simply, he felt old.

Curiously, I quickly lost interest in all this. I felt their pain but didn't feel it necessary to become a part of it. Certainly, the history of it all fascinated me, but my purpose here was not a history lesson.

As that realization took hold, the TV purged me back out in my media room. I noted that Pal's appraising gaze didn't faze me. "Excellent. You learned much quicker than Nigel. You may go when you wish or remain and explore for curiosity's sake. I would explore, if I were you," Pal said enthusiastically. Her projected voice portrayed wonderment, with a hint of jealousy at the opportunity I could undertake.

"I learned quicker than Nigel?" I couldn't help but allow some satisfaction to creep into my voice. "What exactly did I learn quicker?"

"Don't let that go to that voluptuous vapid head of yours, *Brandy*," Nigel's irritated voice popped from everywhere and nowhere.

Was I in training to be what Nigel is?

"That's for you to conclude in your own time," Pal answered, not responding to Nigel's intrusion.

"I know, I know." I chose to ignore Nigel as well.

"I have enjoyed our time together, but after all, time is only relevant as a tool, nothing more," Pal said.

With that last paradoxical statement, Pal flew directly at my chest and disappeared into me. Was this Pallas creature a part of me?

Swoondalini

Now I was left to my own devices. What to do? What to do? Should I explore one of my favorite subjects, history? That was a very tempting prospect, having just been shown that I could literally walk in on history and be the proverbial fly on the wall. The prospects were overwhelming. USS Missouri? Appomattox Courthouse? Apollo 11?

It did occur to me that while it was made clear that my time here was indefinite, if it existed at all, it did need to be well spent. The point of this epic journey seemed to be about myself. Perhaps that was what I should do rather than fret over whether to witness Gene Sarazen's "shot heard round the world" or the beginning of the War of Northern Aggression at Fort Sumter. Perhaps the Emancipation Proclamation or the Gettysburg Address? The list was endless, but nowhere as daunting, as the one great frontier seldom explored by man, or woman, in my case, the exploration of one's self. Self-exploration is the final frontier. After all, that's what I was led to do this entire time. It seemed it was time for me to take the bull by the horns for myself, rather than being led to it.

All that being considered, I suppressed the history buff in myself and chose to keep things simple. I would explore the people, places, and events that made me—me.

***

The questions of what, how, and why would have to be answered at a later date, but where to begin with the when was the question that would determine the destination of my first stop in, "This is your life."

The TV screen displayed a text, reading, "Might I make a suggestion?"

With relief and trepidation all at once, I responded, "Sure, take your best shot."

The text disappeared to the sound of a heartbeat. I could feel the bass of the subwoofer all the way to my core. "Thump, thump, thump, thump..." Then the music of one of the best-selling albums of all time kicked in to take me to another world. It was instantly recognizable as Pink Floyd's *Dark Side of the Moon*.

I loved the album, but really only became familiar with it when combined with weed and *The Wizard of Oz* on mute. Well known among pot-heads is that when one plays the music of the album to the movie, it syncs up in an eerie manner. Simply start the CD on repeat when the MGM Lion roars for the third time before the credits, mute the movie, and prepare to be amazed. Even when viewed sober, it had a cool effect that left the viewer wondering if the band did it intentionally. It was my understanding that the band denied purposefully creating the album to be played parallel to the classic movie. All that aside, add a healthy bong hit or ten and prepare to be enthralled.

I was so fascinated by it that I watched it in this way probably a dozen times or so. Whenever the movie came on TV with the actual sound, I could still hear Pink Floyd's music playing in my mind. The words of the movie became somewhat out of place. Which time in my life would I be visiting? I answered that question at the same moment that it appeared on screen. Instantly, I felt the trepidation well up in my gut. I didn't know exactly what I would find in this time period, but I knew it was some sort of lynch-pin.

I took a deep breath, slowly stood, and rubbed my sweaty palms together. I was only able to walk a couple of steps toward the TV monitor before it enveloped me. What greeted me was the sound of cash registers and an instant of looking over Dorothy's shoulder as she opened the door of her modest farmhouse and stepped into the realm of color, splendor, and danger that was the Land of Oz.

I then took over the point of view of Dorothy in the movie. I looked down and found myself dressed as her. I apparently assumed Judy Garland's place. I was squeezed into the white blouse and blue and white jumper. I felt my hair and discovered pigtails, and Toto was at my heels. At least I wore clothes on this trip, but I was sure if I modified this outfit in the right places, it would do well on my website.

I walked around in the same wonderment that Dorothy displayed when she was deposited in Munchkin Land. I was aware of being watched by the little people Dorothy would be worshipped by as their savior. Quickly, I looked over and saw the two legs that belonged to the Wicked Witch of the East. I was startled by the high-pitched giggles of the Munchkins but pressed on to take a closer look at the fabled "Ruby Slippers."

"Baby, would you buy me a pair of ruby shoes?" I heard my own dusky voice say as if from the depths of a well.

I heard *him*. "I would if I could, sweetness," he responded with sincerity not often heard, much less meant, in this world, and a high-pitched cackle that was the laugh I chased since the day I squelched it.

Apparently, I was in the movie that we were watching. "Anybody but him," I whispered to nobody in particular, and I felt my eyes well up with tears never cried. I plopped down in the middle of the town square and covered my head with my hands, put my face in my lap, and remembered...

Chris Suddeth

***

It was the love of my life, Ronnie Leeman. I tried never to think of him and the times we spent together, but every time I heard the common name Ronny or Ron, I felt a pang in the heart. The same sentiment occurs every time I see a yellow Geo Tracker, but fortunately, there are fewer and fewer of those on the road these days.

Ronnie was my first true love. He was also my first real boyfriend. Come to think of it, he was my only real boyfriend. In my profession, I play many roles, including girlfriend. I'm a saccharine substitute for things men can't get, but that's all play-acting. Granted, it wasn't all bad, but it wasn't the real deal either. If anything, this journey taught me authenticity. We were together before I became so cynical in my early 20's, before I began using my looks and wits to control people, to sometimes devastating effect, before my daddy and my childhood died, and quite frankly, before I became, for lack of a better word to use, a cunt.

Our relationship started out as many do, as friends. We didn't stay friends for long, though. I was the only one of what I call the Berea High School group that didn't go to Berea High or T.R. High (that's Traveler's Rest to those from outside the Upstate). I was kindly welcomed into their group.

Outside of Bob Jones High, school-related events, and church, I didn't make it out of the house much. Fortunately, the scant few friends I made at Bob Jones High were of the liberal persuasion as far as the school policies were concerned. You know what they say about preacher's daughters being the

Swoondalini

wildest... Anyway, it's a wonder Ronnie and I even met. I'll call it fate, because Alice would like the sound of that. We met when my father took me over to Bruce's Auto Auction on Furman Hall Road to get my first car. I met his lifelong friend, Deano, too. They were working there and had quite the little system going. Mama did her best to keep me naïve to the ways of the world by placing me in Bob Jones High. Ironically, the undercurrent that always develops in the face of unnatural and unrelenting restrictiveness taught me about the finer things of life, like what weed smelled like; although I was never reprobate enough to smoke it. I was fascinated, and a bit turned on, when I noticed the two large boys smoking grass. One would leave the joint burning on top of a car's tire on the other side of the sales lot, then run to grab another car, and then signal to the other to pick up the joint.

I discovered the joint while my father and I were looking at what was to be my first car, a silver 1979 Volkswagen convertible with a black top. I loved that car, and the freedom it provided from Mama once I learned to drive the standard four-speed. I picked the joint up when my father's back was turned to examine it. It was then that I heard Deano loudly clearing his throat to get my attention. "Put that thang down, please," Deano said in a stage whisper.

"What do you think of this car, Alice?" my father asked without looking up.

"I think it's beautiful, Daddy. And it's a convertible, too." I jammed the joint behind my back as I spoke to my father.

"Moreover, it's not fast at all." He noticed Deano lurking off to the side. "Excuse me, son, what do you think of this car? Is it in good shape?"

Deano cleared his throat and tried to keep his composure. "I think it's a piece of shit, sir." Deano flushed red as he was unable to stop the words flowing out of his mouth. I still laugh when I remember that. Daddy, for his part, wasn't paying much attention, but smirked nonetheless. I think he smelled the smoke. "I mean, I just drive the cars around this lot and make sure they're clean before they go up for auction. I'd rather have a truck," he said as he waved with pride at his black F-150 4X4 with tinted windows. "I can tell you that this car does run, and it's coming up for auction in about twenty or thirty minutes."

"Thanks, bud."

I heard Ronnie yell at him to bring the '79 Beetle up. Deano barely flinched and was still staring at me. I stifled a snicker. I was just starting to become aware of the effect I had on the male species, due to some petty jealousies I experienced from other girls and thought Deano was cute.

Ronnie ran over to see what was going on and, upon laying eyes on me, uttered his first words to me. "You may not be the first, but you *can* be next." He then gave a "what's up?" nod of his head with a toothy grin. Not many men, at any age, can use lines like that with success, but Ronnie delivered them with just the right timing, humor, and confidence to pull it off. I still think he's one of the smoothest men I've ever come across. He kept it simple and never missed a beat. "I'm Ronnie, this is mah buddy Deano and we're going to a party tonight. Wanna come?"

Daddy was evaluating the scene and Ronnie quickly introduced himself. "Sir, is there anything I can help you with on this car?"

"Nope," Daddy said with a challenging, but affable smirk.

"Mister?"

"Please call me Jim."

"Mr. Jim, my buddy and I will take good care of your daughter and make sure she has a real good time."

"It's the 'real good time' part us fathers worry about," Daddy stated.

"Yes, sir, I know. We promise she won't turn up pregnant." Ronnie, cutting to the chase with a smile on his face, also cut the tension. Ronnie had a way with people.

"You don't miss a thing, do ya, boy?" Daddy was trying extremely hard not to break a smile at that comment and was failing miserably. I think Ronnie reminded him of himself at the same age.

"Try not to, sir."

"Alice, want to go to a party with these gentlemen?"

All eyes were on me. "Sure."

"You know your mama won't like it," Daddy said with a glimmer in his eyes.

"I have no doubt."

***

Ronnie picked me up from my house a few hours after Daddy bought the Beetle. In truth, I think he bought it just to piss my mother off. As a result, it was tense around the house, and Ronnie could not have shown up at a better time.

Ronnie came to the door like a perfect gentleman. Normally, my parents, especially Mama, would have been all over him, but they were distracted by yet another chink in the rusting armor that was their marriage.

"Y'all be safe," my father yelled after us.

"Jim, who is that?"

"Don't worry about it. He's a nice kid."

"How do you know? Alice, don't you let him put his pecker in you. It's a sin," she spit at me.

"Mama," I hissed with embarrassment. She was becoming unpredictable and crass of late, even for her. Ronnie was willing to stand there and take it from my parents, but I was ready to go. "Okaaaaaay. Let's go," I said, as I jammed my finger into his rock-hard chest to move him and slammed the door behind us. I felt a pang in my left nipple a moment before Ronnie yelped.

"Ow," he complained and winced as my nail dug into him harder than I intended. When Ronnie turned his back to walk down our steps, I quickly felt my breasts. They were intact, healthy, and perky as always. No pains that were my own. Interesting...

"Sorry, I was ready to go. Was that a nipple ring I felt?" Mallory told me she saw a guy with one at Lake Hartwell last summer.

"Yeah, just got it and it's a little tender," he said, rubbing his chest gingerly.

I didn't know any guys with nipple rings. Matter of fact, Mama was adept at running off most guys, and girls, for that matter, with her abrasive persona.

"Ouch, I apologize for hurting you."

"Not a problem. Make it hurt so good, baby," he cackled.

His laugh was infectious, and I giggled too. I was momentarily caught off guard when I saw Deano and his truck in front of the house. "Oh, your friend's here, too?"

"I hope that's not a big deal. My Geo is not feeling well and Deano was going to the party anyway…"

"Nah, it's cool."

"Hey, we can go get one of your friends if that would make you more comfortable," Ronnie offered sincerely.

"That's very kind of you, but I'm good," I hedged. Mallory was out of town with her father on a mission trip and there were scant few other friends I could call even if I wanted to share these boys with anybody else.

"You sure?"

"Absolutely, now let's go before my mother comes outside."

"I hear ya," Ronnie said knowingly. Apparently, Ronnie heard what my mother said about not letting him put his pecker inside of me. The thought hadn't crossed my mind until she said it. "Ready to go, Hammer?"

"I was ready to go an hour ago, muthafucker."

I giggled at the way Deano spoke to his friend. I wasn't used to that sort of camaraderie. "Hammer?"

"Oh, that's his last name."

"Cool," I said.

"You'll love Deano."

"I already do."

***

"We need to go feed the Mangler and grab some beer." Deano said, simultaneously tapping the fuel gauge and his tummy. "Then we're off to the track."

"The track? Mangler?" I questioned.

"Yeah, Greenville-Pickens Speedway. You've never been?" they asked in united astonishment.

"No, I sure haven't, and I don't have a fake I.D., so I'm not sure we can get beer."

"Don't worry about that. Ronnie knows the fella at the fillin' station."

I would come to find out that there were few people, rich or poor, young or old, white or black, that Ronnie wasn't at least acquainted with in the Upstate area. In subsequent years, I kept up with him via the internet, and he became the mayor of Greenville by a landslide victory. When I read *The Greenville News* online a few years ago and saw the article, I wasn't surprised in the least. In fact, I picked up the phone several times to call in congrats, but decided it'd just be too awkward after so long.

"Well, this is the night to go for sure. All the big boys will be there, practicing for Martinsville."

"Big boys?" I really didn't have a clue about NASCAR. It's no wonder I took up golf.

"Winston Cup. I heard that even Richard Petty is going to be there. He'll be retiring soon," Deano said.

"I thought we were going to a party?" I didn't mean to be a Debbie Downer, but it came out that way.

"Oh, we are, but this is the pre-party. Practice will be over around 9:30 and we'll head over to Washington Avenue for the bonfire. You don't mind, do you?"

"No, of course not. Didn't mean for it to sound like that."

Swoondalini

In the ten or fifteen minutes it took to get to Greenville-Pickens Speedway I felt like I knew these fellas my whole life. Only later would I realize that I just became acquainted with two of the funniest individuals I would ever meet.

"Sorry about being weird earlier, Alice, it's just that you're so hot."

"Dean!" Ronnie admonished.

I giggled. "Nice truck. The Mangler?" I asked to break the ice and change the subject. I used to do that back then, change the subject when the subject was my looks. I wanted them downplayed.

"Thanks."

"Yeah, Deano, you not gonna tell Alice about how your truck got her name?" Ronnie prompted, and then burst out laughing. "Ak, ak, ak, ka." His laugh sounded like Fire Marshall Bill from *In Living Color*.

"Hush, Ronald," Deano ordered, flushing red. "Here we are," Deano's lips turned razor thin. "You got that hogleg rolled up?"

Ronnie shushed him.

"What? Oh. Sorry again. Didn't mean to offend."

"You didn't, but what's a hogleg?"

"Well..." Deano stuttered.

"Weed," Ronnie whispered and glared at Deano.

"I'm getting quite the education tonight, aren't I?" I was beginning to feel a little embarrassed.

They were both quietly awaiting my approval.

"Well, bust out that hogleg, gentlemen."

"Yes ma'am."

The fat joint seemed to appear out of thin air and light itself.

"Here ya go. Just smoke it like a cigarette, except maybe a little slower until you get the hang of it."

I didn't want to admit that I never smoked cigarettes either, so I just took it.

"Holy shit!" Deano exclaimed. "Put it down in between your legs, Alice. Roll that window up."

"What? Oh, hell's bells!"

We all let a cop sneak up on us.

"Shh, shh, shh. He doesn't see us. Okay, keep toking."

The cop was standing right next to Deano's truck.

"See, I knew getting the windshield tinted would pay off."

"That's illegal, isn't it?"

"So is what you're holding, but it's keeping us from getting a full body cavity search. Pass it back down, babe. Then I'm going to get out and throat chop that cop." Deano followed that empty threat with a "POINGGGGG!" and a quick chop to Ronnie's throat that stopped short. It was so fast that it caught me by surprise and made me laugh so hard, my ribs started hurting.

"You ain't gonna do shit."

"He ain't got shit. Cobra strike!" Deano claimed, mimicking a snake strike with his arm. "Then I'll grab his night-stick and ram it up his ass at a medium pace."

"You okay over there, Alice?" They were responding to my choking cough and inability to catch my breath. I cried from laughing so hard. They were both looking at me strangely and with a little concern. Apparently, this kind of banter was routine for them. They could see me struggling with the pot burn. "Don't worry, baby, that's just the cheebah. We'll cool it down with some beer in a minute."

Beer? I couldn't recall ever having beer before that day. I mean, I did all that with Uncle Bobby. But that was adult me, posing as fourteen-year-old me. I wasn't worried or nervous though; just curious about new experiences outside of the bubble I was raised in. Odd that I barely knew these two but felt safe and protected.

"Alright, he's gone. Let's go find the others," Ronnie said.

"Punk got lucky I didn't have to whip out the POINGGGG on him," Deano stated flatly while giving Ronnie another pseudo throat chop.

"Stop that shit," Ronnie said, red-faced from embarrassment in front of me.

When we emerged from the Mangler, a fog chased us out. It made me start coughing all over again.

"You good, Alice?" Deano asked. "Pace yourself now, babe."

"Yeah, I'm about as fine as I've been in a long time. Am I overdressed for the race?" I suddenly worried.

"You'll see all types here, so don't worry about it."

He was right. I saw everybody from Spartanburg white trash with no teeth, to the pillars of Upstate society and everybody in between. Senator Thurmond was even in attendance. Thankfully absent was anybody from Bob Jones. This place would fall under the large sinful umbrella with movie theaters and shopping malls.

When we got to where the Berea crowd was camped out, there was plenty of beer and cheebah to go around. Everybody was so nice and down-to-earth, very low-key. I was blinded to the fact that these kids were buck wild. I was dazzled and, moreover, also high for the first time in my short life.

The introductions blazed by me. All of the girls were pretty, minus the cattiness that typically goes along with women and girls alike. All the guys, save one, were huge, minus the meathead dumbass factor that typically follows boys even into manhood. The one small guy wasn't much bigger than me, but he made up for it in personality.

I was quickly accepted. A friend of one of their friends was good enough for all. I believe all of them knew each other since kindergarten.

A haze of tobacco and weed smoke hung in the still air, marking where the cool kids viewed the event. I noticed that cops usually weren't too far away. After about an hour, I felt compelled to ask, "What's up with the cops? Should we be worried?" I whispered to Ronnie.

"Sort of, but as long as things don't get out of hand, we're usually left alone. We don't allow things to get out of hand. That's why Johnny's not allowed liquor." Ronnie pointed with his head at the small guy. Ronnie started giggling.

"What?"

"Check Deano out. Notice that as he gets drunk, he begins speaking out of the top of his head." He would also randomly yell out comments such as, "I just shit mah pants!" with such a straight face that I sometimes couldn't catch my breath. Apparently, everybody was used to him and gave it a little, "that's just Deano being Deano," chuckle in response.

Swoondalini

At that moment, Deano walked over to us. "You lovebirds doing okay over here?" Deano pointed the top of his head at me and bobbed it up and down as he spoke.

We both burst out laughing. I gently placed my hand on his arm, "Yes, Deano, thanks for asking."

"What y'all laughing at?"

"Nothin," we replied in unison.

"Damn it, am I talking out of the top of my head again?"

"Yeeeees." I was now crying again.

"Well, one of your legs is shorter than the other one." He pointed to my left leg and gave me a, "POINNNGGG! Throat chop! Can ya handle this?" He quickly shot his hands back and forth by the side of my head. Seeing this while drunk and high really messes with one's vision.

I burst out laughing again. "Sto pittt," I slurred. "What do you mean, one of my legs is shorter?" I asked, looking down at my legs.

"He means you're buzzed too," Ronnie supplied.

"Oh," I yelled back at him as what they called "testing" got under way again.

"Man, fucking Jeff Gordon is a faggot, let's go," the largest of the boys, they called Poe, yelled.

It seemed like a good idea to everybody, so we packed up. "Off to bonfire," the little guy yelled as he slapped the lit cigarette out of Deano's hand. Ashes and hot cinders went all over Deano. "Whap!"

"Damn it, Johnny!"

"That's right, I did it. You don't want none, bitch."

Chris Suddeth

***

The bonfire was amazing. It took place at a green house on Washington Avenue. It would have been a long walk, but I could have walked home to Dunean if I needed to. I was under the false impression that we had done plenty of drinking, but the bonfire was where we turned it up a notch. Ronnie advised me to chill with the beer and just smoke a little more "herb". I took his advice and allowed him to lead me to a small upstairs room that was really just a glorified attic. There he shot-gunned me, a process where one person turns a joint's lit end into their mouth and blows out into another person's mouth. Very sexual, if you ask me, and then he kissed me after removing the joint. I've only felt that weak-kneed one other time, so that ought to tell me something about Geney.

Oh, and the food they had there. I didn't realize it then, but most other college or high school parties would have a keg and some nachos, but they put out a spread. Frogmore stew (outside of Beaufort and Frogmore, SC it's called Lowcountry Boil) warmed my heart with memories of my Lowcountry family and filled my weed-fueled appetite. Marinated pork tenderloin with onions and jalapeños, called dove bites, were slow-grilled over charcoal, melted in my mouth. Ronnie came up with odd combinations of both food and drink. Had anybody else proposed pickle juice and Crown Royal, it would have sounded ludicrous, but it was actually pretty good. Years later, I would be taken back to this evening, when I read the shot list at the Ace Hotel in New York City, and noted that they had a pickle juice shot.

Swoondalini

The entire night was a blur in more ways than one. A healthy combination of country, Top-40, and rap music blasted in the house with an intimate group milling around the bonfire, smoking cigarettes. Suddenly, it was 1:30 am and Cinderella was long overdue to get home. I was having the time of my life.

"Ronnie, I hate to do this, but I've got to go. Mama is likely to be sitting up brooding after the fight she and Daddy had. I hope I can just slip in the house and go to bed."

"I understand, babe. Let me get Deano."

"Kay. I really hate to go, Shelley," I said, speaking to one of my new girlfriends who had the most beautiful bedroom eyes I ever saw.

"No worries, girl. We going to see you again?" she asked as she meaningfully looked at Ronnie. I would later find out that these two were very close, but Ronnie would never get serious about her as he considered her "too wild." Wonder what that meant?

"I have no doubt."

"Whew! Go Ronnie."

He blushed at being goaded but seemed to enjoy it at the same time. If it was up to me, I'd be hanging with this crowd any chance I got.

We then walked outside to retrieve Deano by the bonfire, and I was about to speak to Deano when Ronnie shushed me and smiled knowingly. "Listen," Ronnie whispered.

"So, Dean, if you and I went camping and you woke up the next morning sore from my big dick up your ass, would you tell anybody?" Johnny asked with a malicious smile.

"What? Fuck no, man," Deano said sternly.

"Wanna go camping then, big boy?" Johnny delivered the punch line to raucous laughter.

Deano's features blasted beet-red from embarrassment. "Funny man. Whap!" Dean turned the tables and slapped a lit cigarette out of Johnny's hand. "Cobra strike!" Laughter erupted around the campfire again at an even louder pitch. It made it even more difficult to leave the time of my life.

"Deano, let's go, bud."

"Sorry, Hammer. I've got to get home," I said. "Oh my. He's really talking out of the top of his head now," I whispered to Ronnie.

"He'll be alright," Ronnie assured.

"Hammer's just getting started. Don't worry, girl, Mangles has cruise control for times like these," Deano said confidently.

"Cruise control?"

"Yeah, auto-pilot for drunks. The Mangler always gets ya there."

I believed him briefly until we turned the wrong way on Washington Avenue.

"Deano, my house is the other way."

"I have no control over her. She wants what she wants," he responded evenly, as if the Mangler was alive and in control of herself.

"It's like we're on rails. Don't worry," Ronnie said, but I could tell he was worried about Deano scaring me. As the saying goes, we were all, "too young, dumb, and full of cum," to know any better. For a while, we drove around smoothly, obeying all traffic laws to a tee. I didn't realize Deano was actually searching for the right road until I heard him say, "Hey y'all, watch chis."

Swoondalini

The comedians were right about when a Southerner says those fateful words because something stupid was about to happen. Suddenly, the Mangler veered left with its driver's side wheels completely in the ditch.

"Deano, watch OUT!"

One mailbox, then two more, then another and another. Until finally, we took out all of the mailboxes on that street.

"Holy shit! Deano, what the FUCK?"

"The mailboxes offended the Mangler, and they had to be taken out," he responded so seriously deadpan, as if the mailboxes raped his sister. "Now you know why she's called the Mangler, girl." We stopped being scared and shocked. We were absolutely beside ourselves with laughter.

For the third time that night, I was brought to tears laughing. It would always be that way with them. By the time they dropped me off at home, I was on cloud nine.

***

"Are you aware of what time it is, young lady?" Mama said in an icy whisper from the darkened living room as I tried to slip in the house undetected.

I felt Mama's rage and uncertainty. She had always been a character, to say the least, but she went around the bend. Something snapped inside. Up until recently, Mama knew she was crazy, but used and controlled the crazy to her advantage. I sensed she was scared, even of herself. I mean, it's not like I didn't know my mama lost her shit, but to know that and to feel that are two very different things. Thank God above, I now knew how to filter the difference.

"No, Mama, I'm not sure what time it is. I forgot my watch." Although I was acutely aware of the time.

I never saw the closed fist come at me. Even if I did, I was probably too inebriated to dodge it. "Don't lie to me!"

"I'm not lying, Mama. Ouch, why did you hit me?"

"Have you been out fornicating with those boys? Letting them each have their way with you?" She roughly checked my crotch as I was trying to pick myself up off the floor. "You dirty little harlot," she said through clenched teeth.

"What?" I was punch drunk now, to top it all off. "Stop," I said, shooing her hand away from taking my pants off. "No, why would you say that?"

"I saw the way he looked at you."

"Mama, all men look at both of us that way." That was the wrong thing to say. *SLAP*. She slapped me so hard from the other direction, the entire left side of my face went numb with stinging pain.

"Don't backtalk me, girl. You're never to see that boy again."

"He's a nice boy, Mama. Would you please stop hitting me?"

"Hush, you'll wake your father."

"Good, you know he doesn't approve of you hitting me."

She grabbed my face with surprising strength for a woman of our size. "Don't you threaten me, young lady."

"I wasn't threatening you, Mama." I was pleading and crying by this point. Snot and blood were running out of my nose.

"Is that alcohol I smell?"

"No, ma'am." I lied twice in the same night to my mother. That was a first, but it wouldn't be the last. I would learn to deceive much more deftly after this.

"I can smell it. That does it. And smoke to top it off. Have you been taking pot?"

"It's smoking pot, Mama."

Again, the wrong thing to say. She wheeled me around and quickly slammed my head against the wall and held me there with her forearm. I didn't dare fight back, even if I could have by this point. She ripped my shirt's back off and pulled my pants down and began lashing my back with my own belt without mercy.

"Vengeance is mine, sayeth the Lord," were the last words I understood her to say. I don't know how long it went on for, but evidently, we were making enough noise to rouse my heavy-sleeping father.

"Jesus, Janice, what are you doing!" Daddy rushed to my rescue by grabbing the belt out of Mama's hand and easily flung her to the floor. That was the only time I ever saw my daddy lay a hand on my mama.

"She's been out whoring all over town, Jim. If you're not going to stop her, I will." She was speaking like a woman possessed now.

"Do you intend to stop her by killing her?"

I fell in a crumpled heap to the floor, trying to cover myself and lick my wounds.

"Alice, honey, are you okay?"

"Alice, honey, are you okay," Mama mocked. Spittle was running down her chin now.

"I think so," I lied. I didn't know what to think or feel.

"Go clean yourself up and go to bed. We'll talk about this in the morning."

"She won't see morning if I have anything to do with it."

Daddy focused all his attention on me, thinking that Mama would stay down where he threw her. He was wrong, and never saw the fireplace shovel that brought him to his knees with a loud crack that echoed through the mill house.

I only caught glimpses of the viciousness inside Mama over the years. I never saw it fully out in the open until I saw her land her petite foot square into his groin to take him the remainder of the way to the floor. One would have thought that she would be finished then, but she bent down to retrieve the shovel. I knew at that point that there were two things I could do: 1) Lie in the corner and play dead like I was trying to avoid a bear attack or 2) Save Daddy and probably myself from Mama killing us both.

I chose option number one and it still rips me apart to this day. I could forget many things, but I could never find a way to suppress my cowardice of that night. She turned the narrow part of the shovel to his head and hit him as hard as she could. She meant to kill him for daring to usurp her authority.

"Stop it, Mama, you'll kill him."

"You'll be joining that man you call *DADDY* in Hell soon enough, *WHORE*," Mama ranted. I would not have been surprised if her head started doing a Linda Blair.

Fortunately, a neighbor heard my pleas for help and called the cops. They got there before she was able to do any lasting physical harm to us. I became a believer in both miracles and evil that night. Despite Mama's best efforts, Daddy only had a concussion and made a full recovery. The EMT's were able to patch me up, and as a concession for attempted double-homicide, Daddy talked the deputy (a close, personal friend of his) into having Mama committed to Marshall-Pickens for a mandatory three-night stay in a padded cell. Looking back with the objectivity this journey of my soul has granted me, I don't know who was more negligent with our future, the cops for not hauling her crazy ass downtown or Daddy for talking his good ole buddy Deputy Dipshit into believing this was just an aberration in her behavior.

"Ever wonder how she got to be this way?" Nigel projected gently in to my psyche.

"No, I have not wondered how she turned in a pious, raving, fuck-tarded bitch."

"Yes, you have."

"No, I haven't."

"Yes, you mostly certainly have. You've wondered, because you've always worried about losing touch with reality. Your conception was the turning point for her. She met your daddy shortly after becoming pregnant with you and fell in love for the first time. She never forgave him for loving her back unconditionally. She bought your grandparents Jim and Tammy Faye Baker routine and actually used the Good Book to judge herself harshly and without mercy. Hence her pious, raving bitch routine. Standard operating procedure for those unwilling to let go of the resentment, regret, and rejections they experience on God's green earth."

"Whatever," I said petulantly.

Nigel volleyed back by forcing Mama's mindset on me. Her fuckedupedness was so justifiable when looked at from her point of view.

Anyway, Daddy couldn't bring himself to press charges against the "mother of his angel on earth," as long as she promised to stay up on her meds and see a therapist that Uncle Bobby recommended. "The little green devil pills," she called them.

There were no apologies or pleas for forgiveness. It was just the status quo.

***

I forgot I was in a Technicolor wonderland until Toto began to bark at me. The annoying barking served to right the ship of my spinning head from the disturbing visions that were my home life.

"Yes, dog, I know this isn't in the script. Now, shoo!"

I put my head back in my hands and bent over to lie in my lap. I wanted to wallow more in my memories, but was denied further wallowing by a warm, wet sensation. That mutt that generations found so cute was pissing down my leg. He really wasn't very happy with my departing from the script.

Now, I've never kicked a dog before, but every girl has her limits, and I reached mine.

"Better to be pissed off, than pissed on, I always say," a Munchkin said in such a chipper fashion that I became even more peeved.

Did they even say "pissed off" back in the 30's?

"Very funny, now go away," I said. I lunged at the little guy to run him off. I was in no mood...

"Is something weird going on? What was in that bong?" I heard myself say in my "stuck in a well" voice.

Swoondalini

"Just weed," Ronnie responded in an equally distant voice. The phone started to ring, and we both tried to ignore it, but it wouldn't stop ringing.

"My head is really spinning. Open a window please."

"Damn it, I need to get the phone." I heard the merciful sound of a window being thrown open as Ronnie grabbed the phone. "Pause it, baby."

I knew from experience that pausing the movie would be a pain in the ass because it would screw up the sync between the CD and the VHS tape.

I heard a loud crashing sound and looked up to find the TV had indeed been dropped from nowhere in the middle of the town square. It was no worse for wear. I got the feeling the TV liked dramatics. "Would you like to go see yourself as a couple, or would you prefer to stay here, wallow, kick puppies, and threaten Munchkinlanders?" the text read.

"That dog pissed on me," I appealed to the big black box in the middle of the *Yellow Brick Road*. Toto began to growl at me. "Never mind… I don't know what I should do. What do you think?"

"REALLY?"

"Yeah, guess you're right. I should face it."

"That's better," the TV praised.

I could feel the meaning of its text the same as if it were a person.

"How do you know I'm not a person?"

I had no answer for that one. "Fine, let's go."

"Wait one second. Look, that last memory you did of your own accord. We didn't drop that bomb on you. You did."

"I know, and your point is?"

"Nigel was right about you. You poor child, you haven't been able to see past your beauty in a long time, have you?"

I opened my mouth to answer, but the text came up rapid-fire.

"You *are* making progress, Alice. Come on and give yourself credit."

I was waiting for the punch line, for the rug to be pulled out from under ole Alice again.

"There is no punch line, girl. You are coming along nicely. Now, are you ready to step through the TV?"

"Yes ma'am," I said to the TV in a voice that sounded as if I were resigned to being sent to the principal's office.

"I CAN'T HEAR YOU!" The voice of R. Lee Ermey from *Full Metal Jacket* came from the TV's speakers.

The effect was to clean out some of the cobwebs and turn the tear faucet off. I ripped the wisecracking Munchkin's cravat off his neck to a satisfying gagging sound when it briefly choked him before releasing. I blew my nose and wiped the dog piss off my leg with the cravat while glaring at the Munchkin, daring him to challenge me. There wouldn't be any glory in kicking his ass, so I threw the cravat back at the Munchkin that mocked me and was satisfied to see it catch him square in the face. I flung the basket at Toto, but he skittered out of the way. I could feel the TV laughing as the Munchkin threw the rag onto the Yellow Brick Road in shocked disgust. Toto yelped the dog equivalent of the middle finger at me.

"Yes ma'am. I'll be right with you."

I stomped at Toto to see him scurry off and got a good chuckle before stepping through the TV. I emerged in Ronnie's living room, still wearing the Dorothy outfit. My young doppelganger did not notice me, so apparently; I would be invisible for this leg of the journey.

"You are correct," the large floor model TV texted. Gone was the sleek flat panel LCD to be replaced by a TV that Nana was probably still watching. "Hey, don't laugh, you gotta learn to blend."

"This was probably sometime right after the incident with Mama. I started dating Ronnie pretty seriously at this point." I was talking it out, remembering as I went along.

Ronnie was still talking on the phone to the other person. I believe it was Johnny, if memory serves. "Yeah, hang on, bud. Lemme ask her."

"Wow, you're doing much better. The old Alice had most of the first twenty or twenty-five years of her life blocked out," the TV complimented.

"Babe?" Ronnie called out while cupping his hand over the receiver.

"Yeah?" Both of us responded in unison.

"You want to take a road trip with the crowd?"

"Sure."

"You sure your mama's not going to mind?"

"Fuck her," I said. I developed a potty mouth when not around my mother in an effort to thumb my nose at her ways and forge my own way. Mama became the elephant in the room to my father and me. We never spoke of it, but we both had an uneasy feeling she was a ticking time bomb. Hindsight being twenty/twenty, we should have done something, but we thought that maybe if we ignored and mollified and made sure she took her 'little green devil pills' that we'd have what passed as our "normal" home-life back.

"Need me to call Rev. Randy to see if we can get in?" I heard Ronnie ask Johnny. "You already talked to him? Alright, will do. We'll meet you there in an hour," Ronnie said and hung up the phone.

"Where are we going?" young Alice asked.

I responded with a whisper a moment before Ronnie did. "Pretty Place."

"Pretty Place, up on the North Carolina/South Carolina line?"

"You sure we should go?"

"Absolutely. Last month was just a little mix-up is all. What are we doing?"

"Just going to go up and hang out with the crowd. Got a couple of girls coming down from Brevard, too."

"Deano going to visit Bud Light?"

Bud Light was our supplier.

"Yeeees," Ronnie replied with a huge smile.

"That does it. Let's go."

I now recalled that at this point in time, I spent most of my available time with Ronnie, Ronnie and his family, and/or the Berea contingent. I even began to push to transfer from Bob Jones to Berea High. Daddy was wisely discouraging this. His argument of a better education, despite the dogma, swayed me and not the fact that it would probably set Mama over the edge. The teenager in me wanted to push the issue.

"Probably wanting to redeem your perceived cowardice, while your father's life was threatened by your mother," the TV prompted.

"Perceived?" I looked at the floor, still feeling the shame twenty years later. "I was a coward that night."

"*You* were barely more than a little girl."

I knew the TV was right, but I didn't want the charity. It's amazing how forgiving we could be of others in our life, but when it came to forgiving ourselves, we could be very rigid and brutal.

"I should have grown up a little quicker."

"You were also blind-sided, drunk, and high."

"Anyway... Let's move on."

"Yes, let's," the TV texted slowly.

I didn't want to think about it anymore. I wanted to feel what it was like to be here again, to be in the last pure relationship I ever experienced, maybe the only pure relationship I ever had. Could I forge that kind of relationship with Geney?

My younger self and Ronnie were out the door and driving off in his yellow Geo Tracker before I could catch up. So, I simply willed myself to Pretty Place.

It truly was pretty. Pretty Place is an outdoor chapel at the top of the YMCA's Camp Greenville, where people booked for a year in advance two-hour slots to get married. I could see why. The only reason we were able to get in is because it was an odd day in the middle of the week.

"Good for you," I heard Pal in my head.

"You're back?" I said, astonished.

"Or did I ever really leave?"

"Riiiight..."

"Besides, I blend in a little better than a flat screen television, don't you think?"

"Absolutely. So why here?"

"You should know."

"It's the beginning of the end."

"Wrong, it's just the end of your life in your hometown."

"Followed by my downfall into the prostitution of my soul?"

"You said it, I didn't. And you're speaking as if your life is over. Why is that?"

I turned and gazed out past the altar and into the expanse of the Blue Ridge Mountains beyond and ignored Pal's question. *Shouldn't it be obvious why I was speaking that way?* But the question remained.

"That's fine. You don't have to answer now, but you will have to answer in your own time."

"I know," I whispered.

I could hear all my friends arriving outside, and I rushed up the steps to watch. I hadn't even thought about some of these faces in years. I loved most of them dearly at the time and would have gladly given my life for any of them.

"That would have been easier and would have appeared very noble, wouldn't it?" Pal said, not unkindly, but the words stung like lemon juice finding its way into a paper cut.

"Does Reverend Randy know you're bringing all your delinquent friends up here to party?" Cami asked.

"Yes, but he hopes that we'll see the *Light* shine forth from the beautiful environment," Ronnie answered in his best Baptist preacher Sunday morning sermon voice.

"You ever come across Bud Light, Deano?"

"Yeah, he had something a little interesting."

"What's that?"

"Acid."

"Hell no."

"Watch your language," Cami admonished. "You sure we should do the heavy stuff here in a chapel?"

"We'll do it on the roof," somebody shot the answer back reasonably. Why not climb up on a roof, on the side of a mountain, and trip on acid? Great idea.

"OH NO!" Ronnie said. "Last time I tripped acid at Myrtle Beach, the sand started bubbling like I was in the Redneck Riviera's version of a volcano, and I swore I never would again."

"Take the panties off," Deano taunted. "Just one more time. It's a kinder, gentler dose and it's all we have. It was either this or horse tranquilizers."

"I would have preferred the horse tranqs."

I seconded that emotion. I did not then, nor do I now, believe in the heavy drugs. (AKA drugs other than alcohol and weed.)

"Well, it's all we've got, and there's not shit to do in town with Johnny's mama on the warpath." It was Johnny's mama's rental house, which was never rented, where we had most of our bonfires. I knew all too well how it was to have a mama on the warpath.

"Hook me up, Deano," I volunteered.

"You sure about this?"

"No, but I am sure I don't want to go back home sober."

We were off and running.

We all had a really trippy time, for lack of a better way to put it, on the roof of the Fred W. Symmes chapel. Time was timeless. We were up there for ten minutes, if we were up there for ten hours.

I was lying on my back, watching tracers and brightly colored Disney characters dancing to the music I felt I could only hear. This was not to mention the stars speaking directly to my essence. I couldn't have been more at ease and secure in this very moment of time.

We were being led in the rousing party song echoing chorus by Johnny of, "Beer then liquor, beer then liquor, beer then liquor, then LSDeez..." Who knows how long we sang. The party came to an abrupt end for me when I saw 911 and our home number come across my pager. Only Ronnie and my father had this pager number, and Ronnie was obviously here with me.

"You don't really recall exactly why or how you came to leave Greenville, do you? You just remember that you had a very good reason for leaving," Pal projected my way.

I was beginning to feel sick as I viewed my younger self having the time of her life, before the rug got jerked out from under her. I allowed myself to enjoy the easy banter of good friends in their prime, with their whole lives ahead of them, until Pal brought me back to my original mission.

"No, Pal, I can't say that I recall." I projected irritation and distress all at once.

I heard my younger self say to Ronnie, "Baby, I'm sorry, but I've got to go. Look." Young Alice handed Ronnie the pager, and he shook his head quickly while concern flashed across his face. Ronnie had the unfortunate advantage of seeing our family from the outside, and it scared him.

I could feel the very fabric of my younger self's sanity begin to unravel.

"Be careful with the *shoulds* of life," Pal warned. What was she talking about? Was this a stronger dose than Deano led me to believe? Was I ever going to come down? How did I go from a wonderful, relaxing time to having a turd dumped in my punch bowl in the same minute? *How? Why?*

"You sure it's not a mistake?" Cami asked hopefully.

"No, Daddy's never done this before in the six months I've had this thing. He prefers me with all of you than home anyway. You best take me home, Ronnie."

"Alright, I'll get us back as soon as I can." Ronnie resigned himself to the party ending prematurely for the two of us. "Sorry, y'all. I'll call you tomorrow, Deano. Peace out."

I recalled Ronnie and teen me fighting all the way down the mountain. He was naturally pissed at having to leave the party, but more than that he insisted on going inside with me. I knew his presence would only aggravate my mother and whatever was going on. Besides, even though Ronnie knew my family situation, it was a far different thing for him to witness the embarrassment that was my home life. The more he wanted to escort me inside the more I dug my heels in.

I projected myself to my parents' front porch to await my and Ronnie's arrival. I looked down, and yes, I still wore the ridiculous Dorothy outfit. I huffed and tried to force out a calming breath as I recalled the harrowing ride down the mountain to Greenville. Harrowing, yes, but I remember thinking that I didn't give a shit if Ronnie drove us off of Caesar's Head and not knowing why. "Pal, please, can I change clothes?" I asked, shuddering involuntarily.

"You know you can, but it won't change what's to come," the owl said.

"I know, but I have to do something."

"I understand."

I thought that I'd like something more appropriate and was quickly outfitted in the garb of a lady that would be attending a funeral, say around the time of the War of Northern Aggression. "Oh, hell no!" This propelled me to panic. I paced my childhood home's front porch. "Sweat-shirt and jeans again, *please*," I begged and closed my eyes.

I opened them slowly to confirm my choice of attire and heard Ronnie's Geo Tracker's tires scream as he slammed the brakes in front of the house. My hands were shaking, and my younger self didn't even kiss Ronnie goodnight. I heard myself call out, "I'll call you tomorrow."

"You sure you don't want me to go in with you?"

"No, for the hundredth Goddamned time, no!" I snapped, not caring if my mother heard me take God's name in vain.

"Sorry, call me if you need me," Ronnie yelled to my younger self's back, but it fell on deaf ears as she already plowed my shoulder into the door, to walk into the last thing she expected to find.

I walked in on the heels of the teenage me to discover the scene that altered the course of my life. The walls were breathing rapidly, like a dog panting in the summer. All the memories rushed back into the perfect storm of an evening. I recalled that the acid made it feel as if thousands of little needles were sticking me in every place imaginable. My spectrum of vision altered to where color was reduced, and life was mostly black and white. More like black hole and white out.

"Hey, Alice, did you have a good time with your friends?" Mama said in a chipper manner as she looked up from her *Southern Living*. The cover picture featured a beach home on Fripp Island. Who was this person? She looked like my mother. Had my father misdialed? He had fallen asleep in his recliner as he watched an Atlanta Braves game.

"Yeah, um, Daddy called me, I think."

She went back to thumbing through her *Southern Living*, "I don't know, honey. How would he call you?"

The three of us spotted where his right arm was limp, and the cordless phone dropped on the floor. Mama picked the phone up, but we didn't take our eyes off Daddy. "Oh, that silly man must have dialed in his sleep. It's still on." Mama switched off the phone and calmly refocused on her magazine again. Our collective feet were nailed to the floor, and our eyes went to Daddy's chest. It wasn't moving. He wasn't breathing.

"Mama?"

"Yes, baby?"

She never called me baby. "Have you been taking your green pills?"

"Oh no, I've been saving them up."

"Saving them for what?" my younger self dared to ask.

"For you and your daddy, of course," she said as she flipped a page and sniffed a perfume sample. "There's some chicken pot pie on the stove and some fresh sweet tea in the fridge, if you're hungry. As a matter of fact, you look like you need to eat. It'll calm your nerves. Isn't that what you two are always telling me?"

"Mother, what have you done?"

"You and your father were so keen on me taking those pills from Satan himself, so I thought maybe you'd like to try."

I noticed a large empty bowl and a nearly empty glass of sweet tea by the remote on the table next to Daddy's limp form. We were still standing in the same place.

"Aren't you going to come in and shut the door? You're letting the A/C out. We can't afford to let the A/C out on your father's salary."

"How much did you put in the tea and pot pie?"

We both felt vomit rising up.

Mama pursed her lips and stared straight through me before responding, "Oh, 'bout a month's worth."

I stared in horror as young Alice wretched orange juice and ham sandwich all over the carpet.

"Baby, you're going to have to clean that up. You're much too old for Mama to be cleaning a little spit-up."

I wiped my mouth on my sleeve and struggled to maintain balance, much less consciousness, and asked, "How long has he been this way?"

"Oh, you know your daddy. He'd sleep through a fire alarm." Mama coolly looked at her watch. "I'd say nearly an hour."

Oh my God, he was dead. The first man I ever fell in love with was dead. I dreamed dark dreams throughout the years about this night, but thought they were just nightmares. He remained loyal to her unique from of crazy and raised her bastard child because he loved us. He kept her secret from embarrassing her at church, and she'd killed him for it.

"There's a little more to it than that," Pal stated.

"I said, shut the door, Alice," she demanded as her hand shot under the couch for Daddy's .38 Special.

I ran out the door as fast as my feet would carry me. Bless Ronnie's heart; he had been driving around the block repeatedly, to make sure I was okay. Now that I was reminded of that fateful night, I would have to thank him for going against my wishes and saving my life. He didn't see me, but I dove head first into the open back seat. *"Drive, drive, drive, for God's sake, Ronnie!"*

"Shit! What the fuck happened?" Ronnie asked as he gunned the four cylinder.

"I threw up all over Mama's floor and didn't clean it up."

***

The dawn's light woke me the next morning at Ronnie's parents' house with a horrible migraine. Ronnie's family practically took me as their own daughter since we started dating. Was what I witnessed last night real or a horrible side effect of some bad acid?

There was a soft knock at the door and Ronnie's mother entered. "Alice, honey, there's a detective here to see you."

Guess it wasn't the acid. Oh, maybe the detective is here to do a drug bust. That would be nice. "Okay, Miss Becca, I'll be right out," I said in groggy pain.

My vision was blurred due to the headache, and the tracers were threatening to upset my weak constitution. Ron Sr. plopped down some coffee for the detective and me before pouring himself a cup and taking the seat next to me.

The detective offered her condolences on the untimely death of my father and began to hammer me on the mental state of my mother. I didn't hear much after, "so sorry about your daddy, but…" I did hear Ron Sr. ask if I needed a lawyer, to which the detective replied, "That is her right, sir, but she's not a suspect. May I proceed?"

"Yes, I suppose so. Alice, your uncle Bobby is on his way up from Beaufort."

"How nice, I'd love to see him," I heard myself say, as if he were coming up for Sunday dinner.

"I understand you need to do your job, detective, but she doesn't seem up to this right now. Can you come back tomorrow?"

"I only have a few more questions. Her mother has made a full confession, such as it is…"

"What's going to happen to Janice?" I heard Miss Becca ask, but she sounded so far away.

"Hard to say, ma'am," the detective said while sucking in a thoughtful breath. "If I had to guess, I'd say she'll spend the rest of her life in the psych ward."

I heard everyone gasp as the detective speculated that I was, in effect, an orphan now. I was numb and unaffected. All I had to do was drink my coffee and forget.

I looked in the corner at the Leeman's console TV that was powered off and noticed the text, "Now, you're wondering how you ended up from here to the strip club, right?"

"Now that you mention it…"

"Let's fast forward to tonight before you go to bed. Your boyfriend made a rather bad attempt at levity," the TV texted.

I quickly found myself in Ronnie's guest bedroom, as he was putting me to bed after a long struggle, several secret shots of Jager, as Ronnie's parents were fairly conservative; several Xanax pills and Bud Light forwarded on to me with his condolences.

"What am I going to do now?" I heard myself ask for what must have been the hundredth time that day.

"Baby, I don't know what to tell you," he said, as he looked down at my chest, and it was as if a light bulb went off. "You realize you could make a ton of cash at a titty bar, right?" he asked as he cackled, hoping I would laugh. The Berea gang just got back from Johnny's bachelor party, and Ronnie talked about how impressive Twin Peaks in Columbia was.

"I didn't realize that," I mumbled.

"Sorry, I was just trying to lighten the mood a little. I know you would never do such a thing."

"No, it's okay, babe. That's a great idea."

"What? Alice, I was just kidding," he hastily said.

"I know. So was I." But I wasn't. "Ronnie, I'm really tired, so I'm going to sleep now."

"Yeah, alright, I love you. Sleep well," he said as he kissed me and turned out the lights.

"Mm hmm," I said and felt my jaw tighten. Before this moment, I could and would gladly and instinctively say I love you to the moon and back, or I love you more, or ditto, now that *Ghost* was out, but my mouth was stuck. My tongue could not communicate those words and mean them.

Suddenly, I was out in Ronnie's front yard at around one in the morning. I was facing his Geo Tracker, and beginning to wonder what I was doing here, when its engine screeched to life. My older perspective was blinded by the high beams my younger self clicked on.

"I stole my boyfriend's truck to become a stripper in Columbia due to a bad joke?" That had the makings of a good country song.

"That's the long and the short of it," Pallas responded sympathetically from the Japanese maple I helped plant in Miss Becca's flower bed.

I now recalled strained conversations with Ronnie's parents. They missed me and only wanted me to come home and be a part of their family. Can you believe that shit? I did eventually pay Ronnie back double what the Geo was worth, but that was obviously beside the point. There was no returning it after I decided to see how fast I was. I put the Geo on one of the many train tracks in Columbia and jumped out at the last possible second. The Geo did as well as our relationship after that, broken into tiny little pieces that could never be reassembled.

I just realized it was Ronnie who gave me my first Ben Franklin while stripping. That had to be the hardest thing he ever did in his young life. Ronnie even came to visit me a few times after that in D.C., as one would expect a young man in love to do, but things were never the same, and in time, he wisely left me to my own devices to save himself. His departure was cause for a celebration of my freedom. Freedom from what?

Chapter 16

"Golf is the closest game to the game we call life. You get bad breaks from good shots; you get good breaks from bad shots—but you have to play the ball where it lies."

-Bobby Jones

When I came to, I was again on the couch of my media room. Apparently, I blacked out from emotional overload again, something I was growing accustomed to.

"There she is," TV texted encouragingly.

Pal was staring at me, perched on top of TV with a concerned feel about her.

"I'm fine, but I don't think I can take much more of that," I said breathlessly.

"Yes, I believe you're done. Toast. Finished. Consider that last trip a bonus. You're welcome," the text on the screen deadpanned.

Oddly, I wanted more. I was growing accustomed to the abuse of reliving my life, or lives, as I came to know, and didn't want to stop until the job was done.

"Alice, the job will never be done."

"Never?"

"We are eternal," they both projected in unison.

"If anything, I've learned that I have amazing endurance."

"It's not about having to endure. You've now been given the tools to survive and now you must learn to thrive."

"I gotta ask. It took a team of angels for just me?"

"Angels. I like that term," Pal said, preening.

"Well?"

"When one of our own makes a mess of things, it can. But don't go feeling sorry for yourself because it happens to the best of us."

"Nigel said I had one more stop?"

"True. And before you get worried, know that you will love it."

"Really?"

"Yes, no tricks, no play on words, no double meanings, just bliss."

"Bliss, now that's something I haven't felt in a long time."

"That's something you've never felt in this particular lifetime, but blissful love is where we all hail from. It follows that if we don't know how something feels, then we can search for something until, as they say, the cows come home, and never find it even if you were swimming in an ocean of it."

"I see." But I didn't really. "What did you mean one of our own?"

"We are best described as assistants," Pal said.

"You are in training," TV stated.

"Training for what?"

"This life was, is, and will be your final Earth-bound incarnation. You have not often been beautiful or handsome in most of your other trips to the physical plane among other similar realities. In fact, your higher self shunned it as 'too easy'—"

"It's been anything but…" I said quietly.

Yes, we know, which is why we suggested you try it. You did, and then you went overboard and allowed it to distract you," Pal explained patiently.

Throw in a crazy-ass mother and it's a recipe for disaster.

"What am I being distracted from?"

"From your final life on Earth, of course."

"You mean to tell me that reincarnation does exist, and this is my last time?"

"You're really asking that after growing balls and being hunted by the Japanese for thirty-six days in 1945? And no, it may not be your last time, if you keep dawdling."

"I don't feel like I've been dawdling," I said, genuinely confused.

Hundreds of quick flashes of me smoking weed dashed across the screen. Hundreds of images of me spreading my legs while greasing my own palms flashed by. I was lazy. I was "dawdling". These images felt as if they were being ripped through my chest.

"Stop! I see your point, damn it," I said through gritted teeth.

"We're not saying you shouldn't indulge in 'wasting' time from time to time. But as the great Buddha said, 'Everything in moderation, even moderation.'"

"Alice, whether you realize it or not, you set up before you were born what was to be a challenging life on a very challenging plane of existence. Not that there's anything wrong with sucking a bong or smoking cock for a million dollars a pop, but you can do better. You're selling yourself short."

"What if I like the way things are? Will I go to Hell?"

"If you believe you will, you will. But then again, you've already been there, haven't you? People take the Bible too goddamn literally." Painful images of my life flashed on the screen, and again there was that ripping feeling in my chest.

"Good and evil, right and wrong, light and dark... It's all subjective, really. It just is. Feel me?" the TV asked.

My logical mind didn't know what she was talking about, but my heart and intuition were informing me that such was the way of things. "Yes, I feel what you mean is true," I affirmed.

"Good, you're doing better than we expected."

"Really? So, what now?"

"Change your ways."

"Not that I don't plan on changing, but what happens if I want to continue to "smoke cock" for a living?"

"Fair enough. The 'worst' that happens is that you'll feel like a failure after your sultry, big-breasted body dies. You'll then feel compelled to go back and do it again."

Slightly confused and more than a little overwhelmed, I asked, "And I wouldn't want that, would I?"

"Of course not, now get your head out of your ass."

I couldn't believe I was just dressed down by a TV with a psychic owl on top of it.

"Now what?"

"That is, and always has been up to you."

"Anything else I need to know before I turn you off to summon Nigel?"

"Yes, that you're not a failure. This is part of your learning process, too. It'll make you stronger, for want of a better way to put it. And we didn't do any of it to torture you."

"Felt like it." My voice cracked as I remembered all I was reminded of, all that I had been through.

"I'm sure it did," Pal said.

"Damn right, but I figured out along the way it was for my own good."

"We had to get your attention."

"I was pretty dense and dulled most of the time, and the rest of the time, I spent on golf and patting myself on the back for being an 'independent woman'."

"We're all connected, and there is no true independence in the sense you're talking about. Moreover, don't knock golf, girl. It's very important to you and can be very spiritual. How do you know you didn't invent the game in another lifetime?"

"Did I?" I asked, astonished and felt the history-buff in me perk up at the same time.

"That's not important—"

"How can it not be important?"

"Because in this lifetime, you are Alice, not Brandy, and definitely not somebody from the 15th century that fathered the great sport. While past lives color and influence what you are now, they must be kept in the correct perspective," Pal explained.

"I see." But I didn't really see what harm it could do if I knew that little tidbit.

"Do you?"

"Yes," I murmured.

"Nothing squeezes the juice out of life more than being right here, right now." U2 started playing in surround sound. But surround didn't completely describe completely feeling, seeing, and, yes, hearing such a powerful song.

What to do now was the question.

"Much as we'd like to keep kicking your ass across the decades, we think we've gotten through to you," TV generously offered.

"Thanks, I think. I'm going to take you up on that. I'm spent." I was proud of my progress, appreciative, and worn down all at once.

"You've earned it. And just a hint, your final stop will be different than any of the others."

"Nigel touched on that, but different how?" I was tired now, prepared to surrender.

"Nothing to worry about," Pal said reassuringly. "None of us has lied to you so far, have we?"

"That much is true," I admitted.

"There ya go then. Enjoy. You've earned it. Mash that power button," TV texted.

"You know what? No. I'm not going to mash it just yet."

"Just because you can hold your hand over a flame longer than the next guy, doesn't mean you should," Pal warned.

"I understand," I said. "TV, would you please pull up *Dallas*? Just do a search for J.R. Ewing. Thanks."

While in my hand, the remote morphed into a more traditional remote with an actual VOD (video-on-demand) button for me to mash.

Swoondalini

"Thanks, y'all."

"Not a problem. Take your time," TV texted kindly. Still odd that I could feel meaning in his words, but I suppose I shouldn't be surprised. Words have a power and energy all their own. "Again, when you're ready for Nigel, hit the power off button and he'll be here."

"Thanks again."

With that, the *Dallas* theme song permeated my pores and gave me more than my usual chills as I anticipated hanging with my favorite TV villain, J.R. Ewing. I even had a t-shirt that read, "Who Shot J.R.?" Was this the future of home theater systems? Entertainment you could feel to your core?

This was perfect. I've seen all these episodes so many times, yet never tired of them. Mindless TV was in order since my mind was toast from my travels through the decades of my existence.

I lay down gingerly on the couch, covered all but my eyes, and allowed the emotions and "new" memories to flow in and out. The sands of Iwo Jima, the links of Fripp Island's golf course, Twin Peaks and my twin peaks, Ronnie Leeman and Geney's menthol bong (among other phallic things regarding Geney), Uncle Bobby, Nigel, my daddy, my father, my looney tunes mama, my grandparents, even President Johnson and everything in between waxed and waned. I fell into deep and restful sleeps a few times. I woke up for the final time just before the most illustrious moment in TV history and watched in awestruck shucks as if it were the first time. Pal drew in closer to perch on the back of the couch and figuratively had her bottom beak hit the floor when Kristen shot J.R. (although we wouldn't find out it was Kristen until four episodes into season four.)

The third season of *Dallas* stood the test of time. Would I?

"Okay, Pal, enough of that. I'm ready to get on with it."

"Then get on with it," Pal projected. I felt she was sorry to see the end of *Dallas* and wanted to watch J.R.'s sorry ass get shot over and over again.

"Okay, here goes." I sucked in a deep breath and held it. When I mashed the power button, something unexpected happened. Nothing.

Then the music started. It was like the U2 song in that I felt the music starting at the crown of my head all the way past my hips to my toes. It resonated with my being. It was the Masters' theme song that the CBS broadcast played incessantly during the tournament, and I loved it. One thing was always certain, and that was the fact that one week out of every year, I could be counted on not to be counted on. I would disappear from everybody's radar Master's week. Wasn't so hard for me, as I just screened my business cell phone, even from the Green Jackets. Brandy wouldn't muddy the waters on this profound week, and Alice certainly wouldn't.

"A tradition unlike any other, *The Masters*," the voice of Jim Nantz proudly announced.

Going to Augusta was a tough necessity for me. I was drawn there. Sure, I had clients there, but it was more than that. The town itself sucked, not to mention its close proximity to Greenville, South Carolina, but I felt I belonged there on a soul level. Excitement grew as I considered all the possibilities that Nigel might have in store for me.

Anyway, some people thought that all the pomp and circumstance of Augusta National and the Masters amounted to little more than stroking the cock of every Green Jacket within sight. Lord knows I stroked my share. Augusta National held more true power at its core than Washington D.C.

Swoondalini

It was so much more than a professional thing there with me. Mandy and other colleagues voiced their opinion that went a little something like, "Fuck'em, if they won't let women in." Me, I fucked as many of them as I could, often without charging because they did indeed put on the greatest sporting event in the entire world right down to the pimento cheese sandwiches they charged a dollar fifty for. What most people didn't know was that the current chairman was quietly working to get the first women in. It was joked about among the membership that I would be first. In a rare moment of selflessness, I quieted the jokes. I didn't think it would be proper to have a glorified prostitute as its first female member, despite how much money I possessed.

In retrospect, I think they were just being nice, but either way, it always gave me the chills when I saw the first Jim Nantz commercial every January, featuring *the* theme song, along with the Hogan Bridge and Golden Bell in the background.

Thanks to my connections and golf abilities, that surprised all who played with me the first time, I visited Augusta more times than I could count to view the games and to play on its hallowed grounds. I always treated the place with a reverence that was uncommon for me and could never explain why until now.

Text scrolled across the screen as if in closed caption. "Go ahead and step up to the screen. Don't be skerred."

"I'm not skerred, just so excited, I'm in shock."

"Well, come on then."

"You don't have to ask twice," I said as I stood up and hustled around the coffee table.

Instantly, but with a gentler touch, TV gobbled me up into an Augusta Green vortex that deposited me softly at the entrance to Magnolia Lane. I looked behind me and was pleased to see that Washington Street and Augusta proper were a blur. They were secondary and, therefore, didn't matter. I strolled down Magnolia Lane, taking it in. This was an Augusta National on steroids. When I got to the clubhouse, I called tentatively for Nigel.

"I'm here," he answered back. His voice possessed a melodic timbre. He emerged from one of the famous trees for which the driveway approaching the old clubhouse was named.

"So, are you going to put me on the driving range, picking up balls for eternity without the protection of a cage?" I jested with a little giggle.

"No." He snickered. "However, I feel you'll like the improvements the Green Jackets effected to the range for the occasion of your visit."

"Really? I'd be great with just working the range."

"Yes, really. Why don't you have a look-see? But, if you like, we could arrange for a little unprotected range duty for you."

"No, that's quite alright." I chuckled. I couldn't stop spinning in place and looking. I didn't know which way to look, so my vision switched to 360 degrees. I experienced it once or twice during my out-of-body excursions, and it felt natural, not having to turn my head. "It's perfect," I said, tears welling up.

"I thought you would say that."

What appeared before me was not Augusta National's driving range, but my driving range that Pappy made for me, including the iron stakes representing fifty, one hundred, one-fifty, and two hundred yards. It even had the centuries old live oak, draped with Spanish moss, at exactly one hundred forty-five yards from my tee box, with the St. Helena marsh in the distance. I first started learning to shape my shots around that tree.

Swoondalini

"I smell cigar smoke," I said to Nigel.

He smiled in return.

To complete the authenticity was Pappy's 1965 Aqua Rambler where he would park it and nap. "Want to warm up on your driving range?" Nigel asked.

"Nigel, how could I have blocked so much out? Even after all I've seen, I can still think of holes in my memory..."

"It was the only defense you possessed in your arsenal, but it could only defend you for so long before it exacted its toll," Nigel explained.

"So, no water torture in Rae's Creek?"

"No, mum, only if you plunk your ball in the drink." Nigel smirked, looked down at my body and nodded for me to do the same.

I complied, fully expecting to be nude again or inhabiting some other body. But it was none of the above. I had no body. I felt a moment or two of panic. Had Nigel, and his band of misfit toys, finally killed me off this deranged sitcom of a life?

"No, you're not dead yet. You are simply a point of consciousness. Cool, isn't it?" He smiled again. It was a smile I wasn't used to seeing from him, benevolent, shimmering, and conveying approval.

"Yeah, I guess it's cool," I reluctantly agreed, as I was a little nervous about not having any body at all.

"C'mon, you're as fast as a thought in this form."

"Kay, I'll take your word for it," I said apprehensively.

He placed his arm around my figurative shoulder to steady me. "Want me to clue you in?"

"Yes, please. You would do that?"

"This is the last place you will need help, but I will provide it if you'd like." His smile switched to a smile identical to Daddy's when I would do something cute as a little kid. It endeared me to Nigel and made me miss my daddy's kind touch.

"Very well, what is it that you always say or think about this place?"

"That—that this must be what Heaven looked like, if there was such a place," I answered slowly.

"Right then, cheers," he said before he blipped out of my existence. Was he suggesting that this was Heaven?

"I'm not suggesting it," Nigel said in a funny little huff in my ear.

I always hoped that I might change my sinful ways at some point in my life, preferably five minutes before my death. Being a sinner was more fun than being a saint, or so I always forced myself to believe via being destructively adept at denial. Besides, wasn't it only an issue of perspective sometimes?

I wished fervently that Heaven had a golf course and it would only follow that that golf course would be Augusta National. I mean, it was like stepping into a painting, even on the property's worst days. Last year, I was there when it snowed. Odd-looking, like snow on the beach. A strange, silent beauty all its own.

Could this be Heaven? Not everybody liked golf or what Augusta represented, for that matter. Perhaps it was only my version of Heaven? Whatever it was, it was time to explore. The sounds of this place were almost more important than the azaleas and the perfect grass. At some points, I swear that I could actually hear the vivid colors and see the sounds. It was intense and intoxicating. I could feel the profound silence, but the energy of the Augusta

Swoondalini

Sunday Back Nine's expectant roar was just beyond perception. One only had to still themselves to feel the Big Three navigating around Amen Corner. However, I appeared to be alone.

Time to walk or float around or whatever it was I was supposed to do here. Suddenly, I felt the urge to play. Instantly, I was at the number one tee box, and my body was back, dressed in my favorite spring golf outfit.

Gene Sarazen made my tee time official and announced me to a crowd that only he could see. "Fore, please. Miss Alice, to tee off," he announced in regal, old-world tones. He kindly shook and kissed my hand, then wished me luck on my round. He even said my real name, even though Brandy was the only name they knew in Augusta. "Greens are at tournament speed, Miss Alice," he offered kindly.

"Thanks, Mr. Sarazen. I will be careful not to fire at every pin," I said through a permagrin smile.

Mr. Sarazen, the 1935 Masters winner via the "shot heard around the world," with his albatross on #15, faded away into the sound of Augusta patrons. I then began my first round of golf in green Heaven. This was the Augusta unlike any other. Even though the real thing seemed other-worldly, gone were the annoying reminders that one was on the planet Earth. The pollen, buzzing insects, and bad weather were voted down by the great Augusta National Board of Trustees in the sky. I found that the temperature hovered around seventy degrees with a pleasant breeze.

The layout and the landmarks were the same. Hard to imagine, but the grass was brighter and more uniform. When I took a divot, the grass grew back before my eyes. When one got close to the azaleas, they sang a soft lullaby. Other times, I heard Huey Lewis and the News harmonizing acapella.

The challenge of golf was still intact. I would have been disappointed if slices, hooks, chunks, and thins were left behind. I was so distracted by the majesty of the place that I played poorly on the front nine.

As I made the turn, I was determined to play better, but refused to sacrifice better play at the cost of ignoring my surroundings. Before hitting, I noticed an older gentleman waving to me from the lawn of the Eisenhower Cabin. He wanted me to hold up for him. I guess I was getting a playing partner for the back nine. I waved him over, and it was, in fact, President Eisenhower. It was Ike! My mouth dropped open. I always enjoyed reading the history of his life. He flashed his famous charismatic grin at me and offered his hand. "You're not the only one to make this their Heaven, you know."

"No, I suppose not," I said as I took his hand and stared at him, starstruck.

"Mind if I join you for the back nine?"

My mouth dropped open further. His smile widened when I still held his hand after an embarrassingly long time. "I'd be honored to have you join me, Mr. President." I followed that with a poor approximation of a curtsy in my skort.

"Oh please, none of that here. Call me Ike, Miss?"

"Call me Alice, then."

"Alice, very nice to make your acquaintance."

"Nice to meet you, Ike," I said with stars still in my eyes.

"Ladies first, Alice." He motioned grandly to the forward lady's tee box.

"Oh no, Ike, I'll play from your tees, thanks." I threw a tee in the air, and it landed pointing toward Ike. "Your tee box then."

"Oh, no, ma'am."

Swoondalini

"You'd better take it. You may not get it back."

He chuckled and gave a salute. "Yes, ma'am."

We walked and talked the back nine, conversing about every subject from politics to recipes. Amen Corner did do him in. By the time we finished sixteen, I was two holes up on him. I pegged the tee in the ground on number seventeen and looked down the fairway to see one noted difference.

"Mr. President!" I scolded.

"Well, Alice, this is my heaven, too, so you can't expect me to have left that damned tree there, can you?" He covered his mouth in embarrassment. "Excuse my language, ma'am."

I laughed a belly laugh not felt in so long, probably since Greenville with Ronnie. "You may swear all you like, Ike, and it won't bother me one bit. I have always hated that *damned* tree, too."

"I knew I liked you the first moment I laid eyes on you, my dear," Ike said. He swung for the fences, and his drive crept toward the top of the hill. It went right through the spot where the famous Eisenhower Tree grows on Earth.

"Nice ball."

I teed the ball for a low hook, swung out, and held my hips off. My ball rocketed up the right side of the fairway and drew to end up fifteen yards ahead of Ike.

"Show-off!" He grinned and flicked his Lucky Strike to the side. It disappeared in a slightly more magical way, but still very similar to the real Augusta National.

I giggled. "Thanks. So how long have you been here?"

"Not sure. Doesn't really matter," he said as he shrugged. "When did I die? You just came from there, so you tell me."

"You can tell I just came from the physical world? Am I still alive? Nigel tells me I am, but I'd like to hear it from somebody else. If I'm still alive, how am I here talking to a dead President? I have plenty of dead Presidents in the bank." I hit Ike rapid-fire. Even I sounded a little crazy to myself.

Ike arched his eyebrow and projected, "It's okay."

I felt it was okay, and instantly my emotions calmed. But the question still remained.

"I'm not concerned with time," Ike said, matter-of-factly. When he could see his answer didn't satisfy my curiosity, he went on to explain, "Time is only used there and has very little meaning here. It's more of a tool for learning, like children playing with numbered or lettered blocks."

"That's nice," I said quietly, thinking of the implications of man's number one enemy: time, being little more than a child's training wheels.

"No, it just is." I heard that before.

"General, you are away."

"My, you are a sassy lady."

"I know." I couldn't believe one of the most powerful and influential men to ever inhabit the Earth just called me a lady. I could earn, and get used to, not having "of the night" attached to it. He hit his shot short of the green.

"Damn it!" His happy face didn't match his tone.

Another question occurred to me. "So, I guess you've been here over fifty years then?"

"Guess so." He sounded mildly interested.

"So, do you ever want to leave?"

"From time to time, I do. Other parts of me are incarnated as we speak. But since this incarnation led such a full and stressful life, I'm content to stay where I was most content in life. Make sense?"

"Absolutely. So, this is not everybody's version of Heaven?"

"No, but it is popular, as you may imagine. Life is no different here than on Earth, or any other plane of existence, though."

"Really? How so?"

"It is what you make out of it. Things are just more reactive here."

We played the remainder of the round in silent contemplation, and before long, we putted out on number eighteen, and Ike was shaking my hand.

"It's been a pleasure, Ike."

Again, with that broad, charming, trademark grin that decided the fate of millions in his lifetime, he said, "For me as well, young lady, although I can see that your soul is an ancient soul."

"Really?"

"Yep," he said as he motioned around my aura with his hands and lit another Lucky Strike.

I neglected to notice my aura until Ike pointed it out. I then took note of the yellowish haze surrounding him. "Geney did mention a purplish haze…"

"Well, again, I enjoyed our time together. You should listen to this girl, Geney."

"Oh no, it's a guy." I giggled.

"Whatever, just do yourself a favor and make sure you commune with the azaleas down in Amen Corner before you leave."

"Yes, sir," I said, saluting him. My Marine Corps incarnation gently asserted himself as I stood ramrod straight.

He returned my salute and said, "See you in forty or fifty years, Alice."

"Kay," I said, and I was still waving at him when he shut the door to his cabin.

I watched my arm gradually disappear along with the rest of my body. I was again a point of consciousness. Strange thing was that I didn't feel strange at all, and it didn't disturb me in the least. I merely found it curious, and it felt as natural as breathing in and out, natural as eating when I was hungry or sleeping when I was tired.

With that in mind, I decided to float slowly down to Amen Corner, enjoying everything along the way. I was determined to take my time, even though this experience taught me time doesn't really exist in a strict sense, other than as a tool. It was a torturous, and often times, brutal illusion. But somehow, it made sense and felt right. I could easily wrap my mind around the concept.

As I neared the lowest point on the property, christened Amen Corner by writer Herbert Warren Wind in 1958, I allowed the grounds to soak into my soul rather than before, or when I played on the "real" golf course. But it was always here. The greens were greener. The browns browner. The white marble sand traps whiter. The pine trees, minus the Eisenhower Tree, were grander. And finally, the flowers richer, deeper, more vibrant, more fragrant, and thicker.

I was standing on thirteen's fairway, listening to the melodic trickle of Rae's Creek, lost in realization, when the breeze died down. Was the breeze ever there, or was it just a prop? I suppose I could have asked if Earth was really a prop, too, but that would just be too much to contemplate. We distracted ourselves from living our lives by trying to figure everything out.

Swoondalini

In the stillness, I began to hear tinkling whispers, like hearing a baby's laugh in a distant part of a big home. It dawned on me that it was the azaleas. I could hear them, no, feel them, now that I allowed myself to listen. Was this the secret of life? Could it be so obvious?

"It just is," tinkled the baby's high-pitched giggle. I drew closer to the melodic chorus of efflorescence. I then merged with Mother Nature herself. Became her and she became me. We all came from the same place. The same Source. The same Creator. The Same.

It's unimportant as to the hours, days, weeks, months, or seconds I spent communing. Does it matter? I suppose not. What did I learn? Nothing much, only the secret to life, and the fact that it wasn't a secret, so much as it was just hidden in plain sight. I was only reminded to emulate what the flowers and animals are telling us daily on Earth. "NOW!"

I do know that I've never felt so at peace in my life and couldn't get enough of that baby's laugh tickling my soul. Funny thing was that I never felt a matronly instinct in my life. This was mostly due to the fact that I lacked much positive influence from the mother figures in my own life, but I still made the choices and lived the life. I knew that physical damage, incurred in the line of duty, took my ability to have children. Up until now, I felt it a blessing to my professional life. It would help me maintain my pristine size and leave me unencumbered.

Now, I began to ask, was it really a blessing? Alas, it just was, or is, or will be.

Also, on my increasing list of revelations while reliving and revisiting my burning bush was how we're weighed down by the three R's: resentment, rejection, and regret. Put that in your pipe and smoke it. You'll be guaranteed to choke.

These realizations gently began to pull me away from the enchanted flowers. It was difficult to leave the womb, but not excruciating. I had an open invitation to return, and part of me would never leave, and never left. There was no sense of urgency, but I knew my time here was coming to an end. Most souls currently incarnated couldn't, or wouldn't, come here, and even if they did make it here, they probably wouldn't remember it. Would I remember it? For this eye-opening experience, I'll spend a lifetime in gratitude.

I bid my friends in Amen Corner a warm farewell and set out to float around the property for one final glimpse of glory. Glorious it was, but it wasn't my time to be here and, therefore, it was my time to go, at a leisurely pace, of course.

***

After one final inspection of the Augusta National in the sky, including a bucket of balls on "my" driving range, I was drawn to the Champions Locker Room. Oh my, the memories in that place. I was a popular girl around there. I'm merely stating facts of this in hindsight and am no longer proud of my exploits.

I was pulled, no, compelled, to go to the showers. As I neared there, the compulsion became stronger. This must be what it's like as one approached the precipice of Niagara Falls. The sound was deafening, yet soothing, all at once. Initially, the showers appeared as a large blooming lotus. It was as inviting to me as if I was a worker bee robbing it of pollen to produce nectar. A thousand petals began to drop away as a warm, bright light, brighter than a thousand combined suns, yet gentle and beckoning, asserted itself. My body reappeared, transparent at first, then opaque, and finally solidified as I walked in. I could feel my own weight return.

A thought occurred to me and was confirmed by a gentle whisper from Nigel that this was what it was like being born, and it truly felt like I was going into the birth canal. I would find that being born was an event that was a larger shock to the system than dying, an event I experienced more times than I could, or should, count. However, I wasn't alone, was never alone, for even a split second of life, or death, or birth. I was supported by unconditional love each and every time.

Chapter 17

REBIRTH

If I thought Iwo was a shock to the system, boy, did I have another think coming when my essence zipped back to my body in the shower cave. I was momentarily disoriented but was quickly and painfully brought to full awareness as I tried in vain to move. Fortunately, due to my hot water on demand system, the hot water still flowed all over me. That's where my luck ended.

If one looked down on my body, it would appear like a corpse that had fallen from a high place. Sore wouldn't begin to describe my discomfort. My right arm was completely under the weight of my torso. My left arm was wrenched behind me as if somebody was twisting my arm. Somehow, my right leg was jammed up under my hips, and my left leg was the only appendage that was straight. One of the shower heads was blasting down upon my head and plastered my hair in my eyes. My hair and the steam effectively made visibility nil. I didn't have to see to know *he* was there.

I obviously hadn't moved in quite some time. I gingerly moved my left leg and was rewarded with pain. How long? I guess time made a difference now...

A constant groan emanated from deep inside and with a grunt or two, I managed to lift my head off the shower floor. I caught the stream of water up my nose and began to choke. In a plucky move, I decided to rip the band-aid off and pushed against the wall with my left leg to roll my body over. The pain was exquisite as blood pounded back to my starved extremities. It felt as if a million little men had a million hot poker needles jamming and ramming, twisting and turning in me at the same time.

As the pain began to subside into an acute ache, I opened my eyes again and swiped the hair out of my face. That small move brought pain again, and I sprawled out and thought I was going to start crying like a little girl who skinned her knee.

I opened my eyes again, when I could, and saw an opaque Nigel having a good hearty laugh at my expense. "Goddamn it, it hurts! How long have I been here?" I said with fury I didn't feel. He could have dropped me back in my body near the moment I left, but I figured he dropped me back at least a couple of hours after I passed out, probably more, knowing Nigel. I started laughing with him and that was painful too.

Nigel vanished into the steam with a swipe of his arm indicating he couldn't take it any longer. I wondered if I would ever see the suave devil again.

Time to take stock of the situation: The all-important boobs that weren't so all-important any longer? Check! No penis? Check!! Vajayjay intact? Check!!!

"Owww…" I moaned as I rolled to a sitting position and flopped over with a thud in the water. Apparently, my right leg wasn't prepared for that yet.

"Water?" I rasped, in the realization that I was dehydrated. Without careful consideration, I lunged up to turn off the hot water, so I could drink. "Whew! Holy shit!" I was startled and surprised at how refreshing the cold water felt, temporarily, at least. I lapped water like a dog for several minutes and switched back over to the hot water.

"Here goes. Standing position!" I did my best impersonation of a drill sergeant. "Standing position, *sir*," I said through gritted teeth. I achieved a half-standing position, as I stood like the Hunchback of Notre Dame for several minutes. Why was I talking to myself? This took out-of-body experiences to the next level.

I turned the water off and limped out of my shower cave and shrugged my terry cloth robe on. Then the basic questions started occurring to me: What time is it? What day is it? Perhaps I should ask who the President is. When did I last eat? I was ravenous.

I picked up my cell to order pizza as I peeked outside and noticed that the sun was going down. I had the local pizza joint on speed dial in the number one position. I held the button down. "Yes, Brandy? You want the usual, ma'am? Brandy?"

It took me a beat to recall who Brandy was. My voice hadn't been used in a while, and it screeched. "Yeah, Marty," I whispered. "My usual, please."

"You don't sound well. You okay?"

"Yeah, just tired."

"Um... we're a bit backed up here. Could be a while..." Marty qualified and waited for my answer.

Feeling sleepy again, I surprised myself by agreeing. "Take your time, babe. I'm here, but if I don't answer the door, I've fallen asleep. Tell Toni to let herself in. She knows where the spare key is."

"Cool. Out."

"Out," I whispered as I flopped face first, still wet and robe open, into a dreamless, THANK GOD, sleep.

I awoke to Toni the pizza girl whispering, "Brandy, you ordered some pizza, didn't you?" I did convey that she should let herself in, didn't I? Toni witnessed some crazy shit over the years.

"What? It's Alice."

"No, you know my name's Toni."

"No, I mean—never mind," I said in a confused voice muffled by being face first on the bed. I didn't know where I was, a feeling I became accustomed to long ago in my line of work. It took me a second to get my bearings, and then I felt the concerned eyes of Toni upon me. I tried to get up quickly and paid for it, "Owww! Shit!" I tried to rub the kink out of my neck.

"Holy shit! What happened to you? You look like you've been in a fight." Her voice was full of astonished worry. "Do you need me to take you to the doctor?"

"*No*," I said quickly. I realized I probably looked horrible. "If you only knew," was the only response I came up with. Fighting for my soul was more like it.

I twisted my body around slowly to stretch it out. I looked up to see Toni's pierced, furrowed brow starring back at me. My neck didn't seem to want to turn at this moment. Toni's eyes shot down my body in a lascivious look that you could tell she regretted due to my condition. I didn't dare make any sudden movements to close my robe. Toni always had a crush on me... Poor thang. I certainly wasn't attracted to women, especially the butchy kind, and they better be one rich butch. I usually charged twice my normal rate.

"Do you mind?" Toni prompted.

I was still slow on the uptake. "Oh yeah, you know where I keep the bong and stash. Help yourself. Lemme get you some cash for the pizza," I said.

I was starting to come around and feel more alert. I stood, and my right leg nearly gave way in the process that shot a sharp jolt up my spine, as my neck and right shoulder caught. Toni naturally reached out to help me. I struggled to keep from laughing and had no trouble making my smile look like a grimace.

"You'll have to read the book," I responded to her unasked question. "Now, as long as you're here, take me to the pizza please, babe."

"O...kaaay," Toni said and put her arm under my shoulder.

My BAD shoulder. "Ahhh." I winced. "Easy, Toni. It's just tight."

"Over on the couch?"

"Yes, ma'am. Sounds good."

Toni looked at me strangely for my politeness. Was I just an arrogant ass all the time? "Can I get you anything else?" She couldn't mask her disappointment as I cinched my robe closed.

I ignored it with a smile. "Yeah, actually, some water. Bring the Brita pitcher over here, a plate, paper towel, and my cell phone, since you were kind enough to ask. Open the drawer on the far right, and there should be some money for you."

"Only a fifty."

"That's fine, keep it. Am I your last stop?"

"No, actually my first."

This came as good news since Toni can be a talker, and I needed to eat, process, and figure out what to do next.

I'm not typically a fast eater, but I finished a slice in the short time it took for her to return. How long was I out if I was this hungry and this thirsty?

"What did happen?"

"Don't know much, honey." I found myself turning my home state accent on as if there was a spigot spewing forth from my mouth. Why was that?

"Miss Brandy, you won't mind if I take a couple of bong rips, do yew?" she replied in an overblown Southern accent that Yankees find so funny, and think they do so well. Even the best actors tended to overcook a Southern accent.

Normally, I'd find that funny, but I was not in a funny mood, nor was I crazy about weed right now after spending countless days doing nothing but bong rips. But it was in the spirit of, anything so you can hurry up and get the hell out of my matted hair...

"Absolutely. I already said you could help yourself," I said with a full mouth, finishing my second slice.

"Damn, slow down. I'm not going to steal the pizza from you," Toni said, pouring me a glass of water.

I lurched at the water awkwardly, ignoring the shooting pain in my shoulder, and gulped down most of the large glass. I felt her worried eyes on me again, so I threw my best weed sack over to her as a means of distraction.

Admiring the blue hairs and fine crystals, then taking a long, savoring sniff, she asked, "Is this what I think it is?" She held up the sack.

"Yep, you've wanted to try it for some time now. The bag is your tip. Geney just finished that crop." Toni was one of Eugene's top distributors. "Be careful to only take one hit if you're going to go back to work. It is guaranteed to rock your world."

"So, I've heard. Are you...?" She was interrupted by the *Friday* ring tone on her cell. She saw the number and disappointment cut across her features. Thank God! I needed to be alone with my pizza. Half-eaten pizza! I really should slow down before I made myself sick. Toni opened her cell phone in a huff. "Yes sir. I'm on my way back right now, Marty. Tons of traffic around the Beltway.

Can't talk." She clapped her phone shut before Marty could respond. "Well, I hate to rip and run..." Her tone indicated that she really wanted to hang out.

"I understand." It was all I could do to conceal my relief that she was leaving. "But take it easy with that if you're going to be driving. You'll be at the North Carolina line before you know what's happened." I raised my voice to be heard over the bong gurgling.

"Gotcha. Well, I'm off."

Thank God. "Be careful."

"Thanks." She held up the bag and the fifty spot, indicating her gratitude.

"Don't mention it." I could tell she was concerned about my questionable condition as I winced again, stretching my leg out on the coffee table. "I'll be fine. Off ya go. Skedaddle," I preempted.

"Alright, call me if you need me."

She slammed the door as I said, "Thanks."

I breathed a sigh of relief that didn't last long. My stomach began to knot up, which could be due to consuming all but one slice of pepperoni and mushroom pizza. Could be, but I knew better. I knew it was due to what I was about to do.

I grabbed my cell phone and called Uncle Bobby's house phone I still knew by heart. On the second ring, "Hello," answered tentatively. I could hear a bunch of pots and pans in the background clanking in anticipation of Thanksgiving dinner. I was silent for a moment. Now that I called, I didn't know where to begin. That regret part of the three R's was showing its ugly head. I was glad I could still do something about it.

"Is that you, Alice?"

"Mm hmm." I couldn't speak as the emotions coiled around my vocal cords. I didn't realize I missed him until I heard his familiar voice. The voice that sounded just like Daddy's with a dash of effeminate. "Uncle Bobby, when did you get caller ID?"

"People change, Alice—"

"Who is it, Bobby?" Nana asked. It filled my heart with joy to hear her voice in the background. Unfortunately, it also filled my heart with regret at all the years I missed.

My uncle Bobby always shunned technology and I pictured him speaking to me on the same rotary phone that was in his kitchen, when I was last there as a child. His voice sounded like what water must taste like to a woman dying of thirst. "Alice, what are you doing, baby? Mama, it's Alice."

"What? Dallas? We don't know anybody from Dallas."

Bless my grandmother. She never could hear, even in her younger days. Some sort of thing happened with her eardrums when she was a teenager. The sound of her voice was bringing tears to my eyes.

"ALICE, Mama. Your long-lost granddaughter," he yelled at her so loudly without cupping his hand over the receiver. It made me hold the phone away from my ear.

"Oh, Alice. Bless her heart. I sure would love to see her. Pray for her all the time," I heard my nana yell and drop another pan.

"Are you alright, Alice?" He could hear me sniffling.

"No, but I will be," I said with conviction. "So, I was just calling to wish you a Happy Thanksgiving."

"Well, Happy Thanksgiving to you, too, but we haven't heard very much from you lately."

Oddly, I kept in touch with Mama, but kept the side of the family that was more balanced and capable of unconditional love minus the manipulations and delusions at arm's length with occasional phone calls. Rejection made one do strange things.

"Yeah, I know," I said quietly. "Umm, so I was wondering if you had a place for me at the Thanksgiving table?"

"Always one saved for you," he said without hesitation.

"Great. I'll leave right now."

"You've had an epiphany, haven't you? I've been having dreams about you, strange dreams."

"That doesn't surprise me in the least."

"Alice, I don't care why you're coming, I'm just glad you're coming."

"I love you, Uncle Bobby, and tell Nana I love her too," I blurted out and hung up before I completely lost control of my emotions. I heard him shout to Nana that, "Alice is coming to Thanksgiving."

She replied, "Well, now, that's just grand," before I disconnected.

***

For the second time in as many days, I looked every bit the crazy woman as I limped out the door of my town home with uneven wet hair and still wearing my terry cloth robe. Driving ten hours in this shape didn't excite me, but the destination did. I needed to make my way back to my condo, so I could pack, put on some real clothes, and switch vehicles.

"Holy shit! I'm going to South Carolina," I said breathlessly, as I pulled into the parking garage of my luxury condo complex.

I wiped my tears and nose on the sleeve of my robe. I gathered my thoughts and realized that I hadn't been back to South Carolina since I left Columbia. I didn't really count going into that shithole, Aiken, sometimes when I visited Augusta. The prospect of returning to my home state threatened to bring all the pizza back up, and I instinctively reached for the roach in the ashtray.

"NO, I can't be doing that now," I whispered and recoiled my arm. Even though I was very functional while high, packing a bag was not among the things I could do, even on my best days. I'd end up with no underwear, fourteen pairs of socks, no shoes, ten pairs of pants, one shirt, no toiletries, and plenty of sweaters for a two-day trip to Miami. Once, I packed all formal wear for an out of town golf tournament and forgot my clubs.

All that aside, I felt that there was more than just my inability to pack as to why I was reluctant to toke, but I packed my little bat and dugout just the same. Old habits die hard, and I didn't want to be without my crutch. The adrenaline and excitement of a road trip plus some stretching was easing the tension both mentally and physically.

I packed a little bit of everything, as I didn't know how long I'd be staying, not to mention that in South Carolina for Thanksgiving, it could be eighty degrees or thirty degrees. I attempted to pack conservative attire, but my looks often made conservative look like a naughty librarian if I wasn't careful.

"Alright," I said to my icepack as I grabbed my keys to the Escalade and hit the lights as I limped out the door. Ten minutes later, I was on I-95 South and snarled in typical D.C. traffic that was exacerbated by Thanksgiving. Normally, I would curse having to be in this traffic with the rest of the common riff-raff of the world, but today, I didn't care. I was going *home.*

I called Uncle Bobby again while I was stuck in traffic to ask if there was anything else I needed to bring. As expected, the answer was a definite, "Hell no, there'll be plenty of food, too much, in fact. You just bring your sweet little ass home."

"Yes, sir."

"You going to be alright, driving all night?"

"Yeah, I'm definitely well-rested. Once I get out of the Beltway traffic, and it gets later in the evening, it'll probably be safer this late in the game."

"Well, you've got a point there. I know you can take care of yourself; you've proven that, but are you packing?"

"Always, Uncle Bobby," I said in mock exasperation. I needed to remind myself that I just saw and spent several days with him, but as far as he was concerned, we were practically incommunicado since the mid-90's. All that aside, it was nice to have a father figure tell me what to do.

"Alice, not that I'm not glad you're coming—"

I interrupted, "But what prompted me gracing you with my presence after all this time?"

"Yeah, something like that."

"The full story can wait for your porch, beach music, and some beer, but for now, let's just say, I've seen the light."

"Good enough. Alright then, be careful."

"Will do. It looks like traffic is moving..." It was barely moving, but I really just wanted to hang up before we got too deep.

"Alright, see you in the morning." Taking my cue, Bobby hung up quickly.

One more phone call to make. Geney should be back in our mutual home territory of the Upstate of South Carolina with his family by now.

"Geney."

"Yo."

"Guess what?"

"Chicken butt. I dunno. Listen, I'm in the middle of World War fucking three with my father, soooo…"

"I'm coming back to South Carolina for Thanksgiving."

"Huh?"

"I'm headed back to South Carolina."

"Really? Wow, I didn't think you were ever coming back, other than driving through it to get somewhere."

I could tell his patience was thin, and I knew I wasn't his favorite person since I ran off any female who tried to pee on his tree, so I cut to the chase. "Don't know how to ask, so I'll come right out with it…"

"Okay," he said tentatively.

"Have you had any strange dreams?" I also wanted to ask if he brought that Juanita girl home with him for T-day, but that was definitely none of my business at this point.

"Yeah, I'm living a fucking nightmare right now. I'm hiding in my wrecked Ventura and smoking a little herb before I go back to face a house full of loud Italians. To top it off, the parents are harping on me to go to Mass, so I'll feel more 'grateful.' Happy Goddamn Gobble Day."

Swoondalini

I laughed at his statement and tone. The mention of "gobble" reminded me that it was Ronnie who I first saw put his nutsack through his zipper and make turkey calls. Hilarious…

"What's with you? You sound giddy," Geney pointed out.

"Sorry I asked. Yeah, I guess I am a little giddy. Anyway, I thought you fixed the Ventura?"

To say that Eugene was a car expert was an understatement. Weed wasn't the only thing he had a knack for. At twenty-one, he was qualified to judge classic Ferraris in major car shows across the country. He was also one hell of a driver and taught me a few tricks. As payback for the aforementioned blue balls and scathing, he scared the shit out of me on a mountain road. Geney even had this little trick where he'd do a double finger-snap as he drifted around a turn.

Inspiration for his law career began with a desire to search for antique cars that were lost in much the same way as Rembrandts that were stolen from Jews during World War II. It was an obscure, but lucrative, subsection of law technically called civil litigation that specialized in antiquities and archival matters. Why he had to be a lawyer for that? I don't know. He explained it me, but he also made my head spin in more ways than one.

I probably shouldn't have asked about the Ventura. It was often a sore point with him. "Well, ya know, my fucking dad backed it into a mailbox, going about sixty in the snow. He's been bitching at me about the bald tires on it. I told him not to drive it until I got back because tires were the last thing I needed to complete the restoration. But no, hell fucking no, it's my fault I didn't warn him. I specifically took him out to the goddamn barn and pointed at the fucking tires and said, 'Just crank the car every few weeks because the muthafuckin tires are shot.' I even left him some money to get tires if he wanted to drive it. That money went into buying a new top for his shitbox Z3 four cylinder."

"Sorry to hear that, Geney."

But I took delight out of the relationship he and his father had. It was a sick pleasure for me, but truly, I'd give anything to have a relationship with a father figure. Never knew I needed one until my...

"Why are you coming back anyway?"

"I can't get into that right now. What I did want to talk to you about was our relationship."

"Relationship?" The way he said it back to me made me think he heard me say, "dead puppies," rather than us...

"I've been shitty to you and you're really one of my only friends."

"Oh, okay." He sounded relieved. Was I really that bad? I guess looks could only get you so far. I chose to table the conversation, for now... At least until I could get him face to tits. No! Bad Alice! Only Brandy operated that way.

"Say, listen, as long as I have you on the phone. About your dreams---" At that time, I heard Eugene's father start yelling in the background. Apparently, he found Geney.

"I'm on the phone, Dad."

"What?"

"PHONE! I'm on the Goddamned phone!" he yelled to his father. "Sorry, I didn't hear a word you said. So, you're on your way to Greenville then?"

"Not coming to Greenville but headed to Beaufort. The Lowcountry is the best place for me to start out."

"Gotcha." His voice was questioning, and it was doubtful he heard me.

Swoondalini

"Wanna meet me down in Beaufort?" I couldn't believe I just blurted that out. I knew I sounded desperate, so if I spoke faster, it may not sound so bad. I looked over to my passenger seat and saw the real estate essay about oyster stew; of all things, peeking out of my purse. "I'm going to look at real estate and spend time with the family, if they'll have me." He still hadn't answered my original question, and I chose to let it go due to his mood. "I'll call you in a few days to explain. By the way, is your brother bringing his wife and his girlfriend this year?" His family stories killed me. My own family stories were more painful than funny...

"Yep, and they're fixing a *pot* pie again. They noticed it quiets Dad down. You okay?"

"Guess I should get used to that question." I was glad to hear him ask it though.

"What? He's fucking yelling again. I gotta go."

"Nothing. Yeah, I'm fine for now. I'll call you later." I winced as my back caught. It'd probably take a few days to get over my shower experience physically. Emotionally and spiritually, I hoped I never fully got over the shower.

When I placed my cell in the console, I took stock and discovered I didn't have anybody else to call other than client "friends." Did that really count? Should I call Mandy to let her know where I was going? It was definitely too late to call Senator Sam. Although I truly liked many of my clients, I couldn't, nor should I, count them among friends and family. The cold hard facts depressed my mood, but I decided to shake it off with some music. First up was *Going Back to Cali*. I was fortunate enough to meet Biggie on a few occasions before his demise. I had a tendency to believe that there were only three rap artists, two of which were dead. I didn't see them at that great golf course in the sky, but would I have seen them and known them there? Tupac, Notorious B.I.G, and Snoop Dog made my music rotation for the first few hours of my trip until I decided to switch gears to the likes of Billie Holiday, Dinah Washington, and Frank Sinatra.

As the trip wore past midnight and the South Carolina line was fast approaching, I chose to vent the sunroof and listen to the wind instead. The cool night air kept me alert as I grew bleary-eyed at I-95's count-down of mile markers.

One would think that South Carolina being imminent would have made me extremely nervous. Curiously, that wasn't the case. I suppose my lack of nerves could be an indicator that I was doing the right thing. I looked back over at the essay on oyster stew and thought for several monotonous miles about buying property. I could have written it off as just passing the time, but it was more than that. Truthfully, I didn't know what to think, and maybe that was a good thing.

I was mostly excited at seeing my remaining family. My lungs noted the acceleration of my secret vice of menthol cigarettes. I looked at my dwindling pack and decided to smoke away, because after this Thanksgiving weekend, I would be leaving this naughty habit in the dust. "I'll always love you," I spoke to the menthols in a mock break-up speech. "It's not you, it's me, but we'll always be friends. But I did love you," I replied as if the cigarettes were speaking back to me. "And I do love you. I'm just not in love with you anymore." The road must have been getting to me. But it was true. I meant to quit for years since I started smoking in earnest at the age of thirty. Who starts smoking at thirty anyway?

Swoondalini

The mile markers blazed by, and I crossed the South Carolina line at two a.m. on the dot. When I passed the Palmetto State sign on I-95, my radio turned on of its own accord. The Tams' *What Kind of Fool,* was Nigel's song of choice for me. At least, I assumed it was Nigel and not a defect in Cadillac's top of the line truck. Who else but Nigel?

As soon as The Tams went off, I realized I'd be hitting Beaufort at dawn. To keep my mind off being in my home state, the radio went back on as loud as I could stand it with The Eagles' *Hell Freezes Over* album. It seemed very appropriate to be listening to this album at this particular junction in my life. I liked them so much that I went against my own anti-concert guideline and went to a show.

"Last menthol. Oh no, Mr. Bill!" I was getting loopy and needed to stretch, in addition to needing more lung darts and gas, so I pulled over at South of the Border.

I took a lustful look at my bat and dugout in my purse and quickly decided against driving and flying. I felt that perhaps I should arrive in Beaufort completely sober. Exit 38 Yemassee came a bit too quickly. It was around five in the a.m. and getting off I-95 onto a country road made it all the more real. I felt that I was driving into my future.

I was reminded again of my past as I drove past a sign advertising the Yemassee Mud Run. The mud run took place on the same property where Daddy took me shooting for the first time; thankfully the only time. It was staggering, the sheer number of events during early life I repressed.

What's real, though? Obviously, what I thought was a great reality turned out to be a sham. What now? I knew I could continue my life as it was, but also now knew I could do better. However, change was hard. But change was the only constant in life. I knew that for a long time; or more accurately, I should have known it, but consciously ignored it.

Why not? Why should I change? I was making bank every year doing the same shit, but how much money did I really need? Shouldn't I give back? I could still pass for twenty and got asked for my I.D. occasionally, but how long would that last?

"Wow!" I said in wonderment. Old Sheldon Church Road was unchanged. It was still spooky by dark, and the live oaks burdened by Spanish moss made it otherworldly by day.

Garden's Corner was changed, however. There was a new development called Bull Point, and South Carolina Department of Transportation was reworking the intersection.

It wasn't much further into town now. I could feel my anxiety level rising as I drove down Highway 21. Ten additional minutes and I admired the new jet displayed at the entrance to the Marine Corp Air Station. I was pleased that, *"The Noise You Hear is the Sound of Freedom,"* was still the slogan on the sign. It always made me feel safe as a girl to have all those Marines nearby.

Dawn broke and the Spanish moss looked as if it were licking the salt breeze of change as I turned onto Bay Street. I drove about ten miles per hour, and then decided to pull over. I drank my filling station coffee, watched the tide shift and witnessed the birth of a new day before proceeding to Uncle Bobby's house. After only a few minutes, the coffee kicked my nerves into high gear, along with my bladder and bowels. What did they put in this Hess station brew? My hands were shaking, but it was all life-affirming.

Swoondalini

It was time to see Uncle Bobby. I took one last admiring gaze out across the Beaufort River to Lady's Island and up the river to Port Royal and Parris Island beyond. I pulled back onto a Bay Street that was deserted due to the holiday, the early hour, and out of tourist season. It was a short ride down Bay and a quick left, and there I was.

Uncle Bobby actually lived in a home near where *The Great Santini* and *The Big Chill* were filmed. Over the years, I watched those movies in my media room just to see a little bit of home. I pulled up to the house and cut the engine. I inhaled a deep breath and opened my door to the bouquet of the Lowcountry. The marsh had a distinct aroma, especially at low tide, that was an acquired olfactory taste, but once acquired, you could never filter it from your blood, assuming you wanted to. In the humidity of the dog days of August you could taste the perfume.

I picked up the "Beaufort Gazette" out of the yard, but before I could get to the door, it opened. "Hope it's not too early, Uncle Bobby," I ventured.

"No, baby girl, you're late, but better late than never." His voice was heavy with emotion.

We both started crying, and I ran to him like I did when I was a little girl.

"I'm so sorry I've been absent for long."

"Shh... No regrets," he said, drying my tears with his sleeve. I could hear him sniffling a little, too. "What matters is that you're here now."

"I know but—"

Uncle Bobby mashed his finger firmly up against my lips to shush me. "Let me look at you," he said, as he held me away from himself and looked me up and down. "Good God, girl! Other than your questionable hair choice, you haven't changed a bit in nearly two decades. You had any work done?" I touched my hair and recalled my embarrassing encounter with Marge. I would need to find someone to fix my hair. "You know your nana could probably fix your hair for you." Uncle Bobby was always direct.

"Nope, no work done." I giggled while doing a pirouette. "I may just hit Nana up for a little trim. Where is Nana?"

"Well, you look great," Uncle Bobby said, and then shot his eyes up to the sky. "Yeah, Nana insisted on moving out to the driving range property several years ago. I didn't really want her out of my sight, but since she still gets around okay, I couldn't exactly stand in her way. We never went out there after Pappy and your father passed, so I offered to clean the property up, haul off Pappy's Rambler, and build her a nice little home. She actually told me she'd kick my ass if I ever touched that Rambler while she was still breathing. I've never heard her talk like that, so I wisely left it alone. Anyway, Nana will be along after a bit. She wore herself out cooking yesterday when she heard you were coming."

It hurt seeing Uncle Bobby's face, but not because of his resemblance to Daddy, but rather the time I allowed to pass between us. Not to mention not knowing where my grandmother lived. "Thanks, I've found my looks both a blessing and a curse. Didn't realize the curse part until recently, hence the trip South."

"I say it's neither. It is what it is and what you make of it. You're at a crossroads, and that's what brings you here," he said. I forgot how precise and sure Uncle Bobby could be in such matters.

"I suppose you're right, but I don't want this to be my last holiday in Beaufort."

"That's good to hear. Come on in the house. Want me to help you with your bags?"

"Please. I only have a couple."

"Not a problem."

I was nervous to say what I was about to say. "Uncle Bobby, on the ride down, I started thinking of a change of scenery. Maybe put down some roots here."

"Alice, you've always had roots here. There's plenty of room out at Nana's or even here. This is a big house."

"Thanks, that means a lot, but that may be a bit too much, too soon. Probably need my own space," I said, genuinely touched, as we bounded up the back steps into a kitchen that hadn't changed since my childhood, a kitchen that smelled the way Thanksgiving should, home and sanctity.

"What did you have in mind? Let's just put your bags down here and we'll take them up later. Want some coffee?"

"Na, I'm coffeed out, and I have to poop. Nothing like pooping at home."

Uncle Bobby giggled. "Happy Thanksgiving mimosa?"

"Yes please," I said in a huff of frustration at not being able to project everything I meant. I needed to get this out for my own sanity. "I thought very hard on the way down about buying some property here." I didn't realize it until now, but that real estate recipe essay seemed to be keeping me company on the way to South Carolina.

"Really now?" But there wasn't an ounce of surprise in his voice. It was so strange being with my daddy's twin after all this time. I could see Daddy lying peacefully in that chair. "So, what did you have in mind? Need a good realtor?" Uncle Bobby mercifully interrupted my morbid remembrance.

"No, I have one in mind out on Fripp," I said, and glanced over at my purse to ensure the essay was still keeping its vigil.

"Want me to go out there with you?"

"Na, I can handle it. I think I'll be in good hands with this guy."

"Well, there's a shitload of property for sale, that's for sure, with the *Great Recession* and all. Here's your mimosa."

"Thanks. Can we sit out on the veranda for a while?"

"Great idea. As I said, Nana will be around a little later. Bless her heart. That's okay. It'll give us a chance to chat." He looked at me pointedly. "Anyway, it's supposed to be seventy today, but I'll grab some blankets for the morning chill. Had anything to eat?"

Now that he mentioned it, I was pretty hungry. The entire pizza I ate was several hundred miles ago. "You got any biscuits?"

"Who do you think you're talking to?"

I clapped my hands in glee. Glee was a foreign emotion in my adult existence, and I was grateful for its return. Was I just dead inside my entire adult life? "Sausage, egg, and cheese?"

"My baby girl's coming home for the first time in for-FUCKING-ever, so your nana and I pulled out all the stops."

"You're the best. I don't know why I stayed away for so long."

"Yes, you do and we're going to talk about it," he said.

"Yes sir." I felt like I was just smacked on the hand by a ruler.

"I promise to be nice. First things first, though. You said you needed to freshen up? You remember where your room was?"

"Yes. Was?"

"You didn't think that I'd keep it the same, did you? Pining away for you to come back and see the fam?"

"Well, no, I just--" I stammered.

He softened his tone with a warm smile. "Actually, the light was great in there and it faces the water, so I turned it into my office."

"I see," I said.

"No, you don't see," he said with a toothy grin, eyes glistening.

"What do you mean?"

"I knew you'd return someday. Even if I was wrong and you didn't, I also knew that I needed to start somewhere on home renovations... So..."

"Yeah, you were never much for updating. How'd you know I'd be back?"

"Hush. You know your Uncle Bobby knows things."

"That's true." I laughed and pouted.

"So, your grandmother and I redid the room across the hall. Oh, other people have stayed there, but we both knew it was for you without really discussing it. Off ya go. Get settled and I'll get the biscuits and do up more mimosas."

"I don't know what to say."

"You can say thank you and take your stinky ass upstairs to check out your new digs."

"Thanks, Uncle Bob-O," I said as I pecked him on the cheek.

"You're welcome, child. Now go, before I mist up again," he choked out, giving me a hard slap on the backside.

After becoming intimate with the bathroom, I looked around the old house in wonderment. So much time passed by, physically at least. The common areas were just as regal and traditional as they were in my memories, absent of any obvious signs of technology. I experienced a brief flash of the few Thanksgivings that Mama allowed the family to take the trip down. I could see myself as a little girl sitting on Pappy's lap. Was it really so long ago or was time really so transparent that I could step through its shroud to the past and experience it all again?

Bobby wasn't lying. The upstairs was snazzed-up, with special attention paid to my room. I hurried to unpack a few things, toiletries mostly, wash my face, and get back downstairs. I wanted to be done with our vital discussion before Nana and half of Beaufort arrived. She should be here any time, and if Thanksgiving was anything like it was in the past, we would have a huge breakfast, followed by an even larger late afternoon meal so that we could have plenty of time for dessert before we passed out fat and happy in our beds. Oh, and don't forget the fried turkey. We were frying turkeys down South before the rest of the country hopped on the culinary bandwagon.

I bopped back downstairs to find Uncle Bobby already out on the porch with a plate of sausage, egg, and cheese biscuits accompanied by a large pitcher of "mater beer" (tomato juice and beer). Mater beer saw me through many a bad hangover.

Bobby spotted me out of the corner of his eye and reached for the ever-present pack of Marlboro Ultra-Light Menthols. I held out my hand for one, and he simply gave me his and lit another for himself. "Decided on mater beer instead of more mimosas," Uncle Bobby said without breaking his gaze at the marsh.

"I'm quitting smoking after this weekend," I ventured for a less sticky subject than the one we were about to delve into.

"Good, I will if you will. Lord knows I need to," Uncle Bobby said, while staring at his cigarette.

"Really? After all this time?"

"Uh huh," he said quickly. "Alright, let's have it," he prompted, and locked his eyes on mine.

"You want the long version or the short version?"

"I deserve to hear it all," he stated.

"That you do," I conceded. "Here goes," I said, taking a long pull on my cigarette.

"Alright, I'm all ears." He flashed a warm, encouraging smile. He knew how hard this must be for me.

"First off, let me apologize for not communicating much since Daddy's death. I hope you can eventually forgive me. For now, all I can say is that I'm a changed woman. Also, let me say that you're probably the only one I'm going to tell the full story to. Everybody else would probably just think I'm crazy."

"Honey, we're all crazy at some point or another in our lives," Uncle Bobby offered. "You sure I should be the only one you tell your story to?" he asked with a glimmer in his eyes.

After that, I dove right in, not omitting any gory detail. Uncle Bobby, for his part, merely listened attentively, refilled my glass, lit my cigarettes, and asked a few key questions here and there.

When I was done, I breathed a sigh of relief. I hadn't realized how good it would feel to get the past two decades, especially the last couple days, off my chest. Uncle Bobby was silent and contemplative.

"Well, what do you think?" I prodded him out of his thoughts.

"I think it's wonderful. And it would explain my dreams."

"Okay," I said, waiting for more. "Wonderful? What type of dreams did you have?"

"Yes, it confirms what I've always thought about you. You went through a 'dark night of the soul'," he said with air quotes. "Sounds like an extreme case of Kundalini syndrome, if you ask me. Have you done any energy work lately? The dreams are fuzzy, but no less intense feeling at this point. I do recall something about a teenage girl waxing my ass on the golf course. As if that would happen," Bobby said with a playfully raised eyebrow. "Golf seemed to be some sort of metaphor. Lord knows it's the one game we are truly playing against ourselves."

I giggled at the mention of golf and how it figured so prominently in my journey, not to mention everyday life. "I hadn't even considered the attunement. You think? Well, there was Ifetayo's attunement..." I was heartened by his understanding and felt my jaw go slack as realization began to wash over me.

"You listened to me?" He sounded pleased. "Yes, your spirit guides must really care for you."

"I didn't delete all those emails or voicemails over the years. What have you always thought about me, Uncle Bobby?"

"That you were destined for greatness," he said, stubbing his cigarette out and rising from his chair abruptly. "Time to work on the yeast rolls before I get too hammered," he called out over his shoulder as the screened door slammed behind him.

Uncle Bobby left me in a haze of emotions and cigarette smoke, staring out at the marsh to confirm that, yes, I was at home in the Palmetto State. I lit up another menthol to clear my head, and then made my way inside. I felt spent after telling my harrowing tale to Uncle Bobby. I found him in the kitchen where he said he'd be.

"Anything else come to mind?" I asked.

"I think we're very lucky that you have the spirit guides that you do. I doubt many souls get that kind of attention," Bobby said while kneading dough.

"That's what they told me." I chuckled.

"What?"

"Nothing. It's just that I can't believe I'm here and we're having this conversation. I always thought that you were weird when you'd mention things like spirit guides and such."

"I know, and that's why I didn't speak on the subject too often. Now you're a freak like me."

We both laughed hard at that.

"What do I tell everyone?"

"The truth."

"The truth?"

"Yeppers. You fell in the shower, hit your head, and it removed the narcissistic asshole out of your personality. Biff, bam, boom, here you are to stay. You are staying, aren't you?"

"Thanks, I think… Yeah, it depends on how tomorrow goes, but I'm seriously thinking of moving here. I need a fresh start and a clean slate with some roots to keep me grounded."

"Well said. Prepare yourself for the Slowcountry then. I was born here, but when I came back from Southern California, it took me a while."

"I realize the pace will take some getting used to, but I'll adjust," I said with a confidence I wasn't entirely sure of. I felt this was the right thing to do, but could I do it? Could I really undergo a radical mastectomy of my personality and reconstruct Alice without the tortuous guidance of Nigel and his friends?

"I'm sure you will. I'm proud of you."

"Are you serious?"

"Yes, absolutely. Always have been."

"Even though I am, or was, for all practical purposes, a whore?"

"You survived and were a very successful one. Don't forget that part. But you're a lot more than that, and until you realize it, you'll never live up to your full potential." He stabbed the air with his rolling pin for emphasis.

"Thanks, Uncle Bob-O," I said and gave him a big hug and sobbed. "I won't let you down."

"Work on not letting yourself down, baby, and I'll be happy. Now pull yourself together before your grandmother gets here. Go wash your face off and make her a pitcher of mimosas, will ya, babe."

"Yes, sir."

***

Thanksgiving Day 2009 would be one for my personal record book as the best ever. The family that I avoided for so long welcomed me back as if I never left. The food was out of this world, on top of it all.

As I lapsed into a food-coma that night, I was left with the question of why I allowed so much time to pass and why I endured so much alone, just to avoid this reflection of me. Perhaps it was my reflection I was living in fear of? Up until now, I chose only to see my mother's reflection staring back in the mirror. There was so much more, and I determined, as I fell into slumber that night, to discover the "more" of life that we all deserved.

Chapter 18

Black Friday dawned another cloudless day in beautiful Beaufort by the sea. The temperature topped out at sixty degrees. I awoke to butterflies in my belly and the smell of bacon. The hunger instinct quickly overrode the butterflies, as I washed up and rushed down to see Uncle Bobby. I missed his influence so much in my life in more ways than I can innumerate.

"Ah, there she is. Didn't slip out in the middle of the night, I see."

"Nope, done with those tricks."

"Okay, there's some bacon, coffee's ready, and I'm going to do up some French toast."

"Yum."

"You still headed out to Fripp today?"

"Yes, I do believe I am."

"Sure, you don't want me to go with you? Haven't been out there since I sold my place. Even though I got a shitload of money for it before the bubble burst, I wish I still had it. Otherwise, I just planned to sit on my ass, eat turkey biscuits, and watch football," he said. His voice was full of concern, but he avoided my gaze.

"Thanks, I wouldn't want to interfere with such a day of relaxation. I will take a rain check on that for next year. I need to do this myself."

"I understand, and you wouldn't be interfering. I will, however, hold you to that date for next year," he said with a hopeful grin.

Chris Suddeth

Breakfast flew by, as time seems to be fleeting not only when having fun, but when one is apprehensive to what's coming. Not to sound trite or cliché, but this was the first day of the rest of my life. I suppose every day can be seen that way.

Nana did fix my hair; brilliantly, I must say, but I never took so long to get dressed. I just couldn't find the right thing to wear. My whole frame of mind was altered, but it was going to take some getting used to. I was still proud of my body but felt the need to be more discerning about when and how I showed it off. To that end, most of the clothes that I owned or packed were either too nice and/or too slutty. I finally went out on a limb and settled on a Tommy Hilfiger sweater and jeans. I was chagrinned when I looked in the mirror at the sweater. Conservative as it was, it made my breasts look even larger than they were. And the jeans, well...

"Fuck it," I said in a huff of exasperation, as I noticed that the clock was already reading half past ten in the morning. "It seems that I have the opposite problem of the proverbial lipstick on a pig," I said to myself. I jammed on lipstick and eyeliner, all the makeup I ever needed or wore, double-checked to ensure the printout of the realtor's essay about Fripp and oyster stew was in my purse, and hit the door with a quick peck on the cheek to Uncle Bobby.

By this point in my life, I was used to major purchases. Hell, I was used to being a major purchase, but this was to be my biggie. It wasn't the money. This would be my new home, a critical part of my salvation. Did I want salvation? Did I deserve salvation? Maybe what it comes down to was I ready for success? True success. Fear of success has doomed great and small alike. All these ego demons and more came at me as I prepared for the thirty-minute ride to destiny. I fought the overwhelming urge to vomit bacon and French toast along the side of my Cadillac.

I held it all down and began with the small step of just pulling out of Uncle Bobby's driveway. I turned left on to Carteret and headed toward Fripp. As I crossed the Woods Memorial Drawbridge that took one from Beaufort to Lady's Island, I realized I was driving toward my adulthood. Granted, I was thirty-four, but it fit the bill. My growth stunted when I left South Carolina, and now it was time to put on my big girl panties. The view and the charm of that bridge transported me back to the first time I recall going over it as a little girl.

Lady's Island was definitely a metropolis now, compared to my memories. Gone was the Winn-Dixie, replaced by Grayco Hardware. According to Uncle Bobby, Grayco had everything you never knew you needed until you walked in and saw it there. There was a new Publix and Food Lion since my last time here physically. Sam's Point Road sprung out of nowhere. As I drove further along the five-island chain, Saint Helena Island remained much the same, aside from a new bridge. Gone was the bridge that posed for the Alabama/Mississippi state line in "Forrest Gump," replaced by a wider, sturdier span. Gone was the waterslide Pappy took me to as a little girl. I did take a detour by Nana's house and my now overgrown driving range. I pledged to return it to its glory days.

My stomach got more twisted as I approached the island that was the official farthest point out in the Atlantic of any other in South Carolina. Once on Fripp, that was as far as one could drive.

I pressed on toward Hunting Island State Park. Of course, it remained unchanged, according to mandate. Hunting Island passed in a wavy blur, literally. The road always felt a little like bouncing on small waves.

Finally, there was the Fripp Bridge. I noticed a pier to my left, that I didn't recall, and the same Fripp sign from my childhood memories announced one half mile to the security gate. Here we go. The heartbeat sound of the bridge and the truck soothed my raw nerves. I felt like I was coming home. I knew then that I was on to something. God, the view was better than I remembered it. The vista was an elixir for my soul. It could have something to do with my senses being more sensitive since the shower incident. I looked to my right at the extraordinary expanse of marsh and Old House Creek. On cue, a dolphin at play jumped in the distance toward what is known as the "shark hole." They didn't have that in D.C. Did I want a marsh view? Then I looked left at Fripp Inlet and the Atlantic beyond. Or would I prefer an ocean view? Now, instead of nervous, I was excited.

"Hmm, they moved the security gate up."

I veered right into the real estate/rental check-in office. I entered, clutching the copy of the essay that led me to the man that would lead me to my new home. When I went around the corner to the real estate side of the building, there was an otherwise handsome sixty-something year-old man at the desk. The first thing I noticed was the toothpick he worked end over end with his tongue. His shirt was opened one button too low to show off his gold chains dangling in his salt and pepper man sweater that probably covered his entire back. He sported penny loafers, with the pennies, sans socks. He must fancy himself a lady's man at the Beaufort Shag Club with his "Just for Men" jet-black hair and goatee... He didn't notice me, so I rang the bell.

Startled, he looked up, and upon seeing me, jumped a little and muttered, "Goddamn," a bit too loud in a thick Southern accent as he leered at me.

Swoondalini

I veered right into the real estate/rental check-in office. From outside, I could hear *Magic Man,* a.k.a Nigel's song, as I would call it from now on, blaring like the place was a club. I almost chickened out upon hearing that song. I took a deep breath, then steeled myself, and bravely entered the office, clutching the copy of the essay that led me to the man that would lead me to my new home. When I went around the corner to the real estate side of the building, there was an otherwise pretty, fifty-something year-old lady grooving in a suggestive manner behind the desk. She clearly wasn't aware of my presence. She was working a toothpick end over end with her tongue. Oh my! Her shirt was opened one button too low to show off her gold chains dangling in her cleavage. She sported penny loafers, with the pennies, sans socks. She must fancy herself a swinging chick magnet with her "Just for Men" jet-black hair, sporting the typical butch mullet... I took another deep breath and rang the bell.

Startled, she looked up, and thankfully muted *Magic Man*. Upon seeing me, she jumped a little and muttered, "Goddamn," a bit too loud in a thick British accent as she leered at me. British accent? Would he ever quit toying with me or was I reading too much into an accent? I was used to this sort of reaction, but today, I would take nothing but professionalism. I crossed my arms over my ogled chest and indignantly stared her down until she made eye contact.

"What can I assist you with today, ma'am?"

I looked down at the name and contact information attached to the essay, as if I needed to. "Yes, I'm here to see Jon Sutton. A friend forwarded me his info, and I'm looking to move here. I figured that anyone who felt strongly enough to write like this should sell me a home." I spit the words out awkwardly, like I was doing a middle school book report and wanted to get back to my desk and out of the spotlight.

Very quickly, surprise and a slight sneer flashed across her face. So quickly that one really had to be paying attention. Then the veneer of a perfect sales person responded, "He's no longer with us."

"Oh." All the wind went out of my sails. What was I going to do? "Where is he working now?"

"He went to inactive status to be Mr. Mom." She cackled a bit to giddy for my taste. "His daughter is about three months old, and with the market the way it is, something had to give... May I help you, doll? My name is Angelique, and oh yes, it fits." She flashed her teeth at me again.

I absolutely did not want help from this person. *Doll! Angelique? WTF?* "He lives on the island, right? Can you call him?"

"To look at property? No, I'm afraid he can't legally do that in this backwater state." She took obvious satisfaction in telling me this.

"Backwater state?" I bristled. I could talk smack about my state since I was from here, but... I would not be deterred. "To make it legal, you may accompany us on the sales tour."

"Why would I want to do that? Why would he want to do that when he can't get paid?" she asked.

Handling men was my trade. She would be no different. The sort of juvenile thing I was about to do was something I sometimes took pleasure in when the mood struck me. I decided to exact some satisfaction. "Because I can easily buy the most expensive house on the island and will go elsewhere if you don't find this guy. Don't think you can afford that these days, can you? Not

2005 anymore, is it?" I was drawing this out and took note of her face. "Here is a general statement from my bank as to my worth and my banker's contact number in Switzerland. I have an American banker you may speak with, too, if need be." I carried the letter around for just such occasions when I saw an investment opportunity, and I slapped it on the desk. I looked in my purse and was surprised to find a large wad of cash I neglected to put in my safe. That neglect would now provide ammunition as a thin smile of discovery turned into a childish game. "Ah, here it is." I slowly pulled out twenty-five grand in cash and threw it at her phone, knocking it off its cradle. "That will be earnest money or a retainer for whatever Jon finds me. As for Jon, he'd probably do this out of the goodness of his heart, but I'll take care of him on my own."

Her mouth dropped open, and she stammered about. An idea to take care of Jon and clean some clutter from my own life popped in my head and left me smiling. It was perfect, and it would help me transform my image at the same time. "But I doubt you'd understand that sort of thing, would you?" Let her draw her own conclusions.

She missed my last comment, which was just as well. Her eyes were still wide, and then they drifted back down to my chest, then to my letter, then to the cash that knocked her receiver off the base, then landed squarely back on my chest. I snapped her out her confusion. "Now, would you please call him?" I asked with acid sweetness, invoked my native South Carolinian tongue, and fluttered my long lashes for good measure.

Her head started bobbing vaguely up and down before she responded, "Yes, ma'am!"

The conversation that followed was entertaining from my end.

"I know I told you I didn't like working with men on your way out the door, but she's ready to buy right now and will only talk to you," she said in quick, hushed tones with her back turned to me in an effort to retain some of her dignity. This was definitely worth the trip. I'm sure Jon was enjoying it too.

"She said she'd take care of you," she explained as she picked up and inspected the wad of one-hundred dollar bills I threw at her phone. "I have no reason to doubt her." There was a long silence, and she finally said, "Please."

She listened for a little while. "Okay, lemme ask her," the broker said, cupping her hand to the receiver. "Jon's wife just left the house and he has his little baby girl," the broker relayed to me.

I mulled it over for a second, and then said, "Yeah, bring her along. It won't bother me. I like babies." It wasn't a lie, and I was actually excited to be around one for the first time in longer than I could recall, no doubt spurred on by my Amen Corner experience.

She nodded. "Yeah, bring her on up here. Thanks, buddy," she said. I thought Jon already disconnected.

"He's on his way. Can I get you some coffee or something while you wait?"

"No thanks. I'm coffeed out. I'll just scan these listings and review the map. Have you got any other literature I can look at?"

"Sure. You ever visited Fripp before?"

"Yep," I said. "So, I'll just take this and wait over there," I said, curtly dismissing her. I could have been nicer, but old habits die hard.

Jon Sutton arrived fifteen long minutes later, which was pretty quick for a man with a three-month-old. He wore a green t-shirt with stick figures that were fighting and text that read, "Chuck Norris doesn't break hearts, he breaks legs." I suppressed a nervous giggle. Wow, Jon was a 6'2", dark and sexy Mr. Mom, about my age, with a definite Upstate accent. The things that might have been or still could be. "Hmm?" I pondered aloud. "No matter, Brandy's days of home-wrecking are over," I whispered to myself.

Jon didn't see me and went directly to shake the hand of his Angelique. Classy. She whispered something quickly as I approached and then introduced us.

"Well, hello," he said with an easy smile. "This is E.B., stands for Ellie Beth, and I'm Jon Sutton."

"Nice to meet you. I'm Alice." It felt hopeful to introduce myself as myself. "That has to be one of the prettiest babies I've ever seen," I said with a pang that thrust deep inside me. She truly was a beautiful child.

"Hope you don't mind her coming. She'll probably go to sleep in this sling. Her mama had some errands she couldn't put off."

"No, not at all. I understand I caught you by surprise, and you're not even in real estate anymore. Thanks for meeting with me."

"Absolutely, I'm happy I could help," Jon said sincerely. "Angelique here tells me you read my recipe. That makes me feel good that somebody liked it that much to come see me."

He hadn't even checked me out yet. Wait, there he went. I would have been wounded if he didn't. To his credit, he recovered quickly.

"So, what would you like to take a look at? What's your price range? Did you have a location in mind?"

"To start with, I would like a brief overview of the island. I was a teenager the last time I was here. I can afford the most expensive house on the island, but that may not be what I need."

"Understood, well, let's get started. If it's alright, can we just ride with you? We won't need a car seat if you'll just obey the Fripp twenty-five mph max rule," Jon said with a warm smile. "I didn't really expect this, and my wife took the car along with the car seat. Besides, the inside of my truck is a bit small for showing property."

"Not a problem."

"Lead the way, Miss Alice. Angelique, you have a map, some keys, listings?" Jon asked rapid fire.

"Working on it," Angelique said in a harried voice.

"Alice, let's hold up while Miss Angelique gets the info together, and we'll go over that large map to refresh your memory."

"Good idea."

We briefly glanced at the map as his daughter nodded off to sleep. We found that we were from the same hometown, even roots in the same part of town, Dunean. I wasn't quite ready to go deeper into my background, so I shifted the focus back to him.

"So, do you do anything else, Mr. Mom?"

"I've always done a little odd job here and there, but what's really holding my interest is I'm starting to offer some alternative healing sessions when sweet thang here allows daddy." He smiled lovingly, as he giggled at her snoring.

I was about to inquire as to what he meant by alternative healing when Angelique walked up.

"Ready?"

"Yes, ma'am," we said in unison.

Jon scanned the listings. "Good, we'll start with the movie theater house after a brief tour of Fripp."

"Cool."

The island was larger than I remembered it. I enjoyed listening to Jon. His obvious love and enthusiasm for Fripp showed through in his tour. He spoke of watching dolphins play and feed in Skull Inlet, and I felt as if I could literally see the dolphins' breath on a cold day through his eyes. I heard Angelique huff often at Jon's ways of showing me property. I have been around some high-level pitch-men with my varied investments around the globe. Jon was definitely not of the "you must buy this now or you'll simply burst into flames" ilk, which is what I needed right now. So, I slipped Angelique a look of daggers that quelled her.

Fripp added a new Davis Love III designed golf course and communities where *Jungle Book II* and *Forrest Gump* were filmed. I realized I would have two courses to hone my skills on. Bonus! Both golf courses were in great shape and gave me further incentive to buy...

"Well, this house certainly is nice," I commented on our first showing.

"But you're not feeling it, are you?"

"Not really."

"Three mil is a bit much since the largest closing on the island was two-point-one back during boom boom days. It's a different game now."

I felt Angelique tighten as Jon disclosed the facts, but she kept her mouth shut, to her credit. She was smarter than she looked.

"That's certainly part of it. I like the bar and the movie theater, though. However, it just doesn't fit my taste," I offered. What was my taste these days anyway? The flashy side of me died on that shower floor, that much I knew, but was I really ready to buy a home, not knowing what I liked with my new attitude? Perhaps I'd know it when I saw it.

We looked at several other houses that were fabulous, and then E.B. woke up fussy. Despite this and me shooting down the best houses he came up with, he was not discouraged.

"Ahhhwww... I know it..." Jon cooed to his daughter as she cried. He turned to me as we were walking down the steps of another listing I didn't feel. I had golf course views at Congressional, after all. "Okay, my wife should be home now, so we can drop E.B. off, and while we're there, I want to show you the home site next door."

"Home site?"

"Yes, ma'am," he said as he bounced E.B. gently in a futile attempt to soothe her.

"No 'ma'ams' please, just Alice. We're the same age, I think. 1975?" Actually, I felt we were the same age.

"No shit, me too!" he exclaimed and immediately put his hand over his mouth. "Excuse my language."

"Don't worry, I have a potty mouth, so cuss away."

"Yes, er," he stopped short, struggling with the polite Southerner within. "*Alice*—you've shot down some of our best ideas for you. I don't blame you on the 'movie theater' house, as it was way over the top in price and everything else, but I want you to consider building your own house so that you can have exactly what you want."

"Haven't even thought of that, but I like the direction you're going," I mused. "What about the meantime?"

"Meantime? Oh, you want to move here right away? I should have asked you that in the beginning."

"I should have told you that in the beginning, but I'd like to move here yesterday, if possible." That sounded good to say, but did I really want to move here that fast?

"That's cool. Miss Angelique, is that Fiddler's Ridge tree house still available? Okay, okay," he said to E.B. "Alice, apologies, but we need to take her home."

"Yeah, they're pretty desperate to get out after completing all those renovations," Angelique responded, oblivious to E.B.

"Sounds good. I think you'll like it, Alice."

"Not a problem with your little one. I understand. What have you got in mind with the home sites?" I yelled over a hungry and wet three-month old.

"You're obviously very specific about what you want, and you should be at these prices, but we haven't found it, *yet*."

"True, but I'm not trying to be difficult."

"Believe me, you're not. I think we just need to regroup. You feel me?"

"I feel you," I said with a smile. In the past, just to prove a point, I would have taken him to task for being familiar, but now I found it reassuring. "May I hold her while you drive back to your house?" I asked, as I reached for her and offered my keys in exchange.

"Absolutely," Jon said handing Ellie Beth over to me. "Well, this home I have in mind has a mother-in-law that you could do any number of things with. Two-bedroom, two bath that's just been redone, and you'll have the best view of the Fourth of July fireworks of anybody on the island. Let's look at that in a minute and we'll also walk some home sites."

"My nipples are getting hard. Tell me more."

Jon naturally looked down and laughed easily, revealing a down-to-earth sense of humor. Angelique merely gawked, causing me to involuntarily turn away and look at the view.

"You're funny. Anyway, it's got a long-distance marsh view, which is my personal favorite."

"Really? Why?"

"Well, the ocean is nice. Don't get me wrong, waking up with your coffee and a view of the Atlantic certainly has its upside, but the ocean is a desert. I love the golf course as I love the game, and the family has always had a home there. But the marsh, the marsh is so peaceful, and there's so much to see, rampant with life. I just really like the idea that the marsh is nature's filter," Jon explained. As if Jon cued it up, an osprey flew over with a fish in its talons. "Alright, so let's get this surly girly fed, and you can look at that home site next to me."

"You want me as your neighbor? You sure about that? I might be crazy…"

"I don't think so. You're ready for change."

The hairs on the back of my neck stood up. How could he read me so easily? Sounded like something Uncle Bobby would say to me.

Swoondalini

"We need a good neighbor. Besides, it's got a lot of elbow room and is located on one of the highest points in terms of elevation on Fripp. I have two others to show you, and then we'll go look at that tree house."

"Tree house?"

"Oh, that's what people call most of the houses on Fiddler's Ridge," he explained as I began to recall golf cart rides to my favorite little peninsula on the island. "Yeah, so I'm thinking you can buy or lease with the option to buy. I'd seriously consider buying though, and after you move into your custom-built home, you could rent the tree house out and have it pay for itself. It really is a good deal."

He made so much sense, the way he spoke to me. He had my best interests at heart and that put me at ease. I couldn't show that just yet though.

Jon whistled. "This Escalade is smooth," Jon said, turning on to his road. "Never driven one of these before."

"Special edition," I added, thinking back to the former owner that made it 'special'. "Sounds like a brilliant plan to me."

"What?"

Boy, I really held out a long time. "What you just said."

"Glad to hear it. This won't take long. Y'all want to come inside?" Jon asked as he parked in his driveway.

"No thanks," Angelique said. "Need to make a phone call."

I was nervous about meeting his wife. Women tended not to like me. But I always presented other girls with Brandy. Perhaps she'd like Alice. "Sure, I'd love to meet your wife."

Chris Suddeth

***

They showed me an ocean front home site and a marsh view home site in addition to the one next to the Sutton family. The ocean front home site got to me. It was only a couple spots down from where Uncle Bobby's house used to be. I could still see Daddy surf fishing with Uncle Bobby. What I would do with the property? Who knew? But I had to pay attention to my feelings now. Since I had the means, why not give myself options for the next chapter of my life? To Jon's, and even Angelique's credit, they saw I was upset and waited by my Escalade while I walked down to the water.

Jon then took me to the tree house. Or should I call it tree home? As soon as I walked up the steps and viewed the marsh vista, I was done. I was home. Yes, my nipples did actually get hard and I didn't mind Angelique staring. I heard nothing of the particulars about the home but nodded politely anyway. I dutifully followed them on their tour. It was small, and it was kind of a dump compared to what I was used to, even though they felt it was updated. Definitely couldn't fit a shower cave in this place without a little reworking. Perhaps that was a good thing, I pondered as I sat down in the lone chair on the small back screened porch. Fripp's marina and the Sawgrass community could be seen in the distance.

"Alice?"

I could live on this porch. I would never leave it except to use the bathroom and cook.

"Alice?" Jon beckoned me softly back to the present and placed his hand on my shoulder. His hand was there only briefly, but it still felt as if it was there.

Swoondalini

"Hmm?" I responded absently.

"Alice, do you not like it? It was just an idea. I always assume everybody likes this part of the island just because I do. Come on, we'll run back to the office and grab another couple listings," Jon urged.

"No," I said.

"Yeah, I hear ya. No more Fiddler's Ridge."

"No, I mean, no more listings. This is it. I don't care. Make it happen," I said with more passion than I mustered in as long as I can remember. "I'll take it. Thank you, both," I said with mist in my eyes as I stood up and hugged Jon with all my might. I wasn't a hugger, at least Brandy wasn't. Hell, I didn't have many people to hug, truly hug, that is. Perhaps Alice could be a hugger. "Yep. Yes sir. Yes ma'am. I'm done. Take me back."

When we arrived back at the office, I asked Jon, "So, that's your truck there?" I made a show of kicking the tires.

"Yeah," he replied tentatively.

"Looks like it's in pretty good shape," I went on.

"Well, it is, for being ten years old. I pride myself in taking care of things."

"Good habit to have. I need an old truck that's in good shape down here. Mainly to change my image, but I'm sure I'll actually need it." The "I'd Rather be Driving a Titleist" sticker, GOLF with the University of South Carolina Gamecock representing the "O" license plate, and a Dale Earnhardt Jr. 88 sticker made it perfect.

"No disrespect, but I wasn't looking to sell it."

"None taken, but would you take an even trade?"

"What!?"

"I think you'd come out about fifty or sixty grand ahead on the deal."

"What are you talking about?"

"I told you I'd take care of you, and since you can't take a commission and I don't want this beast anymore... Well?" I asked, shaking the keys in his face.

"You're serious?"

Angelique was watching in rapt interest, her mouth agape.

"Yep."

"Well, if you're sure, then you have yourself a deal," he said, holding out his large hand.

"I'll need you to take me back to my uncle's house, but it's yours," I said, grinning from ear to ear, and taking his hand in mine.

"And you want my truck?"

"Always wanted one like that, bumper stickers, license plate, and all. It does run, right?"

"Just about as good as the day I bought it."

"Figured as much. Alright, Angelic one, if the two properties comp within reason, I'll take the oceanfront home site in addition to the tree home at full asking," I said, and enjoyed taking liberty to be familiar with her name. "I am not in the mood to play around over a couple thousand here and there. Just get it done." Brandy would have taken all three home sites and the tree house just because she could. Perhaps even the movie theater house to boot. I was done with being so ostentatious and thoughtless.

"Okay," Angelique said slowly.

I just blew their minds. Much less of a mess than other things I normally blew.

"Let Jon go over the paperwork before you bring it to me in town tomorrow. Jon, here's my card. Call me with any concerns. Can you set up some builders for me to meet when I come back?"

"Would love to," Jon said enthusiastically. "You sure you need both? That tree house— "

"*Tree home,*" I gently corrected.

"Right, tree home. That tree home seemed like it was the *one.*"

Angelique huffed predictably.

What was up with this? Someone looking out for me. Somebody looking out for *Alice.* I could get used to that. "I hear ya, but why not? It'll be a good investment and I have some history on that stretch of the beach," I said, recalling my father passed out in the incoming tide. I inhaled sharply as I added up the last few days' events in my head. "I've got to go back to D.C. to close down that chapter of my life."

"I'll be in touch, Alice," Angelique said, offering her hand. I gave Angelique a hug instead. I did give her a hard time earlier. Perhaps a hug would make up for it. When I let Angelique go, she looked like she was going to get moist. "You mean you're going to take the oceanfront home site and the tree home?" she asked, grinning at my chest.

"I'll need a receipt for that cash I gave you," I said, poker-faced.

"Yeah, I'll run get that."

When Angelique went inside, Jon inquired with a smile, "You don't like her very much, do you?"

"Like I said, I'm closing certain chapters of my life." I knew I was being cryptic but didn't care.

"I understand."

I felt he really did.

***

We left for town soon thereafter and Jon wisely brought his excited wife and daughter with us for the return trip to town. An escort would have been necessary with Brandy, but I was gaining confidence with Alice now.

It felt good, listening to Jon and Sookie gush the whole ride to Beaufort. Apparently, Sookie always wanted an Escalade. It was very cute. For some reason, I felt comfortable with them, and they would become my good friends and neighbors.

"Are you shitting me?" Jon asked as I gave him the final few turns he had to make to get to Uncle Bobby's.

"What?" I asked, taken aback.

"Is your uncle Bobby?"

"Yeah, why?"

"Well, Bobby is a good friend of ours and a mentor on top of that. He's the one that started me in my alternative healing training."

"The hell you say?"

"Yes, ma'am."

"No wonder I was drawn to you."

"You think he's up? He hasn't seen E.B. since he stopped by Beaufort Memorial after she was born. Naturally, we've all been so busy since then."

Swoondalini

"Naturally," I whispered wistfully. "Oh yeah, he's up," I said as I observed the porch light flip on.

"I love your uncle so much, OMG," Sookie said.

When Uncle Bobby came out, Jon gave him a big bear hug.

"So, this was the real estate agent you went to?" Uncle Bobby asked, still holding on to Jon's shoulder. "You got a good one, Alice, but I thought Jon gave up the game for Mr. Mom status."

"Yep, your niece took me off the bench for the day. Come here and look. Ellie Beth's fallen asleep in the back."

"Oh, my goodness," Uncle Bobby gushed. "I've only seen pictures on Facebook so far. Alice, this baby is even prettier than you as a newborn. Now look at her." Bobby angled inside the Cadillac for a closer look at Ellie Beth and gave her a gentle kiss on the forehead.

"You're on Facebook and not Myspace, Uncle Bobby?"

He only smiled in answer. "So, tell me what happened on Fripp today, Alice."

I felt my stomach flutter as I reviewed in my head what I did with the real estate agents on Fripp. "You could say I got into the spirit of Black Friday."

When we gave Uncle Bobby the rundown of what transpired, he had a look that could only be described as worried elation.

I felt like I knew the Sutton family forever, and Uncle Bobby clearly thought highly of them. They said their good-byes and vowed to get together the following week on Fripp. I was invited but declined. I decided I wouldn't return to Fripp until I moved there. The tree home wouldn't close until the first part of the year. That would allow me plenty of time for loose ends and to work out what I would do with the rest of my life.

Uncle Bobby turned to me as Sookie excitedly slammed the driver's side door of their new Cadillac. "Baby, not that I'm not glad you're going to be around more..."

"But what am I going to do? I was hoping you could help me figure that out."

"Sure, you could probably start in Greenville," Uncle Bobby said gently as he looked over his reader glasses pointedly.

"I was afraid you might say that."

Chapter 19

"Wow! Look at that yellow cloud, would ya," Uncle Bobby said, breaking the long silence he endured since leaving Beaufort.

I grunted in response to his reference of the pollen that blanketed South Carolina in the last week. It was spring of 2010. Well, still winter, if you looked at the calendar. I just moved to Fripp last week. It was time to handle business of a more personal nature.

"You sure you're ready for this?" Uncle Bobby persisted. His face showed concern and apprehension.

"Didn't know I had a choice in the matter," I said.

Uncle Bobby chuckled. "Oh, you don't, I just want to make sure that it's not too soon."

"We're already in Columbia," I pointed out. "Look, there's Williams-Brice," I said excitedly as we passed by I-77's beginning, featuring the distinguished stadium of the Fighting Gamecocks in the distance.

"I can easily turn this vehicle around," he countered.

"You're nervous about seeing her too, aren't you?"

"Mostly out of concern for you, but yeah, she did kill my twin, so you might say I'm a bit on edge. Funny, I always thought you and I would reconnect, but never considered ever seeing her again."

Swoondalini

How selfish was I? I always thought about losing *my* father and never considered Uncle Bobby lost a brother and Nana and Pappy lost a son, not to mention a niece and granddaughter for a while. I was so glad that Uncle Bobby was going with me. I just didn't realize until now that he needed this too, maybe not as much as me, but he did need to do this.

"Let's rip the band-aid off."

"Alright then, to G-Vegas."

***

Visiting Mama at Marshall-Pickens was no doubt, a watershed moment for me. She could still pass for my older sister, but she seemed so small and insignificant, even though she always was physically a little larger. She was a shell of a human being, and I was taken aback by the pity I felt for her. Naturally, the pity was swirled in with a dash of fear, but pity was indeed the overriding emotion rather than rage.

Mama was lucid only twice during our reunion. The first was upon our arrival, when she assumed that Uncle Bobby and I were there for the funeral.

"What funeral is that, Mama?"

"It happened last week. Remember when you hung up on me?"

"Sort of, I haven't hung up on you recently," I mumbled. I was confused and the emotion of just seeing the devil herself was overwhelming. Actually, the last time I hung up on her was before I passed out in the shower.

"I told you your grandparents got into a little tussle," Mama prompted.

I couldn't recall if she told me or not. It dawned on me. "Did they finally kill each other?"

"It was an accident. Granny fell down the steps, and when your granddaddy went to catch her, she pulled him down that beautiful staircase. Remember when you used to slide down that staircase, Alice, before you entered your life of sin?"

I started cackling uncontrollably. They were likely hammered off of prescription pills since it was doctor-approved.

"Alice, baby, are you okay?" Uncle Bobby asked.

"Sorry, the final scene from *War of the Roses* flashed through my mind's eye. Mama, those two fed off each other right up until the very end," I stated as if she would understand.

"Yeah, you're right, it probably went down something like that, knowing Jenny and Billy." Uncle Bobby laughed derisively.

"What are you doing here, Jimmy?" Mama glared at him.

"I'm Bobby, Janice. Jim was my brother," Uncle Bobby explained, sounding wounded.

"What?" Mama asked lethargically. Uncle Bobby later speculated what drugs she was hopped up on. It was staggering.

"Never mind. Listen, Janice, your daughter has come a long way to see you and we have to go soon," he patiently explained in soft tones reserved for sleeping babies and dangerous animals. "We're not sure when we can come back, so do you have anything to say to her?"

Her eyes cleared a little and the second moment of clarity descended upon us. She took my hand and pointed to Uncle Bobby. "I have a confession to make to you both. Jim here isn't your real daddy. Adam still lives on McDaniel Avenue, no less, right around the corner from your grandparents. I apologize to you both for my deceit and ask for forgiveness in His name. Oh, Sweet Baby Jesus. Hallowed be thy Name," she said and put her hands above her head in supplication.

"Sure, you don't want an apology from Daddy here for never making enough money to get you on McDaniel?" I fired back and pointed mockingly at Bobby as if he were Daddy. I was getting hot now.

"Alice," Uncle Bobby said with a reproving tone.

I always felt Daddy wasn't my daddy. Obviously, that feeling was confirmed after witnessing Mama's Yuletide Log assault of 1974, but I never expected her to own up to my paternity. Uncle Bobby and I stared each other down. Mama brought us out of our reverie. "Do I have your forgiveness?"

I felt my head about to implode. "You killed the man that raised me as his daughter and would have killed me if I didn't run for my life. You're just worried about going to hell, aren't you?"

"Yes," she said without hesitation.

I got a nudge in my memory right then that replaced my rage with suspicion. "Mama, when I was fourteen, what happened?"

"What do you mean?"

"You know what I mean. I mean, why did Daddy flip out, start getting hammered all the time, and put me, barely out of pigtails, through Marine Corp Basic Training?"

"Alice, where do you think you're going with this?" Uncle Bobby asked.

"Trying to fill the holes in my memory, *Bobby*! That okay? You insisted we come all this way," I lashed out, without breaking eye contact with Mama.

"Your daddy misinterpreted something your Granddaddy Billy did, that's all," Mama explained as if she were clearing up illegible writing on a grocery list.

"And what was that?"

"Jim thought he made a pass at you."

"Sure, it wasn't more than that, Mama?"

"No," she said, barely audible. Then she stood up and put her finger in my face and asked, "What do you expect with the way you dress?"

Uncle Bobby grabbed my belt as I lunged for her. I never tried to attack anybody in that manner and my raw animosity cancelled out my logical mind.

"Time to go, Alice, I think we've all had enough."

I was still fighting him.

"*Alice!*" Uncle Bobby said through gritted teeth, digging his fingers into my arm for emphasis. "Am I going to have to carry you out of here?"

"No, sir," I said as I relaxed. For a moment, I thought about stomping Bobby's foot, so I could have a real go at her, but old, entrenched memories began to dampen my adrenaline.

"Good, let's go. Janice, if I never see you again, it'll be too soon."

"Bye, Mama," I said, through hot tears.

We sat in the parking lot with the A/C pumping for about ten minutes before Uncle Bobby spoke. "What happened in there, Alice? I felt for a second like you were going to knee me in the nuts, so you could get to her."

"I wouldn't have done that to you," I said quietly as I stared out the window. "I remembered what happened," I said, finally.

"What do you mean?"

"I mean, I remembered the memory that taught me to euthanize my memories."

"Would you care to share?" Bobby gently asked.

"Not really, but I will anyway." I sucked in a bracing lung-full of air before continuing. "I lost my virginity to Billy," I blurted out. I was careful not to say grandfather. That honorific belonged only to the likes of Pappy. "He told me I needed to experience a real man, to know how to handle real men. That 'real man' got me pregnant and I had to take a trip up to the Dark Corner that wasn't for a jar of moonshine. Mama and I disappearing for a couple of days obviously tipped Daddy off." My voice quivered. "She never owned up to any of it. Daddy was able to put two and two together after a while. That explains why Billy wisely never set foot in the Dunean house again."

Bobby gasped and gazed out his driver's side window at the hospital in the distance. We sat in stupefied silence until I asked, "Did you just see a white owl fly into that tree?" It had to be Pal.

"What? No. I don't even know where to go with this revelation, Alice. That's one of the most fucked up things I've ever heard, and I heard it all in my professional career." I didn't look at Bobby, but I could hear him fighting back tears. "He kept this to himself," Uncle Bobby said in disbelief. "I wish I knew—"

"Knew what, Uncle Bobby? You mean so you could have gone crazy like my father?"

"Or worse," Bobby said in a far-away contemplative voice. "You know you're going to have to forgive her. Apparently, I will too. There was a part of me that wanted to let you have a go at her while I held her," Bobby finally said.

"Me? Forgive her?"

"You know, true forgiveness is not about the person who slighted you, right? It's about redemption for you and allotting another, more appropriate spot in your heart for that person. The anger will be the hell of your own creation. Like you drinking strychnine and waiting for the object of your hatred to die. Hate will be your downfall."

"It almost was. Interesting you should mention strychnine," I said softly, realization washing over me. "I've allowed her power over me all this time. That's coming to an end."

"Good. You ready to go see your biological father, on McDaniel Avenue, *no less*?"

"Uncle Bobby, are you shitting me?"

"I shit you not. Look, I know you've had a trying time, but it's almost over and we're already here, so why not?"

"Why not? I'll tell you why not." I honestly couldn't come up with a reason not to see the man that was practically raped into being my sperm donor, but not for lack of trying. "You know, I've got no real reason not to, so let's go before I invent one," I said, drying my tears.

"Atta-girl!" Uncle Bobby beamed and honked his nose.

God, I was glad he was here. I pulled the sunshade mirror down. "I've got to get myself together."

Uncle Bobby looked at me and laughed. "Yes, ma'am, you do. You look like you might have just been released from the insane asylum."

***

Swoondalini

On the short ride over to my father's house, I kept reminding myself of the maxim: It's rarely as bad as you think it's going to be, or as good. I was also thankful I wasn't afforded much time to get nervous about this reunion.

"We didn't even call ahead, Uncle Bobby. Won't that be a bit strange?"

"Honey, this whole situation is 'strange'. I mean thirty-four years, and 'Hello, Father'. I don't think there's any protocol, and that's my professional and personal opinion. If he's not there, or doesn't want to see you, then it's not meant to be."

"My stomach hurts, I think I'm about to pass out."

"I'm sure it does, Alice, but you won't fall off the face of the Earth," Uncle Bobby said, empathetically. "We don't have to do this right now, you know."

"You and I both know that's not true," I said, breathing heavily, trying to keep the tunnel vision from seizing my consciousness. "Keep driving."

The ride over to McDaniel Avenue was less than five minutes from the loony bin Mama was incarcerated in for the better part of two decades.

"I'm not exactly sure which house it is, Alice."

"I'll know it when I see it. Wait, wait. Back up, Bob-O."

There he was, cutting grass at the very same house I visited in my journey.

"Let me out, please."

I hopped out before Uncle Bobby rolled to a complete stop. "Wait here."

I ran through the freshly cut grass to a man who didn't see me coming. I noted that the lawnmower he was using was like using a cruise ship on a pond. He made a turn around a magnolia tree, came to a halt when he spotted me, and powered down the engine immediately. We sensed who the other was.

"OH-MY-GAWD!" he said.

"I'm Alice," I croaked out.

"I know who you are."

"We look alike," we said in unison.

We took one another in for a while before he embraced me and said, "I wanted to know you when you got old enough to understand, and even laid some groundwork with your daddy, and then, well, you know what happened," he explained hurriedly.

I held up my hand. "I don't even want to get into that right now. I just came from seeing Mama for the first time since that night."

By this time, Uncle Bobby made his way to where we were standing. "I'm Bobby, obviously, er, Jim's brother."

"Yes, sir, I figured as much. Adam," my father said, and extended his hand in greeting. Adam broke the silence and blank stares that followed. "Well, I was about to go to a baseball game. How bout I buy you two supper, and treat you to box seats?"

***

The awkwardness between Adam, myself, and Uncle Bobby quickly faded as we ate supper at the Liberty Tap Room before the game. Surprisingly, I had no interest in blame or who knew what and when they knew it. Was that called growth? While Adam probably could have done more during my childhood, hindsight is twenty/twenty, and my mother was, and obviously still is, a force of nature. He would never replace Daddy. A girl only got one daddy, but he could be my friend. I needed true friends in my life, and rarely treated myself to that luxury.

Swoondalini

One of the highlights of the trip to my town of birth was getting to see how much the place changed. It became positively cosmopolitan in my absence. Downtown was the complete opposite of how I remembered it. When I fled Greenville, there were parts of downtown that a person needed to carry a pistol through to make it to the other side. Now, high end restaurants and a baseball stadium were among its many attractions.

And, as fate would have it, as I was flanked by my uncle and Adam, I witnessed the mayor of Greenville, my old flame, savior, and my past, throw out the first pitch to kick the Drive's season off. I wanted to run down on the field and kiss him like I was in some Drew Barrymore movie, but that was not to be as the stadium announcer asked his wife and children to stand up several rows below us. Their beautiful faces were splashed up on the Jumbotron.

Uncle Bobby observed the emotions wash across my face as Ronnie Leeman pitched to the spirited applause of his constituency. He was popular among the people. No surprise there.

"I have to try to see him, Bob-O."

"Big day for you today, babe," Uncle Bobby empathized.

As I got up to run down to the field, Uncle Bobby slapped me on the ass and leaned over to Adam to fill him in on the Mayor's significance to me.

While meeting my biological father turned out to be anything but awkward, seeing my first and only love certainly was. I got to him right before his wife and kids did and we shared a stiff hug, and stiff introduction to his family. I quickly apologized for everything, congratulated him on his life, gave him a hard slap on the back that moved even his large frame, and wished him well in the next election. A moment of understanding and appreciation passed between us and was over in a flash.

"Gotta go buy a hat and a t-shirt. Thanks for saving my life all those years ago. I just reclaimed it recently. Bye, now!"

What would be my future? Who knows? I'm just living out this dream called life. I choose to call this period of time, "odyssey of the soul," rather than declaring it the dark night of my soul.

EPILOGUE

The curtains lick my bare body as I step out on to my back deck overlooking Fripp's marsh and ponder the last four years that have transpired since the shower cave. I chose to improve my life since that night. I split my time living between Columbia, South Carolina and Fripp Island. I earned my degree in English literature, and the book you are now concluding is for my Master of Fine Arts degree.

I built a fabulous beach front house that appeared in *Architectural Digest* but chose to remain living in the tree home on the marsh. Uncle Bobby and Adam developed a special bond that revolved around their love for me, so I was pleased and heartened for those two to be able to spend time in the house and make it a beach front home. Bobby was glad to dust off the *SEREN-FRIPPITY* sign to affix to that home. I got my "morning coffee on the beach" fix by buying into "The Camp" on Lil Capers Island, just down the coast from Fripp. It's only accessible by boat and I'm partners with some wonderful Fripp neighbors I met through the Suttons.

Gone are all the fabulous cars, aside from my old Ferrari. If it was good enough for Thomas Magnum, it's good enough for me too.

Geney is still in my life. As a matter of fact, it went to another level. No, not marriage, I've destroyed too many marriages to deserve a good one myself, but we're in a committed relationship. We're all a work in progress, right?

Gone is all the fabulous jewelry, save the platinum Rolex. I wanted a physical reminder of that day and a nice watch, so it made sense to keep it. Most of the time, the only item in the way of jewelry I wear is the amethyst amulet that was given to me on the day Brandy died. I was just Alice now. Brandy is now a name that hasn't been applied to me in a long time.

Gone are the daily bong rips and menthol cigarettes. A girl's got to keep her wits about her.

I always wanted to take my golf game to the next level, but I never found the motivation until reading an old article on an LPGA South Korean Golfer by the name of Mi-Hyun Kim. Uncle Bobby saved it for me, feeling that I would one day be back and read about how in 2007, after winning the SemGroup Championship, she donated one hundred grand of her winnings to the town of Greensburg, Kansas. A tornado wiped it off the map and she felt that after all the money she made in the United States, she wanted to give back. It touched me enough that I decided to lose my amateur status on the driving range where it all began.

It took me a couple of years, but I found my swing in the sandy soil of St. Helena and on Fripp's beautiful courses. I took pride in and enjoyed keeping up that old driving range where Pappy started it all, not to mention the quality time it afforded me with Nana. I qualified for the Women's British and U.S. Opens, placing top-ten in each. When I announced my professional status and pledged all winnings to the Make a Wish Foundation, a whole new world opened to me. My clubs attracted the attention of the cameras, my looks, that "it" factor everybody else calls charisma, and philanthropy cemented it. The looks haven't faded, but that annoying white spot in my hair did, and I enjoy a longer mane since my self-imposed incarceration in our nation's capital. Unfortunately, my back has twice the mileage as most of the twenty-somethings out there, and if you count my former profession, I probably have the back of a ninety-year old woman. So, yoga became my way of life.

From there, I launched my own active wear women's clothing line; dubbed *Namaste Active: Salute the Spirited Within* that bore my silhouette doing the Virabhadrasana pose. (Yes, we have a sports bra especially for golf.) Being accused of not being able to see past my own bodacious tatas struck a chord. To that end, I chose to think about boobies, other than my own, and donated all profits from the golf sports bras to the *Save the Tatas* campaign.

Here's the kicker about all the charity: I make more money now by giving away money than I ever did in my former life.

As to what happened in the shower, I'll leave it to the reader. Just to be on the safe side, I did see my doctor after my brief return from the Lowcountry in the winter of 2009-2010. He suggested everything from the "strength of the Mary Jane" these days, to an "obvious" concussion from my unfortunate fall in the shower. Whatever it was, I refer to it as the most fortunate slip and fall I've ever had. I would never have met Nigel and would not be the woman I am today.

Shortly after Bobby and I left Mama that day, she chose to exit this life by consuming as many pills as she could get her pretty hands on. Apparently, she had a guard that was sweet on her. As she was taking her last labored breaths, I had no doubt she was armed with every justification she needed to pass through the *Pearly Gates* unimpeded. I would like to think that her passing via "little green devil pills" was her penance for Daddy. I did not shed a tear but slept sounder knowing there was less crazy in the world.

Life in the Lowcountry did take some getting used to, but it turned out to be just what I needed. The noise I hear when the Marine Corps jets fly over my home on Fripp is, indeed, the sound of freedom. My freedom.

Just for today, I live today. For my life today, I am grateful.